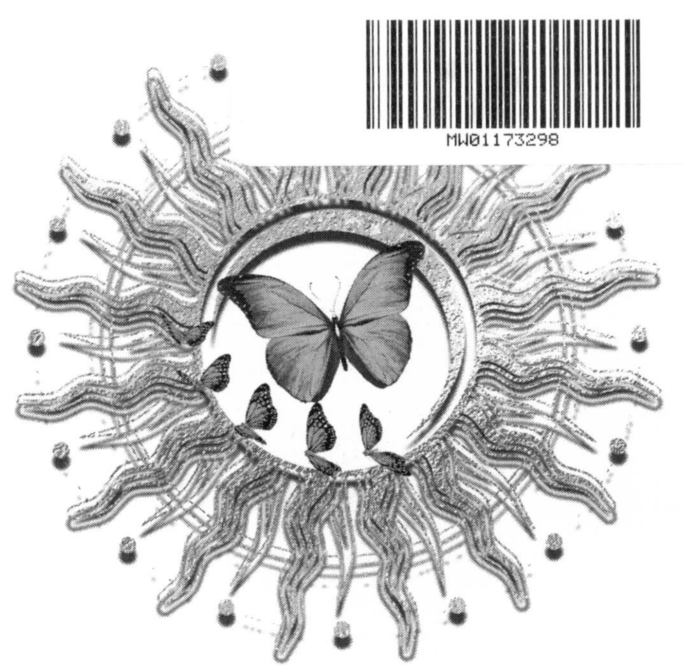

THE TREASURED ONE

HANNAH LEVIN

aethonbooks.com

THE TREASURED ONE
©2024 HANNAH LEVIN

Aethon Books
www.aethonbooks.com

Print and eBook cover and formatting by Steve Beaulieu.

Published by Aethon Books LLC.

THE GOLDEN CHILDREN

The Treasured One

N
W
E
S
AVRILLE
LEIMOR
KERETI
Vhalder
Munarzed
The Rift
Miderrum
WYSALAR

This book is dedicated to my friends and family for their endless support and encouragement,

and to you, you beautiful person you, for giving this book a chance.

PRONUNCIATION GUIDE

In the Ishameti language, Rs are pronounced with the tongue glancing off the roof of the mouth, creating a sound closer to an L or D. This is indicated with the symbol "r/l." A double n is spoken with a nasal quality as opposed to a singular n and is indicated with "ng." For names, the second syllable is usually stressed, except in the case of names derived from the old language (such as surnames, Ralif the king, and Neyes the seer). Riel is an exception, as he purposefully chose a nickname that was easier for humans to pronounce.

NAMES:

Luenki (loo-EN-kee), House Wysalar's diplomatic envoy and ambassador to the U.S.
Solois (so-LO-iss), the first prince of House Wysalar
Astonriel/Riel (ah-STON-r/lee-el)/(REE-el), the second prince of House Wysalar

Wysalar (WHY-sah-lar), one of the 12 fae Houses

Farisen (fa-R/LEE-sen), healer / mender employed by House Wysalar

Leimor (LAY-more), one of the 12 fae Houses, neighbor to Wysalar

Juris (JOO-r/liss), House Wysalar's head cook

Oyanni (oh-YAH-nee), Riel's beloved riding beast

Ralif (R/LAH-liff), Head of House Wysalar, father to Solois and Riel

Elokima (eh-LOW-kee-mah), Lady of House Wysalar, mother to Solois and Riel

Neyes (NAY-ez), seer serving as advisor to House Wysalar

Seersthri (SEERZ-three), renowned healer / mender, resident of Miderrum

Naigatiy'ana (nai-NGAH-tee-ee-YAH-nah), Queen of the *Aminkinya* people

For a glossary of fae words and phrases, see appendix.

PROLOGUE
24 YEARS AGO

A TALL, cloaked figure made its way up a winding stone staircase. Sparks of dust performed a mischievous dance where the figure stepped, and the air took on a distinct chill as they climbed. There was no light to see by, save for the pale glow of moonlight from windows every few feet along the outer wall.

As the figure reached the top of the tower, an ornate oak door with iron hardware came into view. They hesitated a moment before lifting one slender, sculpted hand to knock.

"Come in," a voice called from within. The language they spoke was not English. Indeed, it was not a language spoken on Earth at all.

The door opened of its own accord, and the cloaked figure stepped into a room furnished only with the necessities: a wrought-iron bed frame with a wool-stuffed mattress, a sturdy bedside table with a washbasin, a massive wardrobe, and a single chair by a fireplace, where embers dwindled into ash.

The cloaked figure looked about the room before settling their gaze on the bed, which was half-hidden in shadow.

"You know why I'm here?" a mature, feminine voice inquired, the words spoken with a surety that made the question sound more like a statement.

"I do," a youthful voice responded from the shadows. "You feel it. We all do."

"What is it?"

"The magic."

The cloaked figure stood there, head cocked in question. When the voice in the shadows made no further attempt to speak, they grew impatient.

"What about the magic?" they demanded.

"It grows." The voice sounded contemplative. "It seeks an escape."

"An escape? What ever does that mean?"

"If it doesn't find one," the voice continued, unruffled by the cloaked figure's agitation, "it will create one. I believe it has already begun."

The figure tensed. "And then what?"

"Then it will no longer be alone. Neither the magic, nor our world."

"For Valuen's sake." The cloaked figure threw up their hands in frustration. "This is not the time to speak in riddles. Tell me plainly, what must I prepare our people for?"

There was a beat of silence.

"I shrugged," the voice explained helpfully, since the action wasn't visible in the dim light. The cloaked figure whirled about and began to pace before the door.

"It can't leave us!" they exclaimed. "The magic has been ours for millennia; we cannot function without it now. We were chosen by the Goddess! Why would She desert us?"

"Perhaps She does not desert us," the voice mused. "Perhaps, She is simply choosing to bestow others with Her blessing as well. It is not our place to question Her will."

"Keerya spoke true," the figure spat, eliciting a gasp from the shadows.

"You will invoke the Goddess's wrath with such profanity," the voice chided. "Be calm. She has not revealed Her intentions, but I sense no animosity toward our people. I believe this is no punishment, but rather an opportunity. A sort of test—a chance to prove our worth."

"I don't like it," the figure grumbled. "Why must we prove anything?"

"You must walk carefully, my queen. Soon, you will come to a crossroads. The decisions you make will affect us all, and your success or failure may very well decide our fate."

CHAPTER ONE
THE GOLDEN CHILD

WHEN THE WORLD found out the fae existed, everything went to shit.

Pardon my French.

It happened twenty-four years ago. An irreparable tear—dubbed The Rift—appeared out of nowhere, cleaving the sky in two and creating a permanent bridge between two planes of existence. Our world leaders scrambled to make a good impression on the impossibly strong, inconceivably beautiful beings that existed on the other side. Science as we knew it became obsolete. Governments collapsed and were reformed. New religions emerged.

After some time, it became apparent that The Rift was a momentous accident, and the fae wanted nothing to do with us. They kept to their side; we kept to ours. But as it turned out, the presence of The Rift had introduced more than just the fae to our world; it also introduced magic—in the form of a select few individuals known as "Golden Children."

When I was eight years old, I discovered that I had the power to heal others. My parents couldn't deal with the resulting chaos, so I was brought to Washington, D.C. to live at the White House at the tender age of fourteen. Marcia, a girl from Brazil who could manipulate her appearance at will, was also brought to live there, and the two of us became friends. We were given everything a teenager could want, with the only downside being that we couldn't leave.

Of course, that didn't stop us. One day, we snuck out, prancing into the wild that was the city with more courage than brains. I was found and brought back, though irreparably traumatized. Marcia wasn't so lucky—she didn't come back at all, and though they searched for her for years, it was like she'd disappeared into thin air. I made a vow to myself that from then on, I would be grateful and do whatever was asked of me. I couldn't risk upsetting my government caretakers—not when everything I had, everything I was, hung in the balance.

So every month, it was the same affair; I'd go out to the White House fence and heal a handful of the terminally ill people who waited there for me. It took weeks to get used to their presence. In the beginning, the screaming kept me up for days. I piled things against the windows in desperation, wrapped myself in layers upon layers of blankets, and rocked myself to the closest approximation of sleep I could manage. Eventually, the ruckus became background noise, and I settled into a routine. Noise-canceling headphones were a lifesaver. Still, I never could shake the feeling that everything would fall to pieces someday.

Little did I know that day would come sooner than I thought.

Standing in an opulent dressing room, I studied my reflection in a floor-length mirror. I was bathed in tiers of white chiffon and gold-tipped feathers that were meant to make my reddish hair pop. Like everything I wore for these healing events, the dress was a designer piece. I'm sure the effect was meant to be magical. In actuality, it looked more like a hotel room after a bachelorette party pillow fight: goose down and champagne on every surface. The dozens of fluffy layers, combined with the apprehension that always plagued me at these events, made it hard to breathe.

The thought of pillows brought my attention to my tired face, framed by limp bangs. Since when did I have dark circles? Even with a more than generous smattering of freckles—which were par for the course, being a ginger—and ample amounts of makeup, they were still noticeable. And had my cheekbones always been this prominent? My body felt so heavy. All I wanted to do was curl up somewhere warm and quiet and… not feel for a while.

Oh, well. Duty called.

I didn't have the right to be miserable. My meals were curated by top-notch chefs, and a bevy of private tutors oversaw my schooling. I had access to a movie theater, tennis courts, and a pool. I spent most days watching YouTube videos and playing computer games on a high-end PC with dual monitors and surround sound. Last Saturday was my birthday, and the president was there. How many people got to say that? I was living my best life. Sure, I couldn't travel the world, but I was safe and cared for, and that was far more than most people had.

Reminding myself of that, I frowned at my reflection and turned away from the mirror. Beside me, my stylist was taking her time picking through hairpins, but I put a hand on her shoulder to stop her. "Let's get this over with," I said, gathering fistfuls of my dress so that I could walk unimpeded. "Nobody cares what I look like."

That wasn't exactly true. Photos of me from today would be popping up all over the place, as they always did after my healing events, but I couldn't summon the energy to worry about what news outlets and influencers thought. The only people that mattered were my "patients," and I could be seven feet tall and bright pink all over with seaweed for hair for all they cared.

Skirts in hand, I made for the door. Devon and Chris, my

personal security detail, were on the other side as usual, never more than a shout away. Although we kept things professional, they were the closest thing I had to friends since Marcia disappeared. Devon was of European origin and six feet of too-serious, ex-military muscle in a tailored suit. With the right incentive, I'd admit to having a teensy crush on the man; the man bun really did it for me.

Chris was Asian, a little shorter than Devon, and kept his dark hair cropped close to his scalp. A total goofball, he was the kind of open, easygoing person that made anyone comfortable. He had recently gotten engaged to his long-term boyfriend, and we regularly joked that his partner must have undiagnosed issues if he was crazy enough to settle for him.

The two of them made things a little less lonely… most of the time.

"New dress?" Chris asked with one bushy eyebrow raised, trying and failing to stifle his laughter as I emerged from my room in a flurry of feathers. I shot an exasperated glare his way.

"I'll have you know that no less than twenty baby swans died to make this dress," I responded with a solemn air. "The least you can do is respect their sacrifice."

"Cygnets," Devon corrected me matter-of-factly, face blank as he adjusted his suit cuffs, "Baby swans are called cygnets."

"Oh my God, thank you, that's so good to know," I drawled, my voice dripping with sarcasm even as a smile tugged at my mouth. "You must have been popular in school. In all seriousness, I'm sure someone paid a lot of money for me to wear this. Who am I to turn them down?"

"An up-and-coming star in the fashion world from Wisconsin," my stylist supplied from behind me. "The collection hasn't been officially launched yet. Such a treat to see this piece in person. Thank you." Her thanks were directed at Chris, who had reached over to shut the door behind her since her arms were full of bags and tools. She directed a megawatt smile at me.

"See you next month, Ms. Nelson," she said, bobbing on her feet in an almost-bow. "Good luck with your healing!" In a flash, she was gone.

Without meaning to, my gaze lingered on her retreating form, and a pang of longing went through me. If I saw her more than a couple of hours every month, maybe we could have been friends. Heaven knew it got stifling at times without many other young adults around.

"Well, then. Shall we?" Chris offered me his arm, but I shook my head.

"Thank you, but I'll need both hands to get this dress and myself outside in one piece," I said wryly, gathering up my skirts once more and following my bodyguards as they led the way to the Entrance Hall. The closer we got, the more I became aware of my heart pounding away in my chest. A clammy sweat began to develop along my exposed neck. I'd been doing this for years with no incidents—today would be no different. I just had to keep telling myself it was safe. There was a fence and guards; nobody could get to me here. I was safe.

We were met in the foyer as usual by George Kepler, the official Secretary of U.S. Rift Affairs. He was one of the few human beings who had been through The Rift and seen the fae in person. He was also the one who made most of my decisions for me. I couldn't help thinking that such an important position called for someone who didn't look like they might keel over with a stiff breeze. He'd been old when I first met him—surely the man was pushing eighty by now? I liked to think that he had my best interests at heart, even though he was as much a slave to the system as I was. He had always been nice to me, at least.

"Good morning, Miss Avery," he greeted, politely ignoring the mess that was my dress.

"Morning, George. How's the turnout?" I asked, peering past him. It was nearly impossible to see the edge of the grounds from inside the Hall, but it was habit to try nonetheless. Part of me always expected the shadows from my past to be lurking just past the threshold, malicious strangers waiting to pounce the moment I let my guard down. I still remembered how easy it had been for hostile hands to pluck me off the bustling streets of D.C., even in broad daylight and with Marcia mere feet away. The memory gave me chills.

"Excitement is high as always," George reported, a touch of weariness in his tone. "We've estimated 7,000 attendees. Plus representatives from the major news outlets, of course."

A lump developed in my throat. I was grateful for my healing powers, grateful for what they could do for others, but they didn't go very far; I could only heal a handful of people before succumbing to exhaustion. Recently, that number got smaller and smaller, and the familiar pull of magic became harsher. The last few times, using my abilities had bordered on pain and left me weak for days instead of hours. Even if all went well and I did great, I knew a thousand people would be left disappointed for every one I helped. "Great." I tried to keep my tone light rather than let despair creep in, but couldn't resist a touch of sarcasm in the face of the situation. "Let's not keep my adoring public waiting, then."

"Be my guest." George gestured for me to walk ahead. Already, the muffled roar of the crowd outside was making me itch. Devon stepped forward to get the door for me, and I no longer had time to hesitate. My eyes closed for a brief moment. As the door opened, I was inundated by screams. Inside, the walls muffled the worst of it, but the intensity was something else. I would never get used to the sight either, the thousands of people that filled Pennsylvania Avenue, barely held back by thin strips of wrought iron. Armed military personnel lined the path to the fence just in case. No one had tried any funny business recently, but they couldn't be too careful with me and the president living in the same building.

A cool breeze met me at the threshold. I savored what little comfort it brought me. If Devon and Chris noticed my hesitation, they were too kind to comment. Taking a deep breath to steel myself, I raised my chin and headed down the stairs toward the visitor's entrance where the throng awaited me. At the front, immediately within my line of sight, a wheelchair-bound lady with an oxygen mask grasped the bars with arms that were skin and bones. Next to her, a man who appeared healthy held a baby up as high as he could while shouting something incomprehensible. The weight of their attention was palpable, the miasma of desperation so thick that it hung in the air and made it difficult to breathe.

I didn't let my steps falter, but my nerves started getting to me, and dread weighed down my feet. What if I couldn't even heal them both this time? How long had they been waiting for me, finally feeling hope instead of despair for once? Now I was all that stood between them and a future, and if I wasn't strong enough, I was taking that from them.

I stopped a few feet away. The man was drenched in desperation; he practically shoved the baby through the bars to me. Its howling screams joined the others to the point that they blurred into an indiscernible cacophony of sound. The woman was hardly able to hold herself upright, much less call out to me, but her eyes pleaded with me. All of them did—there were thousands of eyes on me. My head spun, and bile crawled up my throat.

"You okay?" I could barely hear Chris over the crowd.

"Yeah," I lied. My voice was a whisper. I nodded, half for his sake, half to convince myself. Swallowing down the nausea, I pressed my lips together and stepped toward the bundle of joy. Tears of relief streaked down the baby's father's face as he realized that I approached them. As I went, I began to brace myself for the harsh pull of my magic.

I was careful not to reach past the bars. In the early years, before we'd worked out a system, someone had yanked me off my feet and nearly taken off my arm. As terrifying as it had been, I understood why, and I didn't blame them. It bothered me that this was the only way I could help. One of the baby's sock-clad little feet stuck between the bars, so I carefully extended my arm enough to secure my fingers around it.

It took me a moment to determine the problem. With my eyes closed, I could sense the body's processes. Normally, it functioned like well-directed traffic flowing along the highway. If I focused, I could find the flaw, the traffic jam holding the rest of the commuters back. It was a sense of something *wrong* that begged to be corrected. In this child, it was more like a multi-car pileup. That told me that whatever ailment they had, it was serious.

Heart swelling with sympathy, I reached for my magic without delay. It was a constant presence, like a flickering flame in my chest. For some reason, it was harder to reach than it usually was. My nerves must have been getting to me. Eyebrows knitting together in concentration, I put more effort into it. Eventually, warmth signaling the flow of magic rolled through my body. I shuddered at the feeling, as though something vital was wrenched from me. How much more of this could I take? The queasy feeling got worse.

Abruptly, the baby stopped crying. The foot was yanked from my hand, and in the second it took for me to open my eyes, the man and the baby had been swallowed by the crowd. Exhausted and blinking back tears, I turned to the lady in the wheelchair. Gray spots danced at the edge of my vision. When I stepped forward, my feet wobbled. In an effort to stabilize myself, I caught the frail hand that reached for me through the bars. I had to grit my teeth against the urge to lean against the fence for support. One more, at least. These people were in pain, and I was the only one who could help them. Giving up wasn't an option.

"Let's get you well," I whispered, closing my eyes again. I found the problem even faster in the woman than I had with the baby; her sickness was more advanced. She had weeks left, if that. I reached for the flicker of magic within me. Had it always been so small? Worry crawled up my spine. I got a hold of it, but this time, it *fought* me. My eyes snapped open in confusion. The lady's expression hadn't changed, still so hopeful. She wouldn't have registered that something was off; she had no idea how this worked. I had to try again, for her sake.

"Sorry, one moment..." With a frown, I closed my eyes once more and focused harder. The flicker of my magic winked in and out, barely there. Perplexed, I braced myself and tried again, straining for the flame and attempting to cajole it into action. With significant effort, I was able to grasp an ember, a spark. My hands began to warm around the skeletal extremity I was gripping, and I was relieved. *I'm strong,* I told myself. *I can do this.*

The magic flared suddenly, sending scorching threads of pain through my body. I dropped the lady's hand with a gasp. A distant voice called my name. I spun around to face Chris, and the world continued to spin even as I stopped moving. I couldn't breathe—either the dress was cinched too tight, or something had stripped the oxygen from the air.

"I-I can't," I stammered, swaying on my feet. The sounds, the smells, the light—it was too much. The nausea amped up. My ears rang. Something roiled underneath my skin, foreign and angry. Overwhelmed, I struggled to remember how to speak. "It's not working... I don't know what went wrong... I..."

My voice fell away as the scenery began to tip to one side. The last thing I saw was Chris rushing forward to catch me before everything went black.

CHAPTER TWO
THE SICKNESS

When I came to, I didn't recognize my surroundings at first. Chills ran down my spine, and the shadows throughout the room became sinister in an instant. I could only think that it was happening again, that they found me. I froze, momentarily trapped in the memory of my kidnappers' hands around me, of feeling powerless as they dragged me kicking and screaming down into that dark, musty basement. I should have fought harder, but back then, I didn't understand the lengths that people would go to get what they wanted. *The gates and guards weren't enough. I knew they wouldn't be enough, and I let my guard down anyway—*

As I sat up, the memories of before I collapsed came rushing back.

"Whoa there, sport." Chris appeared at my side, arms outstretched in a pacifying gesture. Though my heart still pounded with fear, I was so glad to see a familiar face. "Take it easy. Devon's getting the physician. You shouldn't try to get up."

"Wha—" My voice came out as a garbled squeak. I cleared my throat and tried again, attempting to shake the paralysis that had seized my vocal cords. "What happened? I was healing that lady and then… is she okay? Did I do it?"

Was she left disappointed like all the others?

"I don't know," Chris said apologetically. "But you don't need to worry about that right now. You collapsed by the gate. You're in the vice-presidential medical suite."

Once I was able to process his words, I took stock of the facts. My head pounded, and the nausea hadn't yet faded, but the tightness in my chest and the sudden, unusual pain I'd felt before were thankfully gone. I reclined on a medical cot, hooked up to an IV. Some kind of monitor beeped away to my right. The view through the window told me it was dark outside. "How long was I out?" I asked, dreading the answer.

"Just the rest of the day," Chris replied. Relieved, I sank back against the pillows and closed my eyes. Out of curiosity, I tried reaching for my magic. Not that it ever did anything for me—for whatever reason, it only worked on other people—but I wanted to reassure myself that it was still there. When I found that familiar flicker, I sighed in relief.

But it was barely there. Something was wrong.

Just then, there was a knock at the door. A middle-aged man in a doctor's coat entered, followed by Devon and George; all wore grim faces. Chris went to sit in a chair by the door. Most times, I could read him like an open book, but I couldn't tell what he was thinking now. Not sure what to expect, I turned my attention to the doctor. I'd been to the medical suite in the past for the occasional ailment, but I didn't remember meeting him before.

"Ms. Nelson, I'm Dr. Connor Walsh, one of the White House physicians on staff here. I've heard a lot about you and your talents. You were close to putting us out of a job." He grinned, and the corners of his eyes crinkled deeply, which told me this was not the first time he had foisted a joke of questionable nature on a patient.

"Nice to meet you." I tried to sort through all the questions I had. Was I okay? Did I manage to heal that lady? Did they know what was wrong with my magic?

"Same to you. How are you feeling?"

"Fine." The answer came automatically, the same one I always gave when someone asked how I was. When silence followed, the corners of my mouth turned down. "So, what's going on? Is everything okay?"

"Well, I took the liberty of running a few tests, since we're not sure exactly what happened and you have no prior conditions on record. I'd like to go over the results with you." The doctor raised his clipboard. "Maybe it's best we speak in private?"

"Oh… sure." I cast an uncertain look at George, half waiting to see if he would object and half hoping to glean something useful from his expression, but he was careful to keep his thoughts to himself. Chris stood, and he and Devon left the room without a word. George stepped closer to the doctor and said something I couldn't make out, then patted him on the arm and followed after my bodyguards. When the door closed behind them, Dr. Walsh fetched the chair that Chris had vacated.

"Ms. Nelson, have you injured yourself recently?" he asked as he took a seat by my cot.

"No," I responded with another frown.

"Have you noticed any discomfort? Shortness of breath, dizziness, swelling, anything?"

"Not really, I…" I started to shake my head, but thought back to that morning and had to amend my answer. "Well, I was a little dizzy and nauseous this morning. I mean, my nerves got to me today. I guess I haven't been sleeping well lately, and I was stressed out, so exhaustion caught up to me."

"Perhaps." The doctor didn't seem convinced. "Ms. Nelson, I ask because your organ function is concerning. This sort of system distress is usually caused by sepsis, an advanced infection, but we can't find evidence of that. Frankly, your symptoms are baffling for someone of your age and general health. We've gone ahead and given you some antibiotics, and we'll continue to monitor things, but… we may have to transfer you for more thorough testing."

My thoughts were clamoring before he finished speaking. The irony of the situation was palpable—the special Golden Child with healing powers was sick. If something happened to me, what would happen to all those people outside? They'd be left without any kind of support. Would they riot in the streets? Would they just shrug it off and go back to wherever they come from? "Am I dying?" The question came out before I could stop it. In the background, the beeping of the vitals monitor sped up.

"I didn't say that," Dr. Walsh said quickly. "There's some ways to go between this"—he indicated the clipboard—"and that. You're not in the danger zone, so for now, we're going to keep monitoring your condition and see if you respond to the antibiotics. Once we figure out what's going on, we'll be able to put a more effective treatment plan together."

So, essentially, they knew nothing. Great. I nodded, digesting his words, when a thought occurred to me—coincidence, or something more? "Is this… could this have something to do with my magic?"

The doctor blinked. "Ah… I can't say. Unfortunately, your abilities are beyond the scope of modern medicine. Do you have reason to suspect that could be the case?"

"Well…" I hesitated. If my powers were gone, what would that mean for me? Would I still be able to stay here, draining government resources for nothing in return? Was there anything I could do for those people without magic? Then again, I couldn't hide it. Even if I didn't say anything, they would find out sooner or later. It was probably best to be honest. "I had some… difficulties earlier. Just before I fainted. When I tried to heal someone at the gate, it was harder than usual. I'm not sure it even worked."

"I see. And you don't usually have any trouble?"

"Not really. This is the first time."

"Hmm. Well, that is concerning. Unfortunately, there's no way for me to test anything related to your abilities, since we were never able to find physical evidence of your magic, and we still know little to nothing about the effects they have on a human body. Even if I had to guess, I couldn't say if your healing ability is causing the issue, or if it's the other way around, and your illness is interfering with your powers."

I could only nod again. That was old news—back when Marcia and I had first moved to the White House, we had to put up with a myriad of tests. They never did make any headway on finding out what made us different. At least, not that they told us.

"In any case," Dr. Walsh continued, getting to his feet and moving the chair back to its place by the door, "I'm sure this is overwhelming for you. Take some time to process. If you'd like, we can inform your family of the situation."

"No, that's fine," I said quickly. They didn't need to be bothered with this. While my parents and I still talked on occasion, it was more for the sake of staying in touch rather than out of care for me. My mother and I had been close before everything went down. When word about my healing abilities got out, people filled our lawn, banging on the windows and begging for me to come out. We couldn't go anywhere or do anything. It was a relief when the government came knocking, and as far as I could tell, Mom and Dad didn't miss me all that much.

At first, the lack of contact hurt. I was still a child then, and I didn't understand why they gave me up. Now, I knew that it was necessary; normal people didn't have the resources to deal with something like that. In the years since, the pain faded, and I wasn't all that bothered about being close with the people who gave me life. Plus, they got a generous monthly stipend out of it, so they were happy. The people that mattered most to me now were the ones waiting outside of this room. "Do the others know?" I asked, gesturing to the door.

"While we're not a public hospital, doctor-patient privilege still applies. We can tell them as much or as little as you like. Though, I will say that Mr. Kepler is particularly invested in your condition."

"Of course he is," I muttered. George was unlikely to say it to my face, but this was a disaster. My spirits were at an all-time low. I fidgeted with the edge of the sheet as I mulled over my options, trying my hardest to see if there was anything positive that could come of this. "You can tell him, it's fine. Can I get my phone?"

"Certainly. I'll have some personal things brought to you." Dr. Walsh's expression softened. "Please know that we will do everything in our power to get you on the road to recovery. You mean a lot to the members of this household, not to mention to the world."

"Yeah, thanks." I tried to sound grateful, but I wasn't sure I managed it. While people meant well, that sort of praise became rather empty after the first few times. Dr. Walsh and everyone else probably assumed I enjoyed the fame, not realizing how stressful that kind of attention could be. If there was a way I could stay safe and keep helping people anonymously, I would do it in a heartbeat, but the fact of the matter was that would never happen.

The doctor left and silence fell, punctuated by the steady beeping of the vitals monitor. My gaze swiveled up to the fluorescent lighting set into the ceiling and I took a long, slow breath to center my thoughts. What if I had noticed something was wrong sooner? Would that have helped? It had been too easy to say that the fatigue and decreased appetite were because of stress. Or, heck, a vitamin D deficiency. I'd grown used to the tightness in my chest, which had been a near-constant companion since my anxiety became noticeable during my preteen years. And to be honest, I'd been rather pleased with the weight loss—at first, anyway. No use crying over spilled milk, I supposed, even though it was easy by now to lose myself to the land of what-ifs and should-haves.

There was a knock at the door. The handle turned, and Chris stuck his head in.

"We're putting together a list of things to get from your room," he said cheerfully. "Besides your laptop, phone and charger, toothbrush, and some clothes, is there anything else you'd like? Doc says the med wing bathroom is stocked with toiletries."

A pang of gratitude for him warmed my tired, aching body. Truly, I had everything I needed here. "Uh... no, I think that's good. You got all the essentials."

"Okiedoke. We'll reach out to your tutors too, to put things on hold for a bit. If you think of anything else you need later, just say the word."

"I appreciate it, Chris, thanks," I responded gratefully, and he ducked out of the room. The door shut behind him, and I was left with nothing to do but ponder the fragility of mortality and the potential consequences of my failure.

Days passed. My condition didn't take any turns for the worse, but neither did I show any signs of improvement, so Dr. Walsh had me transferred to the National Military Medical Center for further testing. They took blood, ordered X-rays and ultrasounds, and did numerous scans. The doctors became increasingly frazzled as results came back and they were no closer to figuring out what was wrong with me.

Bored out of my mind, I passed the time with sleep and mind-numbing reality TV. Every so often, I attempted to access my magic, but it slipped through my fingers every time, and I was rewarded with a bout of vertigo for trying. At some point, George visited to assure me that he was working on a solution and I didn't need to stress about the next healing event. Despite his relaxed attitude, I still felt the inevitable creeping closer, and the dread did nothing to ease my symptoms. The nurses were kind, but they couldn't tell me what was going on. No one could.

Finally, two weeks and two days in, George stopped by again, this time accompanied by an official I didn't recognize. She wore a navy pinstripe skirt suit, and her coily hair was slicked back against her scalp. Her deep ebony skin was smooth and tight, not a line or age spot to be seen, but I got the sense that she was older than she looked. Immediately, my guard went up. Was this going to be the moment they told me I was getting cut off? Panic coursed through me, my heart all of a sudden trying to leap out of my ribcage.

"Miss Avery, this is Vivian Pierce, the Lieutenant Governor of Ohio." George introduced the woman with a flourish. She gave me a smile that didn't reach her eyes.

"Pleasure to make your acquaintance, Ms. Nelson. I've heard a lot about you," Vivian said, reaching forward with one hand proffered. Eyeing her warily, I sat up to shake it.

"Your situation is unprecedented," George started in an apologetic tone. "As such, I've had to consider our options carefully. There aren't many." He hesitated a moment before resuming. "Given the state of your health, and the concerns related to your abilities… and, especially, to prevent any rumors from floating around… I believe that the best course of action would be to recruit some outside help. How much do you know about the fae?"

If I'd been standing rather than nestled in a throne of pillows, I might have fainted. As it was, something fluttered wildly in the pit of my stomach, but I wasn't sure if it was excitement or fear. Pouring all the strength I had left into keeping my tone even and controlled, I responded, "I mean, just whatever everyone else has heard. They're beautiful and strong.

The Rift gives us access to their world. They're secretive about their culture and history, but we know they have magic."

"That's the short version," George agreed. "We've made some diplomatic progress over the last few years, but there's a lot we still don't know. They're polite, but guarded. That being said, we're on decent terms with the royal family. I've spoken with their ambassador regarding your condition, and they believe they can help. However, they won't treat you here."

My eyes widened. Was he saying what I thought he was saying? There was no way.

"Vivian here"—George indicated the lady at his side—"has come to escort you to Ohio, where you'll meet with an envoy sent by the fae royal family. If you agree to it, and if all goes well, you'll begin treatment with their medical experts across The Rift."

Full stop. Did he hear himself? I'd never even left the East Coast before. The last time I tried to leave the White House grounds, I was kidnapped and held in a cellar for four days. I could have died. I may have gotten Marcia killed. Was the idea of meeting the fae thrilling? Sure. Hell, the excitement was making me dizzy again. But there was no way.

Then again… I wasn't getting any better, and I needed to resume my healing duties as soon as possible. If I couldn't, I would no longer be of value… and what then? Would they turn me out on the streets and expect me to fend for myself? I was an adult, but I'd never be able to have a normal life. I had no money, no job history, no degree. Maybe my parents would take me back, but what if they didn't? I'd probably be torn apart by my admirers before I even made it home. The thought had me clenching the sheets so tightly that my knuckles turned white.

I had no choice. None at all.

"Okay," I said at last, trying to put on a brave face to hide the emotional turmoil that simmered under the surface. "What do I need to do?"

"Great." George shared a relieved look with Vivian. It did

nothing to ease the fierce pounding in my chest. "Take the rest of today to collect your things," he suggested, not noticing my distress. "Tomorrow, you'll be escorted to the presidential hangar in Maryland to catch a flight. Lieutenant Governor Pierce will accompany you to Ohio, where you'll meet with the fae representative. They'll be assuming responsibility for your treatment from here on out."

CHAPTER THREE
THE BASE

"SO, WHAT SHOULD I KNOW?" I asked. Somehow, I'd made it past the White House gates without incident and was settled into a seat on a small private plane across from the lieutenant governor. A private nurse came with us to monitor my condition during the flight. I couldn't remember ever feeling this fragile, physically or mentally; I think I made the trip from the medical center to the airfield through sheer force of will. They'd had to send police out to part the crowd like Moses and the Red Sea so we could get through, but we made it.

Ashamedly, I'd been so overwhelmed that I hadn't even thought to do some Googling in preparation the night before. The public didn't know much about the fae or their royal family —only what had been leaked by daring journalists who caught a peek during their visits to this side of The Rift. When The Rift first opened, people coped as best they could. Some people stuck their heads in proverbial sand and lived like nothing had changed. Others literally worshiped the fae and prayed that they'd be taken away from here to live on the other side with them. While I fell somewhere in the middle, everything I knew was due to the major news outlets and a handful of blurry photographs. Who knew how accurate that would be?

The more I thought about what was coming, the more my nerves got to me. I'd slept little, haunted by the recurring nightmare of what happened the last time I left the White House grounds. I tried to think of the positives—I was going through The Rift to meet the fae (!!)—but that hadn't been enough to distract me from the weight of impending doom.

Vivian's gaze fell on my right leg, which bounced in agitation.

"First off, take a deep breath," she ordered, not unkindly. "I know it seems like a lot, but we'll handle all the important stuff. You just need to focus on your health."

I nodded but made no attempt to take a calming breath. *Does that ever work?*

"In case George didn't mention it, the issues with your abilities should stay on a need-to-know basis." Vivian turned to the open window before answering my initial question. "Let's see. The North American section of The Rift runs from Missouri to Ontario. There's an opening over Lake Erie, on the grounds of what used to be a National Guard training facility called Camp Perry. Over the past few years, it was converted to a military base for Rift-related matters. The area is guarded at all times; you'll be safe there."

"Oh." Helpful, but not what I was hoping for. "I appreciate that. But I was thinking, what should I know about the fae? I don't want to offend anyone accidentally."

Vivian hesitated a beat. "They're... perfect. Highly intelligent and physically faultless. They speak fluent English. Like George said, they're polite, but guarded. As a result, we don't know much about their culture. We know they are religious and don't eat meat. And magic is widely used, of course, though they don't tend to use it in our presence. They're governed by a royal family: a king, queen, and two princes."

"Princes, huh? Are they hot?" I thought a light-hearted joke might serve to ease some of the tension. Going by the images floating around, it was a perfectly fair question. Instead of sharing a laugh with me, however, Vivian served me a look that had me shrinking in on myself. "Um, never mind. Have you been to the other side of The Rift before? What's it like there?"

"Hmm. I would say it's reminiscent of the European countryside."

"... Say that you were talking to someone who'd never been to Europe?"

"Oh. Well, it doesn't feel that fantastical, just different. The terrain and flora are very similar to what we have here. The same colors generally exist in nature, and they experience seasons as we do. There's no technology—they get around using riding beasts like horses. Many of their animals are similar to ours but more intelligent. It can be disconcerting—"

Vivian stopped and glanced up as the nurse approached.

"We'll be taking off momentarily," she said cheerfully, drawing a small cart alongside us. "The flight will be a little over an hour. How are you feeling?"

I nodded. "Not bad, a little tired. Mostly, I'm just nervous."

"May I?" the nurse asked, pulling out a blood pressure cuff. I presented my arm, and she wound the cuff around my bicep and inflated it with the flick of a switch. After a moment, she removed the cuff and jotted something down on a pad of paper. She took my temperature, made another note, and offered me a small smile.

"You're good to go," she announced, stowing her cart behind the seats and claiming the open spot next to me. "When we touch down, there will be a medical transport ready to escort you the rest of the way. You might feel a bit faint when we take off. If at any point it gets overwhelming, or you're in pain, let me know."

"Will do, thanks." I turned back to Vivian, intending to continue our conversation, but she examined the view outside her window in a way that told me my chance had passed. My shoulders dropped in disappointment. I played it off by fiddling with my belt buckle and pulling it tighter over my lap.

The flight was short and uneventful, with the nurse making small talk with me for most of it. When we landed, the nurse took my temperature and blood pressure again, proclaimed me unlikely to die within the next five minutes, and helped me to my feet.

The pilot saluted Vivian on the way out. By the time we descended the steps, the medical transport had pulled up alongside the plane. Vivian got into one of two SUVs, and the nurse helped me into the back of the transport. It was like a smaller, more luxurious ambulance, with a cot in the middle, plush bench seating on one side, and cabinets labeled with medical supplies.

The cot didn't look comfortable, but I was already exhausted, so I elected to lie down when the nurse asked me what I would prefer. She clipped a heart rate monitor to my finger as the car took off. In moments, I was lulled to sleep by the purr of the engine.

"...ry? Avery, we're here."

I was startled awake at the sound of my name. It took me a moment to recognize that the person giving me an apologetic smile was the nurse I met on the plane.

"Sorry, I didn't mean to surprise you," she said, disconnecting the heart rate monitor from my hand. "We just arrived at the base. Can you walk, or would you like us to wheel you there?"

"I can walk!" I hurried to sit up. As I did so, my vision swirled, and the nurse put a hand out to support me before I went toppling over. She gestured to someone out of sight.

"I think we'll get you that wheelchair anyway. But feel free to take a moment to get your bearings," she suggested. "We're in no rush."

I blinked in rapid succession to shake off the dizziness. It was hard to tell at this point if the butterflies in my stomach were a sign of something physically wrong with me or simply more nerves, but it was easy enough to ignore. When I felt comfortable enough to stand, the nurse helped me toward the back of the transport, where a guy in a paramedic uniform waited with a wheelchair.

"Welcome to Camp Perry," he said good-naturedly, holding the wheelchair still as I got settled in.

"Ah, thank you," I replied awkwardly, grateful for both the warm welcome and his support. As we ambled along, I had the chance to take in my surroundings. The road we came from was flanked by empty fields. The open space felt so freeing compared to the city, like I could just take off anytime I wanted and run for days.

Well, if I weren't dying, anyway.

In the distance, the fence surrounding the property held back a large group of people. While nowhere near the amount that always waited for me at the White House, it was still an impressive number. Somehow, I managed to hold it together; in my condition, it was a miracle I didn't break down at the sight. As it was, I couldn't hide a grimace. "How did they know I'd be here?"

The paramedic slowed to follow my gaze. "Hm? Oh, they're not here for you. Those are the fanatics and missionaries who want to go through The Rift. Hope springs eternal, even if civilians aren't allowed access."

"Oh." It was a small relief, but enough to ease some of my tension, for which I was grateful. I hadn't even thought about that, but it made sense.

A cold breeze whistled by, and I shivered involuntarily, moving my free hand to gather the front of my jacket closed. It had been warm in D.C. the past few days, but it was still not quite spring, and the air in Ohio had a noticeable chill to it. Perhaps I should have packed more layers. I wasn't sure what to expect; with what little Vivian had told me, there was no anticipating what the weather would be like on the other side of The Rift.

"Well, this is it." Speak of the devil. Vivian came up from behind me, and I followed her gaze to the immense concrete building before us. The stale gray color theme and limited number of windows made it appear like a prison. Uniformed personnel hung around outside, lending to that vibe. Vivian gestured to a well-traveled dirt road between buildings. "We're waiting for the go-ahead from the fae envoy, so we probably won't be leaving until tomorrow morning. The guest clinic is just down that way. You'll be housed there in the meantime, where the physician on staff can keep an eye on you."

"Tomorrow?" My voice came out a squeak. "Um, I mean, so soon?"

The tension returned with a vengeance. I had expected weeks of navigating the bureaucratic red tape before a date was even set for my trip through The Rift. Was my situation truly that pressing?

Vivian pinned me with one of her signature stares, but her expression softened at whatever she saw on my face. "Whether you realize it or not, your well-being is a priority for the American government," she advised. "If this is all too much for you, you're still welcome to back out."

I understood what she was saying—or, more importantly, what she wasn't. "I get it," I replied quietly. I didn't need to be babied; I knew what was at stake. "No, I'm not backing out. I appreciate everyone's efforts. It's just… a lot to take in."

"It would be for anyone," Vivian acknowledged. She glanced down at her watch. "Get some rest," she suggested. "Your things should be delivered shortly, along with something to eat. I'll be around if you need me."

"Thank you," I said, and meant it. As she strode off, I turned my attention to the direction of the medical building and remembered that the paramedic was still there, ready and willing to push me the rest of the way. "Oh my God, I'm sorry," I exclaimed, embarrassed by my lack of awareness.

"You're fine." The paramedic laughed. "We're supposed to be keeping an eye on you. Come on, let me help you to the doc and get you tucked in."

My cheeks warmed. "That won't be necessary," I groused, but let him guide me nonetheless. The clinic was a short walk from where we had been dropped off, and I was able to make the trip without incident. An enthusiastic nurse in military scrubs greeted us at the entrance. "Welcome to Camp Perry!" she exclaimed, hurrying to prop the door open so that we could make our way inside. "Come in, come in. *So* excited to meet you. Huge fan of your work."

I offered her a weak smile and waved away her words, embarrassed all over again. It had only been what, thirteen, fourteen years since I became a center of attention for my healing abilities? I was bound to get used to it sooner or later. Any year now.

"You'll be right this way," she continued, guiding us down the hall. "We don't have private rooms here, but there's no one else in the east wing, so you'll just be sleeping with a bunch of empty beds. Honestly, that's better company than the soldiers!"

"That's fine, I'm not picky," I assured her. I could put up with anything for one night.

"I mean, I'm sure you're used to much nicer conditions in the White House," the nurse gushed. She leaned in and lowered her voice as if sharing a secret. "What's it like? Is it like living in a palace?"

"Uh... I wouldn't know," I answered honestly, shifting awkwardly in my wheelchair. "I haven't seen many palaces. It is pretty nice, though."

"Of course not, silly me!" She tittered. "Well, it must be

luxurious. Our tax dollars at work, as they say. Anyway, we have a few folks that are dying to see you, you have no idea—"

"I'm sure Ms. Nelson is exhausted after her journey," the paramedic behind me interjected. "It's probably best we settle her in and have the doctor check her out as soon as possible, given how intense tomorrow will surely be."

"That's fine!" The nurse's cheery attitude was unaffected. "The doctor will be by shortly. You're in here." She stopped by a large set of swinging double doors. "All the way to the end on your right. The bathroom is the door in the corner. Have you had a chance to eat yet?"

"Not yet," I admitted, flustered. Everything was happening so quickly, and this level of attention was new even for me. Having dedicated staff with me at all times? My own medical wing? Doubts clamored in the back of my mind.

"I'll bring something for you!"

Looking forward to a moment of peace, I thanked her and let myself be wheeled inside. To my surprise, the room was large, housing about two dozen beds with a curtain for privacy between each one. The paramedic helped me to the end of the row and pulled aside the curtain to the bed the nurse had indicated.

"Well, I guess this is where I leave you," he remarked, parking the wheelchair next to the bed. "You feeling alright? Want some help getting into bed?"

"No, no, I'll be fine. You've been a huge help. I appreciate it," I said gratefully. "Sorry to make you come all this way."

"Just doing my job, ma'am." With a roguish grin, he tipped an imaginary hat my way. Even with everything that was going on, I ducked my head to hide a smile.

Once he was gone, I swiveled around to take in my surroundings. There wasn't much. A vitals monitor and IV pole stood next to a medical cot complete with the tightest sheet tuck I'd ever seen. My bags, I was glad to see, waited for me on the foot of the bed. My phone and charger were in the side pocket of my overnight bag where I'd packed them. I plugged the charger into the nearest outlet, then sat on the bed to pull up my group chat with Devon and Chris. Scrolling through our messages, I felt a pang of longing. They'd be worrying for me, I knew. *Best to keep things light.* My thumbs moved across the digital keyboard.

I sense you guys are having too much fun without me *thoughtful emoji*

Chris: fuck how did u know

Chris: u got spy powers now too??

Devon: Lol not really. Feel like something's missing tbh

Aww stop Dev, I'm not used to you being so sentimental

Devon: Dev? Really?

Chris: ew quit flirting. my eyes *barf emoji*

Chris: hey i'm expecting some hella awesome souvenirs from faeland k make it happen

Yeye I'll do my best

With a sigh, I put the phone down. Now that things were calm, I could feel the exhaustion creeping in. I also found the lack of faint screaming in the background unnerving... Perhaps I'd gotten too familiar with the sound during my time at the White House. Luckily, I wasn't given enough time to spiral into undesirable thoughts.

The doors swung open to reveal a larger man with graying

facial hair in a white coat, flanked by a middle-aged nurse. I could make out several curious faces in the hallway behind them, and a myriad of hushed whispers filtered through the open doors. Anxiety began to rear its ugly head, along with unpleasant memories of being swarmed by people back at my childhood home in Connecticut.

"Avery Nelson, the national treasure," the doctor's voice boomed, echoing throughout the mostly empty room. "It's an honor. I'm Dr. Gregory."

"Felicity Hammon, Field Surgeon," the woman I thought was a nurse introduced herself. She wore a starstruck look I was intimately acquainted with. While I prayed I was mistaken, I suspected that those waiting outside were soldiers with horrific injuries who hoped for magic.

Dr. Gregory continued. "We received your records from the hospital and are here to keep an eye on you tonight and provide support as needed. Considering your condition has been stagnant for the past few weeks, I doubt there will be any surprises, but if you learn anything in the medical field, it's that people are never short of surprises."

"Sure, thank you." I grimaced but settled into bed without complaint as he summoned a bag of saline. The doors opened again, and the cheerful nurse from before came in with a covered tray.

"Somebody's popular!" she exclaimed. "Admirers are lining up by the dozen. Doc, you'll have to chase them off when you're done. They won't listen to me. Here, Ms. Nelson, I brought you some chicken, greens, and some pretzels. Have however much you can force down."

"Sorry to make you go to the trouble," I mumbled.

"Not at all." The nurse set the tray down on the bed and began to get the IV and vitals monitor set up. "We were all told not to bother you about any healing, but hope springs eternal. Not to mention that not a lot goes on around here; half of them are probably just excited to see a new face! Especially a pretty one." She winked. I barely resisted the urge to roll my eyes, responding with a weak smile instead. Pretty was a stretch—especially with the sunken cheeks and dark circles, which had shown no signs of improvement over the past few weeks.

"For people who are paid to take orders, they certainly are daring," Dr. Gregory remarked, shaking his head. "All right, you're all set. Eat, rest. There's a call button here if you need anything. Same as in the hospital, someone's always around. We'll get an automatic alert if any of your vitals take a turn, but otherwise, you'll have privacy. Even if we have to station a guard at the door for the night."

"I really appreciate it," I said for what felt like the dozenth time today. "Everyone has been so kind and helpful, it's so... so very appreciated."

"You're a patient, not to mention a valued guest," Dr. Gregory asserted, waving away my thanks. "You've made miracles happen, you know, giving dozens of people hope when they had none. This is the least we can do." He swept past the bed and gestured for the others to follow him.

"Leave the tray on the floor when you're done," the nurse told me as she passed by. Felicity lingered while the other two crossed the room.

"I, uh... I know we're not supposed to bother you," she began, her voice low. "My, uh... I lost hearing in my left ear a few years back, during a routine drill. I know it's not a big deal compared to what most people come to you for, but I thought... well, since you were already here, if you wouldn't mind..."

My heart plummeted.

"I'm sorry," I responded softly, trying to ignore the uncomfortable heat that crept up the sides of my neck. "I wish I could help, but... I'm, uh..." God, what kind of excuse would possibly be believable? I couldn't very well say I was broken. "Not feeling up to it at the moment," I finished lamely. As Felicity's expression morphed from hopeful to dismayed, I had to avert my eyes. I couldn't stand that look—the one that said I'd failed someone.

"When I get back from my trip, though, definitely," I promised in an effort to soften the blow. "Just come find me, and we'll get that taken care of in a jiffy."

"Of course," Felicity said hurriedly. "I'm sorry for asking. Just—let us know if you need anything." She hovered a moment, but try as I might, I couldn't find the right response. Face burning with shame, I kept my eyes downcast until she turned on her heel and hastened after the doctor and nurse.

Once I was alone, I could breathe again. I rubbed at my aching eyes, which were now moist with tears. What if this was to be my life now, spreading nothing but disappointment everywhere I went? I hoped to God that the fae had a cure. If not… no, I wasn't thinking about that. They'd seen this before. If they knew what it was, they could treat it.

If they didn't… it was over.

CHAPTER FOUR
THE RIFT

FAIR: an adjective meaning "light of hair or complexion." Once upon a time, I might have thought of myself as fair. When I met the fae ambassador with Vivian bright and early the next morning, the meaning of that word changed for me.

After having more greens and pretzels for breakfast, I was escorted back to the main building to join Vivian. She told me the envoy had finally arrived to meet me, but although I tried to imagine the possibilities, I couldn't think of a single actress or pop star that held a candle to the woman before me.

She was stunning. Modelesque. Statuesque. All the esques. Some half a foot taller than me, for starters, so nearing six feet tall. From head to toe, there didn't seem to be the slightest imperfection. Her form was lithe like a dancer, and just as toned. Her skin was honeyed milk, and her flowing waves were the color of a spiderweb touched by the morning light. She had me practically composing poetry. But God*damn*.

"So, you are the blessed human," she stated, arms stretched wide in greeting. Her voice even tinkled like birdsong.

"Hi. I'm Avery," I managed, somehow, to say aloud. I raised an arm to shake her hand, but she pushed past it and gathered me up in a hug instead. I felt weightless in her arms. My eyes were drawn to her ears, which peeked out from between the long, silken locks of her pale golden hair. The tips were long and curved into elegant points.

"Ishamenarin," she said—or something like it—as she released me. "The Goddess be with you," she translated upon noticing my blank expression. I realized then that I was absolutely, woefully, horrifically underprepared for this entire thing. In disbelief, I cast a sidelong glance at Vivian, who had the decency to look borderline apologetic.

"I am called Luenki," the fae woman continued. "I have been granted the honor of communicating with the humans on behalf of our leading family. We have been told of your circumstances and would like to invite you to our home as an honored guest."

"I'm grateful," I replied honestly. "You have no idea. And I look forward to seeing your…" What was the right word? Country? City? "Your world," I finished, cursing myself internally for not preparing so as to make a good first impression.

"We are ready for you," Luenki asserted, untroubled by my lack of eloquence. "The journey will be quick and easy. As soon as your leaders are sufficiently prepared."

"We're getting everything in order now, thank you." Vivian stepped forward. "If I may have a moment with Avery alone?"

Luenki graciously bowed her head and moved on.

"It's really impossible to be prepared for them," Vivian said by way of apology once the fae woman was out of earshot.

"I can see why," I remarked, unable to disguise the annoyance in my tone. "Anything else you think I might need to know? Now's your chance."

"The Rift entrance is over Lake Erie. We'll take a car to the shore, where there will be a boat waiting for us." She hesitated a moment before continuing. "They don't have electricity or cell towers, so you won't be able to communicate once you're over there."

My hand automatically went for the comforting weight of

my phone in my pocket. "There's no way to communicate at all?" I asked, shocked. Vivian shrugged.

"Messenger birds," she offered. "But if you'd like to call anyone before you go, I suggest you do that now. And also... I'll come with you just until we get to shore on the other side, but that's as far as I can go. You'll be on your own from there."

I nodded, trying to hype myself up instead of focusing on the fact that I was soon going to be left alone in a foreign place. And not just any foreign place—a place completely disconnected from modern society, where I would stand out like a sore thumb and probably make an ass of myself the entire time. "Okay. Can I have a minute?"

Vivian gave me a sharp nod before striding off to join Luenki.

I retrieved my phone from my pocket and unlocked the screen. Pulling up my contacts, I paused over the listing that read "Mom." I couldn't remember the last time I'd spoken to her... my birthday, maybe? During the last few months I'd spent at home, she'd felt more like a talent agent than a mom. Would she even care to know about my condition? My finger hesitated over the call button before I decided to hit "message" instead.

Hey mom

I paused. How much could I safely say? I should probably leave out anything about the fae. What needed to be said? After giving it some thought, my fingers moved.

Just checking in. Going on a trip, not sure how long I'll be gone. I'll have limited service in case you don't hear from me for a while. Hope you and dad are good. Talk soon

It would have to do. I pulled up my group chat with Chris and Devon next. Briefly, I wished I had said more than "thanks, see you guys later" before getting on the plane. If I had known I wouldn't be able to text from across The Rift, I might have come up with a more meaningful farewell speech.

kk I'm off, wish me luck. thanks for everything <3

I stared down at my phone for another moment. When there were no immediate replies, I returned it to my pocket and went to catch up to Vivian and Luenki.

"I'm all set," I told them. Vivian raised an arm, and within seconds, an SUV with tinted windows pulled up alongside us. After helping me into the backseat, she offered a hand to Luenki, who took it with the same grace as a lady accepting the arm of a nobleman. Luenki settled into the seat beside me as Vivian rounded the car.

Extremely aware of the personification of perfection sitting beside me, I racked my brain for something to say. "Have you ever ridden in a car before?" My weak attempt to make conversation was rewarded with a brilliant smile from the fae woman.

"A few times since coming into my role," Luenki answered. "It is thrilling to be sure, but I still prefer *avida*. Our riding beasts."

"Oh, I've heard of those!" I was relieved to recall that Vivian had mentioned something about that on the plane the day before. "What are they like?"

Luenki pondered my question as the car rolled into motion. "They are big and strong, with backs so broad they can carry two with ease. The males have whiskers and antlers, while the females have tufted tails. This time of year, they are shedding their winter coats. You will be on top of one before long." Taking in my wide eyes, she tittered. "Have no fear. They will know to be careful with a new rider."

"I've been on one before," Vivian chipped in from the front seat, her addition to the conversation easing my discomfort somewhat. "It is certainly an experience. But she's right, they're very sensitive creatures. Though, no matter how gentle they are with you, you'll be walking funny the rest of the day."

"It does involve some muscle," Luenki agreed. "You must sit tall and hold on with your legs. The proper form takes time to develop."

"I look forward to it," I said, and I meant it.

As we headed down the street, the buildings grew few and far between. Curiously, they also became smaller and more modern, concrete walls giving way to metal and glass. Perhaps these had been built later, after The Rift opened. The driver made a left turn, and then there was a security gate guarded by at least two dozen armed soldiers in camouflage uniforms. Beyond that was the lake, the shore lined with scientists in HAZMAT suits, big pieces of machinery that I could only assume to be testing paraphernalia, and all manner of boats and planes. As we pulled up to the gate and the driver rolled down the window to provide his identification, I scooted forward so that I could see through the windshield. My breath caught.

I had never seen The Rift before. Apparently, pictures did not do it justice. The dimensional tear was a jagged line that cleaved the sky in two from the surface of the water to some twenty or thirty feet in the air. Inside the break was a geometric pattern that reminded me of the crystals inside of a geode, sharp angles fading into a misty mass that twisted and warped as though it were alive. The surrounding water ran from it in tight ripples. Before the opening was a floating platform that extended all the way to shore for easy access.

"It is beautiful, no?" Luenki's voice pulled me out of my momentary fixation.

"Yes," I breathed. "Beautiful." It was, it really was. It also could have been something from a nightmare. I was going *inside* of that? And what the hell were the HAZMAT suits about? A bout of dizziness and nausea hit me together in a rush. I had to sit back and grasp my seatbelt to steady myself.

We passed the gate and pulled up beside several armored vehicles parked in a row. The driver shifted into park. Vivian got out first, and Luenki and I followed her lead. We were only perhaps twenty feet from the shoreline, and the only boat on the water was an unremarkable motorboat that sat no more than six.

"We're going in that?" I asked doubtfully. There were plenty of other options parked along the shoreline that looked quite a bit more comfortable.

"That's all that's necessary." Vivian waved the driver forward to set my bags in the boat.

"Ms. Pierce."

Vivian pivoted at the sound of her name. The soldier who'd spoken saluted in greeting.

"We're all set. Ready when you are."

"Thank you, sergeant. Luenki?"

Luenki looked around. As if on cue, a parrot-like bird with a long, thin beak and marbled green and white plumage glided toward us on the breeze. Luenki held up an arm, and it hovered a moment before landing. "They are ready to receive us," she reported, giving the bird a loving stroke with her free hand before it took off again. I watched in awe as it zipped fearlessly toward the open Rift and disappeared into the churning mass within.

"Well then, let's get on with it," Vivian declared, all business. She made for the boat, the sergeant following closely behind. Luenki lingered, perhaps noticing my trepidation.

"All will be well," she assured me with a soft, knowing smile. "We will look after you."

"I know," I said quickly, not wanting her to think that my nerves had anything to do with the fae. "It's not that. It's just that I've never been very far from home. I don't really travel." Not after the last time I left the confines of safety and the unthinkable happened. Now, I threw myself into an even bigger unknown, with no safety net of any kind. Why had I agreed to this again? My health, my duty… solid reasons, to be sure, but they seemed small now that it came down to it.

Luenki's hand slipped into mine, startling me.

"The Goddess is with us," she proclaimed, marching us forward with her head held high. I would have to ask about this goddess at some point. Sizing up the distance from the ground to the motorboat as we approached, I tried to figure out how to climb in without embarrassing myself, but Luenki didn't miss a beat. She shifted behind me, inserted her hands under my armpits, and lifted me onboard as though I weighed as much as a Chihuahua. I collapsed in the seat next to Vivian, stunned into silence, and Luenki hopped in after me, skirts fluttering in the breeze.

"Thanks," I blurted. She just smiled.

Several soldiers lined up on shore to see us off as the sergeant started the motor. I directed my attention forward, pulling out my phone to check if I'd gotten a response before it was too late. There was only one notification, from my mom:

Mom: ok dear have fun

That was it. A small part of me had hoped that she might show an interest in my life and ask for more details, but I guess that was too much to ask. I sighed and put the phone away.

The Rift loomed ahead in all its glory, appearing even bigger the closer we got, like it was about to swallow us whole. In the disconcerting silence, the steady purr of the motor and the gentle splash of the wake it created were magnified. I chose to focus on the comfort of Vivian's stoic presence beside me as we neared the swirling cloud of mist.

The air felt denser with every foot we traveled, like an intense level of humidity. Goosebumps prickled my flesh, and the hair on the back of my neck stood on end. We crossed the threshold and the haze swallowed everything before us, including the water and the tip of the boat. All at once, the heaviness in the air went from stifling to invigorating. I became deeply aware of my crippling fatigue, which lessened with each cleansing exhale.

"Do you feel it?" Luenki murmured from behind me, sounding excited.

"What is it?" I breathed, heart pounding at the foreign sensation.

"The magic is welcoming us home," she explained, reaching a hand into the mist. It might have been my imagination, but it almost appeared to caress her fingers in greeting before dissipating. It evaporated all around us—a sign that we were approaching the other side? The air still felt charged, but the hazy overcast lightened, and a subtle herbal scent tickled my nose. I could see the water below us again; it was greener than before. The boat slowed as we pulled through and the other side of The Rift came into view.

Stunning was too mild a word for the scenery. The water that stretched before us was a striking green, giving way to a shoreline studded with tall, green grass and transparent bell-shaped flowers that swayed in the breeze. Mountains and rolling hills comprised most of the horizon. Nearer to us, the lake—river?—twisted out of view, and hills gave way to forests with immense, knotted trees wider in diameter than I was tall. Where the trees in D.C. were largely bare this time of year, theirs were draped in leaves of brilliant colors, viridian and peach, like they had been painted with great care before our arrival.

Just before the imposing line of trees, there waited four massive, majestic creatures, three of which had riders. I couldn't make out the mounted individuals from this distance, but the creatures were clear enough. They had little in common with horses besides the general shape: supple bodies with a long, curving neck and four powerful legs. Three of the beasts were lavender and one was butter yellow. Two of the lavender ones appeared to be male, judging by the large maroon antlers. Even the smallest of the four was easily the size of a draft horse, with thick limbs and layers of rippling muscle.

Luenki got to her feet as we neared land, ignoring the sergeant's barked warning to be careful. He needn't have bothered—she cleared the last few feet in a graceful leap. One of the fae had dismounted and advanced toward us. He resembled Luenki in some ways: skin the color of sweet cream, pale golden hair, and a body built for sin. I tried to find some flaw in his appearance, studying his limbs and face intently. The beginnings of crow's feet at the corners of his eyes was the only flaw I could make out. Greeting Luenki with a quick fluttering hand motion, he knelt to grasp the bow of the boat and drew it alongside the shore with one hand. The subtle display of strength stunned me even as I gripped the sides of the boat for balance. Steadier on her feet than I was, Vivian thanked him without missing a beat and moved forward to disembark. The boat swayed, my stomach rolling along with it, and I held my breath, half expecting to lose my meager breakfast to the river.

Then a hand appeared in my line of sight. I looked up in surprise at the fae man, who said nothing but whose expression was open and encouraging. His eyes were such a rich shade of blue that a person could get lost in them... and so I did, I realized, as it registered that I still hadn't moved from my seat on the boat. Gratefully taking hold of the proffered appendage, I stumbled after Vivian onto the grass.

Luenki had greeted the two men that remained mounted. Now, the three of them approached on foot, and I turned my attention to the new arrivals. Despite myself, despite the situation, despite everything that mattered, I gaped—I couldn't help it.

Luenki fitted her forearms on top of each other before her chest and bowed. "We welcome Vivian Pierce, Lieutenant Governor of the Ohio State, and Avery Nelson, the Goddess-blessed human, to our shores. It is my honor to introduce you to the first prince, Solois of the King's House Wysalar, and second prince, Astonriel."

CHAPTER FIVE
THE PRINCES

THE STORIES and fan art flitting around the Internet really didn't do the whole "ethereal beauty" thing justice. Apparently, it was a trait that all fae possessed, including the males. The one that helped us with our boat appeared to be middle-aged, while the two Luenki had indicated to be the princes looked to be in their late twenties or early thirties.

Both were tall, built like athletes, and as fair as Luenki, if not fairer. They were both clothed in deep gray tunics and pants. The tunics were loose around the upper arms, chest, and shoulders but hugged the midsection, with a fine silver piece worn about the middle like an underbust corset. It was impossible to tell if that served a purpose or was purely decorative.

The one in front, whom Luenki had indicated to be the crown prince, had short, pale blond hair with a jagged pattern shaved into the sides. Hooded sapphire eyes glared at me from under thick brows, one of which had a silver piercing on the outer edge. His model-punk good looks were only mildly impeded by the petulant expression he wore, like this was the last place he wanted to be.

The one in back had a dutifully blank expression, but there was a spark of interest in his upturned eyes, which were the color of clear Caribbean waters. His platinum blond hair went past his chin but was tucked behind his ears, leaving the gracefully pointed tips on display. Both were pierced—one side had simple silver hoops at various intervals from the lobe to the tip, the other an earring and cuff with a fine chain dangling between them. He appeared more youthful than his brother, with features that were less harsh and more androgynous: a heart-shaped face, button nose, and fuller bottom lip.

Hel*lo*, hot and hotter.

Focus, Avery. Organs failing. People relying on me. Not *the time.*

Vivian inclined her head respectfully toward the scowling prince. "A pleasure to see you again, Prince Solois. I trust you've been well?"

"Fine," he responded. "You are welcome to return now. We'll take it from here."

I blinked at his brusque tone. Was that what George had meant by guarded?

Vivian didn't appear to take any offense to the dismissal, instead responding with all the grace of an experienced elected official. "I'll be out of your hair shortly. We've taken the liberty of compiling a copy of Ms. Nelson's medical records for your doctors."

The crown prince looked past us and jerked his chin at the fae who had helped with our boat. He had collected my things from the sergeant, but at the prince's unspoken order, he set them down and approached us.

"Are you on the medical staff?" Vivian queried, offering him a folder I hadn't noticed she held. The man hesitated, looking from her to Solois, who made no move to interrupt.

"I am well-versed in mending magic," he hedged as he accepted the folder.

"Please do not worry." The second prince spoke for the first time, addressing me directly. My heart skipped a beat as I met his gaze head-on, finding myself captivated by a pair of fae eyes twice in what seemed like as many minutes. "Farisen is a trusted member of our House, and he has a strong affinity for the healing arts. If your malady is indeed what we suspect, it is easily treated. You will be in good hands."

"I have complete faith, Prince..." I trailed off, mortified. Oh, my god, this had to be a nightmare. How could I not remember his name?

"Riel," he supplied. "Please call me Riel."

"Riel," I finished on a mumble, face burning. He shot me a heart-stopping grin, and I was forced to look away. Seriously, that was some kind of magic all on its own.

"If there is nothing else?" Solois interjected none-too-kindly.

"That will be all," Vivian confirmed. "Please keep us updated as much as you can, and let us know if there is anything we can do, at any point. Ms. Nelson is a highly valued member of our society."

"We will be in touch," Luenki promised. Vivian gave a sharp nod and turned back toward the boat, inclining her head my way as she passed. I tried to keep the uncertainty out of my expression as I nodded back. She was in the boat and making for the open Rift in no time, leaving me alone with four gorgeous beings, two of whom were high-ranking royalty. Farisen was busy loading my bags on his mount, but Luenki and the princes still surrounded me. My nerves were like a solid lump in my throat.

"I-I look forward to getting to know you all," I stammered, trying to think of something, anything to start a conversation and make a good impression. "It's handy you all speak English, huh?" I tried, giving a laugh that sounded awkward even to my ears.

Solois's brows drew together. I could only imagine how much my face paled.

"Things are a lot simpler with magic," Riel remarked, something an awful lot like mirth sparkling in his seafoam-green eyes.

My stomach dropped. "Oh! Of course." *Stupid!*

"Translation magic would certainly come in handy," he continued, his tone taking on a playful note, "if it existed."

At first, I thought I must have misunderstood him. Was the existence of a translation magic not what he implied? For all I knew, they did everything with magic here. Was… was he teasing me?

"At least, it would have saved me the six months I spent learning your language after The Rift opened," he finished.

"Six months?" I blurted in disbelief. "You learned fluent English in six months?"

"I have had many years to become fluent," Riel corrected me. "But yes, I was proficient by six months. It's a relatively simple language."

"Wow, that's…" I trailed off, and my mouth snapped shut. He wasn't asking for validation, for heaven's sake. Could I say anything that didn't sound like pandering? Maybe ask something about their language or the area? Shit, I was making a massive fool of myself.

"Shall we take this dazzling conversation back home?" Solois remarked without humor.

Luenki spoke a musical mess of syllables that I didn't catch —I assumed in their native language—but her tone was sweet and inoffensive. Solois shot a bland glance her way before turning back to his mount. Luenki offered a gentle smile at my puzzled look.

"The princes have had a long day," she said by way of apology. "So long as your condition allows for it, we will make haste for home. We should return well before supper."

"I'll be fine," I assured her. Riel said something brief in their language, gesturing to the steeds. Surprise flitted across Luenki's face, but she inclined her head without protest.

"You will ride with Astonriel," she murmured. I blinked, turning my attention to the beasts that awaited us. One, two, three… ah. I should have noticed earlier that I'd be sharing with someone. Well, that was probably for the best, considering I'd never even been on a horse. At least it looked like Riel didn't mind.

He hovered by the female lavender mount. I hurried forward so as not to keep him waiting, taking in the creature as I went. Up close, they seemed even larger, if that was possible. Her fur was much thicker than a horse's, downy and plush like a luxurious carpet. To my surprise, she had no saddle, only a thick strap running around her chest and underneath her front legs to create a handhold at the base of her long neck.

I became aware of a presence behind me just as strong arms attached themselves to my hips. Before I could react, I was in the air. Apparently, plucking people off their feet as though they were lap dogs was just something the fae did. In a rare moment of wisdom, I swung my outside leg up and around as I was deposited atop the creature's broad back. I managed to land in the proper position, albeit with the wind knocked out of me.

The prince alighted behind me and reached around my body to slide his hand into the loop of the saddle strap, fitting me against his chest.

"Comfortable?" his voice came from right beside my ear. My arms broke out in goosebumps.

"Yes," I squeaked in reply. In truth, my position was precarious at best; my legs were stretched too far apart to be comfortable, and the heat of an unfamiliar but very attractive man against my back was borderline painful, but manners prevented me from saying so.

Farisen, Luenki, and Solois had already mounted and started toward the forest.

"Relax," Riel instructed me, as if my nerves ever paid any attention to my personal feelings. With a brief, gentle squeeze of his legs, the beast underneath us surged forward. I bit down an unfeminine squeal at the jerk of momentum and quickly found a handhold to provide some semblance of security.

But as we rode, my discomfort was forgotten. If this was anything like riding a horse, I suddenly understood horse girls.

The adrenaline boost aside, there was something incredible about being so tall, feeling such strength underneath you, and having the wind in your face. It was the same brand of exhilaration as being on a rollercoaster, as though touching the ground was optional.

Unfortunately, the novelty wore off some thirty or forty-five minutes into the ride. By that point, we had slowed to a less grueling pace, but my knees were screaming, my hips were stiff, and I could no longer ignore the constant undertone of nausea that had been tormenting me for the past three weeks.

The woods looked the same as they had upon first glance, all stone and dirt and magnificent greenery, but surely, we had covered several miles by now? How much farther could it be? And how in the heck were these beasts not showing any signs of fatigue? Despite their large size, they stepped with delicate precision, as though picking each foothold individually.

It registered that my hand squeezed the strap so tightly, it was painful. I switched hands so that I could shake it out, letting blood flow back into my fingers. "Is it much farther?" I ventured to ask, raising my voice to be heard over the wind and footfalls around us.

"An hour or so," came the response. I managed to stifle a groan of distress and instead gritted my teeth in determination, reminding myself why I was here. Even if it hurt, I wasn't about to complain or demand a break—I needed to make a positive impression on my hosts.

By the time signs of civilization came into view, my legs and backside had grown numb, and I grappled with a lingering ache in my kneecaps. We finally reached a proper road, with signposts covered in scratched symbols marking the way and the outline of a city in the distance. Instead of continuing toward the city, we turned right to travel parallel to it.

"Miderrum."

I jumped at the prince's voice—somehow, I'd managed to forget he was there. "Excuse me?"

"The city. Miderrum. It won't be much farther now."

Sure enough, a misty shape in the distance started to take the form of a great manor. Perhaps "castle" was a better term for it, given the height of the hill it was on and the intimidating stone wall surrounding it. Images sprang to mind of an elegant king and queen in all their finery overseeing a magnificent throne room full of lords and ladies. I'd be horribly out of place, but hopefully, most of the fae would be welcoming.

As we neared the castle wall, we slowed from a brisk lope to a lively walk. There were no guards visible on the ramparts, but the portcullis glided open as though sensing our arrival. Even though the entire gate was covered by some kind of climbing plant, I could see that the intricate details of the metalwork showed exceptional craftsmanship.

I wasn't sure what I had expected, but I wasn't prepared for the sprawling courtyard just within the walls. On one side of us were petite structures, perhaps sheds for storage or some type of temporary housing, surrounded by gardens. On the other side was an expansive field dotted with various animals, including more riding beasts. The path we were on led straight to the castle entrance. The building itself was made up of several connected sections, including a tower sticking out from the back, and appeared larger than the White House, though not by much.

Solois brought his beast to a halt ahead of us, and we all followed suit. Riel alighted without a problem and stepped forward to help me off. I fumbled before leaning over and putting my hands on his shoulders. When he lifted me, the pain returned in my legs and back all at once, and I was unsteady on my feet when he set me down.

Solois and Luenki had dismounted and allowed their animals to join the ones grazing in the field while Farisen retrieved my bags from his steed. Facing the palace, I was surprised that there was no one else in sight, not even a footman. I'd expected... more fanfare, perhaps? But maybe that wasn't how the fae did things. Not knowing what to expect unnerved me, but I had to get used to it. That was probably going to be my life for the next few days.

Solois headed up the stone steps, tossing words casually over one shoulder. Luenki turned to me with a strained smile.

"The first prince will inform the king and queen of your arrival. In the meantime, I will show you to your room."

"Okay, thank you," I said, wincing at the thought of a walk.

"I'll take her," Riel interjected. "Rest and recover, Luenki." Luenki and the older fae man both seemed surprised as Riel scooped up my bags and gestured for me to follow.

"I can at least get my own bags!" I scurried forward despite the discomfort in my lower half to relieve the prince of his burden, but he dodged my reaching hands.

"Nonsense," he declared. "Come along, *eseri*."

Although baffled by the situation, I obeyed.

"Well, it seems that the prince has things in hand." Luenki appeared flustered, if it was possible to fluster her. "Then, rest well. Until our next greeting." She inclined her head in farewell as we passed by, and I quickly did the same, then focused on scrambling after Riel in spite of my protesting thigh muscles.

The front door was a single piece of polished wood the height of two men that, like the portcullis, opened automatically as we approached. A brief examination revealed no pulley system, so I had to assume that some invisible magic was involved. Before I could consider it further, my attention was stolen by the entrance hall we stepped into. It was beyond grandiose, with a polished stone floor, evenly spaced pillars, and stained-glass windows lining the walls.

I didn't have time to appreciate it, though. Jeez, the prince walked fast.

He led me to one side, up a wide flight of stairs, then down another expansive hallway, and took a series of turns that had me struggling to keep up. Eventually, he stopped at a nondescript dark door, one of several that lined that particular corridor.

"What's ours is yours, as you say," he commented as he set down my bags and opened the door for me. He stepped aside so that I could enter.

I first noticed that the room was modest compared to the opulence I'd witnessed thus far. It did have a window, which I could appreciate, but the walls were wood and bare stone. A modest bed with a metal frame took up one corner, a massive armoire beside it. There was also a little bedside table with what looked like an old-fashioned gas lamp, but the room was otherwise empty.

"Thank you, it's lovely," I said quickly, remembering my manners. The bed looked comfortable, at least. "Although... shouldn't I be in a medical wing or something?"

"That won't be necessary," Riel responded. I anticipated that he would elaborate further, but no explanation came. Instead, he bent to gather my bags. I shifted my position to provide enough space for him to bring them inside.

"I see. All right, then." I had to assume they knew best; after all, that was why I was here.

"I'm not sure what you're used to," Riel began as he set the bags down by the bed, "but we rise with the sun and eat four meals a day. They'll be brought to your room for the time being." He hesitated a moment before adding, "I don't recommend that you walk about freely. There are those who are... displeased by your presence here."

I hadn't expected to hear it put so plainly. "Why? I mean, if it's not... I'd like to know, did I do something wrong?"

"Not exactly." Riel shrugged and made his way to the exit. "Some things just are."

While I attempted to digest his cryptic words, a thought occurred to me. "Oh, wait!"

Riel paused in the doorway.

"Where is the bathroom?" I asked meekly.

"The what?" He gave a perplexed frown.

"Bathroom? Uh, water closet? For like, cleaning and... relieving oneself?"

"Ah. We don't have rooms for that, but a bucket has been provided. You'll find it under the bed. I'll have some leaves delivered for you to clean with."

A lengthy moment of silence followed his words. "Oh," I managed finally, trying my hardest not to let the dismay show on my face. "Great. Thank you."

Riel watched me for another moment before the corner of his mouth quirked upward. Striding into the room, he stopped at a panel I'd thought was part of the wall design and tapped it with a knuckle. The sound was hollow.

"It slides," he disclosed with a wink. And with that, he was gone.

Well, then. Apparently, one of the only people around here who didn't hate my guts liked to make fun of me. *As if I didn't have enough to worry about.* I hobbled to the bed, wincing as I went. They weren't kidding about those horse things being rough on new riders. I didn't even do any of the work, and I was sure I'd be feeling it for days.

With a deep sigh, I collapsed face-first on top of the bed and focused on getting my thoughts in order. The best course of action was to lie low, I figured. Do what they say, get my powers sorted out, and go home without pissing anybody off. It was a pretty solid plan. With any luck, my problem wasn't that serious, and I'd be right as rain in no time.

I flipped myself over and studied the pattern of the ceiling, which resembled the underside of a tree canopy. The room wasn't that small, but something about it was stifling. It could have been the silence, without a TV to have on in the background or Chris and Devon to chat with. Maybe it was the stone wall, which reminded me of a cellar. Specifically, a dark, dank cellar full of stale air and dirt—

Before I could continue down that line of thinking, I leapt to my feet and dashed to the window. Gulping in the fresh air, I closed my eyes. No good—I'd almost returned to that place.

I snapped my thoughts back to the present instead. "Lie low," I said aloud, nodding to myself. "Be polite, get well, and go home."

I nodded again, but with more conviction.

Lie low. Get well. Go home. Simple enough.

CHAPTER SIX
THE TEST

Meanwhile…

"SHE'S IN THE CASTLE, and still, the Goddess is silent."

The cloaked figure paced before the tower room door in agitation. Another, smaller form, which had been no more than a voice in the dark when this conversation had begun some twenty-odd years earlier, sat cross-legged on the bed. Without the mysterious shroud of darkness, they were rather unremarkable: a short, blond individual of indeterminable age and gender, dressed in a distinctly unflattering but admittedly comfortable-looking frock. Before them lay a wooden board with checkered spaces occupied by carved animal figurines.

"And?" the person asked, their attention remaining on the game in front of them. "Or have you simply come to see me so that you can vent? Your presence is welcome either way, but if it's all the same, I'd rather avoid the small talk today. I'm in the middle of something."

The cloaked figure stopped their pacing and threw back their hood to reveal an astonishing beauty as fair as day, with golden hair like sunbeams gathered atop her head and held in place by a delicate circlet. Although she appeared barely forty years of age, there was a depthless maturity in her face and the regal way she held herself. This was the one and only Lady of House Wysalar, the fae the humans knew as a queen.

"To ashes with your game," she hissed. "I can't be the only one who sees this for what it is. She's working with *them*. This is a ploy to slip a spy past our defenses."

"It could be," the person on the bed remarked thoughtfully, "that they hope to unlock the secret behind our blessing. Given the jealousy they have harbored these past years, it would not be a surprise. It could also explain why the Goddess chooses to remain silent on the matter."

"This must be part of the test. If the Americans are working with House Leimor, then the girl must be dealt with swiftly and without mercy."

"Indeed, my queen."

"Riel has offered to keep an eye on her while she is here. I cannot help but feel that it is a mistake to trust him with something so important. Is this part of the test as well?"

"That, I cannot answer."

"Have you not seen the results of our current course?"

There was a moment's hesitation. "I have."

"And?"

"He will be successful at earning her trust. But there is a great deal of grief in his future."

"Grief, what grief?" the queen demanded. "Will she turn on us?"

"As I have explained to you before, those from Earth evade my sight. But, although I cannot predict her actions, I can see that her presence here will lead to conflict with our people."

"A conflict." The queen scoffed. "You're no help." She resumed her pacing.

The person on the bed shrugged and turned their attention back to their game. "I will let you know if I can glean any more details. In the meantime, I recommend that you observe the situation for now. Riel may yet surprise you. You know he seeks to impress the family."

"The boy serves his purpose as a spare." The queen punctuated her dismissive words with a wave of her hand. "I dare not form higher expectations where he is involved."

"Be that as it may."

After another moment, the queen stopped at the door and loosed a dispirited sigh. "Is there anything more I can do? Anything at all? I cannot bear this… this powerlessness."

"Continue to pray for Valuen's intercession. It is all we can hope for. If the Goddess means for us to know Her plan, She will make it known, one way or another."

CHAPTER SEVEN
VAHELA

It was a sobering revelation when I realized how much I relied upon technology and the Internet. Without it, I had learned that I was not nearly as resourceful as I'd thought. Also, that boredom may very well be the cause of my eventual death.

Hours had passed. The first thing I did was take the initiative to give myself a full tour of the room. I left the bathroom door open, since it made the room feel more spacious. The bathroom was quite nice. I was pleased to find that it was not that far off from what I was used to, complete with modern plumbing.

There was a deep, square sitting tub carved from wood in the center of the room and a tall freestanding spout beside it. After some deliberation with myself, I'd decided that the knee-height box jutting out from the far wall was a toilet. To the right of it was a shelf with a hook, which held an odd cup or vase of some sort and a folded linen cloth. There was no sign of toilet paper. Was that what the cloth was for? I cringed at the thought of having to ask Riel for clarification. Hell, maybe I *did* need some leaves.

After eyeing the setup dubiously, I rooted around the box and walls for some kind of hidden compartment. Finally, I was forced to assume that one was meant to use the cup and towel to rinse and dry, respectively. Either that, or the linen was meant to be used once and tossed in with the laundry, and there was a pile of extras I missed somewhere. Beside the toilet was another freestanding spout, and next to that was an alcove that served as a sink. It had a drain leading into the floor underneath and a mirror above it.

After the frustrating adventure of figuring out the bathroom, I dozed. At one point, there was a knock at my door. I leapt to answer it, heart pounding, and found a tray of food on the floor outside, no person in sight. The food—a thick, somewhat sweet broth accompanied by a small bowl of crunchy little stars reminiscent of rice crackers—proved palatable, if confusing for my tastebuds. I wasn't sure if they were intended to be eaten together, but that was what I ended up doing, since it wasn't unlike soup with croutons.

I estimated about four hours passed before there was another knock. Like before, I sprang up to answer it, only to be met with another tray of food; this time, three balls of a spiced brown mash wrapped in leaves. The leaves were tough to chew. Feeling silly, I just ate the mash that was inside, then stacked my two plates together and put the trays outside my door.

Eventually, the sun began to sink down over the horizon. Without anything better to do, I unpacked my bags and made the bed. I tried not to let the lack of attention bother me. They knew what was going on; if they were worried about my condition, I would have seen their doctor already. As it was, I might die of boredom. Much more of this and I'd start talking to the dust bunnies under my bed.

Another knock. This time, an unidentifiable minced mush patty over a bed of bitter greens. I didn't have much of an appetite by that point, and it was getting late, so I had a few small bites, rearranged the rest to appear half-eaten, and set the unfinished portion outside.

At that point, it didn't seem like anyone was coming back

for me, so I lay down and tried to sort through the many things I felt while staring at the ceiling and twiddling my thumbs. The anxiety made it difficult to calm down. Although I couldn't guess what my time here would be like, I couldn't shake the unsettling feeling that something terrible was going to happen now that I could no longer rely on the safety of the White House.

Another part of me was thrilled. For the first time in... forever, really, I was on my own. Well, relatively speaking. I was hesitant to hope, but there was no denying that this had the potential to be the adventure of a lifetime. How many people would kill to be in my shoes right now? If I handled myself well, made smart decisions, and did what I could to learn about the culture and fit in... this could be good. Maybe I'd even make some friends here. *That would be nice.* I was pleased with myself for coming up with something positive to focus on.

Eventually, I figured I'd best try to get some sleep and settled down for an early night. With numerous thoughts running through my head, I lay awake in the darkness for what felt like several hours before I could relax enough for sleep to claim me.

I woke with a start to a knock that was distinctly different from the ones that had delivered my meals. Sunlight filled the room, a sign that it had been morning for some time. I lay there, dazed, as the seconds passed in silence. *Had I imagined the knock?*

"It is time to start the day, *eseri*!" a chipper voice called from the other side of the door.

I was out of bed in an instant, scrambling to pull off my pajamas.

"Yes, coming!" I cried as I slipped a casual T-shirt dress over my head while wincing at the soreness throughout my body. Pulling on socks and sneakers, I hopped my way to the door and opened it to reveal the second prince, who gave me a brilliant smile and immediately thrust something into my hands. Without thinking, I took the plate from him.

"Humans do like to sleep in," Riel remarked as he scrutinized my room.

"Oh my God, am I late?" My stomach dropped at the thought that I'd kept someone waiting on my first day here. Then again, no one had given me any direction. How was I to know?

"Not at all. We're on no one's schedule but our own. Aren't you going to invite me in?"

"Uh, yeah? I mean, yeah, you can come in." I stepped away from the door to let the prince into the room, still somewhat muddled by sleep and not entirely certain what was happening.

"You'll be starting your lessons today," Riel informed me as he brushed past.

"My huh-*wha*?"

Riel turned to face me and paused as he took in my state of disarray. His lips pursed—in disapproval? Amusement? I wanted to say something but bit back the sharp words. Not everyone was lucky enough to look like a model fresh out of bed.

"Are you going to eat your *raast*?" He nodded down at the plate I still gripped, which contained several colorless square blobs with pieces of something dark scattered throughout.

"Maybe? I was going to brush my teeth and go to the bathroom..." I mumbled the last part of my sentence, having woken up enough at this point to realize that I was underdressed to have a frickin' hot-as-balls fae prince in the middle of my room. Riel must have read the thought on my face, or at least noticed I was flustered, because he took pity on me.

"So be it. Join me outside when you're ready."

He breezed out just as quickly as he'd breezed in, shutting the door behind him. I stared at the space he left, mouth agape, until I recovered enough to toss my breakfast onto my bed and rush to the bathroom to get ready.

Not even ten minutes later, I'd brushed my teeth, put on a bra and jacket, stuffed a few of the breakfast blobs into my mouth, and yanked open the door. Riel waited for me a few steps from my door, eyeing my bare legs as I approached.

"Is this typical garb for you?" he queried.

"What? Why? Is something wrong with it?" Feeling self-conscious, I stopped short, prepared to turn back and change. Riel just made a sort of grunt in the back of his throat, shrugged one shoulder, and turned down the hall, indicating for me to follow him.

"You said something about lessons?" I hurried to keep up with his long strides.

"All will be revealed in time, little *eseri.*"

"What does that mean, esely, anyway?"

"*Eseri.* It is a small, cute mammal that follows predators around and hides in the grass waiting to clean the bones of their prey. The predators do not mind them because they are too fast to chase and not worth eating."

My brows came together in a frown.

Without slowing his pace, Riel added, "You remind me of one. Small. Cute. Following others around. The hair is a similar color as well. Like clouds at sunset."

"Oh." I felt my face warm as his words registered. Namely, the fact that he thought I was cute. Was it a good thing or a bad thing that he was comparing me to an animal? I didn't have the mental capacity to worry about that right now.

"How have you found the accommodations?"

"Good! They're good, thank you. The food is very different. Not bad," I was quick to add. "Just different from what I'm used to. And the room is fine. Perfect! It's perfect." Ugh, I couldn't get a single sentence out without saying something rude. At this rate, I wouldn't be surprised if I was kicked out to sleep in the field with the horse / elk-animals.

Luckily, Riel didn't appear bothered. It was a good thing I had him showing me around instead of the other one; his brother didn't exactly radiate patience. Out of the corner of my eye, I studied his figure. He had his hair up in a short ponytail, and instead of the formal gray outfit from yesterday, he wore a tailored green tunic that looked exquisite against his fair coloring. I was envious of his flawless skin. Not a single imperfection blemished the milky expanse of throat from his collar up to the firm line of his jaw—

Those stunning pale blue-green eyes glanced my way. I snapped my gaze back to the hallway in front of us, but I knew he'd caught me staring. My cheeks warmed. *Shit.*

"Are you sore from yesterday?" He surprised me by changing the subject. "Riding the *avida* is not easy for those who aren't used to it."

"Hm? A little," I admitted, clearing my throat to thwart the beginnings of a lump. "It was fun, though."

We reached the grand room I remembered passing through on our way in. Two regal thrones sat at the end opposite the main entrance. The ceiling was decorated with elegant beams resembling the winding branches of a dense tree canopy. Captivated by the fine details carved into the pillars we passed, I almost missed Riel's response.

"We will ride again today, but not for long."

Riel paused to allow the front door to open for us. I studied the walls on either side, but there was no visible machinery or pulley system, which as far as I was concerned, confirmed my earlier suspicions that magic was at play.

We stepped out into the courtyard. Riel headed toward the field where the *avida* grazed, but I stayed put to look around the closest garden, where neat rows of orange fruit filled luscious vines. Intent on examining the plant, I had just settled into a crouch when the door to the nearest hut opened. I straightened quickly, surprised to see someone other than the royals and Luenki.

All the fae I had seen so far were beautiful, and the young woman who emerged was no exception. However, her clothing was simple in comparison to what I had seen thus far, which made me think she was a peasant. Was peasant the right word? She winced at the sight of me and, just as I was about to say hello, retreated back into the hut, faster than my eyes could follow. Baffled by her reaction, I retracted the arm I'd raised in greeting, and my budding smile transformed into a perplexed frown.

"Don't worry about it." I spun at the sound of Riel's voice to see that he'd retrieved his lavender mount. "They were asked not to speak to you."

"Why not?" I asked, dispirited.

"They don't want to catch it," Riel responded, waving for me to approach.

"I'm contagious?!" I practically shrieked. That was news to me. *Why wasn't I quarantined in a bed somewhere if that was the case? Had I already spread whatever I had throughout the castle? Was I about to be responsible for the next great plague?*

"Ah, no. Sorry." Riel ducked his head in embarrassment. "I was expecting you to ask for clarification, and then I was going to say 'your fashion sense.' Bad joke."

Before I could grow indignant, he had crossed the space between us and grasped my hand to tug me toward the waiting mount. He lifted me up just as he had the day before. I threw my leg over to straddle the broad back before realizing that picking a dress had been exceptionally stupid, and I had to scramble to pull my skirt between my legs to hide my backside.

Riel gave me a moment to make myself decent before he hopped up behind me, kindly choosing not to comment on my predicament. His arm came around to grip the handhold in front of me and he squeezed his legs to signal the beast to start moving. I was sure I'd never get used to the sensation of it shifting into motion underneath me.

We followed the main road for a few minutes before veering onto a path, where Riel slowed his steed to a rolling trot. I didn't recognize the path we were on. That was no surprise—I'd only been here a day, and my sense of direction was flawed at the best of times. Still, I thought that we were heading in a different direction than The Rift.

Riel wasn't lying when he said the ride wouldn't take long. I guessed it hadn't even been half an hour before we came to a halt and Riel dismounted. He helped me down, and we headed along an obscured path deeper into the woods. My uncertainty grew as the trees became sparse, eventually falling away to reveal a breathtaking clearing.

All thoughts I might have had died on the spot. Front and center was a natural waterfall spilling from a massive rocky overhang into a pale green pool below. The pool was surrounded by tall grass dotted with white flowers, and big, fat buzzing insects flitted from flower to flower. The air was alive with energy, like this place was the lungs of the earth itself.

No fences. No screaming hordes. Just… fresh air and freedom.

Riel studied my reaction. I let loose a grin that threatened to take over my entire face. When words failed me, I gesticulated wildly at the view around us instead, attempting to express my awe somehow. Riel chuckled, a warm, genuine sound.

"There are a few springs like this," he began, moving forward to kneel at the pool's edge. "Some believe the Goddess created them as a gift to us to please Her consort, Valuen. The waters provide a rejuvenating effect to magic users. Come, dip your feet."

The invitation was all I needed. I slid my sneakers and socks off to join him at the edge of the pool. Using his hand for balance, I first tested the water with a tentative toe. It was delightfully cool. With Riel's encouragement, I settled beside the pool and let my legs hang off the edge into the water. A deep sigh escaped my lips as tension fled my body. The feeling was comparable to what I had experienced coming through The Rift: an electrifying tingle that chased fatigue away.

"We'll be spending quite a bit of time here over the next few days. The waters will aid your recovery," Riel said, taking a seat in the grass beside me. "Speaking of your recovery. I think it's time to address this condition of yours."

"Please," I responded gratefully. "You're familiar with it?"

"Based on what we've been told by your government, almost certainly. But first, I'd like you to tell me about your abilities and what happened, in your own words."

I took a deep breath, gathering my thoughts before I spoke. "Well, so, as far as we can figure, I just have to touch someone who's sick or injured, and I can sense what's wrong and use my magic to fix it. I don't know how much you know about our world, but we don't have a lot of magic. If someone's sick, there's medicine or surgery, but that isn't always enough. You can probably imagine what the demand is like for what I can do."

"It's a useful ability," Riel agreed. "A gift of that magnitude is rare."

"Tell me about it," I muttered. "So, basically, I have to be under protection at all times, since people can get... aggressive about wanting to get healed. I totally understand—I mean, I'm usually a last resort, their only hope. Otherwise, they're incurable. I wish... well, that's not important." I shook my head, embarrassed. The prince didn't need my life story.

"I first started noticing issues a few months ago. Thinking back, I should have noticed sooner, but I didn't think it was anything to worry about. My anxiety was worse. My appetite started going downhill. I lost weight, and I was sleeping more than usual. Then, last month, I was doing my scheduled healing, and I only got to one person before I fainted. Usually, I can heal four or five people at a time. Or, at least, I was able to before I started getting sick."

Riel was quiet, but I could feel his attention.

"They ran a few tests and said that my organs are starting to fail. It was a surprise to everyone, myself included. I'm not necessarily suffering, but I'm tired all the time. Sometimes, it's hard to keep food down. I get chills, my chest hurts, and… I can't heal anyone anymore. When I try, the magic doesn't come. And I've been like this for weeks; it's not getting any worse, but I'm not getting better. They have no idea what's causing it."

I had no reason to be nervous, but I was anyway. *Was he going to tell me that they didn't know what was wrong with me after all? Had this all been for nothing?* I kept my gaze on the water before me, watching it lap at my skin. A moment passed in silence before Riel responded.

"Can you describe how it normally feels when you use your magic? Before the issues started."

With some degree of difficulty, I recalled the last few times I had used my magic successfully. "It's like… there's a little flame in my chest that's always there, right? When I try to use it, it flares up, and I gather the heat and pass it along. I feel it get pulled from me. It doesn't hurt, not exactly, but it can be unpleasant. After a few times, I'm totally wiped out."

"And when you heal yourself?"

"I can't. I've tried to in the past, but it just doesn't work. Like, I can feel it, but it just stays there instead of going where I ask it to."

At that, Riel startled me by surging to his feet. He caught my wide eyes and pinned me with a meaningful stare. "It's as we thought. You're not sick, Avery."

His voice was so smooth and masculine that hearing my name from his mouth did weird things to me. I almost forgot to process his statement. "Um… what?"

"Most of our children are blessed with a connection to *mana,* the force you know as magic." Riel scanned the trees. "But they are not blessed with control. Before they can wield it properly, they must learn a few basic concepts. That fire you describe feeling, here—"

He stooped to tap one finger against my sternum. If he noticed my flinch, it didn't disconcert him. "That is something all magic users have, an inner thread connecting them to the flow of *mana* in the same way that roots carry nutrients to a tree. It is only to be used as a tool to access and control the flow of *mana*. When that runs out, we call it *vahela*—emptying."

I attempted to absorb everything he told me like a sponge, but a lot had happened in the last couple of days, and I wasn't quite following. Noticing that I wasn't making the necessary connection, Riel simplified things for me.

"Your equivalent would be death."

CHAPTER EIGHT
THE FIRST LESSON

"YOUR EQUIVALENT WOULD BE DEATH."

His matter-of-fact statement rang in my ears.

"Oh," was all I could say to that.

Riel cleared his throat and continued. "*Mana* is a bottomless force, but you're drawing power from your own, limited essence. It doesn't feel good because it's killing you. Once you learn to draw from the right source, you will find that your stamina increases. You should also be able to heal yourself without issue."

"I see." I digested this new knowledge with some difficulty. "So… what comes next?"

"You need rest. I'm guessing you've already been feeling better?"

I contemplated his question and nodded. Honestly, I could tell something was different since the moment I passed through The Rift. The lingering ache from riding the avida aside, I felt good. I'd eaten most of my food yesterday without feeling sick afterward, and I was only occasionally light-headed. The realization made me hopeful that things were looking up.

"*Mana* is plentiful here. It's all around us, in the air, the grass, the water. The same cannot be said for your world. As long as you don't expend any more energy, you should recover on your own, given some time."

"So... you're saying that all of this is the universe telling me I need a vacation?" I couldn't help but crack a smile at the absurdity of the idea.

"Something like that," Riel agreed. "But while you recover, you might as well learn how to properly use your abilities. We'll start from the beginning, with concepts, as if you were a child. When you're feeling better, we'll move on to applying what you learned."

Swishing my legs back and forth in the water, I leaned back on my elbows. "And you're going to be my teacher?" I clarified, not sure how I felt about that. "You sure you don't have anything better to do?"

Riel's face was unreadable. "Some might consider that to be an insulting question."

I quickly straightened up, realizing that I'd gotten a little too comfortable somewhere along the way. "Sorry, I didn't mean it like that. Obviously, you have other things to do. I'm really grateful that you're taking the time to help me instead."

Riel joined me on the bank once more, leaving about two feet of space between us, and cocked his head in my direction. "Don't be sorry. It's a good question," he said with a grin, surprising me. "I don't. Have anything better to do, that is. I'm all yours."

"Oh." I blushed despite myself. "Well, thanks. I appreciate it."

"Since today is your first lesson, I'll let you guide things," he suggested. "Are there any things you have questions about so far?"

"There are," I admitted, worrying my bottom lip. "But do you mind if we start with more general things? I feel like the magic-related stuff is just... too much right now. I've been trying to adjust, since everything is so different here. Like, okay, the Goddess. I don't mean any disrespect, but I'm not religious myself, so please be patient with me. How much is she… a part of everything? Does everyone believe in her? Are there commandments to follow?"

Riel looked up at the sky as he considered my question.

"It's complicated," he admitted. "Some take Her more seriously than others. My mother, for example. You'll meet her eventually. It's part of her responsibility to serve as our people's religious leader of sorts. My generation has been taught the stories, but most of us have never felt the Goddess's presence. At least, not in the way the elders claim to. Some believe She's abandoned us. But regardless, the faith remains a cornerstone of our culture. And there are no commands, but… to say there are some guidelines, perhaps, would be accurate."

"Should I be doing the greeting, then?" I queried. "The one Luenki used?"

"*Ishamenarin*?" Jeez, the word sounded like silk on his tongue. "No, it's not expected of you. It's more of a tradition than anything else; one of those things that people do for a reason no one knows anymore. You may hear '*Keerya savessan*' as well, but that one's not a greeting. Best not to repeat that in polite company."

"Oh?" My interest was piqued.

"Valuen is another deity, the Goddess's consort. When their relationship was still new, a jealous mortal, Keerya, tested them. She claimed that she had slept with Valuen and carried his child. It nearly tore their relationship apart. Luckily, Valuen was able to convince the Goddess that it was a ruse. As he has a soft spot for mortals, he even asked Her to be merciful toward Keerya. '*Keerya savessan*' essentially means 'Keerya spoke the truth.' It is blasphemy, implying that the Goddess was a fool to believe Her consort and have mercy on the woman."

"Ah, gotcha. A no-no word," I mused, nodding along.

"A no-no word," Riel agreed, a smile teasing his mouth. "Do you have anything similar?"

"Oh, lots," I said enthusiastically. Where did one even start?

"There's shit, fuck, damn. Ah… ours don't have stories behind them, though. They're just crude. Shit is, like, poop. Fuck is… well, that's a really versatile word. Technically, it's a crude way of saying sex, or an exclamation for when you have strong feelings toward something. 'Damn' is like 'go to hell.' That one is religious, I guess."

"Hm. I've heard those before," Riel commented.

"Really?" I was impressed. "It's crazy how fluent you are."

"You were born shortly after The Rift opened, were you not?"

"Yeah, that's right."

"As a member of our leading family, I've been involved in discussions with the Americans from the start. It's likely that I've been speaking English longer than you have."

"Pfft." I shook my head at how absurd the thought was. "That's wild. You can't be that much older than me. They had a kid front and center during political talks?"

Riel cocked his head. "You might be surprised. Our lifespans vary somewhat."

I bolted upright from my relaxed position. "Shit," I breathed. "You're not about to say you're, like, 700 years old? I should have guessed."

"Though a connection to *mana* grants us some additional benefits, the difference is not that vast. We are still mortal but live about twice as long. I'm in my forties by your years."

"That's not bad." If I'd been with Chris and Devon, or chatting with my online gaming crew, I might have made some crass comment about that being prime Daddy age.

"I'm glad you think so," Riel remarked wryly.

It was hard to stay focused. Better to change the subject before I let anything inappropriate slip. "What were things like back then, when The Rift first opened?"

When silence met my question, I glanced his way.

"What was it like in your world?" he asked instead of answering me.

"Uh..." I had to think back to what I'd heard from my parents and knew from my schooling. Was there anything I wasn't supposed to mention? I couldn't remember if George or Vivian had given me any topics that were considered national secrets. "Well, I wasn't very present the first few years. But the way my parents talked about it, tensions were high. Nobody knew anything about the fae or what to expect, and a lot of people were afraid that war was coming. I think... our government was concerned that you guys would start pressuring us in some way, or that you'd give another country advantages we didn't get and throw off the power balance. America has a precarious position... a certain reputation to uphold, you know."

"Mm." Riel went silent again. Eventually, he seemed to decide on what he wanted to say. "We had our own tensions to worry about," he began. "There's another family to the west. House Leimor." A muscle ticked in his jaw. "We've been at odds with them since before I was born, but neither of us is willing to go to war. Some of us thought that The Rift was somehow their doing, at least before your government told us there was a section of The Rift to the west too."

A thought occurred to me. "You mean the one in China?"

Riel hesitated, then inclined his head.

"Huh." I wondered if a map of Earth and a map of this world would line up, like alternate realities on top of each other. People suspected that there might be more sections of The Rift that we didn't know about, and that was just scratching the surface of things we didn't know. "Well, I don't remember hearing about that, but not a lot is common knowledge for civilians. There are probably still people that don't think you exist, and the fae are all some big conspiracy theory."

"Our people likely know even less," Riel remarked dryly. "Though, to be fair, they don't have much interest in foreign affairs. We're simple people."

"Yeah?" I was curious what he meant by that. They certainly didn't come across dumb.

Riel made a sound of agreement but didn't elaborate further.

We sat for a while in silence, enjoying the cool water and each other's company. It was unexpectedly nice. At least so far, this was turning out to be a pleasant adventure. I'd never imagined that I would be able to enjoy the outdoors so freely like this.

"It's nearly time for the late morning meal," Riel said, interrupting my thoughts. "Shall we return, or would you like to stay a while longer?"

I felt a pang of disappointment at the thought of leaving, but wasn't about to argue. "Yeah, we can head back, that's fine."

Riel pulled his legs from the pool and got to his feet, and I followed suit, being careful of my skirt. As soon as I left the water, the fatigue came trickling back. I'd miss the pool… not just for the rest of the day, but after all this, when I had to return to my normal life.

We rode back in silence. When we arrived back at the courtyard, I saw a few more casually dressed fae hanging around the huts, but they were quick to make themselves scarce.

"They're actually not allowed to talk to me?" I inquired as Riel lifted me down.

"Not 'not allowed' exactly, but wary. Don't let it get to you," he told me. "They just haven't seen many humans. When Mr. Kepler visited in the past, it was the same for him."

Well, I couldn't say that I understood, but it did make me feel a little better to know that George got the same treatment. That must have driven him crazy. "Are they servants?"

"Employees. We pay them to cook, clean, and tend to the land. Whatever we need. Most of them live in Miderrum, the city we passed when you first arrived."

"I remember."

"Come. We'll eat, and then I'll show you around."

Riel led me back into the castle. Rather than taking the stairs to the second level where my room was, we passed the throne room and headed down a long hallway lined with windows. "These overlook the fields," he commented. A flash of light from outside caught my eye, so I moved closer to see. There was a small crowd gathered in the field in a loose circle. The light sparked in different colors from the center of the group.

"Our soldiers," Riel said from behind me. "They're training."

"Oh!" I squinted in an attempt to make out the distant figures. It made sense that there would be soldiers around, being a castle and all, but I couldn't remember seeing one yet. They must be doing a stellar job of avoiding me. "The light… is that their magic? Why doesn't mine look like that?"

"Good question. You have a different kind of magic. We'll talk about that during your next lesson." Riel resumed walking, and I jogged to keep up. "Down this way," he indicated a hall that led to wide double doors, "is the banquet hall. And here are the kitchens."

We stopped in front of another set of doors near the end of the hallway, and I noticed a tucked-away corner with a spiral staircase leading up and out of sight. In my head, I went over the areas of the castle we'd covered thus far.

"That's the tower, yeah?" I asked, pointing. "What's up there?"

"Spare rooms," Riel answered without bothering to follow my line of sight. Something about that made my bullshit detector perk up, but when he opened the door to the kitchens, the pleasant smells wafting into the hallway made my suspicion evaporate. My stomach concurred with an appreciative murmur.

The kitchens were organized in an L shape, the room neat and spacious. The employees were caught up in various stages of cleanup and meal preparation, so our presence wasn't noticed immediately. Riel, to my surprise, strode right up to a pot bubbling away on the stove. Perhaps hanging around in the kitchens was normal behavior for him. He lifted the lid to examine the pot's contents, and we both jumped in surprise when a spoon swatted the back of his hand.

The gentleman holding the spoon said something in their language, his tone chiding. He glanced at me before turning his back to us to give the pot a stir. "Sit if you want to eat," he said in English. He was the first I'd met so far who spoke with an accent. Riel murmured a response that I didn't catch, then came back to me with an apologetic look on his face.

"We take our food seriously," he said by way of explanation. Motioning for me to join him, he guided me to a large prep table out of the way from the main action. Shortly after we'd taken our seats, the man from before approached. We were each given a small bowl with a steaming sauce and a thick slice of brown bread that was still warm.

Once we'd finished eating, we exited at the back of the room and passed through the banquet hall to end up in the hallway we'd walked through earlier.

"The whole place seems so empty. Is that just because of me?" I asked as we made our way back toward the front of the building. That was the only thing that made sense to me. Otherwise, why have all this space and not make use of it?

"Some of our forces are currently away on business, but it's usually relatively quiet. Those who do live here are well looked after, and our guard, though small, is very capable."

"Does it ever get lonely?"

"Sometimes," he admitted after a beat. Although his body language didn't change, something about his expression seemed pinched. I wondered if that was a sore point for him.

"I know what it's like," I offered, studying the floor so that I didn't have to deal with eye contact. "I was lonely. I mean, the White House is pretty much always full, despite being so big. But there isn't anyone my age. I have my bodyguards, Chris and Devon. They're the only ones I talk to in real life. Everyone else is either there for the president, or there for my healings."

Thinking back, I added, "It could be suffocating at times, more than lonely, I think."

"I know the feeling," Riel confessed quietly. It was hard to put words to the look in his eyes, but I wanted to give the man a hug. Somehow, I got the feeling that we were kindred spirits, as nonsensical as that seemed. Heart swelling with sympathy, I came to a halt. When he noticed I'd stopped, Riel turned back with a quizzical expression on his face.

"I appreciate you." The words fell out of my mouth. It was what I'd always wanted to hear from others, so it felt natural to say, but Riel gave me an odd look. I hurried to clarify. "I mean, you've been very welcoming, which I appreciate. And you're showing me around and explaining things so that I'm not bored and confused in my room the whole time. So… yeah."

"Hm." Riel contemplated my words. I began to think that perhaps I had overshared, but apparently, I needn't have worried. "And I suppose it doesn't hurt that I'm easy on the eyes."

My immediate reaction to his casual comment was an unladylike snort. I attempted to cover it up with a cough, but it sounded unconvincing even to my ears. So much for trying to be supportive. "Well, yeah, there's that," I mumbled in a last-ditch effort to salvage the conversation.

"So, you do think so, *eseri*?" A slow smile spread across his face.

Wait one goddamn second. He was teasing me again!

"No. I don't find arrogance attractive," I responded frostily, stomping past him. "Let's get this tour finished up with, shall we?"

His low chuckle made my cheeks warm.

As I rounded a corner, I nearly ran straight into someone. At the last second, the body shifted out of the way, and I stepped into the empty space it had inhabited. An apology sprang to my lips, only to die as I found myself looking up into a familiar sapphire-blue glare.

"Prince!" I squeaked, backing up to give him space, and knocked into Riel, who was turning the corner. In a flash, he grasped my elbow to steady me.

"Solois," Riel said in greeting.

"Astonriel," Solois responded in an even tone. His eyes flicked to me, then down to where Riel's hand connected with my arm. I apparently wasn't worth greeting as well, as he then looked back to Riel, saying something in their language.

"Indeed," Riel replied cheerfully in English. "We just returned for our late morning meal, and I was giving her the tour. If you haven't yet eaten, I suggest you hurry. We barely made it in time, and Juris was starting on supper before we left."

Solois made a sound of acknowledgment and shot me a look awful close to a glare before stalking off. Gentle pressure on my elbow guided me to start walking again.

"What did he say?" I whispered once I figured we were out of earshot.

"Oh, just making polite conversation, asking after our general health." Riel's breezy tone suggested the crown prince had not, in fact, been asking after our health. The situation both confused and frustrated me, but I let it go. Prying wouldn't be laying low or being polite.

We finished the tour, but my mood was soured for the rest of the day.

CHAPTER NINE
THE SECOND LESSON

THE NEXT DAY started the same as the one before it: I was awoken by an all-too-cheery knock on the door shortly after the sun rose. Sleep-deprived and fiercely missing alarm clocks, I threw on clothes (this time, I was wise enough to wear joggers) and accepted my breakfast from Riel. We rode out to the same location as last time, and I settled by the pool and lowered my feet into the water with a sigh of pleasure.

"You could bottle and sell this stuff for big bucks," I said to no one in particular.

"I'm not sure that would be as lucrative as you're hoping, given that these springs are plentiful, and no one here is lacking in *mana,*" Riel commented from behind me. Today, he'd brought a stiff round brush to give his *avida,* who I'd learned was called Oyanni, a thorough grooming. Judging by the melodic purring sound she made with each stroke, she enjoyed it. Clumps of fur fluttered to the ground as he went.

"Well, humans would pay out the ass for it," I amended, kicking my feet back and forth and watching the water form pearlescent swirls as it moved. "Could market it as some kind of rare healing tonic. Holistic wellness juice. Put a few drops of red food coloring in it and sell it as a health potion to the same people who buy Gamer Girl bathwater."

Riel paused, his arm poised for a downward stroke of the brush. "Bathwater?"

"It was a whole thing. You guys should be glad you don't have the Internet."

"Indeed." He was equal parts baffled and amused.

"Anyway, what's on the docket today, teach?" I asked.

"I thought we'd touch on what you should know about the different types of magic." Riel patted his beast on the rump to signal he was finished. She turned her big head and flicked her chin in a gesture of thanks before lumbering off to find some tasty foliage.

Dusting his hands on his toned, canvas-clad thighs to rid them of any remaining fur, Riel settled in the grass to my left. I quickly directed my gaze away from his legs and back to the water in front of me. "Let's see..." He considered his words. "It's been a long time since I had my lessons, so let me know if you need me to slow down or clarify something at any point."

At my nod of acceptance, he continued. "Put simply, there are four kinds of magic: mending, breaking, changing, and making. In most cases, a person will find they possess an ability that falls into one of these categories. Your healing abilities, for example, are the purest and most common form of mending magic."

"With you so far," I assured him when he paused to be sure I got the picture.

"Good. There is technically a fifth category, but it is uncommon, so I won't bother going into that. Now, rarely will someone only have access to one particular ability, although it happens. More likely, you have a primary affinity and a secondary affinity. Some magic users, given time and training, are able to call upon all four kinds of magic with great skill—we call them *shahim*, hands of the Goddess."

"Like the Avatar." I nodded along.

"I'm… not sure what that is."

"Don't worry about it. Carry on."

"Mm. Well, as someone with a mending affinity, you should know there is a close relationship between mending and breaking magics. Both have to do with the understanding of a structure, its strengths and weaknesses. As such, it is common for someone with healing abilities to develop a secondary affinity for breaking magic."

"So, I'd be able to break bones and stuff?"

"Among other things," Riel agreed. "It is not always in a literal sense. It could involve swaying a delicate balance or interrupting a natural process. Just as mending could be anything from curing a person's illness to restoring a tear in a shirt."

I imagined the possibilities, and my heart soared. Healing people would remain my top priority, but to be able to use my magic in scenarios that weren't life or death? To potentially break things as well as fix them? The thought was intoxicating. "And these are all things I could do?"

"With patience, you could expand your skill set. Generally, it takes years to master a primary skill, which in your case seems to be healing bodies. It's unlikely that you would be able to do something completely unrelated, but repairing objects is within the realm of possibility.

"It becomes more difficult to learn other skills the closer you get to mastering one, as they require different approaches. In other words, the methods you employ to heal won't work the same way to achieve another result. That all comes later, though. Training always starts with determining the ability and its category. We've accomplished that, so we can move on.

"Usually, the next step would be warning you not to use your ability until you've had the proper training, but you've already become well acquainted with the dangers of misuse. Frankly, from what you've told me, it's a miracle you're not already dead."

That, I had no answer for. "Guess the Goddess must really like me." I shrugged.

"Indeed." The corners of Riel's mouth quirked upward to match my smile.

"So, since we have that covered, what comes after the warning?"

"You should learn the difference between drawing energy from yourself and tapping into the flow of *mana*. That can take a while."

Dreading the answer, I asked, "How long is a while?"

"Weeks. Months."

My heart sank. Sitting out in nature with a handsome, charming prince was no hardship, to be sure, but that was unlikely to be all we did. How was I supposed to manage here? How could I go weeks or months without worrying about things back home? Not to mention that I only packed enough clothes for a week. Had they told George how long it would take?

"It depends on a number of factors," Riel continued. "How attuned you are with your body and with nature, how far your discipline extends, the reach of your ability… how skilled your teacher is, how much the Goddess likes you."

Despite myself, I rolled my eyes and huffed a laugh. "Ha! Okay, I'll bite. So how does one do all that? I have to learn the difference between using *mana* and my internal source first?"

"That's right. Most do it by trial and error. Since you nearly reached *vahela* only recently, you won't have that luxury. Luckily, there's an alternative that works just as well. Close your eyes."

With an impatient sigh, I obeyed.

"Breathe slowly, purposefully," Riel's voice commanded. "Focus on the scents. Feel where you are connected to the earth and the water. Pay attention to the itch of the grass underneath your hands and legs and the moisture against your skin. Empty your mind of all unnecessary thoughts. In your case, that means all of them."

My eyes popped open so that I could give him a dirty look. Riel responded with an innocent smile. It was at that point that a realization struck, causing me to grimace. "So… meditation. You want me to do *weeks* or *months* of meditation."

"Every spare moment," Riel confirmed, unbothered by the touch of sarcasm that had leaked into my words. "But these grounding exercises are just the first step. Once you've managed to *feel* rather than *think*, you'll turn your attention inward. You described feeling a flame within. Find that space again, and open your mind to what lies around it. When you are ready to draw *mana*, you'll know."

"Okay, but what am I looking for?"

"When you find it, you'll know," Riel repeated. "It's different for everyone. Some feel as though their inner self is a river, and they must follow it to where it flows into the sea. Some feel they have roots, and they must find the tree above."

Confused, I tried to imagine that place inside me and match it to some kind of higher power. "So, if I see fire, then I'll get… what? A volcano?"

"It's not literal. You can picture whatever you like. The point is that if you're on the right track, you will feel some kind of current bridging between you and the flow of *mana*. Follow that and you find the right source. It will be a well of boundless power. Once you've found it, it will become easier and easier to connect to it and resist draining your own energy."

"Okay, that makes sense." I nodded along before his words registered and then frowned. "But wait. How can magic be boundless? Doesn't that go against some kind of natural law?"

"Ah. Excellent question. *Mana* is unlimited, but your ability to channel it is not. It's like how air exists all around you, but you can only take in one lungful at a time. You can teach yourself control so that you decide when and how quickly you breathe. You can train yourself to increase your capacity so that you can take deeper breaths. But no matter what you do, you will never be able to utilize all of the air in existence.

"You will also find that there are limits on what you can do. No matter how powerful you are, things you create from *mana* will not be the same as the real thing. You can change a stone into food, but it will not provide the same sustenance. And you can turn dirt into clay, or turn clay into bricks, but you would still need to stack them together to form a building."

"Huh." Thinking about the concept made my head throb, reminding me that I was not yet fully recovered. Still, I had to ask. "So, given these… limitations, what are my chances of eventually being able to raise an army of the undead?"

The corner of Riel's mouth twitched. "Unlikely, I'm afraid."

"What about just, like, a dozen?"

"Slightly less unlikely, but unlikely nonetheless."

"Even with years of training?"

"In another reality, perhaps, where you were not limited by a mortal lifespan. I'm not aware of anyone in history who has gained that particular ability."

"Oh, well. I'm mostly kidding." There went that idea. My feet swung back and forth in the water with renewed vigor. "Honestly, it'd be incredible just to be able to heal without killing myself. Though…" I briefly imagined what demand would be like once my powers were no longer limited by my health, and a prickle of apprehension took root. The crowds would swell. The shouting would intensify. Chances were George would have me out there at least once a week, if not every day. I wouldn't have a moment of peace. "I suppose that'll come with some other challenges if the way things have been is any indication."

"Would you like my advice?" Riel's question was a welcome reprieve from my thoughts, which had begun to turn somewhere ugly. He took my dazed blink as permission to continue.

"You're here because you have a tendency to put others before yourself," he said. "That's not a bad quality to have, but it is dangerous. It means that people will take from you, because it's in their nature to do so, just as it's in your nature to give." Riel leaned back and focused on the sky. "We have a saying: *In virani ma onaya kessavi ki, torenna.* 'When blood is shed in the name of kindness, you have gone too far.'

"It's a reminder to be aware of your limits and not harm yourself in the pursuit of selflessness, as noble as that pursuit may be." He paused to let his words sink in, glancing my way to be sure I still listened. Noting my confusion, he went on to add, "What I mean to say is that you have no duty to inform your keepers of what you've learned here. Feel free to define new limits for yourself and communicate those boundaries."

"Easier said than done." Tension twisted my gut. "I have literally thousands of people relying on me. People who are weak, desperate, and in pain. And for most of them, doing nothing is as good as killing them. Putting myself first is a nice sentiment and all, but I can't afford to do that. Not when I can do something to help."

Riel shrugged. "If you were never blessed with your abilities, they would die regardless, no? Each time you choose to help, it is a gift. Your sense of responsibility is misguided."

I mulled over his words and some of the tension lessened. "Yeah, I guess. It's a little more complicated than that, though. I don't know how I could ignore them."

"You don't need to ignore them. Just take care not to abuse your kind heart."

Unhappy with that answer, I made a disgruntled sound and lay back against the grass. My eyes landed on the cloud directly above me, which looked a little like a heart. The puffy edges even gave it the impression of one battered and bruised. Much to my embarrassment, I found myself tearing up. "Geez, when did this turn into a therapy session?" I gave a broken laugh as I tried to wipe at the moisture with my sleeve without being too obvious.

"My apologies." Riel's voice was soft. He kept his attention on the distance, giving me some privacy. "I didn't intend to touch upon a painful topic."

"No, no, you're totally right. I needed to hear that from someone, you have no idea. I think I just… I don't know how to stand on my own feet. I crave validation, you know? It's like, if I'm making a difference in someone's life, if I'm being helpful, everything feels worth it somehow. I feel like I mean something. If not… Gah, I'm a mess."

"Aren't we all?" Riel remarked wryly.

"Yeah?" I cast a sidelong glance his way. "All right, well, you're learning all my secrets, so you next, then. What sort of skeletons does a fae prince have hiding in his closet?"

"I'll have you know I don't have a closet, much less a collection of hidden skeletons." Riel's smile didn't quite reach his eyes. "In any case, my problems are quite boring. I was raised in my older brother's shadow, the two of us competing for our parents' love. I've come to terms with it over the years. My brother bears the brunt of the stress; being born second has granted me some freedoms and opportunities I would not have had otherwise."

"Ah. Still, that must be rough." Not sure how to respond to that, I turned back to the sky and contemplated some things. I knew what having a responsibility to your nation and guardians was like, but it wasn't the same. Their lifestyle was so different. "You guys are a little different from what I expected. We have stories about fae, you know. Fairy tales and folklore. But you guys strike me as more like Tolkien's elves than the fairies from Shakespeare and stuff."

Riel shrugged at that. "It's easier to let the matter be, but it's worth noting that only humans call us fae. Our people are *Ishameti,* the Goddess's chosen."

"Oh… of course you'd have a different word for yourselves. I'm sorry, I didn't know." My emotions were still raw, and to my embarrassment, the tears threatened again.

"There's no need to apologize," he assured me gently. "You

and your people may call us what you like; it's no insult and makes no difference. I have not read enough of your literature to know where we may differ from the fae of your legends. What did you expect?"

Attempting to keep my voice from trembling, I drew in a soothing breath. "I mean, I kind of knew what to expect from the news and such. But in my world, when someone says 'fae'... I guess I would think of a mischievous little person with wings. There are a lot of different interpretations, though. There're fairies, then there are things like imps, and brownies, and leprechauns. They all look different. In general, they're not necessarily good or bad, but they're big tricksters. Some can change their appearance or grant wishes."

"Mm." Amused, Riel explained, "We don't all look the same, you know. Changing magic gives us the ability to perfect our appearances, but we still have different races with their own histories and cultures. I can't say that I see much resemblance to your tales in other ways."

"No," I agreed with a small shake of my head. "But that makes sense. You're more like humans than what most people would think of when they hear the word 'fae.' You guys are tall, for one. And you carry yourselves elegantly, rather than being conniving and mischievous."

"Some of us, anyway. We also don't grant wishes."

"Well, nobody's perfect."

The two of us shared a smile.

"Some of you are a little grumpy," I pointed out, thinking of Solois's surly attitude. Riel's wince told me he knew exactly what I referred to. Given the opening, I ventured to ask another question. "Um… I understand if this is a touchy topic, and no need for details if it is, but I was wondering… Is Solois always that cheerful, or do I just keep catching him at bad times?"

When silence met my question, I began to worry that perhaps it was best to leave that stone unturned. As I was about to introduce a change of topic, however, Riel spoke.

"I told you on your first day here that there are some who are unhappy with your presence," he said, his voice guarded. "Solois… would be one of them. He sees you as another responsibility on top of everything else he has to worry about, that's all. It has nothing to do with who you are as a person or anything you've done. He was raised with rigid, unachievable ideals, and such an upbringing has a tendency to make one… cranky."

"Cranky, huh?" I shook my head. "That's a nice way to put it."

"Do you have any siblings?" Riel asked.

"Nah. My parents were already older when they had me, and honestly, I don't think they really wanted kids. They never admitted I was an accident, but I have my suspicions." It made me uncomfortable to remember how easily they gave me up when things got tough.

He tilted his head. "Are children often accidental in your world?"

I blinked in surprise at the unexpected question. "Sure. The guy pulls out too late, the condom breaks, the woman forgets to take her pill or tracks her cycle wrong… it happens all the time. Don't tell me you guys have magical birth control?"

"Young men are sent to menders to have changes made before they become sexually active," Riel explained with a shrug. "Children are always planned."

"You mean…" Horrified, my voice dropped to a whisper. "You all get castrated?"

"Ah, no. The… er… anatomy remains unchanged."

"Oh!" My breath left me in a rush of relief. "So, like a magical vasectomy. That makes more sense."

"Anyway, we're late for our meal."

I didn't miss Riel's abrupt change of subject, or the fact that the tips of his ears were taking on a rosy shade. Was the prince a bashful sort when it came to topics of an adult nature? I'd just about seen and heard it all with how much time I spent on the

Internet, but they didn't have social media to taint their delicate sensibilities. The thought amused me.

"Shall we?" he asked, getting to his feet and dusting off his pants.

I hid my smile as I pulled my feet from the pool and stood. "Thanks for the lesson," I told him as we walked to where his *avida* waited. "I feel like I learned a lot today."

"It was my pleasure," he replied. "I suggest you begin setting aside time for meditation. Ideally, you will be able to practice a few hours every day." He lifted me into place on the animal's back as usual and took his seat behind me. "Best hang on tight," he murmured as he reached around, the low words sending a strange shiver through me. "We'll have to hurry."

Even riding like the wind, we were tardy for the late morning meal. Luckily, Riel was able to sweet-talk the cooks into getting us something to eat. I returned to my room that afternoon thoughtful and sated, and the next few hours were spent working on grounding exercises. Although I couldn't make it past a few minutes without getting sidetracked, I still felt like the day had been an overall win.

And I slept well that night, despite the stone walls that made me recall less-than-pleasant memories. That made me hopeful that maybe I could be comfortable here for the weeks or months it took to sort myself out and get back to the life I knew.

CHAPTER TEN
THE SHIFT

OUR DAYS CONTINUED along those lines. I got used to waking up with the sun, so I was usually ready by the time Riel came for me. After the first couple of days, he started bringing our meals with us so that we could eat by the pool and stay until the afternoon. In the mornings, we'd meditate for a while, then I'd get another miniature lesson. He'd let me ask questions, and then we chatted more than anything else during the latter portion of the day.

The weather warmed, and my health and appetite returned in full force. At the same time, Riel and I grew closer, to the point where the vibe between us seemed to shift from teacher and student to friends. That was my interpretation, at least, given that we spent more time shooting the breeze than we did doing anything useful.

For example, I taught him 20 Questions. It hadn't occurred to me that it might be a difficult game to play when we had entirely different cultures and experiences, but we managed. We also played several rounds of I Spy, although we encountered similar problems with that since I didn't know the names of the plants that surrounded us. Still, we got by. And because of that, Riel started teaching me about their plants and wildlife.

A large portion of their diet came from nutrient-rich nuts produced by a tree called *vali*. The buzzing insects that pollinated the flowers in our clearing were not bees, but *kainna*. We even saw an *eseri* at one point, which Riel was particularly excited to point out to me. They were essentially a cross between mice and chinchillas.

The closer we got, the more I wanted to know about Riel. One day, I started the line of questioning with, "What was little Riel like? When you were growing up, I mean?"

Given our usual conversations, the inquiry didn't faze him.

"Curious," he answered, gazing into the distance. "Much the same as now. I wanted to learn everything and couldn't wait for the day when I knew it all. I was rather naïve. And you?"

I shouldn't have been surprised that he'd turn the question around on me, but it had been a long time since I'd thought back to my childhood. Although I didn't have many memories from before my powers manifested, the years that followed were crystal clear. How could I forget, with all the issues that period in my life left me with?

"I was quiet," I said, thinking back to before it all began, when I spent most days in my room playing with Barbie dolls and little animal figures. "Shy. I kept to myself and didn't have a lot of friends. At least, until my healing ability kicked in. I was eight. After that, everyone wanted to be my friend."

"How did you discover your ability?" Riel asked.

"Completely by accident," I admitted. "Before my powers kicked in, I went to public school. One of my classmates fell and hurt themselves during recess. When I helped her up, I felt the pull of magic. Her wound closed and her pain disappeared, just like that. I didn't realize what had happened at first, but when I got home, I told my mom. She was crazy enough to grab a kitchen knife and make a cut on her arm. I healed that too. She acted like she'd found one of Willy Wonka's golden tickets." The memory was one of the few happy ones from my childhood. Before the consequences set in, I'd been so excited.

When Riel's elegant brows came together in confusion, I added, "It's from a movie. Or a book, I guess, originally. *Charlie and the Chocolate Factory*."

He made a sound of understanding, although the perplexed look remained. "Your mother must have had a lot of faith in you, to trust your word enough to harm herself."

"Yeah, I mean, our relationship was pretty good back then. But it wasn't that out of the blue—the other kids were all over the news by then. I guess they figured out their abilities sooner. I sometimes wonder if I would have discovered mine earlier if I'd been able to heal myself."

"A defense mechanism of sorts," Riel mused. "You can't fill a cup from itself. Even if you weren't aware that you were using your abilities wrong, your body knew."

"Well, I know that now. At the time, I just figured it wasn't in the cards for me." I lay back in the tall grass with a sigh, wondering how everything would change now. Enough sunlight filtered through the tree cover above that I could feel its warmth. "Back to you," I said, turning my head to face Riel. "What do you do when we aren't hanging out? Royal paperwork?"

"Thank the Goddess, no," Riel answered with a chuckle. "I don't have as many responsibilities as my mother or my brother, so I find things to do, whether that's helping to prepare food or tending to the *avida*. If there are disagreements among the staff, I might address the grievance." He gave a long-suffering sigh, then added, "I am a glorified maid."

"Don't say that!" I exclaimed, propping myself up on my elbows indignantly. "That's all important stuff that has to get done. And I'm sure your employees are glad to have your help. I don't know if I could see Solois dealing with that."

"No," Riel admitted. "He doesn't have the patience for chores or petty squabbles." The corner of his mouth quirked upward. "Yet another way in which I am superior."

"Yeah, yeah." I rolled my eyes at his now-familiar sass,

unable to stifle a smile. I might have imagined it, but I thought there was a flash of something different in his expression… something soft, almost yearning, that tugged at my heartstrings. It was gone as quickly as it had appeared, leaving me wondering if I had imagined it.

"The others like you," he said once the moment passed. "Tell me about them."

Marcia came to mind first, causing my heart to squeeze painfully in my chest.

"I don't know any more than most people," I began, forcing the words past a lump that had developed in my throat. "But I remember hearing about a boy who could understand animals and a girl who could change her body into whatever she wanted. There were a couple more too." I tried to lighten the mood with a quip. "I always wondered why there weren't a whole bunch of us, but I guess that just makes me extra special."

Riel made a thoughtful sound. "Magic can work in mysterious ways. It is extremely potent, but it also has a life of its own. We struggle to understand it. Before The Rift opened, everyone could feel that something was different."

My interest was piqued. "Really? Like what?"

"Hmm. It's hard to explain." He contemplated his answer. "The *mana* became unpredictable, harder to harness. And excessive—the air was thick with it. Animals grew restless. Some thought the Goddess was forsaking us, that it was the end of the world."

"That's wild," I murmured. I could imagine how terrifying that must have been for their society, like going through a solar eclipse without understanding what was happening. Panic would have been rampant. "Do you think… it meant to make The Rift?"

Riel shrugged. "Perhaps. Our advisor surmised that it simply grew to be too much for our world to contain. According to their hypothesis, The Rift was an unintentional tear resulting from the pressure, with the excess *mana* drifting into your world. Into certain humans."

"Well, that's as good a theory as any."

"Indeed."

We sat in silence for several minutes, enjoying the fresh air and warm breeze. I couldn't remember the last time I'd been this comfortable in someone's presence. It was crazy to think we'd only known each other for a matter of weeks. Already, I felt as close to Riel as anyone. He had a way of making one feel comfortable, with how insightful and considerate he was. I was no longer nervous to say the wrong thing or be awkward in front of him. It was a strange feeling when I was so used to my every move being watched and judged. *I could get used to this,* I thought. A shame it wouldn't last. For some reason, the idea of going back to the White House after this troubled me.

"Are you hungry?" Riel asked out of the blue.

I perked up at the thought of food. I was ravenous these days; my body had a lot of catching up to do since coming back from the brink of death. "I could eat an *avida*!" I exclaimed. An alarmed snort came from the woods. "Not Oyanni, though," I amended quickly, mortified. Raising my voice in order to be heard, I added, "She's too nice!"

"No need to take it back," Riel remarked as he got to his feet. "Our animals have grown lazy believing that there will be no repercussions for poor performance. Threaten them all you like." He collected the bag he'd attached to his *avida*'s handhold strap and gave her an affectionate pat to show that there were no hard feelings.

I pulled my feet from the pool and crossed my legs to get comfortable. When he returned with the food, he settled next to me, closer than he usually was when we meditated together. I tried not to notice how petite I felt next to his tall, slender frame, but it was like the air was warmer on that side. Goosebumps prickled my flesh in awareness.

Rather than let myself ruminate on what that meant, I

turned my attention to the package he'd retrieved. "What have we got today?"

He unwrapped it to reveal two large, flaky pastries that resembled empanadas or Jamaican patties. I was salivating before he deposited one into my hands.

"*Massiya*," he said, biting into his with pleasure. I eagerly followed suit. Although it was lukewarm and a little soggy, the flavor made my tastebuds come alive.

"The filling is made with ground *vali* nuts and spices," Riel explained. "It's a popular food to pack when you'll be out and about, given how easy it is to eat." He licked a crumb from his thumb, and the movement caught my eye. *What else does that tongue do?* I found myself wondering. *Jesus, Avery. Behave.*

I took my time chewing while I attempted to redirect my thoughts somewhere more appropriate. The spices they used provided some unique flavor profiles; familiar in some ways, yet foreign in others. What cuisine from Earth most closely resembled fae cooking… something Mediterranean, maybe? The cooks at the White House always had something different on the menu, but I felt like I hadn't tried enough foods to say.

"What else is consuming your thoughts?" Riel asked between bites.

"Hm?" His question startled me enough that I swallowed before I'd finished chewing, the dry bite sliding down my throat with some amount of discomfort. The face I made must have been a sight, as Riel appeared amused by my reaction.

"Did you have any other questions?" he clarified.

"Oh! I'm sure I could think of some more." In truth, I had them lined up. I'd spent more time than was healthy thinking of things I wanted to know about Riel and the fae—finding something appropriate, that was the challenge. "You've mentioned your mom, and of course, I've met your brother, but what about your father? What part does he play in all this?"

Riel made a disparaging sound in his throat. "I suppose he is the most agreeable of the three," he admitted after a moment's hesitation. "He is not an overly kind man, but he is fair. And he can be reasoned with, most of the time. He is often away for long periods, visiting family in other parts of the region or going on diplomatic trips to other territories, so my mother and brother handle the day-to-day activities here."

"Gotcha. Is he the head honcho, or do decisions go through advisors, or…"

"My father has the final say in matters of policy. My mother holds significant sway, but neither she nor my brother would dare make decisions without his presence. We have an advisor of sorts as well, but they only inform. It is not their place to have an opinion."

I never attempted to understand government processes before; it was all so convoluted. "Huh… sounds like that kind of defeats the purpose of having an advisor, but okay." I finished off my *massiya* and licked the last few remnants from my fingers. "So, next question. What do you do for fun?"

Riel gave a small frown. "Fun? I'm not familiar with the concept."

I raised an eyebrow and held it until he cracked a smile.

"I miss how innocent you used to be," he said ruefully, shaking his head. "You're harder to tease these days."

"I've wised up, old man," I replied with a devilish cackle. "Get on with it."

Riel heaved a sigh. "Let's see. I like to read and draw. I spend more time than is needed with the animals or in the gardens. When the weather is nice, I sometimes take day trips out to the foothills. There's a large spring there that is pleasant to swim laps in."

"Oh? That all sounds lovely." A pang of envy hit as I thought about my hobbies in comparison. Before my health took a turn, I enjoyed swimming and tennis. But over the past few months, I'd done little except watch movies and play video games. That would be a chore to explain, given that they had no concept of television or gaming systems. "Do you have any books in English? It'd be nice to have something to do in the evenings."

"Regrettably, we do not. If you let me know what kind you would like, I will ask Luenki to request some next time we send word to your people."

"No, no. Don't worry about it." I waved away his offer, feeling silly to make a big deal out of nothing. "Honestly, it would become an excuse not to meditate. I try to do it as much as I can, but it's so boring. We sit and talk all day, and then at night, I just lie there. I need a little more excitement in my life, you know?"

"Excitement, hm?" The corner of Riel's mouth twitched. "Well, you are young after all. With time, you'll grow to appreciate the quiet. Most people don't have the luxury of enjoying a relaxing evening of meditation."

I worried that I'd said the wrong thing. "I don't mean to sound ungrateful…"

"You'll get no judgment from me. I struggled through the same adjustment. It's about as interesting as watching *vali* nuts ripen."

He peered over my shoulder at the water then, and a perplexed look came over his face.

"Is that…? It's early in the season for them, but perhaps…"

"What?" Alarmed, I reared backward and followed his gaze toward the water. When I didn't notice anything right away, I leaned forward to get a closer look. "What am I—?"

The shove didn't quite register. What did was the world tipping above me as I went weightless for a brief second. When I hit the water, instinct kicked in, my arms flailing to get me back to precious air. I surfaced quickly, coughing and sputtering and in complete disbelief, to see Riel bent over with laughter on shore.

He extended an arm over the water to help as I made my way back to land. I was tempted to ignore it, but a moment of inspiration struck. With a sweet smile, I accepted his outstretched hand, then braced myself against the edge of the pool and yanked hard.

Nothing happened. It was like pulling on a rooted tree. His guffaws doubled in volume.

I let go of his hand out of principle and, muttering threats under my breath, dragged myself up onto the grass. His shoulders still shook with mirth as I straightened and squeezed as much water as I could out of my hair and clothes, my cheeks burning with humiliation.

"I don't know why you're laughing," I grumbled as I wrung the end of my shirt between my hands. There was no saving my shorts. "You're going to be snuggling against me on the return ride. By the time we get back, you'll be as soaked through as I am."

"You'll dry," Riel responded with a shrug. "Was that exciting enough for you? I know I found it thrilling."

"That's not what I meant and you know it, you prick." I shook my head like a wet dog. Strands of hair plastered themselves to my neck and shoulders. Examining Riel thoughtfully, I asked, "I don't suppose you've got drying magic up those sleeves of yours? Heaven forbid you do something useful."

"Hmm, no." He shook out both arms to punctuate his words. His eyes danced with humor, but as we looked at each other, the humor was replaced by something else. A touch of confusion, perhaps, and… I didn't know for sure what the other thing was, but I became suddenly and intensely aware of the fact that my shirt clung to certain areas more than usual when wet. Feeling self-conscious all of a sudden, my hands began to come up to cover myself.

A colder-than-usual breeze blew through our clearing, and my hands were diverted to cover a sneeze. Riel sobered up quickly. I found myself in the odd position of being equal parts relieved and disappointed that the other look was gone from his face.

"Are you cold?" he asked, tone contrite. He glanced around

as if a coat might appear from thin air. "These springs usually warm up early in the season..."

"Freezing." I drew out the word and exaggerated a few shivers for good measure. In truth, it was a little uncomfortable, but not unbearable. Still, milking an opportunity for all it was worth never hurt anyone. I laid it on real thick, summoning all the acting talent I could muster. "I may be a block of solid ice before we make it back. Oh, woe is me. Have my body launched into the lake and set on fire in a proper Viking send-off."

"Let's return early today," Riel suggested, frowning as though worried I would keel over. I giggled and shook my head at his reaction.

"You can dish it out, but you can't take it, huh?" I teased.

"I didn't realize humans were *that* delicate," he argued, grasping my arm to steer me toward the waiting *avida*. I relaxed and let him guide me into place and help me up like usual.

Once Riel had settled into his spot behind me, I wiggled my hips against him to ensure that he had full contact with my wet backside. "Well? Comfy?" I asked with a smug grin.

"Very." He breathed the word awfully close to my ear as he reached around me and slipped his hand into the loop of the reinstrap. I stopped wiggling, more for my own sake than his, and a blush suffused my cheeks. My brain floundered for a new subject.

"Out of curiosity, what would you have done if it turned out I couldn't swim?" I blurted.

"I suppose I would have had to jump in after you and pull you out."

Hmph. I couldn't find fault with that response. Attractive people got away with way too much. "Well, that doesn't make it okay. Just so you know."

"Yes, my lady. My most sincere apologies."

His tone was light, and since no harm had been done, I let the matter drop. Then, I spent the rest of the ride silently enjoying the fact that he'd called me his lady.

CHAPTER ELEVEN
THE SPARK

SPRING GAVE WAY TO SUMMER. Things were—dare I say it?—good.

Our lessons became less and less about magic as time passed. The more I told Riel about Earth, the more fascinated he became. He was especially interested in how reliant we were on technology. Trying to explain the Internet was a real challenge; at one point, Riel started to muse about its potential, and I had to admit that people mostly used it to share memes and start anonymous arguments with people halfway across the world.

The closer we grew, and the more I learned about the fae and their world, the more I dreaded going home. Eventually, I would be going back to the White House and resuming my healing sessions, because that was what all this was for. Although that should have been my top priority, I found myself less and less desperate to get my magic back. I'd even begun racking my brain for excuses to stay. It was as though I didn't know how to function without some degree of anxiety, so my mind offered up some new things to worry about.

I stretched out in bed while I pondered my situation. Even if I appreciated my newfound freedom here—and the unique connection I'd found with Riel—I was nothing more than a temporary guest. Riel and I were… well, we were literally from two different worlds. There was no way that I could both convince George to let me go and Riel's family to let me stay. No matter what I did, things couldn't continue like they had been forever.

The whole situation was hopelessly frustrating.

Deciding that my brain needed a break, I hopped off the bed and went to sort my laundry. Luenki came by every so often to collect it. She was the only one besides Riel who had shown me real kindness here, even going so far as to fetch me a pain-relief tonic when the cramps were bad during my last period. I wanted to make her job as easy as possible.

As I got my worn clothing together in a neat pile, I recalled earlier that day, when I'd finally seen magic up close. I'd been thinking about how weird it was that the fae didn't sling it around at every opportunity. My curiosity only grew seeing the soldiers practice outside. It had been my intention to see some magic when I asked my first question of the day that morning…

"You never did explain the light that those soldiers were making the other day," I remarked casually, easing myself out of a cross-legged position in favor of stretching my legs.

Riel cracked one eye open from where he sat across from me. "Light is a common side effect of making magic. They practice to improve their speed and accuracy during combat."

"Is there more to making magic than just flashes of light? How is it used offensively?"

Riel gave up on his meditation, opening both eyes and stretching his arms outward until his shoulders—or perhaps his elbows?—made an unnerving crack *that resonated like a gunshot in the small clearing. I cringed in disgust, pulling a face that Riel found amusing.*

"It's not just light, though that could be useful in blinding an opponent," he revealed once he finished laughing at my dramatic reaction. "The aggressor will cast something like fire or lightning. Something that will at least hurt, or ideally, kill. Making magic isn't the only kind that can be used offensively, but it is simple and effective. I

mentioned that things created using magic will not be identical to the real thing?"

He waited for my nod before continuing. "Making something entirely from mana *is the perfect example of that.* Mana *flames will possess the same properties as real fire, but it's not the same. It will burn, but it may take on a unique color as a result of being channeled through the caster. I suppose the best example would be to show you."*

I perked up. "I think that would help," I reasoned, trying not to show how excited I was.

Riel raised his right arm, then began to move it in an arc over his head starting at the opposite shoulder. I leaned forward a bit, holding my breath so that I didn't miss anything. First, I felt a tingle in the air. My hair began to stand on end just before a misty pale blue light coalesced around his fingers, as though he were pulling it from a pocket of air.

He drew his hand downward, and the light solidified before my eyes. The air sparked and crackled with electricity, the only warning I had before a controlled streak of lightning leapt between us. I fell backward in surprise. Riel chuckled at my reaction and dropped his hand. The light winked out of existence.

"Oh my God," I breathed, understanding all at once why magic was such a big deal. Healing was one thing, but if this was a small demonstration of the things the fae could do, the world should *be scared of them. By keeping their abilities under wraps, they had an extra line of defense. Even a country as power-hungry as the U.S. would think twice about trying any kind of political takeover when they didn't understand their enemy's strength.*

Riel observed me, perhaps wondering where my thoughts were running off to. I crawled back to my spot in front of him and sat back on my heels with a grin.

"That was amazing," I exclaimed. "I can't imagine what it would be like to throw lightning around. Geez, healing is so lame by comparison."

"Not at all." Riel gave me a soft smile. "A healing ability of your

caliber is more than impressive. One day, I would rather like to see you in action."

I wasn't used to receiving praise like that. And the way Riel talked to me, it felt like he respected me, like he considered me to be an equal. That wasn't something I was used to either, and it made me feel confusing things.

Dear God… was I developing a legitimate crush?

I mean, he was gorgeous. Anyone with functioning eyes would get it. Hell, if the rest of Earth understood what the princes really looked like, there would probably be a dozen fan clubs, regardless of Solois's winning personality. Not to mention endless amounts of digital art of them in the nude. Possibly even together. Aaand that was the line—no more of that, no sir.

More important than his looks, he gave me a safe space here. Our connection was something special, wasn't it? At least, it was for me. I couldn't remember ever having someone like him in my life. The things he made me think and feel—the way I got butterflies even now, just thinking about it—made me wonder if this was on its way to something more than friendship. I liked him, very much. And despite being a complete virgin, I knew enough about relationships to know that "like" led to another L-word.

But… that just brought me back to my earlier concerns. This thing between us couldn't last. And if I tried to express my interest, that would ruin everything, wouldn't it? He was twice my age and a frickin' prince; it was unlikely that he felt anything romantic for me in return. For all I knew, he had a million women that he acted the same way with. He might tease, but it was innocent. Or was it? For all I knew, that was some kind of fae courtship ritual. Maybe I was supposed to reciprocate? The stakes were too high to risk getting things wrong.

Shit, this was bad. I wished I had my phone to talk to someone about this mess. Luenki! Maybe? No, bad idea. She was busy, I knew that much, with what little I'd seen of her over the past few weeks. Plus, she was probably sworn to let the royal family know anything I told her. It would be bad if I confided in her and then word got back to Riel that I…

Belatedly, I realized that I was manhandling the undershirt in my hands. I quickly dropped it onto the pile of clothes I'd collected and balled my hands into fists before they could do more damage. This was why girls hung out in packs. What I really needed was some good, old-fashioned, heart-to-heart girl talk. I'd never needed it more than now.

In hopes of clearing my head, I went to the window to get some fresh air. I could see a portion of the courtyard and some amount of the land beyond the wall from my room, including the outline of Miderrum in the distance. Today, the horizon was shrouded in mist, but a dark shadow in the distance caught my eye. I shielded my eyes and squinted to get a better look.

It was hard to see, but I could make out movement, glints of light, and dots of pastel colors that could have been *avida*. Didn't that look like an approaching army? I was just starting to wonder if I should tell someone when a horn blared out, making me jump. No one rushed to defend the castle, so there was probably no cause for concern… but Riel would know for sure.

I went to find him, kicking the laundry pile closer to the door on my way out. His room wasn't far from mine—he'd shown me where it was during one of the tours. The hallways all looked similar, but he was on the same level, just the other side of the building. One, two, three… there, the fourth door. I retraced my steps in my head to confirm before I dared to knock.

At first, I heard nothing. Wondering if I had the wrong door, or if he wasn't in, I tried knocking again. That time, a muffled response filtered through the door. It sounded like an invitation to come in, so I tried the door and, finding it unlocked, pushed into the room.

"Riel, did you see—" Hand still on the doorknob, my body came to an abrupt halt. The prince stood by the open door to his bathroom, holding an article of clothing in his hands. His hair was wet, slicked back against his neck, and his ears were free of the usual adornments, which suggested that he'd just finished bathing. That, and the fact that he was half naked.

I thought perhaps I'd willed the sight into existence through an as-yet undiscovered power. He had no shirt, and his pants sat low on his hips, revealing a significant amount of skin. There was no over-the-top brawn weighing down his body; he was built like an animal, lean and powerful, with subtle hills and valleys to his musculature. His chest was as flawless as the rest of him, and there were two identical glints of silver there that could only be… God have mercy, the man had pierced nipples.

All at once, I realized I was staring. Then, to my utter mortification, it registered that he stared back. The look on his face was incredulous, like he couldn't believe the nerve of this human to be peeping. But as I gawked, mouth ajar, his expression began to morph into a delighted smirk that sent something quivering in the pit of my stomach. Without being conscious of the movement, I shut the door. Even face to face with the wood grain, all I could see was his pale, toned chest, like it was permanently burned into my irises. My thoughts short-circuited.

"You might as well come back and see the rest."

The amusement was audible in his voice, adding insult to injury. Face burning with the heat of a thousand suns, I spun on my heel and headed back down the hallway with purpose. *What sort of grand cosmic joke was that timing? And since when did I become the sort of person who would take advantage of another's nudity and gawk? Did I have zero self-control?*

If I was ever brought before a judge for my actions, I'd probably argue that the fae just have an undeniable allure. Would that hold up? Not a chance. I walked a thin line right now—one that, if broken, could very well start the next world war. Worlds war?

Well, that decided it. I was fucked.

I'd only just begun to panic when a knock at my door interrupted my budding plans of sneaking out in the dead of night and returning through The Rift to avoid embarrassment. I had a sneaking suspicion I knew who it was and briefly considered pretending I was asleep before I built up the courage to answer the door. Walking the plank over a vortex of hungry sharks might have been less nerve-racking than the walk across my room.

As expected, it was Riel. I tried not to be disappointed that he had donned a shirt. Too nervous to look him in the eye, I inspected the floor instead. He leaned against the doorframe ever-so-slowly, taking up much of the limited space between us and angling his body so that it hovered over me. His scent overwhelmed my senses—something fresh and zesty, like lemongrass, calling to mind a sea of sunny meadows in the springtime. My throat moved, but no words emerged.

"Good evening, *eseri,*" he greeted me in a very different tone from the cheery morning greetings I had come to expect from him. With the way he leaned forward, his voice was much closer to my ear than I had expected. *Holy shit,* I thought as my heartbeat sped up. This was bad. Indecent, even. *I could close the door? No, I couldn't; he was right there. Maybe I could come up with a distraction. Was it too late to pretend to be asleep?*

"Y-yes, hello. Sorry about that… earlier." Well, I wouldn't be composing award-winning sonnets anytime soon, but words were a start. I wanted so badly to give in to my instincts and invite him in, but instead, I continued to study the floor, refusing to allow my gaze any higher than his boots. If I looked into his eyes, I'd end up climbing the man like a beanpole.

"Not at all." He lingered in the doorway a moment longer before easing back to give me some space. I filled my aching lungs with oxygen for the first time in several seconds. Good heavens, the man had the power to make someone forget how to breathe. "What did you need?" he asked, his voice mostly back to normal.

I risked a glance at his face and saw nothing out of the ordinary there, which got me wondering if I had somehow misinterpreted his intentions. *Had that not been the moment of intimacy I'd thought it was? Was my heart racing for no reason?*

"Um..." Although thoroughly baffled, I pushed some strength into my words. "I just saw something from my window, and I thought I would ask you about it. It's probably not important... sorry to bother you."

Riel frowned. I stepped aside to let him in without a word, and he made his way to the window to peer out. He had no difficulty picking out what I referred to—his senses were keener than mine, and the marching army had come into view by that point.

"My father," he stated, pivoting away from the window. I couldn't tell anything from his tone, but his movements, which had been languid moments earlier, were now tense. "He's been away on business," he explained, mouth set in a tight line. "It would seem he has returned."

He hissed something under his breath and strode back toward the open door. "Stay here until I come for you," he ordered, suddenly appearing more of the prince he was than the friend I had come to know. I reared back at the sudden shift in mood. He paused to spare me a brief glance before adding in a gentler tone, "Keep the door locked."

With that, he vanished, leaving me to wonder what this all meant.

CHAPTER TWELVE
THE STORM

Meanwhile…

RALIF OF HOUSE Wysalar was head of the *Ishameti* leading family in the Northwest, or, as the humans knew them, the fae royal family that presided over the North American territories. He ruled alongside his wife, the fair Elokima. Ralif had been away for many weeks on official business, kept informed with messenger birds sent by his family. Although he did not like the idea of having a human in the heart of their nation, he liked the idea of aggravating the U.S. even less, which was why he had agreed to extend a hand in the first place.

Elokima advised that this request from the humans was part of a test from the Goddess. She planned to delegate the task of watching Avery to her eldest son, Solois, but to the family's surprise, Riel volunteered. While the queen had been hesitant to trust him with such an important job, Solois vouched for his brother. Whether it was out of kindness toward Riel, who clearly wanted to prove himself, or a desire of a more self-serving nature, no one knew.

The queen at that moment sat on her carved throne in the entrance hall with Solois standing by her side. Word of the king's return had made it around the castle, and she planned to fill him in on the current situation. Her thoughts flitted to Riel. He should be part of this conversation; they were due an update.

The front door opened, giving way to a large group of soldiers dressed in layers of white canvas armor. The queen inclined her head in greeting as they bowed and continued on to their quarters to rest and recover after the arduous journey. Finally, a figure adorned in finer clothes than the rest appeared in the open doorway, and the queen straightened. The king resembled his sons in build and stature, and he was handsome for an older man, with thick brows over hooded eyes and a square jawline hidden by a well-kept blond beard. It was clear to see where his eldest son got his looks from, the younger one taking after his fair wife.

"How was your journey, my dear?" the queen asked demurely, lifting one delicate hand in a salute-like greeting as he approached the thrones. The king snatched her hand from the air and brushed a kiss to the back of it before collapsing into the seat beside her.

"Long and exhausting," he sighed. "Leimor and his kin are as trying as ever. It's good to be home. How have things been in my absence?"

"You were dearly missed, but the Goddess watched over us." Elokima sat back in her chair. "Solois collected the season's taxes in your stead and updated the books. Harvests are coming along nicely. Riel has been looking after the American girl. Last I heard, she was approaching *vahela*. He will inform us of anything he has discovered since then."

"Good. Have they given us any trouble, the Americans?"

"Luenki has kept them apprised of the girl's health as they requested. Beyond the occasional message, all has been peaceful." The queen hesitated a moment before continuing. "I… hate to say it, but Neyes suggested that her presence here will lead to conflict. I feel the same. The longer she is here, the more knowledge she gleans. As you know, knowledge makes humans dangerous. They are unpredictable, the ones with magic even more so."

"She doesn't know anything, and she's hardly dangerous."

Startled by the outburst, Elokima turned to the staircase, where Riel descended with a fierce expression on his face. "She knows as much about our ways and our magic as a fledgling," he continued, coming to a stop in the middle of the room. "And her intentions are pure. Your fear is misplaced, Mother. She is not a danger to us."

"Oh?" The queen tutted. "How kind of you to join us, Riel. We were hoping that you could fill us in on what you have learned these past months. Tell me, do you mean to say that Neyes was mistaken? If you believe that she poses no danger, then you discredit our seer."

"I would never doubt Neyes," Riel denied with a shake of his head. "But perhaps they saw only one possibility, or they did not see the whole truth. As you well know, much of what they see is incomplete and can be misinterpreted."

The queen put a hand to her mouth, aghast. "Then, you mean to claim that I, who would never lead our people astray, misinterpreted the Goddess's words?"

Riel gritted his teeth in frustration. "I'm saying she's just a healer," he ground out. "A powerful one, but a healer nonetheless. Her ability is pure mending, and she can't even use it properly. She poses no threat. Is this not a good thing for our family?"

"I'm sure you won't mind telling us what else you've learned," Solois remarked. "Isn't that right? After all, you've spent so much time together. You must have an idea of the reach of her abilities by now, if not her intentions. This is your chance to share."

Riel considered his response. "She is... impressive," he admitted. "From what she's told me, she mended life-threatening injuries and illnesses every month for years of her life. And… she hasn't yet learned how to draw *mana*."

Eyes widened all around at his words.

"She healed from her own power… for years?" The queen looked to the king as if expecting him to correct her. His face had hardened as the conversation progressed.

"The blessed humans may be formidable," Ralif reasoned, "but they are few. And the Americans are hesitant to wage war. I don't expect this healer will give us any trouble." He glanced at his wife. "Though, I've no doubt Neyes spoke true. Tensions have been on the rise for several years between us, House Leimor, and the Americans. This last trip confirmed for me that a conflict is inevitable. We can only pray for a quick and painless resolution."

"Well, if we're anticipating problems with the Americans, it would be wise for us to strike first," the queen sniffed. "Show them that we are not to be underestimated. Otherwise, they might think us soft. We've already welcomed their spy with open arms."

"We could send the healer's head back to them in a box," Solois suggested thoughtfully. His gaze remained trained on his brother to see how his shocking statement would be received.

"No," Riel growled, the passion behind his response surprising the rest of the family.

Solois frowned. "Don't tell me—"

"Starting a war with the humans is not a good idea," Riel stated, interrupting whatever Solois was about to call into question. "We may have the Goddess's blessing on our side, but they have powerful tools and large numbers. We would be fools to think that an empty show of strength would be worth the losses incurred. Not to mention they have been peaceful thus far."

Elokima stood. "You will respect whatever decision we make," she said softly, danger clear in her tone. "It is not the place of a second son to question his elders. Perhaps you have done enough. Perhaps Solois should take over the girl's teaching, as it should have been."

"Stand down, Elokima." The king raised his hand in a pacifying gesture. "Astonriel makes a fair point. I don't doubt that he, too, has the family's best interests at heart." He gave Riel a meaningful look before directing his attention back to his wife. "We have House Leimor to contend with as well. They are waiting for an opportunity to tear us down, and I have not yet secured an alliance with the Southern House. Let us maintain open eyes and ears for now, and we can discuss this further when we have more information at our disposal."

"Of course," the queen murmured. She perked up and clapped her hands together as a thought struck. "In the meantime, Ralif, let us host a party in honor of your return. I feel our house has been empty for too long, and the people are ready for some cheer."

"As you like," the king said, nodding. "But give us at least a day or two to recover, my dear. The last two months have been trying on myself and our soldiers."

"We shall have it on the night of the new moon, then. That will give us time to spread the word and get the hall prepared for guests."

"I'll leave it to you." Ralif got to his feet, running a tired hand through his hair. "Now, if there is nothing more to discuss, I believe a bath and a good night's sleep is in order. Shall we retire?" He offered an arm to his wife, who accepted it gracefully, before turning his attention to his sons. "Keep up the good work," he said with a nod.

Solois lingered, eyes narrowed on his younger brother, as the king and queen swept out of the room. Riel returned the gaze with a blank face, his stance anything but relaxed. Once their parents had gone, Solois crossed the room in a flash. Riel, to his credit, did not flinch, even as Solois closed in so that there was a handbreadth of air between them.

"You seem to have our father fooled into thinking that

you're simply looking out for our family, but make no mistake," Solois warned in a low voice, "I see what you're doing, and I don't appreciate your taking advantage of the situation to goof off. If it comes to war, and you get in between me and the spy, I will have no qualms about taking you out first."

"Confident, are we?" Riel mused. "That won't be necessary. We're on the same side. I'm hurt that you think so little of me, Solois, after everything we've been through together."

His relaxed air and self-assured tone of voice appeared to antagonize Solois. "It's because I know you that I think so little of you," he retorted. "You've always been soft, and if you can't see where this is going yourself, then you're even more half-witted than I thought. Our nation needs strong leadership right now, and you're practically cavorting with the enemy. Ask yourself, brother—is her cunt really worth treason?"

A flash of shadow crossed Riel's face, gone as quickly as it had appeared.

"You are mistaken," he said simply. "The girl is inconsequential, although I do believe her ability could be a benefit to us. I intend to keep our family from making a grievous misstep. Perhaps, if you had bothered to learn about the humans as I have, you would understand that it is in our best interests to avoid war at all costs."

Solois studied his face for a moment, as though expecting to find evidence of treachery there. Riel showed no fear. Eventually, reluctantly, Solois stepped back.

"Killing her would be rash," he admitted. "As you say, she doesn't pose an immediate threat. But don't let this go too far. *We* are the blessed race, not *them*. When it comes down to it, we cannot hesitate to do what needs to be done. Do you understand me?"

"If I believed she posed a threat, I would kill her myself," Riel countered, a muscle ticking in his jaw. He didn't bother pointing out that Avery's very existence showed the Goddess had chosen to bless more than one race. "But I have better things to do than argue. Go to bed, Solois. I plan to do the same. If you can't find something productive to do tomorrow, we can resume this discussion then. Good night."

Solois scowled. "Soften your tongue," he snapped. "You speak to this family's future head." Leaving things at that, he turned on his heel and headed for the stairs.

As his brother disappeared from sight, Riel loosed a breath he had been holding. He lingered a moment longer to gather his thoughts before following, with every intention to return to his room. Fate had other plans, as he found himself outside *her* door instead, one hand poised to knock. He hesitated for a brief second before dropping his arm. It was late, and she wouldn't have waited up for him given the abrupt manner in which he'd left. Even if she had… it wouldn't be right to push things any further. Though it pained him to admit, Solois had not been mistaken about his interest in Avery. It was a good thing she'd the sense to draw the line where she did. He couldn't afford to get carried away; if he did this, he did it properly.

Without wasting any more time, he pivoted to return to his room, keeping his footsteps even and quiet. Even if she would have welcomed him, he didn't deserve the comfort she brought —not tonight. It was too much of a risk. And they would both need their rest in order to survive the storm that was coming.

CHAPTER THIRTEEN
THE FANTASY

WITH NOTHING better to do once Riel stormed out, I elected to take a long bath. With any luck, taking some time to relax and mull over the events that had transpired in the last hour would clear up the clouds of doubt that were gathering on the horizon.

As I turned on the tap to begin filling the tub, my thoughts drifted back to him. Given the way that he talked about his family, I'd been able to discern that there was some tension there. Were things going to be even worse now that his father was back? I needed to find something to do in case Riel was busy with family stuff for the next few days. If I couldn't leave my room, my options were limited.

I tested the water temperature with my hand. Scalding—just how I liked it. I had spent some time wondering how they did all their plumbing, and if magic was involved with that too. But if humans could figure it out, it made sense that other worlds would have similar things.

After stripping off my clothing, I climbed in and settled against the side of the tub. Ah, shit, the soap. For a split second, I debated just soaking for a while without bothering to wash.

Grumbling my displeasure, I pulled myself up and made an

effort to wipe some of the water off before stepping out of the tub. I grabbed my soap, shampoo, and towel and put them to one side. As I washed, I returned to thinking about Riel. It was wrong to think so, but I was grateful for the peep show. I recalled the striking planes of his upper body and that smirk he gave when he caught me watching from the doorway. *Hell, if I looked like that, I'd be arrogant too.*

But then when he showed up at my room, things had gotten too real too fast. I was still reeling, in all honesty. Part of me was relieved we didn't cross that line, but the other part of me wondered… *Would it really be that bad if something happened between us?* My hands trailed down my chest, soap bubbles scattering along the water's surface.

He was tall; it was one of the first things I'd noticed about him. Not that it was unique—all the fae I'd seen so far were model height—but it was a different experience when he was right in front of me. It felt like his body had taken up the entire doorway. What had he thought when he saw me? Did I seem short and plain in comparison to everyone else he knew? Due to my illness, I had been skinny when I first arrived, but I was filling out now. Did he notice? Did he like what he saw?

I called his smirk to mind again. My hands journeyed down to the junction of my thighs. Would he look at me like that if I stood naked in front of him? What if, when I opened the door, instead of just standing there… he had grabbed me? I wouldn't have stopped him. My imagination took hold of that thought and ran with it, the scene playing out in my head:

He slowly leaned against the doorframe, filling the space, and oxygen fled from me. "Good evening, eseri,*" he murmured. I looked up, up, up into his eyes. It was the wrong thing to do. A predator looked back at me, one that had decided I was to be its prey. My breath caught.*

Before I could react, he pushed into the room, the door slamming shut behind him. I quickly backed up, but he didn't let me put space between us. In an instant, he wrapped an arm around me and brought his body flush against mine, the heat from his hand scorching my lower back. He walked into me, forcing me to stumble backward until I hit the wall with a gasp of surprise. I was caged in by his body, at his mercy like a butterfly pinned to a bug board.

His eyes appeared to glow in the low light of twilight. They were set on my parted lips. He was transfixed by them, like he was already lost in imagining their taste. My heart pounded in my chest. We shouldn't, *I wanted to say. But I couldn't bring myself to stop him—I wanted it as much as he did. Instead, I found myself pushing up on my tiptoes at the same time he tilted his head downward, and our faces met in a clash of lips and teeth.*

Whatever awkwardness there was at our first kiss faded quickly, replaced by desire for each other. His lips teased mine from edge to edge, as though learning their shape so that he could identify them even in the dark. His leg came between mine and applied upward pressure, calling my attention to a spot down below that had begun to throb with every heartbeat.

Swallowing my whimper, he took the opportunity to slip his tongue inside my mouth. My hips jerked of their own accord. In an effort to ground myself, I fisted a desperate handful of his shirt. He responded by adjusting his grip from my lower back to my hip, his touch searing a line across my skin where my clothing rode up.

In the bath, my left hand drifted upward to grip the opposite side of my hip, imagining Riel's broader hand in place of my own. My right hand slipped in between my legs.

I didn't notice his other hand until I broke off our kiss to come up for air. He caught my jaw as I turned away. "Look at me," he ordered. Struck dumb by the authority in his tone, I could only crane my head upward to meet his eyes. His lips curved in that familiar cocky smile, and he started trailing kisses from my jaw down the expanse of skin now bared to him. "Good girl," he said against my neck. My cheeks flushed in response to his praise.

A euphoric giggle escaped me, momentarily interrupting the

fantasy. Maybe that was taking things a bit too far. But a girl could dream, couldn't she?

"Shouldn't we go to the bed?" I whispered, eyes half-closed in pleasure as his lips made love to my collarbone. He straightened without a reply, bringing his hands around to cup my rear end. With an unexpected shift of his powerful body, I was lifted up and away from the wall. He was depositing me on my bed before I could panic. My hand still gripped his shirt, and as I fell back, the fabric came with me. Buttons scattered throughout the room.

"Oh my God, I'm so—"

He claimed my lips again, cutting off my apology and making it clear that the shirt was the last thing on his mind. I melted against the bed as he set a toe-curling pace, attacking my lips and tongue with expert technique. Any thoughts I may have had died before they had the chance to form. Eventually, the throbbing between my legs became insistent, and I squirmed beneath him in an effort to ease the ache that had developed there. His body lifted away from mine to put space between us—enough for his hand to play with the waist of my pants.

A desperate sound arose in my throat. He chuckled in response and slid his fingers between my skin and the fabric. Impatient, I wiggled my thumbs into the waistband and twisted until it slid down enough to reveal my underwear. At that point, Riel batted my hands away and took over, ignoring my indignant huff. Once my legs were bared, he tossed the piece of clothing aside and reared up to remove the remains of his tattered shirt. I took the opportunity to lift my shirt over my head as well, letting it join my pants on the floor.

His hands drifted down my body the moment I settled back against the bed. I responded in kind, reaching up to learn the lines of his torso. His skin was smooth and hot to the touch, and I imagined that I could feel his power shivering underneath the surface as though it were alive. My thoughts were consumed with wanting to feel more—his weight on me, his presence between my legs, that power inside of me.

"Touch me," I begged, my voice breaking with need. His hands hadn't left my body, but he understood what I meant. He resumed worshiping my neck and shoulder with his mouth, trailing kisses

down toward the swell of my breasts. I reached between us to yank down my bra, unwilling to wait a moment longer, and didn't miss his sharp intake of breath as my chest was bared to him. He wasted no time in giving me what I wanted, as his hand snaked between us to tease one of my nipples. I moaned my encouragement.

I brought my hand up to grip one breast, releasing a shuddering gasp as the motion sent an electric signal straight down to my clit. My other hand moved faster between my legs, seeking a climax that rapidly approached. Everything but the fantasy fell away, nothing but my craving for release mattering at that moment.

He attended to my other breast with his mouth. The combined sensations from his tongue and teeth on my nipple sent a jolt of pleasure throughout my core, and my thighs rubbed together in answer. Finally, his fingers drifted where I needed him the most, skirting across my ribs, over my abdomen, and past the waistband of my underwear. My body was already primed, and when they found the place I ached most, a sound escaped me that would have been embarrassing under any other circumstances.

"You respond so sweetly to my attentions, eseri*," Riel marveled against my breast, "Had I known you were this desperate for me, I would have come to you sooner."*

I couldn't formulate a response, captivated as I was by the movement his finger was making inside me. It was somehow perfect and not enough at the same time. As a second finger joined the first, I was brought that much closer to the brink of relief. He barely thrust them, somehow applying slow and steady pressure to a certain spot in a way that would have made my legs weak had I been standing.

"Yes, yes, yes." I arched into his hand. It was almost enough, but his mouth was too gentle for my liking. "Bite it," I demanded breathlessly. Riel didn't hesitate, nipping my flesh hard enough to make me gasp. My hand shot up to find my lonely clit and rubbed insistently, amplifying the sensations tenfold. The multi-pronged assault on my senses brought that elusive pinnacle of pleasure within reach, climbing, climbing until—

"Oh, shit!"

I bit my lip to stifle a whimper and jerked against the wall of the bath as the tension in my core at last hit its peak. Handfuls of lukewarm water sloshed against the floor below. A haze of gratification flooded my brain, leaving me limp and pliable, and the next few moments were spent trying to collect myself. As the thinking half of my brain caught up to the horny half, the residual pleasure from my orgasm began to morph into a queasy mishmash of horror and shame.

I stood abruptly, ignoring the splash as I did so. Setting the tub to drain, I collected my towel, wrapped it haphazardly around my body, and sprinted into the bedroom. Two thoughts yo-yoed back and forth in my head while I wrestled pajamas onto my wet limbs: "Did I seriously just do that?" and "What the fuck was I thinking?"

Cheeks burning with shame and hair soaking the back of my shirt, I collapsed face-first on the bed. As if it wasn't bad enough that I was plagued with inappropriate thoughts about a foreign dignitary when my nation depended on me, now I actively transformed those thoughts into full-blown fantasies. And as if *that* wasn't bad enough, I *touched* myself to them like some kind of degenerate pervert. Then again…

No, it didn't matter how attractive he was! There was no excuse for that kind of behavior. I needed to get a grip. God… what was this place doing to me?

The noise continued clamoring around in my head until finally, mercifully, exhaustion carried me away into dreamland.

Unfortunately, the mercy was short-lived. That night, my tumultuous thoughts inspired a familiar nightmare, one I'd been lucky enough to avoid for the past few weeks. While my subconscious took certain liberties, it always began and ended the same way. First, I saw a series of memories from my teen years, which included a girl with long chocolate-brown hair, rich bronze skin, and an athletic build. Although she never revealed her identity in the dream, I knew who she was: Marcia, the Brazilian girl with changing magic.

We were both fourteen when we met. We were complete opposites, but we were kids, and kids didn't need to have anything in common to be friends. I saw snippets of our time together, as I always did: the day she showed me her abilities for the first time, becoming one of the Secret Service dogs in an instant. The day we gorged ourselves on a platter of tuna salad sandwiches that she'd stolen from the kitchen. The day she taught me how to float in the White House swimming pool. And finally, the day we decided to sneak out.

I saw her back in the crowd, silhouetted by the sun. It made for a beautiful picture. Her shirt was cornflower blue, with ruffles along the sleeves and neckline. Her hair hadn't been trimmed in a while—the split ends caught the light. She walked with her shoulders back and head held high ahead of me. People passed by, oblivious to our identities. To them, we were unremarkable, just two more people on the street going about their day.

When the nightmare began, the sunlight coalesced into three blurry faces surrounding me. There was laughter, then darkness. The smell of stale air and dirt. Cold stone against my back. My tears wouldn't stop coming, and my throat was hoarse from shouting. I was alone and terrified, trying to stifle my trembling so that I could rest my heavy head on my knees.

Muffled voices filtered in from somewhere up above me. They scarcely managed to drown out the growling of my stomach, which cramped from hunger. Had it been hours? Days? Weeks? The terror was my only companion in the dark, along with a single thought that repeated itself over and over again until it was all I could hear: *Am I going to die here?*

At some point, I had the unnerving feeling that the dream had ended long ago, but a part of me was still there in that cellar. She was still a lonely, terrified sixteen-year-old girl whose sobs echoed in the darkness. No matter how long she waited, no matter how much she screamed or how hoarse her throat became, help never came.

CHAPTER FOURTEEN
THE PREPARATION

THE NEXT DAY, I woke well past sunrise to a puffy face and a pillow damp with tears. I'd nearly forgotten how much those memories hurt. But although I coped, I'd never fully healed; the nightmares were a reminder of that. They always came back with a vengeance when I was emotional, as though my brain was a sadist that liked to throw more challenges at me during times of stress. I lay there in bed, deep in thought, before it registered that the sun had risen a while ago and no one had come to get me.

After throwing on clothes, I checked the hallway and brought in the tray that was waiting for me. The day's breakfast was a trio of white balls smothered in fragrant syrup. The inside was dense but moist, with a cakey texture and nutty taste. The syrup was thick and sweet with a floral, honey-like quality to it. It was so delicious that I forgot where I was until I was licking leftover syrup off my fingers.

When the knock came, my heart damn near burst out of my chest. Wiping my hands down the front of my shirt, I leapt up and made my way across the room. My chest began to tighten with anxiety as I debated how I would face Riel given the events of the last twelve hours, but to my surprise, it was not him on the other side of the door.

"Luenki!" I exclaimed, my shoulders dropping in relief. "Good morning."

"*Ishamenarin*, Avery," she greeted with a warm smile. "Are you well this morning?"

"Yes, thank you. How have you been?" I stepped aside to make room for her to enter, figuring that she had come by to say hello and chat for a bit.

"I am well," Luenki replied, lingering in the doorway. "Are you ready?"

"Oh!" I hesitated. "Is, um… is Riel not…?" I trailed off when I realized I wasn't sure what I wanted to ask. Was he busy, or was he avoiding me because of the weirdness last night? And… did his not being here make me feel relieved, or disappointed?

"The second prince is otherwise engaged." Luenki's tone was apologetic. "But I am happy to be your companion today. A woman's company is perhaps more appropriate anyway—I am taking you to our clothier to have new attire crafted for an event."

I'd begun to lean against the doorframe, but her words made me straighten in interest. "An event? What kind of event?"

"The king has been away for many weeks, but now we celebrate his return. Guests will be coming from the city, and there will be food and entertainment. Do you like to dance?"

Those niggling worries started up again. Somehow, I got the vibe that she didn't mean freestyling. "Uh, you mean like ballroom dancing? Waltzes and stuff? I can't say that I do."

Luenki waved away my concern. "Not to worry. It is informal. Most people use these events as an excuse to wear nice clothing and socialize. Shall we go?"

"Oh, yeah." Trying to keep my thoughts optimistic, I focused on looking forward to the nice clothing as I stepped into the hallway and shut the door behind me. Another thought occurred to me unbidden. "Heard anything from Vivian and George recently?"

"Not since we were last in touch," Luenki responded. "Our exchanges remain cordial. They are glad you are feeling better, but… well, there is not much news to share."

She didn't say it, but I heard what was left unspoken—they were hoping to hear that my powers were back in full force. Any other news was inconsequential. Although I'd been meditating almost daily and had more energy than ever, I still hadn't managed to make any progress toward drawing *mana*. When I tried, all I felt was my familiar little spark of magic. Riel assured me it took time, but I couldn't help but feel frustrated at the lack of progress, even as the part of me that wanted to stay as long as possible was secretly pleased.

"Consider what style of dress you would like," Luenki suggested, interrupting my brooding. "Our clothier works quickly, so it is a good idea to have an image in mind."

I examined her peachy A-line gown as we walked. She often wore dresses, as she did today, the style somewhere between '90s prom and costumes out of a Renaissance Faire catalog. But I had seen some of the female employees wearing slacks, so perhaps something with pants would work, like a romper. Having this kind of design power was daunting.

"I'd appreciate some guidance," I admitted, not ashamed to rely on Luenki at this point. "I don't even know much about fancy clothing where I'm from, much less what sort of styles would be acceptable here. I always just wore what I was given."

Luenki beamed, pleased at the thought of assisting me with my selection. "Long skirts are popular for events such as these. Sleeve length depends on the weight of the fabric. A shapely waist and low neckline would be good, to show off your figure. As for color, blue would suit you nicely." Her gaze raked critically over my form. "Or green, perhaps. Something deep and vivid to complement your light coloring."

"Sounds good to me," I agreed. "Anything that I should avoid?"

"Hmm… yes." I was taken aback as Luenki leaned in and lowered her voice to a conspiratorial whisper. "You should avoid the king and queen as much as possible. The first prince as well, if you can. They will be greeting guests over the course of the evening, so it should not be difficult. It will be best if you stay close to me during the festivities."

Of course. Because why would a party here be a chance for me to relax and enjoy myself for once? "Got it." My chest tightened in a familiar way, and a sense of frustration and dread began to brew. *Damn it all—couldn't I catch a break?* "I don't suppose anyone would notice if I just hung out by the food for a while and then turned in early?"

"We shall see. You are a guest of our House, so it's important that you are seen, but I may have the opportunity to make an excuse for you at some point. Though I hope that you will be able to enjoy yourself before it comes to that."

I made a sound of agreement, but it came out more miserable than I had intended. Luenki slowed her steps, perhaps noticing the shift in my mood.

"You will be looked after," she assured me with gentle confidence. I nodded, feeling a swell of gratitude for her supportive presence, and elected not to meet her eyes lest the waterworks start up. Her footsteps halted, and the hallway fell silent.

"Is there… something else I can do for you?"

Her question was so genuine that I almost poured my heart out then and there, but after everything she'd done for me, the last thing I wanted was to pass my worries onto her.

"No, no." I took a deep breath and faced her with a smile on my face. "You've been so wonderful. I honestly don't know what I would do without you."

Luenki returned my smile, but her eyes continued to study me.

"Does Astonriel treat you well?" she surprised me by

asking. Of course, my traitorous brain responded with memories of last night: the sight of Riel half naked in his room, his presence filling my doorway, and his confusing departure. The bath that followed.

"Oh, yes," I said quickly. "He's great. So nice. I mean, he's a very professional teacher. Patient and... and knowledgeable. I'm learning a lot from him." Internally, I couldn't help but cringe. *Real smooth, Avery. The word vomit will definitely throw her off the scent.*

Luenki cocked her head. "I am glad," she stated, her tone bright and innocent. "Although he has always been fascinated by humans, I will admit I initially found his interest in you curious. Even concerning. I am happy to hear he has not forgotten his place."

It was a bait; I was sure of it. Nonetheless, I latched onto her words like a drowning man.

"What about his interest was... uh... curious?" I tried to be casual about it, but Luenki was giving me a knowing look, her eyes swimming with mirth. *She knew Riel better than most, right? And she should understand where I'm coming from.* Desperate to get my most recent dilemma off my chest, I dropped the pretense and started babbling. "Okay, here's the thing. Respectfully, I find him attractive. I mean, he's objectively hot, right? But I don't know if the flirting is just something he does or if it means something. I just don't want to misunderstand things and make an ass of myself. Do you think... I mean, you know him better than I do, right? Is he just being himself? Or is there something I'm missing?"

I had begun to cross into frantic territory toward the end of my spiel. After casting a glance down the hallway to be sure we were alone, Luenki stepped forward and grasped my hands in hers. "Breathe," she ordered. I obeyed, sucking in a big breath. At her pointed look, I released a forceful exhale and repeated the calming motion.

"You are young," Luenki remarked, drawing soothing

circles on my hands with her thumbs. "When you are young, emotions are wild and strange. Nonetheless, you are their master." She waited until my breathing had evened out before continuing. "I was not born here. When I was young, my parents both passed away, and the leading family took me in. I have known the second prince since he was barely able to stand upright, and he has always been kind, thoughtful, and well-mannered. But he appears to be more than that with you."

"We've only known each other for a couple of months," I said in a broken whisper.

"You spend every day in each other's company," Luenki pointed out. "I only know what I have observed, and that is that he rises early each morning in his eagerness to see you again. Whenever you are together, the two of you share smiles like old friends. It has been a long time since he has had someone so close to him, someone he can be at ease around."

"It's not like that," I protested. "But… even if Riel does like me too, what do I do with that? We're from two different worlds. It's not like we can ride an *avida* off into the sunset, settle down in a nice cottage in the woods, and have beautiful magical babies together. Or… or live out our lives enjoying piña coladas on a beach in Bora Bora."

Luenki blinked as she processed my words. "I cannot assume what your future may hold," she hedged eventually. "But if this bothers you, I suggest you speak with him so that you may work out a solution together. You are clever and brave, Avery. Your heart is gentle, and your manner is kind. I cannot find fault with his interest."

My cheeks warmed at her praise.

"Nor yours," she added matter-of-factly. "He is, indeed, objectively hot."

An unattractive snort of laughter burst out of me. "Hey, now, I called dibs," I joked, pulling my hands from hers and giving my cheeks a quick pat to get the blood flowing again. It felt as though a heavy burden had been lifted from my shoulders. "Thanks, Luenki. I really needed to talk about this with someone."

"I am happy to be of service," Luenki responded with her signature grace and warm smile. She started walking again, and I followed, relief making my steps light. This event would be another matter entirely, but with a clear sense of direction now, I felt a little better equipped to cross that bridge.

We arrived at the elegant double doors of the banquet hall, with palace soldiers in white leather armor stationed on either side. I was surprised to see them indoors. Luenki nodded a greeting to the men as we approached, and they eyed me up and down but made no effort to respond. Perhaps like the other castle employees, they had been asked to leave me be.

Luenki paid them no mind, striding forward to set her palm on the wooden door above the handle. It swung open soundlessly, revealing a large room with a line of banquet tables covered in rich fabrics of every imaginable color and type. A tall, painted screen obstructed one corner at the far end of the room, and three ladies waited before it with armfuls of materials. They had been chatting but fell silent as Luenki and I entered.

"See if anything catches your eyes." Luenki gestured broadly at the assortment of choices. "Take whatever you like. When it is your turn, we will show them to the clothier and she will design and fit your dress behind the screen."

"Wait, like she sews the dresses on the spot?" I wasn't sure I understood correctly. How was anyone supposed to create an entire custom dress in a day? And for more than one person?

Luenki examined a handful of shimmery sky-blue velvet. "With the Goddess's blessing, anything is possible," she remarked with a twinkle in her eye.

"Man, you guys give new meaning to fast fashion," I muttered under my breath. Running my hand over a thick, patterned red-and-cream fabric, I thought about what I might like to wear. The idea of something vibrant appealed to me. If

I was honest, having to wear a big, heavy ball gown did not. I'd had enough of those kinds of getups back at the White House.

I shifted a pile of burgundy fabric to the side to reveal a light, flowy material that was colored deep indigo with a slight sheen to it. The blue-purple color reminded me of the night, dark and mysterious. It wasn't something they ever would have let me wear at the White House—they liked to put me in things that were bright, cheery, and innocent, like whites and pastels; things that suited my supposed image. I stroked the fabric thoughtfully.

A bolt of rich green was thrust into my line of sight as Luenki held it up to my shoulder. "This would be stunning," she said, nodding approvingly.

"What about this?" I asked, lifting up the indigo fabric. Luenki set the green aside to examine it.

"Yes, I think this will do well," she agreed. "Several layers, perhaps. With the right accompaniments. Let me..." I stepped back for her to gather up my selection, and then she was breezing past me to another table, which held a collection of accent fabrics, straps, gold and silver chains, lace, and other accessories.

I looked past her to the fitting area at the end of the room. The screen had been pushed aside, revealing a slim woman in layers of yellow examining her reflection in a floor-length mirror. Another shorter woman stood behind her, running her hand over the back of the gown with a length of extra fabric tucked into the crook of her arm. As I watched, a sash appeared in her hand as though it had sprung from her palm.

Of course. Magic.

Luenki came to my side, arms overflowing with items she'd collected. Full of wonder, I took the opportunity to examine her dress. I hadn't noticed it before, but the piece was without a single visible seam. Fabric joined fabric as if adhered by glue.

"Magic really is convenient, isn't it?" I mused aloud,

returning my attention to the remarkable sight of a gown being formed before my eyes.

"A blessing," Luenki concurred, seeing what I had noticed. She shifted on her feet to knock her elbow against mine, shaking me from my fixation on the clothier. "Come, let us join the line," she suggested. I followed her toward the fitting area. As we approached, the two ladies who had been waiting changed their minds and rushed past us for the exit. I might have been insulted if I didn't find their over-the-top reactions so ridiculous.

The clothier was finishing up with the lady in yellow, who examined her reflection appreciatively in the mirror. She said a few quick words that sounded like thanks and spun around, letting her gaze linger on me before inclining her head to Luenki and sweeping past us. The sound of the door shutting behind her reverberated in the room. With her other customers gone, the clothier's attention turned to me, and I stiffened under her critical stare.

She was shorter than most of the fae I'd seen thus far, only a couple of inches taller than my 5′5″. Her hair was even lighter than Riel's, just barely off-white, and smile lines accented her eyes. That got me wondering how many years had to pass before a fae started showing outward signs of old age. Luenki stepped forward, a greeting dropping from her lips. I echoed it.

After a moment, the clothier graced me with a small smile. She and Luenki began to speak in their language, and Luenki leaned in to show her the items she'd picked out. As they talked, I awkwardly studied the toe of my boot and shifted my weight from one foot to the other. Except for a term here and there, Riel always spoke to me in English, so I hadn't been picking up the language at all. If I was honest, it was a little frustrating to not know what was going on.

The clothier flicked a hand in my direction, drawing my attention.

"Are you comfortable removing your clothes?" Luenki

asked, turning toward me. "I can wait on the other side of the screen if you would prefer privacy."

"Oh, yeah. No, you're good, I have underwear on." I went to undo the button on my jeans. The clothier tutted and moved to orient the screen so that we were hidden from view. Once I stood before the mirror in my mismatched, everyday-wear bra and panties, she began rifling through the pile of fabrics and accessories Luenki had selected.

The first piece she held up was a shiny dark gray. She started by wrapping that around my waist and having me hold it in place. Then, she added a layer of the indigo fabric I had picked out. She went around a few times with that one until there was a bit of poof to the skirt's shape. When she pulled the bolt of fabric away, the cloth split effortlessly.

The next few minutes passed in a blur. She ran her hands around my hips to secure the skirts and then had me spread my arms while she fitted the bodice and sleeves. Every so often, she would check in with Luenki for directions. The fabric around my middle firmed up as she handled it, providing a structured waist and neckline. When the sleeves were complete, she attached finishing touches—midnight-black laces to close the back and delicate silver chains to line the neckline, wrists, and waist. Finally, she pulled out a box full of rhinestones and knelt to attach them to the bottom of my skirt.

When she straightened and stepped back, I felt like I was Cinderella, and my fairy godmother had just waved her wand over me. The result was significantly better than anything I could have come up with. The dress flattered what few curves I had, accentuating the dip of my waistline and the modest swell of my breasts. The dark color and silver accents lent an edgy feel that I loved. I would have never been allowed to wear this at the White House.

"Beautiful." Luenki beamed as she adjusted the lay of my skirts with one hand.

"It's gorgeous," I breathed, admiring the way it sparkled

when the stones on the skirt caught the light. I meant the words, but a part of me worried that it didn't suit me. Big, floofy dresses had never been my style before, and now I was dressing myself, so I could choose what I wanted. A thought occurred to me, and I ducked my head sheepishly. "Is it too late to change a few things?"

Luenki translated for me, and the clothier shook her head with an accommodating smile. I explained what I envisioned, describing the best I could with words and a series of gestures. The clothier nodded along and played with the design while Luenki translated. A few minutes later, I couldn't stop smiling at my reflection, even as my cheeks began to ache.

"Yes, it's perfect," I exclaimed, giddy with excitement. "Oh my God. It's giving… moon goddess meets goth witch at a high school formal. I love it."

"This is different," Luenki said slowly, sounding uncertain.

"I never liked fancy dresses," I admitted, still unable to drag my gaze away from the mirror. "I used to wear them for my healing sessions, and it was a headache more often than not. But this is perfect. If it's not inappropriate, I'd like to wear this."

"It is not inappropriate," Luenki assured me. "It is not a style we have seen before, but it is a lovely idea to make it your own. Though… you may attract unwanted attention."

I shrugged and swayed back and forth, admiring the outfit as it moved with me. That was something to consider, but I'd have to get over my fears eventually. And what I felt looking at my reflection in the mirror—not to mention embracing my freedom and doing what I wanted for a change—that was more valuable right now.

No matter what, I wanted to enjoy this feeling as long as I could.

CHAPTER FIFTEEN
THE PARTY

I DIDN'T SEE Riel the next day, or the day after that. Luenki, bless her heart, did her best to keep me comfortable and calm. She brought me more clothes and several books in English, which someone must have transported through The Rift at some point. To pass the time, she told me stories of Riel's childhood, which I devoured eagerly, and taught me several games. One involved a carved board with many colorful little stones. That led to her teaching me the numbers one through ten in the *Ishameti* language, as well as a few additional words.

Despite Luenki's best efforts, by the time the day of the party came, I was reduced to a bundle of nerves. The grounding exercises seemed to make no difference, so I'd all but given up on them by that point, and the guilt was getting to me. I also hadn't gotten much sleep, too busy stressing over whatever might be going on in Riel's head on top of trying to figure out how best to navigate this event without any issues. More than once, I'd caught myself petting my party dress, as if the repetitive motion would somehow relieve a portion of the anxiety I was feeling.

The morning before the event, the castle was abuzz in a way I had never seen it. By the time the first rays of sunlight began streaming through my window, people were up and bustling around, the hallway outside my room noisy with traffic. The morning was uneventful, but when I stepped out to get my late morning meal, or what I'd affectionately dubbed "elevenses," I almost walked right into a pair of soldiers who were patrolling up and down the hallways.

I quickly retrieved my tray, scampered back, and shut the door behind me. After deciding to stay put until I heard from Luenki or Riel, I spent the next couple of hours playing the fae version of chess with myself and trying not to succumb to the jitters.

It was getting to be early afternoon before there was a polite knock at the door. The part of me that missed Riel was disappointed when it turned out to be Luenki once again, although I was happy to see her. She wore a stunning sleeveless pomegranate gown with a high neck.

"How are you doing?" she asked, studying my face for any signs of distress.

"Hanging in there," I replied, making an effort to school my features into the picture of serenity. "You look gorgeous. Did you want to come in?"

"Thank you." Luenki beamed. "But no. I came to let you know that preparations are complete and guests have begun arriving. There is no formal ceremony to commence the event, so you may join us in the Great Hall whenever you are ready."

My hand tightened on the door. "Oh, yeah, sure. Give me a few minutes." I started to draw back when a rare burst of courage hit. "Actually, uh… that's the main room right when you enter, right? I know the way. You can go on ahead, so I won't keep you waiting."

"Are you certain? I do not mind accompanying you there."

"I'll be fine," I promised, shaking my head. "You're too good to me, Luenki. I'll come find you in like… twenty minutes, how about that?"

She considered my proposition.

"If you are sure," she conceded, albeit hesitantly. "Then, I will see you soon."

"See you soon!" I raised a hand in farewell. Luenki bobbed her head before disappearing down the hallway, and I retreated back into my room.

It was strange no longer having a personal stylist to attend to my outfit, hair, and makeup for events like these, but I was determined to make the most of it on my own. I started by getting into my custom dress. "Ah, shit," I said out loud upon realizing that turning Luenki away meant I had to cinch up the laces on the back by myself.

I moved to the bathroom to use the mirror. By contorting my neck and looking over my shoulder, I was able to thread the laces and draw them tight one by one. It was a painstaking process, and by the end of it, my neck was sore. I needed to ask someone if I could work my healing powers into dress-making ones, because that would be ridiculously helpful.

It took more than twenty minutes to make myself presentable, but when I saw myself in the bathroom mirror, I was pleasantly surprised. I'd twisted my copper hair up into a bun and secured it with a claw clip, since that was nicer than leaving it down. I'd also bumbled my way through a touch of eyeshadow. I finished off the look with sandals with a wedge heel. While I wasn't going to stand out compared to any of the fae, the result was acceptable.

I was especially happy with the changes I'd made to the dress. Where it had originally featured an ankle-length layered skirt, now it had tight-fitting pants made from the same midnight indigo material underneath a skirt overlay that flared out from my hips. Business in the front, party in the back—just the right amount of formal, still modest, but a little more me.

Knowing that Luenki was probably going to be waiting with bated breath until I showed my face, I headed out without further delay. As I made my way to the throne room, I could already make out a swell of murmured conversations and folky string music. The tension that had gripped me the past few days doubled, but I forced my legs to keep moving.

I was familiar with social events involving foreign dignitaries and VIPs. If I treated this like the others, what was there to worry about? Really, this should be easier. Then again, there was no reason for a member of Congress to kill me where I stood. *Was that what this was about—a fear that I wouldn't make it back to my room in one piece?* That was a stretch, even for me. Nothing I'd seen or heard so far gave me the impression that the people here wanted me dead. And I was under the protection of the leading family, wasn't I?

I set my shoulders back and raised my chin as I approached the staircase that led down into the room. *Fear is the old me,* I told myself. Today, I was just another guest, here to enjoy the food, pleasant conversation, and dancing the same as anyone else.

The wall gave way to open space. They'd really gone all out with the decorations. The beams on the ceiling, which resembled tree branches, were studded with flowers. The floor had been polished to a mirror-like shine that reflected the colorful dresses, the pillars gleamed like a dragon's hoard, and even the color of the walls was different—a warm blush that flattered the artistic touches of silver. *How much of this was done with magic versus by hand?*

Pausing at the top of the stairs, I looked over the sea of faces in search of familiar ones. It was a challenge given the number of attendees with some version of blond hair and blue eyes. As I took in the crowd, however, I noticed several fae that were closer to average human height and had darker coloring. Interest piqued, I continued scanning the area for anyone that stood out. There was a man and woman standing by the musicians that were barely three feet tall. I even spotted one lady who was sky-blue from head to toe. Her dress appeared to be see-through, but I couldn't tell if that was a trick of the light.

Realizing that I was staring, I forced my eyes away. I hadn't seen Luenki or Riel yet, but I did notice tables of food at the far end of the room, and that was good enough for me. To my immense relief, no one stared as I made my way down the steps to join the revelers. The music played without pause, attendees mingled and chatted in their beautiful lilting language, and I was only given a few curious glances when I stepped onto the floor.

I made a beeline for the tables brimming with goodies. The first one was covered in tall, elegant glasses with a pale, golden liquid inside. I helped myself to one and took a sip, expecting champagne. It had no bubbles, but the flavor was exquisite, sweet and smooth with a citrusy zing. I finished it off, savoring the pleasant warmth as it traveled down to my stomach. No sooner had I drained it than an employee relieved me of my glass, so I helped myself to another.

"You may want to go easy on that," a voice said from behind, startling me before I had the chance to place it. I spun around, and my shoulders dropped in relief when I saw that it was Riel. He was dressed in a satiny silver getup similar to what he'd worn when I first met him. Like that time, he had a delicate corset-like piece around his middle. I gathered that this was formal wear. His impressive earrings, practically chandeliers capping each ear tip, all but confirmed it for me.

His head dipped as he returned the perusal, taking in my figure from head to toe. Then he inclined his head at the glass in my hand. "Our nectar wine has been known to cause adverse effects in humans. Lowered inhibitions, spontaneous laughter, an increase in poor decisions…" He paused a moment before adding, "In extreme cases, a propensity for promiscuity."

"Sounds like a good time," I retorted, raising the glass. "Where I come from, we have entire buildings dedicated to the sale and consumption of alcohol. I know what it does." I took another sip and licked my lips, savoring the sweetness. Riel watched the motion intently before glancing around the room as if to make sure no one else had seen. I started to ask if everything was all right, but I didn't have the chance.

"Would you like to dance?" He changed the subject.

"Probably shouldn't. I've got two left feet." I wiggled my toes in my sandals to emphasize my words. Riel glanced down, puzzled. I hid a smile behind my glass as I imbibed another mouthful. The warmth that spread through my core was addicting. It also granted me a much-needed push to be brave. "You know what?" I said. "I changed my mind."

I looked around for a place to leave my glass. Not finding one, I shrugged and downed the rest of my drink. It joined my first on the castle employee's tray.

"Shall we?" I offered my hand with a flourish.

Riel blinked at it. He recovered quickly and, hiding a smile, stepped in to link his arm with mine instead. His heat suffused my side. On our way toward the musicians, I caught sight of Luenki through the crowd. Her eyebrows rose, and I made a subtle gesture that I hoped came across as "all's well." To my relief, she inclined her head to show that she understood and moved on. I returned my attention to the task at hand, determined to tackle it with grace.

Riel guided me to the section of floor nearest the musicians, which seemed to be allocated for dancing. We joined several individuals and couples who were already swaying to the music and engaging in more complex dances. Upon seeing that, my courage began to wane. Even if it wasn't that formal, I doubted that Ridin' the Pony would be socially acceptable here.

As if reading my mind, Riel took me off to one side of the floor. He gathered me into a starting position with his hands on my hips, then led me through a simple dance that went along with the music. I floundered at first, but after a few steps, we were back in the starting position. On the third repetition, I got the hang of it, and a wide grin split my face.

"This isn't nearly as bad as I thought," I exclaimed, pleased with myself.

"It is said a capable partner can teach even an *avida* to dance," Riel remarked.

"Do they say that?" I wondered, calling to mind the mental image of a dancing *avida*.

"I did," he admitted. "Just now."

I swatted him on the shoulder as we passed each other back to back.

"Well, I'll take the capable partner, even if he comes with an attitude." I heaved a wistful sigh, wishing for more moments like this. "I wouldn't know the first thing about dancing to this kind of music. I've got the disco finger or *Thriller* in my repertoire, and that's about it. I could probably fumble my way through a waltz if I tried, but it's been a while."

"Perhaps I could be the student for one evening," Riel offered, pausing to convey his willingness. "Show me your dances. I'm sure I can learn them."

I tried to imagine the fae prince doing the disco finger and a smile tugged at my mouth. Shaking my head, I pushed him gently back into motion. "I think not. But it's sweet of you to offer."

We reached the starting position again, with his hands resting on my hips. This time, instead of beginning the dance, he lingered there. I shot him a questioning glance, and his eyes caught mine and held them. The intensity there caused a pleasant tingle to travel throughout my body, from the pit of my stomach all the way down to my toes. God, I could happily drown to death in that color. The world could end right now, and I wouldn't even be mad.

"You are radiant," he said softly. "Always, but this evening in particular."

I turned my head to hide my blush.

"Thank you. I can't remember ever having to dress myself up for anything. Honestly, it's a miracle I managed it. Well, the dress wasn't me, of course—that was thanks to Luenki and the dress lady. That's probably the coolest magic I've seen yet. I guess the only magic I've seen, aside from yours that one time. Not that yours wasn't cool!" Aaand I was babbling.

Riel chuckled and swept me into another dance. When that song ended, there was scattered applause. Another began, this one more lively than the first. Judging by the way the other dancers split off, it was not meant to be a couples dance, but Riel stayed close anyway. We made something up, his motions spontaneous and yet controlled. Without guidance, I couldn't do much more than awkwardly sway from side to side and move my arms around.

Eventually, there was a lull in the music, and I seized the chance to take a break.

"I need a drink," I excused myself, abandoning the dance floor in favor of the table full of not-champagne. I helped myself to another glass and downed it quickly, then took a moment to catch my breath. *This is more fun than I've had in ages,* I thought, still reeling with joy. Why weren't balls a regular thing back on Earth? We were missing out.

Riel appeared at my elbow and took a glass for himself. He savored the drink rather than making it disappear as I had. Although he'd relaxed somewhat since taking me to the dance floor, there was still tension in the way he carried himself. He appeared more alert than usual too. I surveyed the crowd, uncertain what he knew that I didn't. Nothing stood out to me.

"Are you all right?" I asked, keeping my voice low in case there was something nefarious afoot.

"Yes, thank you," Riel responded lightly. The tension remained.

"Are *we* all right?" I revised my question, raising a meaningful eyebrow. He seemed to pick up on my concern then, angling his body toward me to give me his full attention.

"We are," he assured me. "I apologize for my inattentiveness. The last few days have been… stressful. I kept thinking that things would settle down, but they haven't yet."

I nodded and returned to a relaxed position. I should have

left it at that, but I couldn't help but ask. "Is that why you've been avoiding me? 'Cause it's fine, I totally get being busy."

Riel's face flooded with shame. "You should know that I intended to return to you that night," he told me earnestly. "But there are things at play that…" The glass in his hand wobbled as he tried to find the words. "I can't afford to draw the wrong attention to you."

"That's fine," I hurried to reassure him. I'd have time to worry about what he meant by "the wrong attention" later. "It's fine. It's complicated, I know. And I'm doing okay. I mean, I miss our hangouts, but obviously, I don't want you to get in trouble."

His lips pressed together in a thin line, betraying his frustration.

"If there's anything I can do to help, let me know," I offered. I knew it was an empty offer. There wasn't really anything I could do, except… "If it's just not a good time right now, I'm sure I could go back to the military base for a while and come back when things are better. I've already taken advantage of your hospitality for so long." I gripped a handful of my skirt as I spoke, fighting to keep my voice even so as not to show how much I didn't want that.

"No. I want you close," Riel said quickly, only appearing to realize what he said after the words left his mouth. My heart soared at the confession, but he made a sound in his throat and turned away from me in embarrassment. "That is to say, it helps to know that… you're being looked after," he amended, taking another sip of his drink. "Even if I can't be there. I trust Luenki explicitly."

"I'm sure Vivian could look after me just fine," I murmured, taking a fourth glass of wine in hopes of drowning the swarm of butterflies in my stomach. "But, um… I appreciate that."

"I care about you, *eseri*."

I glanced his way, surprised at both his choice of words and the serious tone, but Riel's attention was focused on the last inch of liquid in his glass. Just as well, because it was hard enough to breathe without his eyes on me. He didn't appear to expect a response, but I was feeling particularly brave with the alcohol coursing through my system.

"I care about you too," I said softly. My face felt a little too warm for comfort, but my response came out steady. I directed my own gaze downward. "But, if I'm being honest, you're a little confusing. It's kind of hard to know where we stand right now, what with the teasing and then giving me goo-goo eyes and then running away and avoiding me, and now this… I don't want to misunderstand anything, so maybe you could clarify what you mean by that?"

He hesitated, and I thought the worst. My stomach twisted itself into knots. I tried not to let it get to me, but my hand tightened on my glass, and I started to think of ways I could gracefully excuse myself and return to my room without anyone noticing.

"You're right," he said finally, resolved. "I should make myself clear."

CHAPTER SIXTEEN
THE CONFESSION

I BRACED myself as Riel resumed speaking.

"From the moment I saw you, I wanted to know you," he admitted in a low voice, sending the butterflies scattering. My eyes flicked upward hesitantly, hopefully, but he still looked away from me. "At first, it was innocent intrigue. The existence of a Goddess-blessed human goes against our teachings. But you were so… genuine. I understood why you'd been given Her blessing. You put others before yourself—strangers, even. It's incredibly foolish."

I frowned and opened my mouth to defend myself, but he cut me off before I could.

"I've never met someone like you before," he confessed. "Someone who doesn't pretend to be something else. Someone who's willing to set their own wants aside to do what's right, no matter how uncomfortable. Someone who's willing to share their own secrets to put those around them at ease. During the time we've spent together, I've watched you try your hardest to make the best of things, putting your whole heart into everything you do. Somewhere along the way, I realized that I wanted to be on the receiving end of that.

"Our lessons are more than just lessons for me, Avery. Of

course, I want to help you—don't ever doubt that. But the more I learn about you, the more I want to know. Our respective situations do make things complicated, but I hope that we can overlook that. I hope that we can continue to speak on equal terms and get to know each other further. And… if the Goddess has willed that you feel the same in regard to me, I hope that you will allow me to court you. Perhaps, someday, we might be able to be more than we are now."

Shit. My eyes were getting moist, and I couldn't blame these feelings on the wine.

"That's…" *How do I even respond to a confession like that?* "That's very nice," I said weakly, cursing myself as soon as the words left my mouth. I cleared my throat to dislodge the lump there and tried again. "I'm… I do feel the same way. I want to get to know you. To keep getting to know you, I mean. I would like to be more with you."

When Riel didn't say anything more, I chanced another glance his way. His eyes were closed—whether in pain or relief, I couldn't tell. He muttered something under his breath before opening his eyes and turning back to me. Some of the tension had left his body.

That is, until a female voice purred, "The blessed human! Riel, introduce us?"

I stiffened, all the fuzzy, warm feelings gone in an instant, and my attention snapped to the woman approaching us. She was about as tall as Luenki and held every inch of herself with grace and poise. Her dress was a stunning mass of silver and white that clung to her form unlike any other in the room, and her blond hair was coiled around her head and finished off with a silver circlet. Over her dress, she wore a metal accessory not unlike Riel's corset, except that hers went from her neck to her ribs, decorating her breasts and shoulders. She also had piercings on the bridge of her nose and both cheeks.

Riel's hand touched my lower back, startling me—I hadn't noticed him come to my side. "Mother," he said in an even tone.

I stiffened further, suddenly regretting all that wine. "This is Avery Nelson, the Goddess-blessed human from Washington, D.C. Avery, this is Elokima, Lady of the House Wysalar, the Right Hand of the Goddess, and… my mother."

"At last!" Elokima exclaimed, fitting her forearms on top of each other and bowing. I quickly mimicked the action, sending up a silent prayer to whatever powers that be that I wasn't making an utter fool of myself. "It is such a pleasure to finally make your acquaintance," she continued. "My son has been doing his best to keep you hidden away." Her words were friendly, but the look she directed at Riel made me nervous.

"The pleasure is all mine," I said quickly, hoping to keep things light. "It's such an honor to finally meet you. Ah… Riel's told me so much about you. Thank you for your hospitality these past few weeks. I've been having such a blast, and I've learned so much. And your English is so good! Everyone speaks such great English here. It's really impressive…"

Elokima tittered, interrupting me just as I'd begun to spiral. "Aren't you a sweet thing?" Assessing eyes swept over me from head to toe, lingering on the glass in my hand and the legs of my romper/dress. I kept a smile pasted on my face in hopes that it hid my crumbling nerves.

"How are you enjoying our celebration?" she asked, her gaze returning to mine. Something about her expression bothered me. Was it just my imagination? I couldn't shake the feeling that if I gave the wrong response, I was going to be eaten alive.

So I turned up the charm, the same way I did when I was meeting a dignitary that was "very important." "I'm having so much fun," I gushed, focusing on keeping my hand steady and my smile genuine. "The music is fabulous, and the wine is delicious. We don't have a lot of events like these where I come from, and it's such a shame. Then again, I'm sure our efforts would pale in comparison to yours. You make an exceptional host."

Elokima chuckled again. "Be sure to try the food, if you haven't already," she suggested, inclining her head in farewell before turning away. "Enjoy."

"Thanks, you too!"

As she drifted off, I whirled about to face Riel. "That was awful," I hissed, my shoulders slouching with misery. "Wasn't that awful?"

"Far from it," Riel remarked as he watched his mother disappear into the crowd. His hand returned discreetly to my back. "You did fine. That went about as well as could be expected."

Just then, my nape tingled with the sensation of being watched. Somehow, my eyes caught surly sapphire ones through the tangle of bodies between us. Solois stood on the other side of the room, his back rigid and his expression tight as he observed Riel and me. Riel noticed him at about the same time I did and snatched his hand away as though I'd burned him. It bothered me, but I could understand where he was coming from—he probably didn't want his brother to see how close we were. That would raise tricky questions.

"I need to mingle," he murmured apologetically. "Go to Luenki. I'll find you soon."

"Okay," I agreed, trying to keep the disappointment out of my voice. "But you're going to have some explaining to do later."

"I will," he promised. He looked like he wanted to say something else. "Later," he ground out instead, the tension and frustration returning in force.

Not wanting to leave things like that after such an emotional breakthrough, I sidled closer and reached between us to pinch his sleeve in a way I hoped conveyed my affection for him. "Whatever's going on, things will work out," I said softly, only just resisting the urge to give him a hug. "They always do, one way or another."

"I truly hope you're right." Riel breathed a sigh brimming

with unsaid words and inclined his head before striding off in the direction his mother had gone.

I finished off my—fourth? Fifth?—glass of wine and, deciding that was plenty, opted to refill it from a pitcher of water instead. Then, I took the queen's advice to explore the food tables. I didn't recognize everything that was there, but it all looked delicious. One table featured a spread of petite sweets in all manner of shapes, while another bore savory finger foods.

Once I'd had my fill, I was off to find Luenki. I circled the massive room twice before I found her chatting away with another fae woman by one of the pillars. Not wanting to interrupt their conversation, I hung out awkwardly nearby. When her companion moved on, Luenki turned her attention to me as though she had known I was there the entire time.

"How is the prince?" she asked knowingly.

"Ooh, things are… things are something, that's for sure." I shook my head, not having the words to sum up what had happened. "I met his mom," I offered.

Luenki's lips drew together in a tight line.

"It went well," I was quick to clarify, not wanting her to think the worst. "Or, as well as can be expected, Riel said. I figure I can take his word for it."

Luenki made a sound of agreement, though she didn't appear convinced. "I am glad. If we are lucky, she will not feel the need to approach you again."

"Is she that disagreeable?"

Luenki's head cocked as she considered her response. "Not disagreeable," she hedged. "But she is wary of outsiders. Our leading family is responsible for the protection of our people, after all. There is much at stake at any given time." One hand indicated the people around us.

"Sure, I get that."

If it was anything like being president, being queen probably came with a host of annoying responsibilities, from mundane things like paperwork and blessing babies to high-stakes duties like drafting treaties and ordering missile strikes. Or… whatever the equivalent was here, anyway. *Did they have missiles? Magic ones?*

"Well, I'm not about to let them bring my mood down." I proclaimed, rolling my shoulders back and extending an arm out to Luenki. "May I have this dance?"

Eyes twinkling, Luenki accepted my offer, and we joined the other revelers on the dance floor. After an hour or so of chatting and dancing with Luenki, Riel came to find us. By then, my buzz had faded, but I'd managed to resist the lure of the wine table. The three of us danced together for a little while longer before I had to call it quits.

"That's enough action for one day," I wheezed, putting my hands on my knees to catch my breath. "I think… I think I'll head back to my room now, if it's not too early."

"If you like," Luenki agreed. Her forehead shone with the faint sheen of perspiration under the light of the sconces, but other than that, she showed no signs of physical exertion. And rather than detract from her appearance, it only made her glow all the more. Ridiculous. "You have more than fulfilled your obligation. It is doubtful anyone would notice if you slipped out."

"Let me walk you to your room," Riel offered, ever the gentleman. Excitement sparked at the thought that we could continue our conversation from before.

"Is that okay?" I murmured, not wanting to get him in any trouble. "It won't cause any problems if they see you leaving with me…?"

Luenki examined the platform where the musicians sat with their instruments. "I will make sure that their eyes are elsewhere," she said, a hint of mischief in her voice.

I could only watch, baffled, as she whirled about and strode past several dancers to interrupt the performers before the next song began playing. Mounting the two wide steps in a graceful bound, she took up a position in front and addressed the crowd in a booming voice.

"'We are grateful for the safe return of Ralif, Second of His Name, Lord of the Northern House Wysalar, Guardian of the Goddess's Chosen,'" Riel translated for me in a low voice as he gathered my arm to lead me from the room. "'May the Goddess continue to smile upon our leading family, and their reign deliver us greener pastures and brighter days.'"

On our way up the steps to the living quarters, one of the stringed instruments started playing. Its sweet music and an angelic voice combined to fill the room with an emotional ballad. I looked back to see Luenki seated where one of the musicians had been, her mouth open in song. She played a large stringed instrument that resembled a horizontal harp.

I turned back to Riel with wide eyes.

"Our ambassador is a woman of many talents," he said, smiling at my surprise.

"So it would seem! Man, you think you know someone."

"She is competent with a blade as well."

"Are you serious? She can fight too?"

"Having a diplomatic attitude is important in matters of foreign policy, but it is equally critical to choose someone who can handle themselves in a fight should anything go wrong."

"I… suppose so." I couldn't help but feel a touch of envy. Apparently, it was obvious on my face, because Riel felt the need to highlight some of her flaws.

"She's a shameless cheat at several games, however. And she loves to make sweets, but has no talent for it. She refuses to follow the recipes; it's nothing short of complete chaos."

"Well, not everybody can be as perfect as you." A grin took over my face.

"Indeed." Riel mirrored my smile. We arrived at my door then, despite the way I'd been subconsciously dragging my feet to prolong the walk. I hesitated to reach for the handle when I still had so many questions.

"Would you, uh... would you like to come in?" I dared to ask.

"I shouldn't." Riel's voice was so near, I could practically feel his presence at my back.

When I turned to face him, it took me a moment to register how close he was. Only a few inches separated us. I pressed my back against the door in an attempt to give myself some breathing room, and he looked down at me with such a fond expression that my pulse sped up. When he didn't make a move like I expected, I moistened my lips and ventured another question.

"You... you said you wanted to court me. What does that mean, exactly?"

Riel was quiet. "What would you like it to be?" he asked.

"It's not fair to answer a question with a question," I pointed out, raising my eyebrows and pursing my lips in a pout. He flashed me another arresting grin.

"It should be illegal to be that pretty," I muttered, turning my head so that I didn't have to see his face. "I guess... I guess I need some things cleared up before I can answer that. But I don't think things need to be all that different. I like how it's been between us so far, and I'd like it if it stays that way. Instead of getting awkward, you know."

"I'd like that too," Riel responded softly. "As for the answers I owe you... I'm still finding some things out, I'm afraid. What I can tell you is that my family has some concerns about whether or not your nation—and you—can be trusted.

"I have told them that these concerns are unfounded," he assured me just as I opened my mouth to interject, "but they can be stubborn. I didn't want them to do anything rash out of a belief that you are somehow manipulating me, so I thought it wise to turn my attention somewhere else for a while. Believe me when I say that it was difficult to leave you alone."

My mouth closed with an audible *snap*, and a swell of pity swept through me.

"I'm still keeping a close eye on my parents and brother," he continued. "As of right now, they're still considering their next move, but I'm doing everything I can to stay one step ahead. Your well-being is my top priority. When I have more information, I'll start working on a plan."

"Oh my God," I breathed, instantly thinking the worst. "Do—shouldn't we tell someone? Vivian and George and the rest of them, they should probably be—"

My hands flapped about in the air, echoing my racing thoughts.

"Luenki knows." Riel snatched up my hands and held them. "Since things are still undecided, I think it's best that your government stays out of this for now. If this develops into a real threat, we will address it then, but I'd rather not involve them if we can help it."

I nodded slowly. "I trust you," I whispered, adjusting my hands to squeeze his in return. *But was staying silent some kind of treason?*

Riel leaned in to press a soft kiss to my jawline, distracting me just as I'd begun to question if that was the right move and consider the possible consequences. I sucked in a breath as my inappropriate fantasy from a few days ago sprang to mind.

"Thank you," he mumbled into my neck before resting his head on my shoulder. I stood frozen, hesitant to even breathe for fear of disrupting the moment. After a beat, I worked one hand out of his to reach up and tentatively caress the nape of his neck. His hair was like silk, and I was in the perfect position to admire his ear adornments more closely.

"I've been meaning to say so, but I like your piercings," I murmured.

Unprompted, my mind's eye flashed back to the day I'd caught him half-dressed. Were his ears and his nipples all that were pierced? And, come to think of it, how come his nipple piercings didn't show through any of his lovely shirts? Was that also some kind of magic?

"Thank you. I did them myself."

I blinked in surprise.

"You did them yourself?" I repeated to make sure I had heard him right. He nodded.

"Traditionally, those with a primary affinity for changing magic, like myself, used jewelry as a way to carry metal with them in case it was ever needed for defense. Nowadays, it's just a fashion, I suppose. My grandfather had many piercings, and I always used to admire them as a child. It was one of the first things I did when I came of age."

"That's crazy. I mean, doing it yourself. Plenty of people get piercings where I come from too, but we go to shops and have it done by professionals."

I almost reached up to trace the beckoning point of one silver ear tip but remembered myself and drew my hand back before it made contact. "They're beautiful. I wanted to get my ears pierced as a kid but never got the chance to."

Riel studied my face, perhaps gauging my sincerity. "I could do it for you," he suggested. "If you like."

Maybe I still rode an emotional high from our conversation earlier, or maybe I had underestimated the influence of all that fae wine, but his offer appealed to me. Hell, I was a girl with magical healing powers dating an alien prince in a fantasy land. What was getting my ears pierced on top of that? Another thought occurred to me—I made my own choices here… what if I didn't stop at my ears? What if I did something else entirely?

"You would?" I imagined little silver hoops donning my own nipples and felt the need to moisten my lips. The buzz of anticipation set off a tingle under my bodice.

"How is your pain tolerance?" Riel asked then.

"Uh… average, I guess?"

"Humans seem to be rather delicate creatures. If piercings are still common among your people, I imagine you wouldn't have an issue, but it can be painful."

"Oh, please." I waved away his concern. "Nobody's that delicate. A little needle prick is nothing."

Riel raised one platinum eyebrow, and the dare was written on his face. I drew my shoulders back and raised my chin in reply.

"Let's do it," I declared.

"Tonight?" His eyebrow stayed raised.

"Fine, tonight," I agreed, not wanting to risk the chance of second-guessing myself. That sexy smirk made an appearance in response to my enthusiasm, and my heart sped up.

"It's settled," Riel decided. He glanced toward the end of the hall, then back to me. "I have to go back now, but come to my room after the sun sets." His fingers caressed the shell of my ear, tucking a strand of hair behind it. "We'll find something nice for those pretty, round ears of yours."

"Okay," I said over the sound of my heartbeat. "See you then."

"See you then," Riel echoed. With one last blinding smile, he left to rejoin the party, leaving me at my door. My legs became noodles, prompting me to lean most of my weight against the jamb and focus on catching my breath. My head whirled. I felt like I'd been injected with elation, but at the same time…

What did I just agree to?

CHAPTER SEVENTEEN
THE AFTERPARTY

I HAD TO BE HIGH. Drunk? Dreaming?

There was a lot I still had to process. The party, for one. Meeting Riel's mom. What he said about his family not trusting me. That was sure to come up again sooner or later, especially given that… Riel and I were dating now? But I could worry about that whenever; right now, there were more pressing matters to attend to.

What was I thinking, agreeing to let him pierce me on a whim?

I've done some crazy things in my life. Not *that* crazy, but as crazy as anyone would with the same resources and opportunities I've had. Having a fae prince pierce my nips would be an unbeatable highlight—that is, if I managed to go through with it. I half-suspected I'd lose all my bravado the moment I saw Riel again, but for now, all I could think about was getting his hands on me. *Thanks, gutter brain.*

As I changed into something more comfortable, I recalled the shiver-inducing words he spoke to me: *I know that our respective situations make things complicated, but I hope that we can overlook that. I hope that we can continue to speak on equal terms and get to know each other further. And I hope that you will allow me to court you. Perhaps, someday, we might be able to be more than we are now.*

Yeah, there really wasn't any misinterpreting that, even for me. Gah, I had goosebumps. Not for the first time, I missed my gaming buddies and my bodyguards. Chris, especially, would absolutely die if he knew what was going on right now. At least I had Luenki to talk to now when I needed someone, but... it wasn't quite the same.

I sat on the edge of my bed and fidgeted. A quick glance at the window told me I probably had another hour or two until sunset, but eyeballing it was far from an exact science. *What I wouldn't give for a clock.* I didn't miss too many things from Earth, but technology was probably the biggest one. Well, technology and pizza. Meditating, board games, and appreciating nature were fun and all, but I missed being able to pass the time with apps or TV streaming services. *I took that for granted, didn't I?*

Closing my eyes, I began the grounding exercises that helped me get into a meditative mindset. It had been a little while since the last time I tried. If I thought about it too much, I started to feel guilty that I still hadn't made any progress toward accessing *mana*. But as far as I was concerned, I had bigger fish to fry. Or, more attractive fish, anyway. If it was meant to happen, it would. In the meantime, it was better to focus on things that lay within my control.

When I opened my eyes again, the sun was not much lower in the sky. I groaned aloud and threw myself onto my belly, splaying my hand flat against the bedding. My options were few. I could keep trying to pass the time with meditation, but with my excitement at the level it was, I doubted I'd be able to achieve the right headspace. My room was spotless, so anxious cleaning was out of the question. I'd already refolded all of my clothes in the armoire a dozen times over the last couple of months. And I didn't feel like working out right now either.

I could take a bath? That was a good idea. I'd be alone with Riel, after all. Who's to say things wouldn't go further than a piercing? If there was any chance I might end up naked, I should ensure I was fresh and clean. Oh, God, was he the kind of guy who reciprocated? Was oral sex even socially acceptable here? Maybe I was getting a *little* ahead of myself. We hadn't even done anything yet, and I was freaking out. This did not bode well for me.

I'd made an effort to be thorough during my bath. *Just in case,* I kept telling myself. When I emerged from the bathroom, smelling like flowers and gleaming pink from all the scrubbing, the sun was beginning to set. I tossed my towel onto the bed and went to pick out another outfit. Eventually, I settled on a light, flowy top and shorts. Was it a little revealing? Maybe. But I was feeling daring tonight.

I paced until the sun was out of view, then waited a little longer. When my room finally fell dark, I made for the door, taking a moment to check the hallway before heading out. The lights had dimmed and the sounds of music and conversation had quieted, hopefully signaling the event was over. I didn't see any guests or guards, which I took as a good sign.

Letting the door close behind me, I padded along the corridor toward Riel's room on the other side of the castle. The journey was quick, but my heart pounded the whole way. Luckily, I didn't run into anyone. It was wild how the castle just shut down at night. Not that I saw many people around during the day—they all stayed out of my way—but still, it was almost spooky. At the White House, someone was always around.

Was it that the security wasn't on the same level here? Or, maybe, if everyone could use magic, there wasn't any need for personal guards. Riel and Solois were able to go where they pleased without accompaniment, after all, and they were royalty.

I didn't have time to ruminate on the thought, as I arrived at Riel's door before long. There was no way to prepare myself for what was to come, but I breathed in and out before knocking.

The door opened almost instantly, flooding the hallway in cool light. Riel stood at an awkward angle, as though he'd rushed to the door and nearly fallen over in his haste to open it. He still wore his silver outfit from the party, although he had since removed the corset piece around his middle. The tie at his collar and the first few buttons of his shirt were also undone, revealing a glimpse of lickable skin. *Did I catch him about to change?*

"Hi," I whispered. *Shit, I wasn't drooling, was I?*

"Hi." Riel's disarming grin had my nervousness melting away. He moved aside to let me in. "I was just getting ready for you. You can take a seat while I finish setting up."

"Oh, you're fine," I assured him. *So fine. More than fine.* I stepped past him and into the room. His room was, of course, larger than mine, and quite a bit nicer too. There was a fireplace on the far side, with a woven rug and cozy-looking chaise in front of it. Sets of shelves covered in books and assorted knick-knacks lined the walls on either side.

He also had a desk in one corner. In the opposite corner was an armoire similar to mine with a large, ornate chest beside it. There was an excessively large bed, which had four carved wood posters and gauzy curtains like something out of a preteen's dream journal, with another chest at the foot of it. The room was bathed in cool light from a strange glass lantern set on one of the shelves.

My wandering gaze caught sight of a set of long, slim needles nestled in a cloth booklet on the bedside table, and I almost hesitated. Almost. "How was the rest of the party?" I asked instead, staring down the needles and willing myself to not turn tail.

"Uneventful." Riel's voice was muffled. I adjusted my line of sight to see that he had disappeared into the bathroom, the sliding door left open a few inches. Although I couldn't see inside, I caught a hint of that fresh, woodsy, uplifting cologne he wore. "My mother was disappointed that you left early," Riel's voice continued.

I winced. "Oh, I'm sorry. I hope that didn't cause any problems."

"No, there was enough going on to keep her distracted." The light in the bathroom blinked out, and Riel emerged in a more casual outfit, one hand held as if holding something.

"What have you got there?" I asked, pivoting to face him.

"The jewelry." Riel opened his hand to show me a flash of silver. "Would you be more comfortable on the bed or the chair? I leave it up to you."

I eyed the bed. Sitting there felt too intimate somehow. "Maybe the chair," I muttered, trying to ignore the little voice in my head that called me a coward. I made for the chaise in front of the fireplace and poured myself into the seat.

"I thought you might not want something too heavy, so I made some changes to a pair of my earrings." Riel went to collect his tools from the bedside table. "They should be small enough that they won't interfere with anything, and you can wear them daily without discomfort."

"Ah, thank you."

This was my chance. If I wanted to take the plunge, it was now or never. I straightened my back and folded my hands in my lap, picturing a confident version of me that always asked for what she wanted and didn't think about being awkward or regretting it later. "Actually, I gave it some thought, and I think I want ones like yours. The, uh… the ones on your chest."

"Hoops? I can modify them, but it might take some getting used to. Hoops are a bit heavier and can get caught on things more easily."

"Oh, that's fine…" My cheeks warmed, but I forged forward. "I meant… as in, rather than pierce my ears, I was thinking I might like you to pierce my, ah, my nipples."

Silence followed my request.

"If that's okay with you," I hurried to add.

Riel kept his expression controlled, but I could see the gears struggling to turn in his head. "Is that so?" he said at last, the question coming out more like a statement.

I nodded, my hands fidgeting in place. Did it bother him? The last thing I wanted was to turn him off, especially when we'd come so far toward understanding each other. I was on the edge of telling him not to worry about it and just do my ears after all.

"Both of them?" he clarified, sounding dubious.

"Well, yeah," I mumbled. "What's the point of just piercing one?"

Riel looked down at the earrings in his hand. "Okay," he said. "Okay." He swayed on his feet as though he wasn't sure what he was doing before swiveling around and heading for the bedside table. I watched his back with bated breath as he fiddled with the jewelry in his hand. Once he was pleased with whatever changes he made, he turned back to me.

"Then, uh…" He made a vague gesture in the air between us with his free hand. I blinked, not understanding, and he made a humming sound in his throat. "If you want to…" A meaningful inclination of his head finally got the message across.

"Oh! Um, should I…? I guess I'll…"

My hands jumped up to the hem of my shirt. Riel averted his eyes, busying himself with sorting out his tools. I couldn't describe why, but a sort of giddy excitement washed through me upon seeing his reaction. I felt… powerful. Like I was the one that held all the cards.

I drew my shirt over my head and dropped it onto the floor beside the chaise in one smooth motion. My hands then moved to my back to unclasp my bra, and when my gaze came up, I locked eyes with Riel from across the room. He hadn't moved, but a slight crease had appeared between his brows, as if he hadn't thought I would actually go through with it.

In a sensual move rather unlike me, I took my time with the bra, holding it to my chest and creeping one strap down my arm. Riel's eyes followed the movement. Switching hands, I pulled the other strap down. Once my second arm was free, I slipped the article of clothing out from underneath the hand that still preserved my modesty and dropped it on top of the shirt that lay discarded at my feet. Riel's eyes narrowed.

Maintaining eye contact, I wet my lips and let my arm fall, baring my breasts to his gaze. There was a moment of silence. Neither of us moved, both of us waiting to see what the other would do next. Maybe it was just my perception, but the temperature in the room felt like it had risen several degrees since we began this dance.

Riel was the first to break. He brought a hand up to hide his face and angled his body away from me. When he spoke, his voice had taken on a rough quality. "Sorry," he said. "Just… one moment."

I gave him a moment. Then another. Sitting there exposed, every second that passed eroded more of my courage. I squirmed in place and eyed my shirt on the floor. Maybe this had been a bad idea. *Maybe I made him uncomfortable by being so forward. The fae women were more demure, after all. And they were religious. Maybe they didn't do any sexy stuff until after marriage—or their version of it, anyway.* Oh, God. *Was he trying to figure out how to get out of this without hurting my feelings?*

I'd been so deep in thought that when Riel dropped his hand, I jumped in surprise.

"I feel… I need to point out that I'm physically attracted to you. Intensely so," he asserted. "I'm going to try my best to be respectful of the situation. I don't want to scare you. If I do anything to make you uncomfortable, at any point, please just let me know."

My breath left me in a whoosh, followed by a short bark of laughter.

"Oh my God." I shook my head at Riel's incredulous look.

"You're the sweetest thing. That's good to know, but I don't think it will be an issue." Summoning all my newfound confidence, I gestured at my chest and added, "Carry on, then. We haven't got all night."

Riel eyed me a moment longer, perhaps to be sure that my mind was made up. Satisfied by whatever he saw in my expression, he swiped the needles from the bedside table and prowled my way. The anticipation redoubled, and I tensed as he closed the space between us in a few long strides. He dropped to his knees an arm's length away. I couldn't help but notice that the movement put his face right at nipple height.

"Good?" he asked, keeping his eyes downcast and bringing his hand up to show me two dainty silver loops. I nodded, and he held them out for me to take. When they dropped into my waiting palm, I took the chance to examine them more closely. A delicate trailing vine design was etched into the outside of the metal. They were beautiful.

And they were about to be embedded in my skin. Goosebumps traveled up my arms.

"It may hurt a moment at first," Riel explained as he selected a needle from the assortment wrapped in cloth. His tone was measured, but I could hear the strain behind his words. "You'll feel a sharp pinch or sting, but it will be quick. You don't have to fear infection; I've sterilized the metal, and I will close the wound quickly."

"You have healing magic?" I asked, my voice coming out weirdly breathless.

"Enough for this," Riel replied, turning to me with the needle in hand. I forced myself to roll my shoulders back even as my instincts screamed at me to curl inward and cover myself. To his credit, Riel remained as steady as a surgeon, even with a faceful of grade-A boobage. He gently took one of the nipple rings from my hand, and I held my breath.

"Ready?" he asked, leaning in.

"Ready." I turned my gaze up to the ceiling.

The pinch of the needle caused me to inhale sharply.

"All right?" Riel asked immediately.

"All right." I nodded and began to release the breath I'd been holding. Riel barely twitched, and the second pinch came and went before I even had the chance to fill my lungs again. My chest flushed with warmth in response to the injury. Just as I went to look down, skin brushed against the underside of my right breast, and a strange sensation zipped through both nipples and down my spine.

An embarrassing sound escaped me. My hand shot up to cover my mouth.

"Sorry," Riel murmured, his shoulders shaking with the effort to hold back laughter as he cleaned off the needle and returned it to its place. "It would seem that my mending is a bit rusty."

"Did you do that on purpose?" I hissed, face burning with shame.

"I didn't, actually." He directed an appreciative glance my way, and his voice dropped low. "But I'd do it again if it meant that you would make another sound like that."

I froze like a deer in headlights, one hand reaching out to retrieve my top from the floor. *Did he just?* That went beyond innocent teasing, surely? It was practically a handwritten invitation. All I had to do was let him know that it was okay, that I wanted this.

"Uh… I mean, you could"—my voice cracked, but I cleared my throat and pressed on, my audacity surprising even me—"maybe try it and see?"

Riel responded by placing a hand on the chaise just beside my exposed thigh and leaning forward. Heart pounding, I snatched up my shirt and held it to my chest as if it would protect me.

"Avery," he said seriously, his face inches from mine, "are you *flirting* with me?"

"I-I—" I blinked rapidly as no witty answer sprang to mind.

My eyes fell involuntarily to his lips. They beckoned to me, smooth and pink and so appetizing that it hurt. All other thoughts faded away. *If I seized the moment and kissed him now, would he kiss me back? Would we go even further than that? Did I want us to?*

My mouth opened slightly, but I didn't get the chance to say whatever it was I had intended to, as the lips I had been admiring found mine without prompting. The contact left no room for doubt—it was everything I'd wanted, and everything I hadn't known I needed. As his lips explored mine with excruciating tenderness, Riel's hand rose to cradle the side of my face, and I leaned into his touch. The motion caused our noses to bump together.

"Relax," Riel whispered against my mouth. I felt his lips curve into a smile. I tried to relax, I really did, but my imagination ran wild. Weren't tongues supposed to be involved? All he did was line my lower lip with feather-light nibbles. The contact was somehow both innocent and provocative, sending shivers through my body to rouse my various pleasure points.

Just as my right hand reached up with the intention to grasp the nape of his neck and demand more, Riel released me and leaned back on his heels. Immediately, I felt the loss, my budding arousal fizzling into frustration.

"You're not stopping me," he murmured, studying my expression as if expecting that I would remember some delicate sensibilities I didn't have and get offended.

"No, I'm not," I agreed. In case there was still any confusion, I let the shirt between us fall to my lap, exposing my breasts once more. Riel's eyes dropped. In a flash, he had me pinned to the chaise, his body invading the open space between my thighs. When his lips met mine again, it was with bruising force, all traces of tenderness forgotten. I gasped in surprise and threw my arms around his neck.

His hands wrapped around my ass at the same time his tongue pushed into my mouth, producing an electric jolt of arousal in response. I had trouble forming a coherent thought, but Riel seemed to know what he was doing. His tongue engaged mine in a passionate dance that caused my eyelids to flutter closed. He tasted sweet and zesty, like orange peels or the fae wine. Everywhere he touched, my body burned with a level of need I'd never felt before.

At some point, the sensations overwhelmed me, and I made a sound somewhere between a whimper and a whine. Riel abandoned my mouth. Just as I began to protest, the room spun, and I found myself blinking up at the ceiling with him hovering above me. His knee found the junction of my thighs, providing delicious pressure. I bit back another moan.

"Oh my God," I squealed in surprise as Riel lowered his head and seized one of my freshly healed piercings between his teeth. Despite the raw hunger that burned in his gaze, he was gentle as he tugged. The unexpected feeling made sparks fly in my groin and my next inhale stutter.

"Good?" Riel asked, the question a throaty rasp.

"Do that again," I ordered breathlessly, my fingers scrabbling for hold in his silky hair. He chuckled and obeyed, continuing to lavish one breast with his lips and tongue and bringing one hand up to tease the other with his fingers. My hips began to jerk sporadically, seeking more stimulation to push me over the edge. Somehow understanding my wordless request, Riel slid his knee up further, giving me just what I needed.

"Shit, shit," I whimpered, clutching at the collar of his shirt as I ground against him. The pleasure grew and grew. He kept playing with my nipples, now slick with his saliva, cycling between nips and licks and pinches and tugs that were driving me crazy. Lost to the symphony of sensations, I didn't notice the impending orgasm until it was upon me. Muscles deep in my abdomen clenched and shuddered, and I let out a soft cry of relief.

For a moment, all I could do was tremble under Riel's ministrations. Wave after wave of pleasure came and went until slowly, lovingly, he brought me down from the peak, transitioning from the arousing contact to trailing slow, deliberate kisses from breast to shoulder.

As I lay there trying to catch my breath, I meant to say something, but words escaped me. *Did I need words?* I couldn't think of anything that mattered enough to say. *What did lovers usually say to each other after their first time together?* Riel didn't seem to mind that my brain had turned to soup, still depositing sweet kisses across my skin.

Once I was able to think straight again, I went to sit up with the intention of returning the favor. Riel retreated to the end of the chaise to give me some space. When I scooted forward and reached for him, he stopped me by catching my hand. My eyebrows furrowed in confusion.

"Thank you." Riel pressed my fingers to his lips, his gaze soft and tender. "I'd like to leave things here for tonight. This time with you has already been a gift, and there's no rush."

"Oh!" I withdrew my hand and tried to ignore the little pang of hurt. "Yeah… no problem. Next time, then." Giving an awkward laugh to hide my embarrassment, I tucked a strand of hair out of my face and surreptitiously rooted around the chaise for my shirt.

"I look forward to it," Riel murmured, his eyes simmering with heat. He dipped down to collect my shirt and bra from the floor and passed them both to me. I opted to pull my shirt over my head and hang on to my bra rather than try to wrestle it on while he watched.

With my important bits covered, I folded my bra in my hands while I racked my brain for the proper thing to say in this situation. "Well, uh… thanks! I appreciate it. The piercings, not the… well, sure, for that too. Thanks for both. That was great."

"The pleasure was all mine," Riel replied, the corners of his eyes crinkling with humor.

He stood when I did. I froze in place as he ducked in for another kiss; somehow, it felt different when we were standing.

Rather than ravage my lips further, he surprised me by planting a chaste kiss on my cheek. While I tried to make sense of it, he guided me to the door with a hand on my back and made sure the hallway was empty before letting me step out.

"Good night," he whispered.

"Good night," I responded, finding it hard to meet his eyes for some reason. I bobbed my head in farewell and pushed on into the darkness without looking back.

No sooner had I reached my room than I threw off my shorts and climbed into bed in just my shirt and panties, not bothering with pajamas. I reached a shaking hand up to one nipple, which still buzzed with sensation, and then up further to touch my lips, where I still felt the phantom touch of Riel's. An elated grin met my probing fingers.

For the first time in a long while, I slept soundly through the night.

CHAPTER EIGHTEEN

THE HONEYMOON PHASE

THE DAY AFTER THE PARTY, life resumed as though nothing had changed. Riel fetched me from my room as he had most days before last week's hiccup. He didn't greet me with a kiss or sling his arm around me or try to grab my butt… but that was a good thing, since I doubted that would go over well with his family. I tried to ignore the foreign feeling of my new piercings against my bra, and also not to grin like a fool whenever Riel looked my way.

He walked a little closer than usual as we headed into the courtyard to find Oyanni. We passed by a couple of castle employees working on the little garden plots, and they surprised me by acknowledging our presence with smiles and nods. I perked up and returned the smile, adding in a cheerful wave for good measure.

"Is the silent treatment over?" I asked Riel under my breath.

"Some of the staff have been curious about you since your arrival." Riel nodded his head in greeting as well. "Seeing you at our celebration likely amplified their interest. Not speaking to you was not a formal order, so I expect some may try to approach you."

"They won't get in trouble if they do, will they?" I bit my bottom lip.

"I doubt it. They do have free will, as much as my mother likes to exert her authority without reason."

"Is she really that mean?" I asked sheepishly. "I mean, obviously, you'd know her better than me, but she didn't seem that bad at the ball. I don't know, the way you talk about her, you'd think she's an evil stepmother or something."

"Unfortunately, there is no doubt that she is my mother by birth," Riel responded as he scanned the herd of grazing *avida*. He made a clicking sound that echoed across the grass, and a lavender head perked up. As the mare made her way to us, her sleek summer coat glinted in the morning sun. "Evil may be too strong a word," Riel continued. "It's complicated. She is practical, and she does care about our people. But she is also self-centered and easily angered. She was not a good mother."

"I'm sorry," I murmured, and I meant it. My thoughts drifted to my own mother. She hadn't been that great, but I didn't have many complaints either. I had several fond memories from my childhood. They were mostly vacations or birthday parties, but some were little random things, like the time I held a baby chick at a petting zoo or when I lost one boot in deep snow and my mother had to carry me back into the house. A pang of longing shot through me. I briefly entertained the thought that maybe we could work toward having a better relationship again, before I started thinking about the logistics and had to dismiss that dream.

Oyanni stopped before us with an excited huff, and Riel beckoned for me. "It's not worth dwelling on," he said as he lifted me up onto her back. "Nothing will change."

"Well, sure," I agreed, settling into place. "But that doesn't mean you can't still complain about it. Complaining is a beloved human pastime, you know. I do it all the time. Sometimes it can be a good thing to just vent your frustrations to someone else."

Riel swung up behind me. Maybe it was my imagination given the activities of the night before, but it felt like he wasn't as careful with space as he seated himself against my behind. I wondered if he'd always been tense before, trying not to be all up in my business in case I would be bothered by that. My little internal "Affection for Riel" meter hit critical heights.

"What is this? My *eseri* having a rare moment of wisdom?" he teased.

"Excuse me?" I scoffed, hiding a smile. "I'll have you know my moments of wisdom are not rare at all. Maybe it's time you got your hearing checked, old man. Or your memory."

Riel chuckled. As we made our way out of the courtyard, he surprised me by nuzzling into my neck. "Watch it," he murmured just below my ear. "This old man bites." He punctuated his words with a sharp nip that had me smothering an indignant squeal.

"Riel!" I hissed his name and went to bat his head away, glancing wide-eyed behind us to make sure no one saw. He dodged my hand easily, laughing with abandon, and kicked the animal beneath us into gear. We took off down the main road at an exhilarating gallop.

Rather than taking the usual path, we continued along the main road for some time. The city appeared in the distance, and we kept going until we reached an open plain covered in long grass. Then, Riel slowed his *avida,* giving us all a chance to catch our breaths.

"Doth mine eyes deceive me, or is this not our usual haunt?" I asked.

"Most of the time, I'm quite proud of my grasp of English," Riel mused from behind me, "But there are other times when I could swear that you just insert a random word into a sentence, regardless of its meaning."

"Sorry." I flashed him a grin in apology. "I meant this doesn't look like the pool."

"I thought we'd do something a bit different today."

Riel brought us to a stop in the middle of the field and dismounted. I didn't see anything of note in the immediate area. Puzzled, I reached for him as usual. But instead of helping me down, he stepped aside to put space between us.

"What are you doing?" I asked, frowning.

"I think it's time you learned to ride on your own," he said with an impish grin. All the warm, fuzzy feelings from a moment before fled me, and I tensed up and made a wild grab for the handhold despite the fact that Oyanni stood still.

"Now?" I sputtered, clinging on as if she would take off at any moment. "Without any warning or anything? And without so much as a training saddle?"

"You'll be fine," Riel assured me, stepping farther away. "Eyes up. Back straight. Loosen your legs and relax. Heels down. That's it, well done. How do you feel?"

"Uh, ridiculous?" I approached hysterics. "Your faith in me is misplaced, and this is a terrible idea. Also, if I don't fall off and break my neck, I'm going to kill you."

"Nonsense," Riel cooed, clearly unbothered by my threat. "You're a natural. Besides, Oyanni knows to go easy on new riders. Back straight, heels down."

He made a clicking sound and his *avida* began to walk. My knees squeezed together as I hung on for dear life. Without Riel's presence at my back, I felt exposed and wobbly, but I had to admit that it was also thrilling. Riel stayed put as we made a circle around him, his *avida* requiring minimal direction. Only a few minutes of that passed before he got to the point.

"How is your training coming along, the grounding exercises? Have you made any progress toward connecting to the flow of *mana*?" he asked casually.

"What is this, an intervention?" I grumbled, trying to focus on maintaining my posture. "Trust me, when there's a big breakthrough, you'll be the first to know."

"Mm. You've been doing the exercises I taught you?"

"Every chance I get." It was the first outright lie I told him.

Perhaps my response came too quickly in my eagerness to reassure him, because Riel raised an eyebrow like he knew. Then he said something that made my conscience prickle with guilt.

"In their latest letters, your leaders have expressed some concern about the rate of your recovery," he said. "We've assured them that these things can take time, but they're becoming rather impatient. I don't think Luenki will be able to hold them off much longer."

I couldn't hide my grimace.

"Can we worry about one thing at a time, please?" I begged. "I know that should be my top priority, but I can't force it. It's just not happening. At least this I have some control over." I gestured to indicate the current situation. "And look, I'm doing it!"

Riel gave me a sweet smile before making another clicking noise. I couldn't tell the difference between the sounds he made, but Oyanni apparently could, as she picked up the pace. I seized the strap with both hands, trying to mitigate the bouncing.

"How the heck are you supposed to drive this thing?" I wailed.

"That's next," Riel assured me. "Heels down, *eseri*. *Avida* are sensitive creatures. All you need to guide them is your body. You start with your eyes, by looking where you want to go. Follow through with your head, shoulders, hips, and legs. Not yet."

I'd begun going through the motions but relaxed again with a huff. As Riel put a hand out, Oyanni turned inward and stopped just in front of him, pressing her nose against his hand. He ran it down her neck and glanced up at me.

"When you're ready, you'll turn your body in the direction you want to go and rotate your hips to apply pressure. You may have to exaggerate the motion at first, but as you get attuned to how she feels and she gets used to your cues, you'll be able to do more with less. We'll try it at a walk until it feels natural. Ready?"

"As I'll ever be." I gripped the handhold once more, determined.

"Give her a light squeeze," Riel ordered. I tentatively reached forward to wrap my arms around the beast's thick neck, wondering what exactly that accomplished.

"With your legs, *eseri*."

Flushing with embarrassment, I let go of her neck, corrected my posture, and engaged my legs. I was almost grunting with effort before Oyanni ambled forward. I went through the checklist of things Riel told me in my head. Raising my gaze to the grassy plain before us, I straightened my back and tilted my toes up.

"Now turn back toward me," Riel called. I looked back over my shoulder and angled my body his way, but it didn't make any difference in our trajectory.

"With more intention!" Riel's voice grew distant.

"I'm intending," I hissed between clenched teeth, pushing my body harder.

Riel caught up to us with ease, his sudden appearance making me jump.

"Put your hips into it," he said, patting my thigh. Without being fully conscious of my actions, I relaxed into my seat and adjusted my body toward him. This time, Oyanni followed the movement underneath me. Although I couldn't tell if she responded to my request or her master's presence, excitement and pride charged through me.

"I'm doing it!" I exclaimed, beaming with joy.

"You are. Well done." Riel walked beside us. "How does it feel?"

"Good! It's still kind of terrifying to be all the way up here by myself, but it's also empowering. I imagine this is how it'd feel like to walk normally if I was a centaur."

That got me a bemused look from Riel.

"That's a half-human, half-horse person. Oh, horses are our version of *avida*."

He raised an eyebrow but didn't seem inclined to press me for more details. Adjusting my grip on the handhold, I raised my gaze once more to admire the landscape. The plains went on for a while into the distance before giving way to foothills. After living in a big city for most of my life, the countryside was something else. I'd probably never get tired of the views.

"Let's do another turn."

Riel's suggestion broke me out of my daydreaming. I sighed and went through the motions of turning my body toward him, starting with my head. This time, I found it a little easier to direct the animal underneath me. After making a ninety-degree turn, we set off in the new direction, still at a meandering walk. I nodded to myself, happy.

"Does everyone here know how to ride?" I asked.

"Most everyone learns to ride. Some bond with an *avida* early on, in their teen years. Not everyone has room to keep companion animals, though. There are other methods of transportation for those that live in the city."

One word caught my attention. "Bond?"

"*Avida* tend to form a close relationship with their main rider. That's not to say that they won't listen to another, but they have their preferences. And over the years, the rider begins to form their own preferences as well." Riel gave Oyanni's side a tender pat.

"Ah, gotcha. So, do you have the same one your whole life? How long do they live?"

"Not your whole life, but if you're lucky, most of it. Seventy or eighty years or so."

"And how old is Oyanni?" I asked, leaning over to scratch her neck.

Riel cocked his head as he considered my question. "She was born late summer during my thirteenth year. So, I suppose that makes her… not quite thirty-four."

"Damn!"

If I could whistle, I would have. Grinning down at my mount, I told her, "That makes you older than me." She responded with a huff as if to say "Duh, that's how math works." "That's really nice. The whole bonding thing. The whole concept of companion animals, really."

"Is it not common for humans?" Riel directed us to perform another ninety-degree turn. "Besides horses, I have been told of dogs, cats, and pet birds during my visits across The Rift."

"Oh, it's very common. My family had a cat when I was growing up. But I never had one of my own, you know? It would have been nice to have something like that—a little animal that's always there, happy to see me and excited to hang out every day. It would have made things less lonely at the White House."

"Someone kept you from getting one?" Riel guessed.

"I never asked," I confessed. "But I figured it wouldn't be allowed. They did their best to keep me happy, especially after… well, especially in recent years. But I also didn't know if I could handle the responsibility, and I didn't want to get a dog just for someone else to end up taking care of it. It just wasn't meant to be for me, I think."

"Perhaps you could choose an *avida* someday," Riel said, staring into the distance. "Ah…" Embarrassment pinkened the tips of his ears. "That is, if you were here enough to need one of your own."

I perked up. "Really? That would be awesome!"

Riel seemed pleased by my reaction. "I'll see what I can do. Once we figure out your magic, and things settle down."

That thought was sobering. Neither of us knew what was going to happen once I recovered the use of my magic. I'd probably be hustled back to the White House and never allowed to leave again. In fact, the more I thought about it, the more that seemed likely. Being in a relationship with Riel didn't change anything, not really.

"Do you think... do you think I'll be able to come back?" My voice was small, the undercurrent of anxiety washing away all joy from the moment.

"Absolutely," Riel replied with conviction. Perhaps noticing the way the mood shifted, he reached up to take my hand and squeezed. "You should have the freedom to go where you like. If your leaders disagree, we can talk to them together. If I request your presence here personally, it would be difficult for them to say no, wouldn't it?"

"Yeah." I found it difficult to keep worrying in the face of his confidence. It was like he always knew what I needed to hear. I rubbed absently at the ache in my chest as I digested this revelation. Having his self-assured attitude around gave me something I was missing in my life, like a long-lost puzzle piece slipping back where it belonged.

"Come," Riel suggested. "I have an idea, something that might help set your mind at ease. Let's practice a little longer, and then we'll head back."

I shook off my train of thought and turned my attention back to the task at hand before I started getting emotional. At his direction, we continued walking up and down the plain while performing a turn every so often. It became easier with each repetition, until we tried it again at a trot. I found it impossible to hold on and steer at the same time and began to grow frustrated.

"That's all right," Riel said eventually. "I think it's time to call it a day. You've made a lot of progress in a short amount of time, though. Good work."

"Thank you." His praise warmed me.

I scooted forward to make room and Riel leapt effortlessly onto Oyanni's back. He didn't reach around me to take the rein strap right away; instead, he let his hands settle on my hips and leaned in to nuzzle my cheek. I couldn't resist turning my head to seek out his lips and was rewarded with a kiss that had my scalp tingling and my toes curling in my sneakers.

"Maybe we could hang out a little while longer and do some more of this," I murmured as we parted, not wanting to let him go just yet.

"Tempting." Riel pressed another kiss to my shoulder. "But alas, duty calls."

Releasing an exaggerated sigh, I sat back against him and grumbled my displeasure. Riel chuckled as he eased Oyanni into a trot.

After a routine ride back to the castle, we pulled up to the steps and dismounted, letting Oyanni return to the grazing herd. As we headed up the steps, Riel broke the silence.

"So, regarding learning to use your magic properly… it does normally take time, but considering the timeframe we're working with, it may be worthwhile to explore other options."

"Excuse me?" I paused between steps to fix Riel with an incredulous stare. "There are other options? And you didn't think to mention this sooner?"

Riel shrugged. "There's doing things the right way, and doing things the fast way. Trust me when I say that I have your best interests at heart. However, it won't hurt to get some advice. We'll get something to eat first, and then I'm taking you to meet Neyes."

CHAPTER NINETEEN
THE SEER

"I'M TAKING you to meet Neyes."

I tried to remember if I'd heard that name before. "Uh... if you could remind me...?"

"You haven't met them," Riel assured me. "Do you remember during your tour when I mentioned there are extra rooms in the tower?"

Vaguely? I nodded, frowning.

"That was a half-truth. There's one room in the tower and a person who stays there. Their name is Neyes. They serve as an advisor to my family, my mother especially."

"Oh-kay?" When my thinly veiled prompt failed to elicit an explanation from Riel, I raised an eyebrow and nodded encouragingly. "We're going to see them because...?"

Riel made a vexed sort of sound in his throat as we entered the castle.

"I think I mentioned this once, but there are five categories of magic. Most often, you'll come across one of the four I told you about: mending, breaking, changing, and making. The fifth is uncommon, and it does not have a direct translation, but you could think of it as something like... a specialty, up to chance.

Essentially, those abilities that are impossible to categorize elsewhere. This person belongs to this group."

"Okay. So, what do they do?"

"Neyes sees visions of the future. Among those who are aware of their ability, it's widely believed that the visions are direct communications from the Goddess Herself."

I blinked as his words settled in.

"Woah!" The exclamation burst out of me before I thought to lower my voice, and my hands shot up to my mouth. "You're saying that you guys have a psychic?"

With a grimace, Riel glanced around to make sure we had privacy. The hall was thankfully empty. "Technically, my mother does," he said. "It's not... general knowledge, exactly. At least, not the true extent of their abilities." He gave me a meaningful look. "It's certainly not information that your government needs to know."

I mimed zipping my lips shut even as my heart pounded with the weight of such a secret. "So, they'll be able to see the future and tell us what we need to do?"

"With luck, they will be able to provide us with guidance," Riel agreed as we headed down a corridor in the direction of the kitchens. "It's unlikely that we'll get a straight answer, since that's rarely how their visions go. But it's worth a try."

"For sure!" I could use all the help I could get. "Anything I need to know in advance?"

Riel considered my question. "It can be unsettling, speaking to someone who seems to know everything," he said eventually. "I'll guide the conversation, but feel free to participate as much or as little as you like. And don't be surprised if something unexpected comes up, or if they act strangely. Some abilities do... odd things to people."

"Okay, good to know." I still had questions, but they could wait.

The kitchens were bustling, with numerous people rushing to prepare trays of food to be delivered to the castle residents.

The head chef—his name was something with a J, if I remembered correctly—spotted us as we entered. He said something to Riel in the fae language as we took our seats at the prep table, and Riel responded with a grin. The cook chuckled to himself and went to fetch us some food.

"He says we must have missed him," Riel translated for me, still smiling. "It's uncommon that someone chooses to eat in the kitchen, but this is one of those second son perks I told you about. I told him he's far more important than either of us."

"Accurate." I giggled, grateful to be included in the conversation. "Food is the backbone of society, after all. Definitely more important than you... maybe a close second to me, though."

"Is humility considered a desirable trait where you come from, or is that only the case here?" Riel asked wryly. An impish smile was the only answer I had for him.

The cook came by with trays. The day's late morning meal was a stuffed egg dish, essentially a spiced veggie scramble served in the shell. Last time I'd had it, I'd asked what they had that produced such big eggs with thick shells, and Riel described an emu-like animal.

The chef gave Riel a wink before leaving, which drew my attention to his tray. To my surprise, he got two plates—one with the same portion of eggs I had, and one with more *raast*, the same white, gelatinous cubes we'd had for breakfast that morning. I raised an eyebrow.

"They know me well," he said by way of explanation.

"You do seem to like those," I commented as I picked up my spoon.

"I'd go so far as to say it might be my favorite food."

"Really?"

"Mm-hmm. I haven't had the pleasure of sampling many human foods, though. For all I know, there's something even better somewhere across The Rift."

"We do have some good stuff. Pizza, chili cheese fries,

falafel, butter chicken and garlic naan..." My mouth watered despite the fact I was already eating. God, I missed how indulgent our food was. Fae food was so elegant and restrained by comparison.

Riel leaned back and sighed. "Someday, I hope that the relationship between our two worlds will be such that I can travel freely across your globe. There are many things I hope to experience for myself one day."

"Honestly, same." Although the thought of crossing through The Rift had once been a terrifying ordeal, I now found myself curious about the world in ways I hadn't been since my teen years. I was proud of the progress I'd made, although I was sure that was due to Riel's influence. Having a patient, capable guide did a lot to ease my nerves. And once I figured out my magic, maybe I could bargain with George for more freedom.

With that thought in mind, I shoveled the last few bites into my mouth and swallowed them down, eager to get going. "Better get a move on," I said, swinging my legs over the bench to get to my feet. "The sooner we can get this sorted out, the better. I'm more than ready to be done with all the meditating."

Riel made a sound of agreement as he finished off his last piece of *raast*.

"It is good?" asked an accented voice from behind me. With a jump of surprise, I whirled about to find myself face-to-face with the cook.

"Oh, yes!" I made a show of patting my belly. "Delicious as always. Thank you!"

The cook nodded, pleased with my response. He said something to Riel, who shrugged and gave a noncommittal reply. I thought I picked up a few familiar sounds, but nothing useful. Though I kept a pleasant smile pasted on my face, frustration brewed beneath the surface. Not for the first time, I wished there was a language app or at least a textbook I could learn from.

As we left the kitchen and headed across the hallway for the spiral staircase, I fell into step beside Riel. "After I get my magic sorted, how about you start teaching me your language?" I suggested. "We'll need something to fill our time with, after all. And I'd like to learn."

"Perhaps." Riel leaned in and lowered his voice. "Though if passing time is the goal, I can think of several activities that would be more desirable than further lessons."

Having a gutter brain, my cheeks colored at his words. He overlooked my reaction and added, "And although I am a wonderful teacher, it is not my primary calling."

When we reached the base of the stairs, Riel paused.

"Ready?" he asked me. "Remember, whatever happens, I have your back."

I nodded to show that I understood and gestured for him to get on with it. Although he meant to reassure me, I found that it became easier to overthink things the more they were discussed. Sometimes it was better to leap in rather than test the water first.

Riel started up the steps with me on his heels. Our footsteps echoed in the tight space. The stairs went up much farther than I had expected, curling up and around out of sight and beyond. Just as I began to wonder if there was some kind of confusing magic at play, an ornate wooden door appeared, signaling that we'd reached the top.

My palms started to sweat. I discreetly wiped them on my shorts as Riel raised a hand to knock. Before his hand made contact, a voice called out from the other side of the door.

"Now, who could that be?" A soft chuckle followed. "Come in!"

Riel and I shared a glance. He reached out to grip the handle and push the door inward. No sooner had a gap been created than a short, blond figure appeared, making me jump.

"The prince!" The person there, who I assumed was Neyes, made a show of throwing a hand up to their mouth and gasping. "What a pleasant surprise." Despite their choice of words, their expression remained slack, without even a lick of surprise.

Riel rolled his eyes and bid me to come in as the person stepped back to give us room to enter. Once inside, I had the chance to examine the figure before me.

They were… not what I expected. A nest of unruly curls sat atop their head, flat on one side and a frizzy halo on the other. Their irises were such a pale blue-gray that they almost appeared white. They were also short for a fae, around my height, and I couldn't tell if they were male or female. It didn't help that the tunic they wore was drab and shapeless, providing an effect not unlike a child wearing a potato sack.

"Um, h-hello," I stammered, realizing that silence had fallen. Holding out a hand, I introduced myself. "I'm Avery. From America, across The Rift. Riel's been teaching me about my magic for the last couple of months."

Neyes's eyes sparkled with delight as they directed their gaze to Riel.

"You told her who I am?" they asked, pointing at me.

"I did," Riel replied, remaining stoic. Neyes directed their attention back to me just as I let my unshaken hand fall back to my side.

"I appreciate your introduction. It is refreshing," they said, turning away from the door and making for the bed on the other side of the room. "Most people come to me assuming that I already know everything. I usually do, but… that does not make for the best conversation."

Neyes sat with a huff of exertion, displacing a board game that had been sitting on the covers. Crossing their legs underneath them, they looked at us expectantly.

Riel cleared his throat. "You probably know why we're here…" he began.

"A good start," Neyes exclaimed, clapping their hands together. "But let me stop you there. I have not met anyone new in decades. Tell me about yourself, Avery."

"Oh!" I scrambled for words. "Ah, I, uh… I'm twenty-two years old. No siblings. Born in Connecticut, later moved to Washington, D.C. My favorite subject is sociology. My interests include video games, social media, reality TV shows, swimming, tennis… uh, what else… I want to learn how to play the guitar someday."

Neyes didn't blink even once throughout my speech.

"How wonderful!" They laughed. "So many strange words, I can barely understand you. And how do you like our world, Avery?"

"It's lovely," I offered. "This area is beautiful, and the weather is so nice. The food is delicious. Everyone's been so accommodating."

"Accommodating? Yes…" Neyes's gaze flicked to Riel and lingered there, causing him to stiffen. Neyes was quick to wave off his concern. "It will be our little secret," they promised, putting a finger to their lips. "If I wanted to tell anyone, I would have to leave this room, after all." Their light chuckle seemed to set Riel at ease—mostly, anyway.

"So… they just keep you locked up in here?" I dared to ask. "All the time?"

The room wasn't exactly a prison, but it didn't look that comfortable either. It was minimally furnished, and without at least a TV to pass the time, it had to get boring.

"What reason do I have to leave?" Neyes responded with a shrug. "I have sunlight, a bed, peace, and quiet. My meals are delivered to my door." As if reading my mind, they added seriously, "And the things I see are entertainment enough."

Questions started jumping to mind. My eyes darted to Riel. He showed no signs of annoyance or impatience, which emboldened me.

"Go on," Neyes encouraged, waving a hand in invitation. "Ask."

Not letting myself be bothered by their sharp intuition, I

launched into the most pressing of my clamoring thoughts. "What's it like?" I blurted out. "Seeing the future?"

"Exhausting." Neyes's expression, which had been open and relaxed until now, sobered in the span of a breath. "Imagine that you are always watching ten different places out of ten sets of eyes in ten different years. After some time, you learn how to filter out the irrelevant material. But even then, you find yourself living the lifetimes of those around you while they go about their business, entirely oblivious. It is noisy and exhausting."

A hint of irritation crept into their tone as they spoke. Before I could start feeling self-conscious and mumble an apology, they'd pivoted back to Riel.

"Shall we get to business, then?" they asked.

"We came to seek your advice," Riel said without missing a beat. "Although we've made some progress, Avery has not yet learned to access *mana*. She was using her mending ability regardless and almost reached *vahela*. If you've seen anything that could help, please."

Neyes's expression became contemplative. "Mm. One that changes, one that mends. One that makes all beings friends." Without elaborating on the random rhyme, they shook their head.

"Unfortunately, I do not have an answer for you. As you know, those from beyond The Rift live outside the realm of my sight. But I believe you do not require my help." They turned a meaningful look on Riel. "If she uses magic in the same way as the *Ishameti*, then the same methods should be effective. There is one way to speed up the process."

Confused, I glanced at Riel.

"No," he said immediately. "It's too dangerous."

Neyes shrugged. "I am no *vahelim*. You came to me seeking the truth, did you not? You can continue with the usual exercises, which may yet take several cycles of the moon, or you can perform the *manaviri*. Those are your only options."

Riel's lips pressed together.

"You lost me," I remarked, hoping for an explanation. Unblinking, Neyes watched us both, letting the silence drag on. Eventually, their expression softened.

"Perhaps the time is not right," they suggested. "Send the girl home for now. Try again in a few years. It may come easier then."

My eyes widened in alarm. "Years? I don't have years."

"We don't have years," Riel echoed, pacing across the room. "Perhaps we would make more progress if we spent more time by the pools?"

He switched to his native language to direct a question at Neyes, who clucked dismissively and shook their head.

"Well, what's the other option?" I asked, looking between the two of them. "Even if it's dangerous, it might be worth considering."

"Too big a risk," Riel replied with a small shake of his head.

"High chance of failure," Neyes added.

Their dismissiveness irked me. I raised my chin and prepared myself for an argument. "Listen, I appreciate that you want to look out for me, but in the end, the choice should be mine. If I want to take risks, that's my prerogative. So please, tell me about this other method."

Riel struggled to find a response, gesturing with one hand as though hoping to pluck the words from the air. "It's believed that when we die," he began haltingly, "the Goddess guides our… life force, our essence, to leave our bodies and join the flow of *mana*. In some cases, if the death was not by natural causes and a skilled mender is present, there is a small window of opportunity during which the two can be reunited and the body revived.

"The methods I've been teaching you, proper education and repeated grounding exercises, that is the usual way a youth learns to connect to the flow of *mana*. There is, however, a *very dangerous* technique"—Riel shot an irritated glance in Neyes's direction—"which involves forcing a *mana* connection by bringing someone to the brink of death."

Before I had the chance to process his words, he stood in front of me, startling me into stumbling back a step. His eyes trapped mine, making it impossible to look away. One of his hands lifted, then dropped, as if he'd thought better of what he was about to do. "If anything goes wrong, you could lose your life," he told me, his voice thick with emotion. My heart went out to him. "You can see why I'm not considering this."

Not wanting to let it go, an argument sprang to my lips, only to die on my tongue the moment he added, "It's not just risking you, although that's more than enough. If you die here, we risk war with your country—perhaps your entire world. We can't afford to take this decision lightly."

So what, my options were crippling boredom or the chance of death? My mouth snapped shut, and I had to settle for a glower. The way he put it, there weren't any options at all.

"I don't suppose you have any statistics?" I muttered.

"What?"

"Like, what's the chance of something going wrong? Twenty percent? Fifty percent?"

The half-shrug I got just ticked me off more.

"Neyes," I said, facing the seer on the bed. "You're the expert on the Goddess. Say that we did give this a try, do you think there's any chance that she'd look out for me? 'Cause I'm a guest here and all?"

"She chooses no sides." Their tone was chiding.

"Of course. Well, how about we sleep on it and see if we can't think of anything better by tomorrow? I'll meditate extra hard this afternoon."

Riel didn't appear pleased by my suggestion. Rather than argue the matter here, I tugged on his sleeve and began steering him toward the door. He slipped past me so that he could open it for us. Before we crossed the threshold, I addressed Neyes one last time.

"Thank you so much for your time," I said with a grateful smile, ducking my head to make eye contact underneath Riel's outstretched arm. "It was a pleasure to meet you."

"The pleasure was mine," came the amused reply as the door shut behind us.

As the door shut behind the second prince and the Goddess-blessed human, Neyes's smile disappeared. They lingered a moment before sliding off one side of the bed. Crossing the room, they went to the large window and peered out. The view of the land beyond was one they had enjoyed numerous times before, but now there was a strange darkness on the horizon. Perhaps not one that was visible to the eye, but Neyes beheld it nonetheless.

They unlatched the window and pulled it open. In moments, a petite bird with white-and-black plumage alighted on the sill as if summoned. Neyes ran a finger along the bird's spine, and it leaned into their touch with a chirp of pleasure. With their free hand, Neyes reached into the pocket of their tunic to retrieve a piece of parchment, which they slid into a discreet metal tube attached to the bird's left leg. With one last loving caress, they whispered a handful of words to the bird, and it took off. Neyes released a mournful sigh as they watched it go.

Responsibility is truly a double-edged sword, they thought.

CHAPTER TWENTY
THE BREAKING POINT

TO NOBODY'S SURPRISE, I didn't magically figure things out overnight, no matter how hard I meditated. In fact, I found it even more difficult to focus with the brand-new collection of questions and concerns plaguing me. As if things weren't frustrating enough.

The next day, we spent the morning with more riding lessons on the plains. Riel was the grumpiest I'd ever seen him —even Oyanni acted surprised by the way he sulked on the ride there and the sharp edge in his tone. After about an hour of riding back and forth and practicing turns with minimal interaction but for the occasional barked command, I finally felt the need to speak up.

"Are you mad at me?" I demanded, relaxing back into my seat to signal Oyanni to stop.

"No," Riel replied, his reaction too quick and too curt. I leveled a frown his way. "No," he repeated, frustration lacing his tone. "I just… I hate being backed into a corner. Nothing is on our side. It's one challenge after another, and I hate it. I hate how powerless it makes me feel."

I felt a pang of sympathy for him, knowing all too well how it felt to be in a relative position of power and still feel powerless. It had been all I'd known over the last few months, ever since the day I collapsed by the White House gate.

"We'll figure it out," I assured him, trying to twist my body around from astride the *avida* so that I didn't have to crane my neck to speak to him. "Somehow or another, the *mana* thing has to click for me soon. Didn't you say these things take time? I know I've been impatient, but I still feel like I'm getting closer every day."

Riel sighed. "Believe it or not, that's not my biggest concern at the moment."

"Oh?" It was impossible to get Oyanni to turn while standing still. Taking pity on me, Riel moved into my line of sight, drawing near to caress her neck. Up close, I could see that his eyes, normally the shade of still Caribbean waters, had somehow become stormy to mirror the emotions that roiled within. Fascinated, I leaned forward to see them better.

Riel stopped me with a hand to my leg before I toppled over the *avida*'s side.

"The situation with my family has not improved," he admitted. "I'm still hoping for more information, but I suspect…" he hesitated a moment before continuing, his hand returning to Oyanni's neck. "I suspect this will not end well."

"Let me know if there's anything I can do." It was still a weak offer, I knew. But I didn't like feeling helpless either, and I especially didn't like to see Riel like this. He felt… fragile. Comparatively, anyway. He was usually so strong and confident.

"Perhaps it *would* be better for you to return home," he said suddenly.

The fact that he thought of that first, with everything that was going on, hurt. I scoffed. "And what, play video games and twiddle my thumbs for months, if not longer? There's nothing for me back home if I can't heal. I'd be dead weight as far as the government's concerned, and they don't like moochers. I just need a little more time."

Riel didn't seem convinced. Not above begging, I added a sincere, "Please."

He didn't get it. But then, my situation was pretty unique. With the way I'd grown up, I had no official education or marketable skills beyond my healing abilities. Hell, I didn't even have my own bank account. The weight of my situation grew harder to ignore the more time passed here. Just thinking about it made me feel sick. It was a miracle that my handlers were still being so patient, but I couldn't rely on that forever.

A flash of movement in the distance caught my eye. Riel glanced up as I raised a hand to shade my eyes and squinted at the speck of color that approached. It looked like one of their messenger birds, coming from the direction of the castle.

Riel raised one arm just as it rolled in midair and dove for the two of us. Spreading its wings to catch the air at the last second, it alighted atop Riel's arm with a cheerful-sounding chirrup. I waited for Riel to retrieve the message from the little tube attached to its leg. His eyes scanned the paper from top to bottom, then repeated the motion. A crease appeared between his brows.

"It's from Luenki," he said just as I opened my mouth. "She says an envoy is coming through The Rift now. Your presence is requested." He gave his arm a slight shake to dislodge the bird and came to Oyanni's side.

"What?" I frowned as I scooted forward so that he had room behind me. Riel mounted and reached around me to take the rein strap. "Like, now, now?"

"Now," he confirmed with a grimace.

Panic seized a hold of me in an instant. "Did she say what it's about?"

"No need. We'll find out shortly."

Kicking Oyanni into gear, he guided us to the road that led to the castle. We continued on that path for a little ways before turning right and making for the woods. I wasn't yet familiar with the way to the river, so as we rode, I took in the sights and tried to commit landmarks to memory. There was a road some of the way, although it was not wide or well-traveled. And for the most part, we went in one direction. Not for the first time, I was impressed by the stamina of an *avida,* as we kept up a loping run that ate up the terrain.

Eventually, the trees began to thin, and vaguely familiar hills loomed in the distance—a sign that we were getting close. I held on tighter. Despite the fact that I'd spent a decent amount of time riding since crossing The Rift, my butt was getting sore. We didn't ride this far when we were just going to the pool or the plains, and Oyanni's walk was much smoother than her run.

When we finally burst into the clearing and the river came into view, the pace relaxed, allowing both Oyanni and myself to catch our breaths. I could see that three people were already waiting for us, the small boat bobbing on the water behind them: two men wearing military uniforms and a woman in a baby-blue suit that complemented her dark skin.

"Oh! It's Vivian," I exclaimed, raising an arm to wave as we got close enough to make out the figures standing on the shore. Ohio's Lieutenant Governor was put together as usual, though her kitten heels were sinking into the soft earth of the river's edge. Her restrained smile told me nothing of her intentions, which had me breaking out in a nervous sweat. It was time to face the inevitable, I supposed. At least the uncertainty was over.

Riel brought us to a halt and swiftly dismounted before helping me down. No sooner had I touched the ground than Vivian was approaching.

"Your Highness. A pleasure to see you again," she said warmly, stepping up to offer Riel a handshake. "Luenki has kept us apprised of your efforts to help Avery regain her healing powers. I was hoping I'd have the chance to extend my gratitude to you personally—our nation is truly in your debt." Maintaining her smile as she turned to me, she continued.

"And, Avery, you're looking much better than the last time I saw you. That has to be a good sign, at least?"

I made a conscious decision to ignore the unspoken question and take her words at face value instead, matching her smile and responding with, "Yeah, I'm feeling a lot better. What a surprise to see you! How have you been? Anything exciting going on at the base?"

"Nothing at all. It's all training drills and paperwork." Vivian shifted her weight. "I apologize for the visit out of the blue. I know you weren't expecting me." Stepping to one side, she gestured to the suitcase that stood between the men behind her. "We packed up some things for you. Toiletries and such, more books, and also some cards, puzzles, and a sketchpad and drawing utensils, in case that tickles your fancy."

"Oh my God," I squealed, my hands flying up to my face in excitement. *Could it be that this was the reason she'd come?* "You're a lifesaver, seriously. The only thing that would have made this any better would be some crunchy Cheetos."

"We'll be sure to put that on the list for next time," Vivian responded amiably.

I went to grab the case, but Riel appeared beside me, gently brushing my hand away to take it instead. Beaming, I turned my attention back to Vivian. "You have no idea how nice it will be to have more things to do when I'm on my own."

"Well… I would hope that you've been keeping busy," Vivian said slowly, eyes following Riel's retreat with the suitcase. Just as suddenly as they'd risen, my spirits dropped again. "Luenki has been sending us regular updates," she continued, "but without much substance. I wanted to see that you were improving for myself. I'm glad that you're feeling better. Have you made any progress with your magic?"

And there it was. I ducked my head to hide my wince. "Ah… I'm working on it."

"Respectfully, we could use a bit more to go on than that," Vivian remarked. "The last thing I want to do is put more pressure on you, Avery, but you have to understand how much pressure there is on us. The president, the press, people hoping to be healed; they're all hanging on our every word. It's getting harder and harder to keep everyone calm. Can you give us any details? Do you have any idea how much longer this will take?"

"I, uh…" Racking my brain for a reasonable response, or at least something I could say to stall, not much came to mind. As much as I wanted to reassure Vivian, I was disheartened knowing that I had no power over the situation. It wasn't like I could meditate any harder. "Maybe you could come back with us, and I can fill you in over the late morning—ah, lunch?" I glanced at Riel, seeking his permission, but he shook his head.

"Although you would be more than welcome in our halls, Lieutenant Governor, I'm afraid that your visit was too sudden for us to prepare," he said, his tone conveying sincere regret. "We didn't think to bring along another *avida,* and if we attempted to reach the House on foot, it would already be time for supper when we arrived."

"Oh, duh." I should have thought of that. "I guess not, then. Sorry. Well, uh… Riel—that is, the second prince here—has been super helpful. I've learned a lot about my kind of magic; they call it mending here. We've been doing exercises regularly. Now that I'm in good shape physically, it should be any day now, honestly. It's just a matter of figuring out the right…"—I groped for the word—"the right technique? But I'm told it's normal for that to take time."

"It is," Riel chimed in. "Especially given all that Avery had to adjust to when she arrived. Even for those who have lived their whole lives around magic, the process usually takes several weeks. And unfortunately, there is no rushing it. Please be assured that we are doing everything in our power to fulfill our commitment."

"We appreciate it." Vivian's eyes drifted to me like she wanted to say something else. Thinking better of it, she sighed instead. The disappointment behind it had me wilting. "Please continue to keep us in the loop. If there's anything we can do, don't hesitate to reach out. Our resources are at your disposal—whatever you need."

Riel inclined his head in acknowledgment of her words.

"This is great," I said without enthusiasm, indicating the suitcase. "Thank you again. I'll keep trying. I'm sure I'll get it soon."

"I'm sure you will," Vivian assured me with a confidence I wasn't feeling. "I'll hold down the fort in the meantime. Seriously—anything you need, it's yours."

"Yeah, thank you. I appreciate it."

An awkward silence fell until Vivian dipped her head in farewell and pivoted back toward the uniformed soldiers waiting on the bank. One officer held the boat still while the other helped her into it. Once seated, she looked back and waved goodbye. The boat pulled away to make the voyage back to the misty abyss on this side of The Rift.

Watching the boat retreat, I couldn't bring myself to feel relief. It was nice to see a familiar face, but it came with a harsh reminder: We were running out of time. I opened my mouth to say as much before I noticed that Riel was no longer at my side. Instead, he eyed his *avida* with my suitcase in hand. I headed over.

"Do you need me to hold on to it while we ride?" I asked, unsure how that would work but willing to give it a try nonetheless.

Riel shook his head. "I've got it."

He put the suitcase down and held out his hands to help me up first. Once I was comfortable, I watched as he tied the suitcase handle to the handhold strap with a length of cord that he had produced from somewhere.

"That won't bother Oyanni?" I asked, imagining it bumping against her side as we rode.

Riel shrugged. "It's not an ideal solution, but she won't have to put up with it for long." He gave the suitcase a tug to test the knot.

My thoughts turned to the matter at hand.

In the past, whenever someone higher up was involved, it was because shit was hitting the fan somewhere or other. I had no reason to believe that this wasn't the case now. I didn't know Vivian well enough to say if it was innocent, or if she checked on my progress because things were devolving into an absolute shitstorm back home. Maybe I could get their recent letters from Luenki to glean the tone. In any case, it was time to get serious.

"Let's go over our options again," I suggested once Riel was mounted behind me.

"The situation won't change because we continue to discuss it," was his tight response.

"No, but maybe we can think through a solution together, you grump. It's worth a shot, isn't it? I can't just sit around with so many people waiting on me."

"It is normal for the process to take—"

"I get that," I interrupted him, trying hard to come across as authoritative rather than pissy even as my patience ran out. "I do. But our circumstances are unique, no? If I was just another kid learning to use my magic, it wouldn't be a big deal. But it's bigger than that, so we've got to weigh the pros and cons." I thought for a moment. "We've got two options, yeah? Either I keep at this, and we have no idea how long it might take, or we try that other method that Neyes was talking about. Both have their risks."

"Can you say that the risks are equal?" Riel argued, his body going taut behind me.

"Maybe they are," I retorted. "Obviously, I don't want to *die*, but you won't tell me what the chances are either. If there's only, like, a one-percent chance of something going wrong, then maybe those odds are worth it. I feel like I might not even get it at all by meditating."

In the moment that followed my statement, all I could hear

was Oyanni's steady footfalls and the sounds of the forest around us. If I didn't still feel Riel's reassuring warmth at my back, I might have thought that he'd fallen off.

When he eventually spoke, all he said was, "It's unlikely."

"Wait, what is?" Frowning, I tried to twist myself around so that I could see his expression but quickly gave up. "You mean the chance of dying from the alternative method? Or there is actually a chance that what we're doing now won't ever work?"

"There is a small chance that the usual methods don't work," he admitted, the words clipped. "Some… aren't ever able to feel the flow of *mana*. As for the *manaviri*… there may be a way to minimize the chance of failure. But the fact remains that it is significantly more dangerous."

"Well, then."

I tried to keep the snideness in my tone to a minimum, but I couldn't help but be pissed that Riel wasn't being more forthcoming. He was just trying to look out for me in his own way, I supposed, but it stung. I'd been left out of the loop plenty at the White House, and that had never bothered me, but Riel and I were supposed to be on the same side.

"Okay." I decided against laying into him for the lack of communication—at least for now. We could come back to that when there were fewer pressing matters at hand. "Tell me what you know about the *manaviri*," I demanded instead. "What could we do to up my chances?"

"I've never seen it done myself, so I don't know all of the details," Riel confessed. "But like any… procedure, magical or otherwise, the best way to ensure success would be to have a capable mender on hand. I know of one in the city who's very highly regarded. It's possible that she would be able to help us."

"Okay, now we're onto something." Pleased that the beginnings of a plan were forming, I summarized. "So, we head to the city, meet with the mender, and pick her brain for a little bit. See what she has to say on the subject. If she knows what she's talking about and thinks it's too dangerous to risk, then we go back home and keep at the meditation, no harm, no foul.

"But—" I raised a finger. "If she's willing to give it a try, so am I. Or, so should we, rather. 'Cause at this point, I don't think we have any better ideas. Sound good?"

Behind me, Riel let out a heavy sigh and muttered something under his breath. "I'll take you to the city," he agreed, his reluctance clear in his tone. "So that we can consult with this mender. But I want your word. If she advises us against attempting the *manaviri,* then we won't go through with it."

I hesitated to make that promise. Who's to say the situation wouldn't continue to get more dire? "If she thinks the chance of failure is more than 10 percent," I proposed. "If that's the case, I won't risk it. I'll just stick with the grounding exercises and hope for the best."

"So be it," Riel acceded grudgingly.

We were silent the rest of the way to the castle. Once there, he helped me down and helped me carry the suitcase back to my room.

"Thank you," I said gently as he set it down by my door. "And I do appreciate that you're trying to take care of me. I just think… sometimes we have to take risks; otherwise, nothing would ever get done. I hope you can understand where I'm coming from."

"I do," he assured me. Glancing down the hall to make sure we were alone, he reached out to run his thumb along my cheek before bringing his forehead against mine in an intimate gesture. "And… I don't mean to… I'm sorry if I come across too… ah…"

"Mulish?" I supplied, lips quirking in a smile. "Obstinate? Bull-headed?"

"Uncooperative," Riel finished, mirroring my smile as he pulled away. "This has been a trial for me. I'm not used to… being in a position where my decisions could mean life or death."

I didn't even think of that, but it made sense. From what I'd seen, he wasn't usually the person making the big decisions. He probably also felt that he was responsible for me in a way, since he'd been my host here. I didn't consider how it would reflect on him if I died.

"I'm sorry too," I said, reaching out to wrap my arms around him. He returned the hug with enthusiasm, as if he'd been waiting for me to initiate it.

"You have nothing to be sorry for," he responded as he slouched to rest his chin on my head. I felt his fingers thread through my hair to tug lightly in an absentminded motion. "I can't blame you for wanting to get back to your people as soon as possible. And I admire your selfless heart, even if it does make things difficult at times."

I couldn't see his expression from where I was, but his tone became teasing as he finished speaking.

"It's not…" I hesitated. I'd been about to argue that I didn't want to go back, but wasn't that what all this was for? No matter how much I cared for Riel and appreciated his company, my whole life was there. And figuring out my powers wouldn't help anyone if I stayed here. "Yeah," I said finally, my voice muffled from having my face in his chest. "Thank you."

Riel let go of me abruptly, stepping back before I had the chance to react.

"What—" I began just before two of the castle guards rounded the corner.

"I'll have some food delivered to you," Riel said as if we hadn't just been having an intimate heart-to-heart. "And tomorrow, I'll show you the city. The change of scenery might be beneficial for your progress. We can stay a night or two if you like. There are several options for accommodations dedicated to visitors."

"Uh, yeah, okay. Sounds like a plan." I stepped back into the doorway and nearly tripped over my new suitcase. I was able to regain my balance on my own, but I didn't miss the way Riel's hand twitched at his side, as though he barely resisted the urge to grab for me.

The guards walked past us, inclining their heads to Riel as they went.

"Take some time today to pack anything you might need and relax some. I'll fetch you in the morning after you've had a chance to eat," he intoned. Lowering his voice, he added, "And I'll have a message sent to the mender I mentioned so that she knows to expect us."

"Okay," I whispered back. "See you tomorrow."

"Until then."

We stared at each other a moment longer, numerous words lying unspoken between us, before Riel eventually tipped his head in farewell and made his way down the hall to fetch whatever was left of the late morning meal. I gathered the suitcase and headed into my room, shutting the door behind me.

After opening the window to let some fresh air in, I settled on the floor by my bed, opened the suitcase, and pulled out the contents. Everything Vivian mentioned was there, from tampons, sunscreen, and toothpaste to books, puzzles, and art supplies. I grabbed one of the bags I'd come with and loaded it with necessities and a couple of outfits. Then, I stowed the hobby items in the bottom of the wardrobe with the books and games I'd gotten from Luenki.

Just as I finished up, a knock at the door signaled that Riel had pulled through. I got my meal, which consisted of a hearty vegetable and dumpling soup. As I ate, my thoughts drifted to the city. Having only seen Miderrum's skyline in the distance, I had no idea what to expect, but I was excited to see it up close. I spent the afternoon sketching the view from my window and daydreaming about the sorts of things I might encounter in the foreign city.

CHAPTER TWENTY-ONE
THE CITY

When he picked me up the next morning, Riel looked like a model out of a fantasy clothing catalog. Gone were his usual extravagant earrings, simple hoops in their place. He wore high-waisted pants with a line of metal buttons and a linen shirt that was better suited to hard work and travel. Around his waist was a utility belt with various pouches and a sheathed knife. To top it all off, he wore a tan cloak with a hood and clasp composed of twining silver vines. He held out a nearly identical one for me to take.

"Look at you," I exclaimed, cracking a smile as I accepted the offering. "That's different. I'm getting… elven pirate prince at a Renaissance Festival. That's a vibe and a half."

I could have laughed aloud at the baffled expression on his face.

"Thank… you?" he tried, not sure how to respond.

"You're very welcome," I assured him, tossing the cloak onto the bed and waving him inside. "Come on inside, but give me a minute. If that's what you're wearing, I need to change into something else." If Renaissance Festival was the vibe, I was there for it.

I went to the wardrobe and rifled through piles of clothing

until I found what I was looking for. Holding the selected pieces to my chest, I rushed into the bathroom to strip out of the tank top and capris I'd originally put on.

"Did you eat?" Riel called from the bedroom.

"Yep," I answered as I stepped out of the pants. "The lack of *raast* was unfortunate."

"Thank you for reminding me what a poor start to the day it's been." The smile was audible in Riel's response. "Then again, I'm not the only one who lives here." A wistful sigh carried through the door. "I suppose the cooks have more than just my tastes to consider."

"It's a tough life you live, being a gorgeous prince in a fancy castle and not getting your favorite food for breakfast every day. I can't imagine," I teased, emerging from the bathroom in a tiered maxi skirt and off-the-shoulder blouse. After collecting my bag and the cloak from where I'd placed it on the bed, I joined Riel by the door. "Ready when you are!"

"A vibe and a half," he said, looking me over appreciatively as he reached out to take my bag from me. It took me a moment to catch on, but when I realized that he repeated my words from before in an attempt to pay me a compliment, I beamed.

"Why, thank you."

Figuring that we were out of sight from anyone who might walk by, I hopped up on my tippy toes to plant a quick peck on Riel's cheek. As I withdrew, he leaned in and looped his free arm around my middle to pull me in for a proper kiss. It was just long enough to steal my breath and wake up certain parts down below, yet over far too soon. When he drew back, I found myself reluctant to let him go.

As if reading my thoughts, Riel chuckled.

"Later, *eseri*," he murmured, his voice low and rich with promise. My face warmed, and I busied myself with pulling the cloak around my shoulders and engaging the clasp before I followed Riel out into the hallway.

Oyanni waited outside for us. In place of her usual simple

rein strap, she wore a more intricate harness that held large bags over her rump. I watched with interest as Riel added my bag to the bunch, attaching it with a series of straps and buckles, before turning his attention to me. He beckoned me over.

"Hang on," I interjected, extending a hand to stop him. "Can you just"—I made a series of vague gestures to get my point across—"just give me a bit of a boost, and I'll sit with my legs on one side so that my skirt doesn't ride up?"

"My pleasure." Riel lifted me up and held me there so that I could sweep back my cloak and skirt before letting me go. It didn't feel as secure as sitting astride, but with straps to grip and Riel at my back, I was sure I'd be fine for the brief ride to the city. This way, I didn't have to worry about flashing everyone on my way in.

We headed down the main road at a brisk walk, my excitement growing the closer we got to the buildings in the distance. Eventually, dirt and grass gave way to man-made fields portioned off by dainty little fences. Gray pinpoints in the distance became grazing livestock beasts as we neared. They resembled cows or bison, except that they were varying shades of gray and their backs appeared to be covered in a layer of moss.

"Those aren't food?" I questioned, knowing the castle inhabitants didn't eat meat. I'd never asked why, but I assumed that it was like Hindus and their belief in non-violence.

"They're called *lya*," Riel answered. "Some of our citizens do eat their flesh, but they are more prized for their milk."

"Oh. I've been meaning to ask; not eating meat, is that a religious thing?"

"Not specifically. A majority of *Ishameti*, my family included, believe that it would be cruel to slaughter another intelligent being for food, especially when other sources of nutrition are so plentiful. We don't judge those who believe differently, though. From what I've heard, the situation in your world is not quite the same."

"I mean, we have a division between the vegans and vegetarians and the meat-eaters, for sure." I thought of the *avida,* of their sensitivity and the attachments they formed with their owners. "I guess our animals aren't as smart, so that's a big part of it. Not that they aren't intelligent," I conceded, thinking then of pigs, cows, and horses. "But not like this. If all your animals are like the *avida,* it's totally different."

We passed close by one of the cow creatures. My heart melted at the sight of little slender birds nesting in the moss on their backs.

"They seem so sweet," I remarked. *They had to be,* I supposed, *in order for those little fences to keep them contained.*

"They are gentle creatures, for the most part," Riel agreed. "Only aggressive when protecting their young. Even then, they have a sense for friends and those that wish them harm."

"The same cannot be said for those," he added as we drew closer to the edge of the city and passed a large pen with big, emu-like birds meandering about. They must have been the ones that Riel mentioned, the ones that laid the eggs we ate. They weren't as large as I'd envisioned, coming up to about hip height. One noticed us, sticking its head out at a creepy angle and ruffling its feathers in warning as we rode by. I felt Riel shiver against me.

"Not a fan?" I asked with a grin.

"When I was young and exceptionally stupid, Solois dared me to steal a fertilized egg from a nesting female. If not for a talented mender, I would still have the scars."

A horrified laugh escaped me. "Oh my God."

"Although it was a long time ago, the trauma is still fresh," Riel acknowledged.

"I can imagine." And I could—trauma was something I was familiar with.

Another moving object caught my eye. Someone tended to the animals with what appeared to be a little motorized cart, like a golf cart or utility vehicle. "Is that a...? I didn't realize you guys had automobiles."

"Not like yours. But we do make use of machines where needed."

"Machines, plumbing... you guys are well on your way to computers."

"Your government has offered to provide us with technology on numerous occasions."

"Oh? Why... sorry, I don't mean to be rude, but why don't you take us up on it?"

"We're happy with the way things are," Riel answered, untroubled by my question. "Everything we need is either handled by hand or with magic. There's no need."

"I mean... things like TV and the Internet aren't necessities, I guess, but they're sure nice to have," I insisted. "Don't you ever get bored with just... books and board games?"

I felt Riel shrug against me.

"We have our methods of passing the time," he said simply. I made a doubtful sound but put the conversation to rest since I didn't want to miss anything as we entered the city. A massive, arching stone gate towered over our heads, flanked by statues that were delicate despite being at least three men tall. One looked like a benevolent praying saint, the other a warrior goddess poised to strike. I couldn't begin to guess what they were supposed to depict.

On the way in, we passed a handful of guards who wore the same uniforms from the castle. They nodded to us as we went by, their gazes lingering on Riel.

The thing that first struck me about the city was how modern the whole place felt. Metal, wood, stone, brick, and concrete came together to create an environment somewhere between the medieval village I'd expected and early London. Every roof, wall, and pillar was crafted with care—using magic, perhaps, if not construction equipment?

There were dozens of buildings with shop fronts displaying

various kinds of merchandise along the main road. An assortment of people lined both sides, going about their lives without sparing us a second glance. I supposed travelers were common enough that we didn't appear out of place. That, or it was a regular occurrence to see the princes.

Many of the townspeople were tall blonds with pointed ears, but not as many as I expected. There were plenty with shorter statures, varying shades of skin and hair, and other unique features. I noted some small, pudgy figures in the crowd that I would have pegged as dwarves if I didn't know any better. Off to one side, a shopkeeper argued with a customer who had horns and furry legs like a faun. Another had dragonfly wings!

"I'm… wow." I found myself afraid to blink for fear of missing anything. "This is… remember when I was telling you about fae? We have all these people in our fairy tales. How did we not know about this? If people back home knew that they existed… well." There weren't any words. I had to settle for, "There'd be a lot more fanfiction, for one thing."

"You're the first human that's been to Miderrum," Riel told me, removing one of his hands from the rein strap to rest it casually on my thigh.

"Huh?" Distracted by the movement, it took me a second to process what he was saying. I met his cool gaze with wide eyes. "You mean… Not even the president? Or George?"

He shook his head and repeated, "You're the first."

I gripped the strap between my hands tighter, marveling at the scene around me with fresh eyes. As I took things in, the general cacophony of the city began to separate into distinct sounds. Many were inoffensive and familiar, like people walking and chatting, the purring of engines, and shopkeepers calling out their wares. But I couldn't help but notice one that was an assault on the ears—a hellish combination of discordant clanging and loud wails interspersed with groans—coming from somewhere up ahead.

"Yeesh. What in God's name is that?" I groused, only just resisting the temptation to cover my ears.

"Ah. That would be *Epitgig* music." Amused, Riel nodded toward a section off to one side, where people gathered around a fountain. "It's not to everyone's taste. In fact, it is sometimes used on the battlefield to inspire fear in an enemy. Here, it makes for a rather brilliant business. No one asks them to perform, but they show up anyway. They're playing by the public well, where everyone gets their water, so they can't be avoided. Most people will give them money in hopes they'll pack up and go home for the day."

"That's ridiculous. Why isn't there some kind of law against being a public nuisance?"

Riel shrugged. "They're not hurting anyone."

The crowd parted just enough that I caught an eyeful of the offenders, a small group of pale gray goblins wearing ratty skirts and playing an assortment of odd instruments. On second thought… that was perhaps too generous a term for what they were doing. One of them appeared to be banging his disproportionately large head against a metal board with great enthusiasm. Another clashed two blocks together while wailing loudly and without any clear rhythm.

"That's just awful," I muttered as the sounds began to fade out of earshot. "Really, I could happily go the rest of my life without ever hearing that again."

"You never know. It might be the first thing you miss when you leave."

"Somehow, I doubt that."

Riel chuckled to himself as he turned us down a side street. We passed by a tall signpost with several wood slats pointing in various directions. I couldn't make heads or tails of the collection of symbols there, but it was safe to assume he knew where we were going. People were quick to get out of our way, but they weren't scraping and bowing at our feet. Either nobody recognized Riel, or they simply didn't care. It was… reassuring.

A part of me had expected us to get swamped with admirers, but with the way Riel and his family regularly interacted with the townspeople, maybe they weren't considered to be a big deal.

It took me a moment to realize we'd stopped before a four-story building lined with black windows. My eyes didn't stray from it as Riel helped me down.

"Is this where we'll be staying?" I asked, leaning forward to admire the pale copper bricks that made up the outside of the structure. It was truly an impressive creation for people who didn't have any factories or heavy machinery. Though, then again, I couldn't assume that at this point.

"So long as there is room," Riel answered, moving to Oyanni's rump to begin untying our bags. After a moment's deliberation, he added, "It's unlikely to be full. So, yes."

As he passed, I made to take my bag from him, but he shifted it out of my reach and continued on toward the steps.

"I can carry my own bag," I protested, chasing after him.

"I have no doubt," he responded with the utmost sincerity. Upon reaching the front door, he placed his own bag at his feet to give himself a free hand to operate the door knocker. I stopped two steps behind him, grumbling under my breath about unnecessary chivalry.

The door was opened, revealing a slight woman with a generous smattering of freckles not unlike my own. She was dressed practically, with a short apron and a sort of cloth turban covering all of her hair. She struck me as being the most human-looking person I'd seen across The Rift thus far, despite her too-wide, upturned nose resembling a pig's snout.

Greeting Riel warmly in the *Ishameti* language, she stepped aside for us to come in. The interior was furnished to be luxurious but welcoming, with solid wooden furniture and a variety of soft, golden-toned accents throughout the room. The lady scampered past us to take her place behind a front desk to our right.

While she and Riel talked, I wandered away to take in the space. A tapestry on the far wall caught my eye. It depicted a woman bathed in light with a tastefully nude man kneeling at her feet, gazing up at her with clear adoration. Behind and to the left of them was a backdrop of darkness and fire, but the woman was bent over and holding out her right hand to provide shelter for a series of small figures that reached for her in return.

Is this… the Goddess? My hand hovered over one edge.

"Avery?"

I yanked it back with a guilty look.

"Would you prefer to have separate rooms?" Riel asked, observing me for my reaction. At the sound of English, the proprietress eyed me with renewed interest.

It took me a moment to process his words. "Oh! Uh…" *Would it be coming on too strong if I said no?* "That's fine, actually. I mean, if you want to just get one room and share, that's fine with me." More than fine, really. My mind's eye was already taking the opportunity to run through the tantalizing possibilities that came with having real privacy for once.

Riel relayed my response to the proprietress, and I returned to examining the tapestry. The skill of the weaver was clear even to me. Each color blended with the next to create depth, life, and movement. Additionally, the threads had a subtle shine to them that made the whole thing glow. It was a work of art, if also a bit creepy. Then again, that described a lot of art.

When Riel pulled away from the desk and gathered up our bags, I joined him.

"All good?" I asked.

"No issues," he replied, a twinkle in his eye. "She has the perfect room for us."

So, we would be sharing a room. I ducked my head to hide the pleasure on my face.

The proprietress came out from behind the desk holding an ornate key. She walked quickly, leading us upstairs and down the hall. She babbled the whole way, with Riel giving short, polite answers in response. I just smiled and nodded along. Finally, she brought us to the last door on the far end of the building and unlocked it with the key. Riel stepped aside to let me enter first, and my eyes widened when I saw the interior.

It was much nicer than my guest room at the castle. It was nicer than Riel's room too. Large windows lined the opposite wall, complete with gauzy golden curtains. Against the right wall was a massive four-poster bed, perhaps even larger than a king, with a bedside table on either side and a large landscape painting above it. On the left side, a wide opening in the wall revealed the bathroom nook. I ventured further inside to get a better look. The bath was even bigger than the one I had in my room, large enough to fit maybe four people. While there was no door, an embellished folding screen sat at the entrance to provide some privacy.

The place was immaculate and tastefully furnished, including an intricate but not too busy rug and a modest writing desk by the windows. It even had a cozy fireplace. The overall effect reminded me of some of the rooms at the White House.

"It's gorgeous," I murmured when I realized I had yet to say anything. Riel had placed our bags by the bed, and the proprietress still stood by the open door. While her gaze remained on me, she directed a question at Riel. He nodded and said something in response. The only word I caught was "American," but our host nodded knowingly. She said one last thing, made a generous sweeping gesture, and was gone. I gave Riel a questioning look.

"She asked about our journey and how long we're staying," Riel translated for me. "I mentioned I've been to the city before, but it's your first time seeing it. She asked if you were from the land across The Rift. She's pleased that you're happy with the room, and she made it clear that we're welcome to anything we need. All we need to do is ask."

"Oh, that's nice of her." I made my way to the bed to feel the covers. They were thick and fluffy but not too heavy. The top layer had beautiful embroidery. "We don't have many royals anymore these days," I remarked. "But when we did, they were treated much differently from normal people. Bowing and scraping and all that. I'm glad that you guys aren't like that."

"We have a place in society, same as everyone else. Respected, but not worshipped."

"I like that." Nodding absently, I continued to explore. On the bedside table nearest me was a glass object somewhere between the shape of a fishbowl and a lantern. I picked it up to examine the base, trying to figure out what its purpose was.

"It's a *mana* lamp," Riel's voice came from right behind me, making me jump. I stepped aside and watched, fascinated, as he made a gesture over the lantern. In an instant, pale blue light sparked into being, lighting the room with a cool, steady glow.

"Making magic is an interesting case, because it involves coaxing *mana* from the environment into a usable form," he explained, withdrawing his hand. "*Mana* does not generally change states by itself, so once someone has manipulated it to achieve a certain effect, it can remain that way indefinitely. For example, in the case of creating light."

"Pretty sure that breaks, like, all the laws of physics," I said wryly. "But I don't know enough about science to argue that, so I'll take your word for it."

Riel chuckled, sliding out from under his cloak and bundling it under one arm. "Which side do you want?" he asked. I followed his gaze down to the bed, and the thought of us both in it together made my face begin to burn.

"Doesn't matter," I mumbled, easing toward the window to put some space between us. "You can take whichever you want, and I'll just have the other one."

"So be it."

He deposited his cloak on the bed and went to retrieve his bag, and I made an effort to appear entranced by the view of the street from our room. For some reason, things felt awkward between us. *Was it just that the prospect of sharing a room made me nervous? Had I used up all of my newfound courage the other night getting my nipples pierced?*

"May I wash your feet?"

Distracted, I turned around to find Riel standing patiently by the bed with a cloth in one hand and a small, stoppered jar in the other. His eyes never left my face.

"I'm… sorry?" I couldn't have heard him correctly.

"It's a courting custom," he offered, raising the items he held to show me. "A way of tending to one's partner after travel. It will only take a moment. Unless you're ticklish, in which case I might be tempted to draw out the process."

He cast a disarming smile my way.

"Uh…" When I remained frozen by the window, Riel took mercy on me, putting down the items he carried and taking my hands to guide me. He brought me to the bed, and I could only watch as he lowered himself to kneel on the floor before me and took up one of my feet. I was torn—*do I let him do this?* There was no harm in it, and he seemed to want to…

"This is kind of…" I fidgeted with my skirt as Riel unbuckled my sandals and slipped them off one by one. He set my shoes aside and paused, looking up at me.

"Does it bother you?" he asked, studying my expression closely for signs of distress. "If so, I'll stop."

I squirmed under his steady gaze. "No, I guess not. It's just not something… I mean, it's a little awkward, but… you do you. I won't stop you."

He nodded and continued, breaking eye contact to lay a cloth down on the floor and set my feet upon it with great care. Picking up my left foot, he reached for the little jar and unstoppered it with one hand. He poured some onto the foot he held, a warm and spicy scent like cinnamon or cardamom filling the air as he did so.

"What is that?" I tried to get a better look at the bottle.

"An oil made from the *vali* nut. It cleanses and softens the skin."

He punctuated his words by taking my foot in both hands and beginning to spread the oil. I shivered as his fingers massaged skin and muscle, adding more pressure when he got to the heel and keeping his touch light as he stroked the arch and delved in between each toe. My eyes started to close in pleasure. Before I realized it, he was repeating the process with the other foot.

Once both feet were tended to, he sat back on his heels and used a clean cloth to wipe off any excess oil. Finally, he collected the bottle and the cloths he had used and stood up. I flexed my feet in front of me, admiring the glow and how warm and baby-soft they felt.

"Thank you. That was really lovely."

I hadn't expected to enjoy it that much, but… huh. *Maybe people who were into feet were onto something after all?* Looking up, I realized with some degree of alarm that Riel had re-stoppered the oil and was putting everything away. "Wait! Shouldn't I do yours too?"

"No need. I just wanted to do that for you," he replied, giving me a sweet smile that, combined with his charming words, made my heart trip over itself. "Also, I'm ticklish," he added, which somewhat dampened the effect of his previous statement.

"Okay," I conceded with an awkward laugh, grabbing for my sandals and pulling them on. It didn't escape my notice that this was the second time he took care of me without asking for anything in return. As much as it warmed my heart, I'd have to find some way to return the favor at some point, or it wouldn't feel right. That would have to come later, though. "I guess we should go find that mender, then, huh?"

"There's no rush. Feel free to settle in first. Are you hungry?" Riel slid his bag underneath the opposite side of the bed and took a seat beside his discarded cloak.

"Not yet. Honestly, I'm more keen on getting down to business, if it's all the same to you. I mean, if you're hungry, though, that's fine, we can eat first!"

"Not enough to merit bothering our host. We can set out now, then, if you're not tired. The mender will be expecting us soon anyway."

Riel got to his feet again, collecting his cloak and shaking it out with a sharp *snap*. He fastened it in place while I finished putting on my shoes and came around the bed.

"Are there any customs I should be aware of while in the city or meeting this person?" I asked as I followed him to the door.

"Nothing comes to mind. But I'll let you know if I think of anything," Riel assured me, putting a hand on the small of my back and letting me exit first.

"Okay, great. Thank you." Having someone reliable with me kept the anxiety at bay for once. Feeling good about this, I stepped out with a smile on my face, and we headed downstairs together.

CHAPTER TWENTY-TWO
THE MENDER

UPON STEPPING OUTSIDE, Riel steered me back toward the main road. Oyanni followed behind us without prompting, as if she'd already been briefed on the situation.

"Miderrum is an old word that translates to 'a place of gathering,'" Riel told me as we walked. "Not very creative, I know. There are several other settlements in the general area, but this is easily the oldest and the largest." There was more than a hint of pride in his voice. "During the last census, we recorded a population of nearly 30,000."

I kept my smile to myself, thinking about how cute it was to be excited about that. If 30,000 was a lot to these people, they'd lose their minds in D.C.

"Is there anything the city is known for?" I asked. "Besides the vicious birds and terrible music, I mean."

Riel gave me a look somewhere between exasperated and amused. "The main thing to appreciate about Miderrum is the collection of backgrounds and cultures you'll find among the people here—everyone has a different story to share. And it's rare to find so much knowledge and skill in one place. The craftsmen and craftswomen that do business here are unequaled. There's also a library with relics and records that span thousands of years."

"Bet George would give up both his shriveled old nuts for a peek in there," I mused. Riel chuckled to himself.

"He has expressed his desire to do so on several occasions," he admitted, nodding. He winced when he realized what he'd said. "Visit our library, that is. Not surrender body parts."

As we reached the larger road, I entwined an arm with Riel's. The last thing I needed was to get separated from him surrounded by strangers in a foreign city. I couldn't remember the last time I'd walked freely around so many people. Actually... I could, but the memory didn't bring me any comfort. I eased closer to Riel, pressing myself against his side.

We headed into the middle of the road and joined the stream of traffic. One or two people glanced our way as we passed, but no one showed much interest in either of us. Chances were they noticed the *avida* following us, and that apparently wasn't a sight worth commenting on. Faced with the truth of the matter, my nerves began to settle.

No one knows me here, I reminded myself. Plus, healing magic was commonplace in this world. There was little chance of getting accosted by hopefuls here. Immensely proud of myself, I relaxed my grip on Riel as I let my guard down and allowed myself to enjoy the sights.

People of all kinds gathered in front of vendors on either side of us. I saw a man with blue skin and nearly transparent clothing that looked like he could have been related to the blue lady I recalled seeing at the ball. In front of one shop, a child with albinism and a pointed prehensile tail sticking out of their clothing stood in a short line. I had to turn away; if I kept trying to catalog all the oddities I saw, I'd go cross-eyed.

Was I missing things like this every day back home? The new experiences, the liveliness, the assortment of sights and smells? If things were different, maybe I could have left the White House long before now. Maybe I could have even traveled the world.

There was a time when I wanted to, some years ago. Recently, I'd been content, even happy, to keep my head down and do what was asked of me. *But could I call that happiness, given what I was feeling now?*

My train of thought was interrupted when Riel tugged me to one side, stopping in front of one of the vendors. I peered around him to see that the shop sold jewelry. A sidelong glance told me that Riel's attention had been claimed by a cuff bracelet with twin chain details and amber-colored stones. He asked the shopkeeper something. Appearing satisfied with the answer, he gave something to the man, and the bracelet exchanged hands.

When Riel swiveled around to show me, I examined the piece with polite interest. "What is that? Some kind of *mana*-storing tool?"

Riel reached for my hand. Puzzled, I gave it to him. He slid the cuff onto my wrist, giving it a firm pinch to make sure it fit snugly. "Just jewelry," he said innocently.

"What? For me?"

"No, for the *Epitgig* musicians playing in the square. Of course, for you."

My eyes widened as I took in the fine workmanship. "Wasn't this expensive?"

Riel shrugged. "Gifts are another traditional aspect of courtship. Is it not also common among humans? How else do you court one another?"

"Well, I guess there is a fair amount of gift-giving," I admitted reluctantly. "But nobody calls it courting. We call it dating. And fancy gifts like these are usually for special occasions."

"If it makes you feel better, think of this as a special occasion. Your first visit to Miderrum." Riel's charming smile had my reservations turning over a new leaf.

"Thank you," I mumbled, fingering the fine chain detail on the bracelet. "It's beautiful."

"When the sun hits them just right, your eyes turn that exact color," Riel said, nodding at the amber stones. Touched by his words, I examined them more closely. If I were a more poetic person, I would probably agree—the color *was* similar to brown eyes in the sun.

"Aren't you charming?" I flashed him a shy smile, which he returned. The thought occurred to me that maybe I should get him a gift too, but then I remembered that I had no currency in this world, and my shoulders sagged. *Oh, well.*

We started walking again. Eventually, we came to a long, sandy-colored building with a series of doors. A panel with labeled buttons was set in the wall about chest height on our end of the building. Riel examined the labels and then chose a button, pressing it with a flourish.

I couldn't believe my eyes.

"That's not an intercom system?" I exclaimed in disbelief, pointing.

"Hm?" Riel followed my gaze to the button he'd pressed. "This? It's a… trigger of sorts. It notifies a specific resident that they have a visitor."

"So, a doorbell." I shook my head. "You've got indoor plumbing and doorbells, but use magic light and messenger birds instead of light bulbs and phones."

"Is that a complaint?" Riel asked mildly. "My sincerest apologies. Please be assured that I will bring your concerns to my parents right away. Your opinion is very important to us."

"Just an observation," I retorted, rolling my eyes at his sass.

Just then, one of the doors opened to reveal a portly, dark-skinned woman with hair cropped close to her scalp. She looked around before spotting us and raising an arm to get our attention. As we approached, I made out several piercings in her nose and cheeks. Her ears were even longer and more sharply pointed than Riel's, with feathery tufts at the ends.

When she folded her arms together and bowed her neck in greeting, her sleeves rode up enough to reveal black markings along both forearms that bled into her hands. Her nails were black and filed into long, sharp points. She said something before turning around with a gesture I recognized as inviting us inside. It was then that I noticed the bulky cape on her back was not a cape at all, but wings that were long enough to skim the ground as she walked.

"Oh my God," I whispered, biting back the urge to ask if she could fly. Riel glanced my way, amused by my excitement. He had to duck to enter her home; the threshold was lower than any in the castle, and the ceiling wasn't much higher.

"I am Seersthri," the woman said in a voice much deeper than I had expected. I couldn't tell if it was just the strong accent, but her name came out sounding more like a toothy whistle than a word. I was certain I had no hope of repeating it properly.

"Hello," I offered. "I'm Avery."

"I know." The woman—Seersthri—gave me a wide grin that I supposed was meant to be friendly, revealing pointed teeth. And her eyes, I noticed then, were striking, round and pale yellow like an owl's. I directed a nervous glance at Riel, but he didn't seem bothered. Well, he'd probably met her before. And for all I knew, the fangs and nails and eyes were commonplace here. *So what if she wasn't what I'd pictured when I imagined a healer?*

"You speak English too," I remarked, relieved for that, at least.

"I speak seventeen languages," Seersthri replied with pride. "It helps my..." She paused and frowned, trying to recall a certain word, before settling on "customers."

"You are tired," she said before I had a chance to respond, heading further inside. "Come. Sit." The mender showed us to a kitchen table. Riel and I settled on the bench seat, and I took the chance to look around. Her home wasn't what I would have expected either. It was homey and rustic, with woven furniture and furs covering the floor. I had sort of expected a cabin with a thatched roof, the interior filled with hanging herbs and jars of animal pieces. Something witchy.

"Thank you for seeing us," Riel began, clasping his hands together and setting them on the table before him. "As I mentioned in my letter, Avery has shown a natural talent for mending, but unfortunately has yet to learn how to access *mana*. At this point, we've begun exploring options beyond the traditional route. I normally wouldn't consider the *manaviri*—"

"Yes, yes, *manaviri*," Seersthri interrupted. She leveled a serious look at me, unblinking yellow eyes peering into my soul. "*Manaviri* can be… dangerous. Not always, but often."

"So I've been told," I admitted, correcting my posture to mirror Riel's position. "But you have to understand, See—uh, Doc—Madam Healer, I really need to figure this out. There are a lot of people relying on me, and the fact is that it's just taking too long. We were hoping that you might be able to help make it not so dangerous for me. With your expertise…"

I trailed off as Seersthri came around the table and held out a clawed hand. Hesitating, I looked from her hand to Riel and back before reaching out. She wrapped her fingers around my hand and tugged my arm toward herself. "Pretty," she commented, nodding down at my bracelet. I hid a shy smile. A second or two passed before I felt it: a distinct rush of warmth, foreign and familiar at the same time, traveling through my body from where we touched.

Expressionless but nodding now, Seersthri patted my hand twice before releasing it.

"Your body is good. Strong," she declared. "Come. We try the *manaviri*."

"What? Now?" Riel shot up from the table, alarmed. In any other situation, I would have laughed aloud at the look on his face. As it was, I probably had the same one on mine.

"Are you sure?" I asked like an idiot, not budging from my spot at the table.

Seersthri paused to regard the two of us. "Your letter said there is no time?"

"We are in a rush," Riel agreed, shooting me an indiscernible look. "But not enough to risk… We came to you because we trust your expertise. What we want to know is, is it safe?"

He switched to his native language and continued speaking, presumably to be sure that the mender understood what he was attempting to convey. I could have sworn that I heard my name. When he finished speaking, Seersthri shook her head.

"I cannot promise," she said. "But I have done *manaviri* before." She stared Riel down. "Her body is strong. I am confident."

A crease appeared between his platinum brows. I watched the minute changes in his expression as he tried and failed to come up with an adequate excuse to give this up and go home. Still, he hesitated to make the call, so I took the burden from him.

"Let's do it," I announced, getting to my feet. "If she's confident, that's good enough for me."

Riel met my eyes, and I tried to ignore the helplessness and concern I saw there. I turned to face Seersthri.

"Let's do it," I repeated, infusing my voice with resolve.

Unfazed, the mender gestured for me to follow her. With Riel close behind, we headed for a back room that held three cots. Having been in my fair share of hospitals as of late, I got the sense that this was where she treated her patients. When she bid me toward one of the cots, I obediently approached and lay down. Seersthri sat on the cot next to me and took my hand, stroking up and down my forearm in a soothing manner.

As her touch imbued my body with the comforting warmth of her mending magic, she spoke, but not in English. Riel listened intently and responded with what sounded like a question. As they talked, I stared at the ceiling and tried to quell the rising nerves. *Between the two of them, I'm in good hands,* I told myself. *This was my idea, for heaven's sake. Chickening out now just wouldn't do.*

After a moment, Riel appeared in my field of vision. "She says she's going to put you to sleep first," he reported in a measured voice. "Once you are no longer aware, she'll stop your heart, and then we wait. The timing is crucial. When the moment is right, I'll deliver a shock to restart your heart. The whole process will be over in minutes."

"Okay." My voice came out a whisper.

Riel looked down at where the mender held me, and his right hand twitched as though he yearned to do the same. When I reached for him with my free arm, he crouched by my other side in an instant, wrapping his hand tightly around mine and raising it to his lips.

"It'll be okay," I assured him, gripping his hand in return and trying to ignore the tenderness of his lips brushing against my skin. When I found myself blinking back tears, I focused my attention back on the ceiling. "It'll be fine," I said aloud, not entirely for his sake. *God, please let this be the right decision.*

"Sleep," Seersthri murmured, still stroking my arm gently. Drowsiness followed, the effect of her magic not unlike a dose of sedative injected into my veins. My thoughts grew sluggish, my limbs heavy. When my heart began to slow, my body responded with a desperate jolt of adrenaline, causing my hand to tighten around Riel's.

"Don't leave," I cried out on instinct. The world around me blurred.

"Never, Avery."

Riel's choked response was the last thing I heard before everything fell away.

CHAPTER TWENTY-THREE
RIEL

I HEARD the moment her heart stopped beating, and mine nearly stopped with it. Every muscle in my body tensed in response, ready to leap into action the moment Seersthri gave the word. I glanced up at the mender across from me. She held Avery's hand, seemingly unbothered by the way the rest of her arm dangled there, lifeless. With her other hand, she rapped two fingers against the edge of the cot to the time of a heartbeat, and her lips moved silently as she counted.

"Give it another moment," Seersthri murmured, her full eyebrows coming together in concentration. "Let her body realize what's happening. A few more beats."

Goddess, how could I have agreed to this? Every second that passed was agony. I shifted my weight, needing to direct this restless energy somewhere, anywhere.

"Now?" I asked through gritted teeth.

"Not yet."

How long had it been already? Ten seconds? Surely that was more than enough?

Avery was so still and pale, not at all like her usual, exuberant self. Trying to keep my thoughts positive, I recalled her smiling face instead. The way the corners of her eyes crinkled and her little nose scrunched up when I teased her, equal parts amused and affronted. The happy sounds she made when she was proud of herself for doing something right. Her orange hair backlit by the dawn when we headed out for lessons in the early mornings.

Seersthri inhaled, and my hands were hovering above Avery before she could speak.

"Now?" I demanded.

"Now," she agreed, giving me an abrupt nod.

Mana leapt to my call, changing from formless energy to light and heat in an instant. The hair on my arms stood on end and my palms warmed as it flowed through my body, drawing from my inner magic along the way to become electricity. The pulse of power left me without delay, crashing into Avery's chest. Her limbs jerked from the force of it, and I winced, worried that I had gone too far. I looked to Seersthri.

Her expression hadn't changed. And Avery didn't move, her chest still quiet underneath my hands. Her lips were turning blue.

"Once more," Seersthri said.

Everything felt too fast and too slow all at once. The realization came from someplace far, far away: she wasn't moving.

It didn't work.

No. No, that can't be. *Where did I go wrong?*

Letting this develop between us in the first place, even knowing the danger my family posed to her. Not sending her back to her people as soon as her condition improved. Bringing her here and letting her attempt this foolish, *foolish* thing. I couldn't deny that it was my selfishness that brought us to this point. I knew the risks; it was my responsibility to communicate them properly. I thought I could have this… this *one* thing, and now…

"Second prince!"

I was ripped back to the present. The look Seersthri fixed me with could have drained a lesser man of all fight. As it was, it affected me to my core, and my spine snapped straight.

"Do it now, or the girl dies," she said, not one to mince words.

It's now or never.

I drew mana like a man possessed, so much so quickly that my veins strained to bear it. The discomfort was nothing compared to the thought of losing her. Channeling *mana* into lightning was second nature, but I didn't dare look away, didn't dare *breathe* lest my concentration falter. My hands shook—from effort or fear, I didn't know—as they delivered another shock to Avery's cooling body.

"Again," Seersthri commanded.

All of me shook now, and with a vengeance. "It didn't... she's..."

"*Again,*" Seersthri enunciated, yellow eyes flashing with resolve. "*More.*"

I summoned everything left in me and prayed. When the current surged from me to Avery, even Seersthri flinched at the intensity of it. Blue light filled the small room, illuminating every corner for a brief moment before winking out. I blinked rapidly to clear my vision.

Seersthri brought her free hand up, casually brushed a ruffled lock of Avery's hair over her shoulder, and resumed stroking her arm with gentle, steady movements.

At first, the only sound I could make out was my own breathing as my lungs worked for air. But then came the slightest flutter from underneath my hands, as delicate as *kainna* wings and more precious than the sweetest ballad. Slowly at first, hesitantly, parts of me that had shattered into pieces began to put themselves back together.

And then Avery breathed in, and I was whole once more.

CHAPTER TWENTY-FOUR
THE CURE

WHEN AWARENESS RETURNED, it was sudden and brutal.

My eyes snapped open to see Riel panting above me, eyes wild, hands still poised on my chest to deliver another shock of lightning magic. He did a double take upon realizing that my eyes were open. Slowly, wearily, he lost all strength, collapsing by my side and lowering his head to the cot. The linen muffled his whispered prayer of thanks.

I lay there and took stock of my feelings. Seersthri still held my hand, her mending magic easing the worst of my aches and pains. My lungs expanded and contracted somewhat reluctantly, but my toes and fingers wiggled without much prompting. Thoughts were slow to come, but the memories of moments ago were still there. Minor aches and heavy fatigue were all that lingered from my brush with death.

Oh, and my nipples tingled.

The mender drew away. Riel lifted his head then, his eyes scanning my face as though to reassure himself that I was alive and alert. I lifted a hand idly, wanting to show him I was okay but unable to do much else while I worked up the strength to speak.

"Jesus," I wheezed once I caught my breath. "Feels like an *avida* kicked me in the chest."

"We are never doing that again," Riel said with finality.

I raised my head to look for Seersthri, seeking confirmation that the *manaviri* worked. She advanced toward us with a glass of water in her hand. Riel helped me sit up. As I went from horizontal to vertical, I could have sworn I felt something slide down my boob and catch on the underwire of my bra, but I didn't have time to ponder that.

"Thank you." I gratefully accepted the glass Seersthri handed to me.

"Slow," she warned as I drank. When I was done, she took the glass back.

"Did it work?" I asked, looking up at her hopefully.

"All is well," Seersthri told me, patting my knee. "We will see soon. Now…" She retracted her hand and got to her feet. "Your body and spirit need rest. Stay, or go. I have work."

With that, she crossed the room, gathered some items into a tote bag, and swept out of the room. I rubbed absently at my chest, where I still felt raw.

"Does it hurt?" Riel murmured from beside me. His hand made slow, comforting circles between my shoulder blades, and I closed my eyes to savor the feeling.

"Not really. Just a little sore."

"I'm sorry. I… tried to be gentle."

"Don't be sorry. Whatever you did, it worked." I offered him a smile.

Remembering the odd sensation I'd felt when I sat up, I tugged my top open and peered down. When nothing obvious jumped out at me, I hunched over and pushed at the bottom of my bra to get a look inside. "Oh, my God. I think… I think my piercings closed."

Angling my body away from Riel and attempting to be discreet about it, I went digging. When I pulled my hand out to reveal the two silver hoops that should have been attached to my nipples, we both stared at them in disbelief.

Then Riel threw back his head and laughed.

"Ahh… I suppose we'll just have to do them again, *eseri*." He punctuated his words with a saucy wink that had my nether regions perking up and my cheeks warming.

"So, what now?" I hurried to change the subject. "Are we going back, or…?"

"That's up to you. Would you prefer to rest here or return to the boarding house? Seersthri would not mind either way, I'm sure."

After thinking it over, I admitted, "I think I'd be more comfortable there."

"Then let's return."

Riel got to his feet and offered me a hand. I swung my legs over the side of the cot without issue, but when I stood up, I was hit by a rush of dizziness. Noticing the way I staggered, Riel seized my arm and wrapped his other hand around my waist to support me, clutching me to him as though I were something impossibly precious. I wanted nothing more than to wrap my arms around him in return and savor the contact, but as it was, I barely knew up from down.

"Ooh, hang on." I put a hand to my head and leaned into him while I waited for the room to stop spinning. It took several seconds. "On second thought, maybe I'd better stay here."

"Oyanni should still be outside," Riel leapt to offer a solution. "If you're able to hold on for a few minutes of riding, I can get you the rest of the way."

My thoughts strayed to the luxurious bed in our hotel room. Fluffy pillows, a weighted duvet, enough room to spread out… the cot didn't compare. And I wasn't sure I could relax in this space; there was no privacy. What if Seersthri needed it for another patient?

"Okay," I agreed.

Needing no further prompting, Riel scooped me into his arms, one arm around my back and the other under my knees. Delighted, I wrapped my arms around his neck and let my head fall against his chest. He showed no signs of struggling with my weight as he carried me through the house. When we emerged from the building, Oyanni trotted up to us immediately. She gave me an inquisitive bump with her nose before presenting her back.

Riel helped me up like usual, and as though she could tell that something was up, Oyanni held extra still. Riel slung an arm around me for added support and we were off.

By the time we made it back to the boarding house where we were staying, the fatigue had settled like a heavy cloak, as bad or even worse than it had been before I crossed The Rift. My eyelids drooped and my muscles protested every movement. Riel lifted me down as carefully as he could, but I wasn't able to stifle a discontented groan.

"Sorry." Riel's expression was contrite. "Just a little farther."

"You're fine," I assured him, relaxing into his hold. "It's every girl's dream to be princess-carried by a hottie. I'm not doing too bad right now, all things considered."

Riel's lips quirked upward in a smile as he made his way up the steps. "Is that so? Our people tend to be generous when it comes to physical touch and affection, but I was under the impression that it isn't the same case for humans."

"Well, in formal settings, maybe. It's different when it's somebody you're dating." My words faded off into a mumble that may or may not have been coherent. I must have dozed off, because the next thing I knew, I was being deposited with great care onto the bed.

"Just a moment. I'm going to leave Oyanni to graze," a voice murmured above me. I gave a half-hearted nod and snuggled into the bedding. A second later, it registered that I hadn't heard retreating footsteps. I opened my eyes to find that Riel still stood there, watching my chest rise and fall with a strangely haunted look on his face.

"I'm not going to spontaneously combust, you know," I remarked, closing my eyes again. He made a doubtful sound in his throat, but my statement worked to break the spell. I felt him fiddling with the ties of my sandals. Snippets of awareness came to me through a haze of exhaustion, with no concept of whether it had been hours or minutes between each one.

Riel returning to the room and dropping something by the door.

The sound of running water.

Hushed voices and the quiet clinking of ceramic dishware.

At some point, someone fed me a few bites of something savory until I turned away. I dreamed that I steered a wobbly canoe down a fast-moving river of curry, dodging giant chunks of meat and vegetables with nothing but a flimsy oar. Eventually, I made it to the shore, where I joined a herd of *avida* that had become unicorns made of ice cream and sundae toppings.

Sometime during one of my more lucid moments, I remember thinking that I'd like to see a dream interpreter try to make sense of that. But then I felt a comforting weight settle at my back, and I drifted off into a deeper sleep surrounded by warmth and the somehow familiar scent of sunshine and spring meadows.

CHAPTER TWENTY-FIVE
THE LESSONS RESUME

WHEN RIEL WOKE ME, I was horrified to learn I'd somehow slept the rest of the day and night away. After a desperate rush for the bathroom and some time spent freshening up, I felt like a new person. The body aches and exhaustion were replaced by uncontainable excitement and an overall sense of vitality. Riel and I had a quick breakfast and headed to Seersthri's, where the mender pronounced me hale and hearty.

Thus, we were resuming my belated magic lessons.

"Let's start with something simple," Riel suggested. He looked around before stooping to collect a piece of straw. He separated it into two pieces and held them out to me.

I raised my eyebrows at the offering. "You're… asking me to heal a piece of straw?"

"Mending is not limited to living things," he reminded me. "Although it's often more intuitive to direct energy into something that has its own, you should be able to put an object back together just as well as you can a person."

"I've never tried," I admitted, still eyeing the straw with doubt.

"It's the same concept," Riel assured me. "Try to fix this piece of straw."

It felt like it had been ages since I tried to access my magic. Plus, I'd been healing people for years, and straw was new. On top of that, the straw didn't care if it was whole or not, whereas there was a bit more at stake with people. Altogether, it didn't bode well. With a sigh, I held a piece of straw in each hand and put the severed ends together. Turning my attention inward, I went through the usual steps.

My flicker of magic leapt to meet me as though thrilled to be back in action. I ignored the temptation to draw directly from it and instead felt around for something new.

During the past few years, I'd become intimately familiar with that place inside me. Normally, it was a yawning chasm of nothing, illuminated only by the faint flicker of my paltry life force. Now, there was a roaring tempest of power surrounding my little flame. It had a presence like the sun, radiant and fierce and bathing everything around it in light and warmth.

There could be no doubt. This was *mana*. This was what I had been missing. I inhaled a sharp breath.

"Avery?" Riel asked, a hint of concern in his voice.

In awe of what I was feeling, I'd momentarily forgotten the task at hand. I held up the straw with confidence, and there was a brief pulse of light.

"Oh!" I exclaimed, so surprised that I dropped the straw. It fell from my hands and fluttered slowly to the ground—in one piece. I stared, shell-shocked.

"Nicely done," Riel praised, scanning my expression. "How did that feel?"

"How did that feel?" I repeated, pivoting to fix him with an incredulous stare. "That was… that was…" No words came to mind. Nothing even came close. Shaking my head, I settled for "Indescribable." With that kind of power available to me…

Faces flashed through my mind—Felicity, the surgeon from Camp Perry who had asked me to heal her ear. The feeble old lady I'd tried to heal outside the White House on the day I lost my magic. Dozens, hundreds, thousands of hopefuls in a crowd, screaming for me to notice them. "I can heal them all." My voice dropped to a whisper as the gravity of the situation became clear. "Oh my God. I can heal them all. Every last one of them."

"Remember, what you're feeling is all the *mana* around you, not just what you can use," Riel warned. "You'll need to take it slowly until you've figured out your limits."

"How can I figure out my limits?"

"You heal," Seersthri said from behind us, startling me all over again. She came through the open doorway with a covered basket and hustled past us into the kitchen. "You heal," she repeated, stooping to sort through some glass jars on the floor, "until you cannot."

"It's found through trial and error," Riel clarified, coming to my side. "Then, like anything else, you practice. With time and training, you'll get more comfortable. You'll learn control, and you'll be able to expand your capabilities."

Seersthri directed a question toward Riel in the fae language.

"She's asking if you would like to help her with her patients today," he translated with a slight frown. "You don't have to. It would be best to take another day or two to rest before you try anything big. We can keep practicing on small things until you've recovered."

"No, I feel great," I was quick to say, my heart soaring at the prospect of helping people again. "And I'd love to help. Do you have a lot of sick or injured?"

"Always something," Seersthri responded absently, transferring some jars to her basket. "Sickness. Accidents. Animal bites, sore muscles, fever, broken bones. Sometimes births."

"Births!" I exclaimed, my eyes widening to a comical degree. How different would it be to treat people who weren't dying for a change? Could I handle it? Usually, I didn't have to see any blood or gore.

Seersthri took her time collecting everything she needed, and we set off to a modest clinic a short walk away from her home. Riel didn't appear pleased by my decision, but he came along anyway. Through him, Seersthri explained that with mending magic being what it was, she and her coworkers didn't often come across a case they couldn't handle. A handful of people with chronic illnesses returned or stayed several days for multiple treatments, but for the most part, people came and went over the course of the day.

I shadowed her for the first hour or so. It was infinitely more boring than I had expected. Even in a city of 30,000, people here didn't get hurt all that often. When they did, the injury could usually be fixed within a few minutes. Thanks to magic, they had no need for a full-size hospital with dozens of staff members, an emergency room, and a recovery wing.

When a blue lady came in with a broken nail, Seersthri called me over.

"Look," she said, pointing. "Simple. You try it."

I moved forward eagerly. Though trying not to stare, I couldn't help but appreciate the lady's form. She was lithe and graceful like Luenki, but her skin and hair were powder blue. Her eyes were azure pools framed by royal-blue lashes, and her artfully draped dress was one or two shades darker than her skin and practically see-through. I desperately wanted to ask Riel what she was but realized how rude that might be.

The situation would have been laughable if the poor lady didn't act as though she'd lost an entire arm. Trembling and sniffling through tears, she extended one dainty hand to show me her injury. Sure enough, one of the fingers on her right hand—one out of six, I noted—had a crack in the long, almond-shaped nail. A drop of blue blood leaked from the wound.

Giving me little time to process, Seersthri encouraged me to take the lady's hand. Her skin was smooth and cool to the touch, like a polished river rock. I went to heal her injury, but the feeling of "wrongness" I was familiar with didn't jump out at me. I dug a little deeper, forehead creasing in concentration.

A faint trace of *mana* came to my call, a single spark of light flashed in my vision, and her nail was whole.

"Huh."

"What is it? Are you all right?" Riel was there in an instant.

"I'm fine," I assured him, releasing the lady's hand and stepping back. "It's just weird. I was healing people with cancer and stuff back home, and it just came so naturally. Even though this was easy, it was almost harder. Is it because I'm using *mana* now?"

Seersthri grunted, catching my attention. "Simple is not always easy," she remarked, ignoring the blue lady as she admired my work and gave a squeal of glee. "We listen to the body. Sometimes, it screams. Sometimes, it whispers."

The patient reached out to grasp my hands, her eyes swimming with gratitude, and babbled something in a language that sounded like all vowels.

"You're welcome," I responded automatically, smiling at her infectious joy. She squeezed my hands one last time and swept past us for the exit. When she had vacated the room, I spun to face Riel with a question on my lips. "Did you see that?"

"I did. You made her very happy." He looked at me with something akin to pride, which only served to amplify the giddiness I experienced.

"Well, yes." I ducked my head sheepishly. "But the little bit of light? When I healed her?"

"Light? No. But that's not common with mending." Noting the change in my expression, Riel added, "I'll watch more closely next time."

"Okay." Turning to Seersthri, I asked, "Can I try something else? Something different?"

"Come," she said, indicating for me to join her. I followed her to another room, where they had more permanent cots set up for long-term patients. There was a young faun in one of the beds there, whom Seersthri greeted briefly. The thought occurred to me that she didn't have the bedside manner one might expect from a renowned healer.

"His body is stubborn," she explained. "The lungs are weak. We heal, but it comes back."

The patient fixed me with a stare that bordered on impolite. Brazenly, I stared back, taking in the curling black horns that jutted out from either side of his skull. The man was somewhat gaunt, with an unhealthy pallor to his skin and tired eyes. I approached him warily, thankful for Riel's comforting presence not far behind.

"May I?" I reached for his hand and paused, seeking permission. He was reluctant, but gave it to me without complaint. His sickness was apparent, like a black rot spreading inside him. Now *this* was something in my wheelhouse. I reached for the *mana* flow to assist me.

The burst of warmth was sudden, thrilling, and didn't hurt in the slightest. Around me, the room appeared to flash gold.

The faun blinked in surprise, taking a breath that started out hesitant but deepened as he went. He repeated the breath and said something in a hopeful tone.

"Your eyes," Riel murmured, hovering beside me to examine my face.

Seersthri stepped forward to take the patient's hand, presumably to check my work. After a moment, her lips stretched wide in a half-grimace, half-smile.

"Well done," she praised, releasing his hand. She said something brief to the patient, and he settled back against the pillows in muted shock. Chattering all the way, Seersthri led Riel and me back to the main room.

"She's seen a mender's eyes glow like yours did only once before," Riel translated as we went. "It's an outward sign of the *mana* you're channeling. Normally, it's a slow draw, and there's a limit to how much you can direct into another body in a sitting. But it seems like you're pulling larger amounts faster than usual, and apparently without any ill effects."

"That's a good thing, yeah?" It was hard to tell with his matter-of-fact delivery.

"She's very impressed," Riel assured me, though he didn't look too happy about it. Seersthri had begun to pack up some items once more. "She wants to take you to see some of the other people they treat with chronic conditions. There are a few of them in the city."

Excitement surged at the prospect. It had been way too long since I was able to be useful. "Let's do it," I agreed eagerly. "Lead the way."

"You *died* yesterday," Riel reminded me in a low voice, putting a hand out to stop me when I started forward. "You should take things slow."

"I appreciate your concern, but I feel fine. Great, even. You're worrying too much."

Even as I told him so, the shadows in his eyes didn't retreat. *What's that about? Is he just concerned for me, or is there something more?*

He made a reluctant sound in his throat but accepted my words. I patted his hand in what I hoped was a reassuring way.

"I'll be careful," I promised. "I just want to be helpful. It's been a long time since I did anything to earn my keep."

"I hope you don't truly believe that you have to earn anything here."

Riel's distaste was apparent in his tone. I wasn't surprised that he didn't get it—he was the top of the food chain here. I'd had my share of luxuries, but I still understood there was a give-and-take at play.

"That's life, isn't it? Adult responsibilities and all that. I mean, it's different for you, but where I come from, we all have to do our part if we want to eat." With an indifferent shrug, I went to catch up to Seersthri. She waited by the door with her basket.

"Tell me if you need rest," she ordered as I approached. "We will walk."

"Sure. How many people are we going to see?" I asked politely.

Seersthri considered my question, gazing down at one clawed hand as she counted. "Hm. Five, six. If there is time."

"We're at your disposal," Riel said from behind me, sounding for the most part sincere. Seersthri's eyes twinkled, intrigued by the prospect of getting to use the prince for menial labor.

CHAPTER TWENTY-SIX
THE PATIENTS

IT WAS interesting to see the different styles of homes as we strolled through the residential areas. Many were not that different from what I'd grown up seeing in suburban neighborhoods, while others were entirely unfamiliar structures.

The first home we stopped at was modest, one or one-and-a-half stories, the size resembling a shack more than a house. The outside appeared to be a mud or stucco-type material, and it had bright yellow shutters. There was a small metal contraption just next to the door, which Seersthri fiddled with. It made a loud clanging sound to announce our presence.

The door opened, and a little face peeked out. At first, the boy began to smile, but then he saw me and Riel. Eyes widened to the size of dinner plates, and then the door slammed shut. Loud voices sounded inside. When the door opened again, a woman not much taller than my waist stood there. She greeted Seersthri and opened the door to invite us in, eyeing me with interest. As Seersthri and I made our way inside, Riel hovered by the door.

"I think I'll wait here," he said, examining the height of the door frame with a critical eye. "Just shout if you need me."

In response, Seersthri barked a short command, taking one

of the jars from her basket and reaching past me to hand the basket to the prince. He took it without complaint, the corner of his mouth twitching with humor. We shared a look as the door shut between us.

The house was cozy, if small. Everything was scaled down for an effect not unlike a child's playhouse. The residents were a mother and two sons. The first son, the one who had opened the door, stood by the kitchen table, while the mother had the younger boy perched on one hip. She began to speak, inviting us to the table.

Without Riel there, I had to rely on Seersthri for a translation. The mender wasn't inclined to help, however, holding a brief conversation with the mother without so much as glancing my way. I remained where I was with a polite smile on my face.

Eventually, Seersthri moved on to the topic at hand. "Pain and weakness," she said, nodding to the older boy. I blinked, taking a moment to catch up to the abrupt shift to business. "Rash. A fever that comes and goes." She approached the boy, who stepped forward and let her take his hand. After a moment, she nodded and released it, waving me over. "Try it."

I moved forward. The boy was slower to give me his hand, likely harboring concerns about this strange person he'd never seen before. I gave him a bright smile and crouched low in an effort to make myself as nonthreatening as possible.

"I'm Avery," I told him gently, giving his hand a light shake. "It's okay, I'm here to help. Let's see if we can't do something to make you feel a little better."

The mother chipped in, saying something to the boy in an encouraging tone. She had hope in her eyes, as if she knew exactly who I was and what I did. It had been a long time since I'd seen that look. Taking a slow, calming breath, I enclosed the boy's hand in mine and reached for my magic.

Like before, the *mana* responded eagerly. It was something I could get used to, having this amount of power just within reach. Adjusting my focus, I delved into the boy's presence, feeling for whatever inside him called for help. Like with the faun, it didn't take much effort. Whatever ailment he had was throughout his entire body.

My magic surged forward in an intense rush of warmth and light. I was beginning to realize the difference—before, it felt disconcerting, even painful. Now, I was one stop along the magic's path, directing it through me rather than from me.

The boy shivered, and I quickly let go of his hand, stepping back so that Seersthri could check my work. In the meantime, my excitement faded as my thoughts strayed to how things would change now. As soon as I returned, George and the others would be eager to work out a new healing schedule. I could be doing sessions every week… every day, even.

Seersthri withdrew from the boy and fixed me with an assessing look.

"The sickness is gone," she announced. As she relayed the news to his mother, I allowed myself to breathe a sigh of relief. Maybe now, I could put a dent in that never-ending crowd. My magic would no longer have to be a luxury for those who could afford to camp out at the White House all day long and were lucky enough to get to the front.

The boy's mother caught my attention as she approached. Before I could react, she had set her toddler on his feet and dropped to her knees on the ground before me, bending at the waist so that her forehead brushed against the dirt.

"Oh, no, that's not necessary," I hurried to say, casting a desperate look Seersthri's way. She observed the situation but said nothing, to my chagrin.

The mother didn't protest as I helped her get to her feet. Once standing, she met my eyes and said something I didn't understand, but that sounded serious.

"Ahh… she is happy," Seersthri supplied the translation after a moment's deliberation. "You are a gift from the Goddess. This home is honored."

"Not at all."

Embarrassed, I waved away her words. I couldn't help the smile that bloomed, though. Nothing came close to the feeling of being able to change someone's life for the better. Even if I was worked to the bone when I went back, it would be worth it.

On our way out, the boy I healed followed us to the door. He got a glimpse of Riel waiting on the other side and became shy all of a sudden—at least until his mother came up behind him to lay an encouraging hand on his shoulder. Then he blurted something out. It was all I could do to nod along and make an effort to appear engaged.

"He says that his parents attended our celebration the other day," Riel translated from behind me. "They mentioned seeing you there, but he never thought he'd get to meet the Goddess-blessed human." A smile tugged at the corner of his mouth. "From their description of you, he had imagined you taller."

"Oh!" I glanced down at myself with a frown. "Uh, sorry?"

The boy's mother tsked and shooed him away, but not before meeting my eyes once more and bobbing her head in thanks. I nodded back and let Seersthri sweep me outside.

The second and third times we stopped, things went equally well. I managed to set someone's gut health straight and do away with a growth that kept returning despite Seersthri's best efforts. Although I was grateful for the chance to practice using my powers properly, I began to flag on the way to the fourth patient. I intended to tough it out and thought I did a good job of hiding my exhaustion, but Riel must have been watching me.

"This is the last one," he announced, having been a quiet and supportive presence until then. He still had Seersthri's basket draped over one arm—she'd taken items out at each place we stopped, but I still wasn't sure what was inside. I would have thought that the jars of liquid were some kind of healing tea if not for the fact that we had magic for that.

Seersthri paused in the middle of the street and pulled an unattractive face.

"You feel pain?" she asked me. "Tired?"

"No pain. A little tired," I admitted reluctantly. "It's okay, though. We're almost done, right? I can keep going."

"We listen to bodies every day," Seersthri said with an exasperated sigh. "Listen to yours also. If the mender is sick, who heals?"

I expressed my understanding with a meek nod. It was easy to get caught up in the flow and not pay attention to how I was feeling, but all the walking and healing *was* exhausting.

"One more," she announced, striding onward with purpose. "Then, you rest."

Riel and I followed dutifully. At first, I thought that we were heading back to the clinic, but we took a detour at the last minute, instead stopping at a multi-story hive-like structure. It had numerous holes from top to bottom and side to side, and as we approached, something began to emerge from them. My lips parted in awe as I realized they were little ghoulishly pale people with multiple sets of iridescent wings—pixies, perhaps, for lack of the actual term.

From a larger hole near the base, another form appeared. This one was no taller than my knee and looked young except for the commanding way she held herself and the resting bitch face. Her lime-green hair lay flat along her head in a series of intricate braids, and she had on full-body chain-link armor and a face full of colorful war paint.

Seersthri strode forward to greet them. When I moved to join her, Riel stopped me.

"Careful," he murmured. "The *Aminkinya* are known to be aggressive to strangers. That one is the queen. Best to let Seersthri introduce you."

I had trouble seeing what danger the little fairies posed, but

I wasn't stupid enough to try my luck and potentially insult an entire people while I was at it, so I kept my distance.

When I heard what sounded like my name being spoken, I eased forward a few steps. "This is Naigatiy'ana," Seersthri said for my sake, seemingly unbothered by the fairy's attitude. "She is… ah… leader for the *Aminkinya*."

Riel stepped forward then, arms arranged in the formal fae greeting. The pixie queen's dark expression lightened. Her wings flicked, making a chirping sound, and dozens of the smaller fairies moved forward to line the ground before us, one arm raised straight in a salute. I swallowed down an awkward laugh and waited for Seersthri's guidance.

"Her wing"—Seersthri pointed—"was hurt during battle."

Sure enough, when I looked closely, I could see that while she had three wings on her left, she was missing half of the middle wing and almost the entire bottom wing on her right side.

"The injury is difficult." Seersthri shook her head to drive the point home. "We tried healing for many moon cycles. Still, she cannot fly. But, you try it."

I eased forward nervously, aware of Naina… Naigat… the fairy's expression and body language. A couple of the smaller ones fluttered their wings as I approached, but I couldn't tell if it was meant to be aggressive or friendly. The queen remained impassive as she gave me her hand. Since I'd never tried regrowing limbs before, I took my time.

Right off the bat, I noticed that her injury felt different from what I'd healed in the past. Although the urgent "wrongness" that came with terminal illnesses wasn't there, the injury to her wing gave off a sense of something missing, like her body yearned to be whole again.

When I opened my eyes, the scene before me was awash in a flood of gold. Frowning again, the fairy queen regarded me with interest, taking in my glowing eyes before shuddering as my magic swept through her. Several seconds passed in silence while I encouraged cells to multiply and flesh to knit together. Her wing began to twitch. It took longer than usual, and I kept having to draw more *mana,* but soon her wings were whole and symmetrical once more.

Drained, I let go of her hand and straightened only to stumble. Riel's arm shot out, wrapping around my middle and keeping me from falling. I looked up to thank him and winced at the disapproving glare I was met with. Wordlessly, he tugged me aside to make room for Seersthri and shifted his body so that I could lean on him if I needed to.

Seersthri stepped in to speak with the fairy queen, and I noticed that the rest of the fairies all eyed me with varying degrees of awe and alarm. They were used to magic, so was it because I was human? I tried not to feel self-conscious.

"You did well," Seersthri remarked, coming to my side. "She is pleased."

"I'm glad I could help," I said truthfully, watching as the little queen stretched out her wings to examine the areas I'd healed more closely. Satisfied, she folded them back and barked an order at one of her minions. The pixie retreated into the hive-like structure and emerged with a small glass vial with a chain.

I watched with interest as the queen drew a small knife from behind her back and deftly sliced off the end of one of her braids. She stuffed it into the vial and closed it, then flicked her hand to let it dangle in the air. The vial was thrust out toward me with a brief command.

"Wh-what is this?" I stammered, confused even as my hand reached out.

"She says the *Aminkinya* are in your debt," Riel murmured, nodding for me to take it. "It's a sort of… favor. They don't give them out lightly, so it would be rude to refuse."

No less confused, I accepted the item and gripped it to my chest. "Thank you."

Almost as one, the pixies turned to head back inside their nest home.

"I… guess that means we're dismissed?" I ventured after a moment's silence. Seersthri made a huffing sound and set off in the direction of the clinic. Riel and I exchanged a glance.

"Are you all right?" he asked.

"Oh, yeah." Embarrassed, I shook his hand off and stepped away. "You don't need to carry me again. I think I can make it back on my own. Thank you, though."

With a slow nod, as though he didn't quite believe me, Riel replied, "After you."

As I'd thought, the pixies' dwelling wasn't far from the clinic. When we made it back, Riel ordered me to wait by the door and went to find me a chair. I sat there with my hands in my lap, admiring the vial of green fairy hair that I was now the proud owner of, while Riel spoke with Seersthri in hushed tones. After several minutes, he came to get me.

"Ready to go?" he asked, offering me a hand.

"Yep. Everything good?" I slipped the chain around my neck and let him help me to my feet.

"Indeed." Riel held the door open for me to walk through. "Seersthri is very impressed with you. She says you are the most talented mender she's ever seen."

"Really?" I beamed, pleased with myself, and was surprised to find that when I stepped outside, the sky was already turning golden. I hadn't realized how late it was getting… *How long had it been since we last ate?* I dropped a hand to my stomach. Too long.

"Hungry?" Riel inquired.

"Ravenous," I admitted, patting my belly. "Do you think the proprietress will have the evening meal ready?"

"I'm sure she will. The main road is closer; would you like to stop by and see what food vendors there are? We can pick up something quick to settle your stomach."

"Oh, that's fine, I can wait. I'd rather be back in our room anyway. I'm pretty tired." As if to back me up, a yawn escaped me. Riel chuckled.

"Let's get you back, then," he said, affection lacing his tone.

The walk back to our hotel was only about fifteen minutes, but I felt every minute of it. *Maybe I should have taken it easy,* I thought, wincing as we made our way up the front steps. The invincible feeling from that morning was gone, replaced by fatigue and dizziness once again. *Oh, well. A meal and a good night's sleep ought to set me straight.*

Riel sent me up to our room while he hunted for food. The room was just as we left it—bed made, Oyanni's harness on the floor by the door, our bags tucked under the bed. I pulled off my cloak and deposited it on a chair, then went to the window to close the curtains.

The room went dark.

"Oh, geez," I muttered, fumbling around to open them again. I'd forgotten that our only source of light besides sunlight was Riel's magic. *Though... Now that my eyes glowed when I channeled* mana, *could my eyes work as flashlights?* That would be something to test out at a later date.

My train of thought was interrupted when Riel returned with dinner. Closing the door behind himself, he set the tray on his bedside table and bent to remove his shoes. I hastened to take mine off as well. Since I was already on my side of the bed, I stowed my shoes and went rummaging through my bag for some pajamas to change into. Once I had my clothes in hand, I caught Riel's attention with a little wave.

"I'm just going to"—I made a broad gesture in the direction of the bathroom—"right quick. Feel free to eat without me."

"Take your time," he insisted. "Your food will wait for you."

Without further ado, I ducked into the bathroom, pulling the screen into place so that I had privacy to use the toilet, change, and brush my teeth. I debated leaving my bra on but decided against it. My boobs weren't terribly large, and I didn't feel like sleeping in the restricting garment. It wasn't like my PJs were particularly sexy either—just a matching T-shirt and shorts set with stars on them. Surely, Riel wouldn't even notice.

When I emerged from the bathroom, the curtains were closed, and the room was lit with the blue glow of Riel's magic emanating from the *mana* lantern. He sat on his side of the bed, his bag open at his feet and a book in his hands. The tray of food sat in the middle of the bed, my portion untouched. I padded over to it, stomach growling in anticipation.

As I drew near the bed, the thought occurred to me that I would not be alone in it tonight. I cast a sidelong glance at Riel, who had his back to me. *Would he try something? Did he expect anything?* We finally had the privacy and time to ourselves that we'd been missing. *Was the prospect of getting cozy with him exciting or nerve-racking?* A little of both, I decided.

As if hearing my thoughts, Riel twisted around to regard me. I almost jumped. "Everything all right?" he asked, studying my expression for signs of concern.

"Everything's fine," I said quickly, dumping my daytime clothes on top of my suitcase. "No problem. It's just that I don't usually share a bed with someone else, that's all."

"We slept in the same bed last night," Riel reminded me.

I frowned, thinking back. "Well… that was different. I wasn't all there."

"You don't have to worry." Riel settled back on the bed and lifted his book. "It's been a long day, and you need your rest. Eat and get some sleep. I won't try anything."

Eyeing the fae prince with suspicion, I began to say, "You don't…" and paused. *Had I really been about to ask if he had mind-reading powers? Could I be any more obvious?* "Okaaaay," I said instead, drawing the word out as I climbed into bed and tugged the tray toward me. "Thanks. Good to know. Glad we're on the same page."

Riel didn't respond, but I kept watching him out of the corner of my eye. When my stomach growled again, I turned my focus to the food in front of me. For the next few minutes, my chewing and Riel's periodic page-turning were the only sounds in the room. When I finished, I stood with the tray in my hands.

"You can leave it in the hall," Riel told me, breaking the silence.

"Oh, okay, thanks."

I put the tray outside and returned to the bed, a yawn coming on as I climbed back in and got comfortable. While I fluffed up my pillow, I snuck another peek at Riel. He was such a picture of elegance, lying there on top of the covers with not a care in the world, his book in one hand and his legs crossed at the ankles. If he put the book down and closed his eyes, he'd give Sleeping Beauty a run for her money.

Sensing my gaze, his eyes slid sideways and locked with mine. In the dim light, they looked almost as dark as his brother's. I didn't know if I'd ever seen eyes as blue as theirs on a human. People would kill for eyes like those... Not to mention that perfect skin. And the height, the physique, the bone structure...

"Would you like a goodnight kiss?"

"Huh?"

Shit, I was staring. Blinking myself back to the present, I slammed my pillow down and threw myself down on top of it. "No, I don't need a goodnight kiss," I asserted into the pillow with more force than was necessary. I waited a second before adjusting my position so that I could breathe, but that made it so that I was face to face with Riel again. He gazed down at me, lips curved as though he were looking at something particularly amusing.

I second-guessed myself. *Why did I need to turn down a goodnight kiss?* After all, it was just the two of us. We were safe from prying eyes here, and we were technically dating, weren't we?

There wasn't anything for me to be afraid of. Hell, we could go all the way if we wanted. If he had his ears and his nipples pierced, maybe he had other places pierced too, like…

My eyes betrayed me by glancing downward, and I could hear my blood rushing in both ears. When I looked back up, Riel's grin had transitioned to something that bordered on predatory. Of course, he hadn't missed it.

"I… you could… maybe just a little one."

The invitation had barely been audible, but that was enough for someone with fae hearing.

The book in Riel's hand closed with a *snap*. As he reached to place it on the nightstand, I drew the blankets to my chin in hopes of finding some courage underneath. The bed was huge, but Riel made it feel small with the way he closed the space between us. When he leaned over me, memories of the night of the party flashed before my eyes. Namely, the feeling of his skin against mine, the heat of his mouth on my breasts, and the way I'd shamelessly brought myself to completion by grinding against his leg.

My breath caught in my throat as a foot of empty space became eight inches, then six, then three. All I could see was those expressive blue eyes and those soft, perfect lips coming closer and closer until finally…

"Sleep well, *eseri*."

He placed a light, chaste kiss on my forehead.

It was exactly what I asked for, the amicable part of me reasoned as he gave me a sweet, self-satisfied smile, turned over, and picked up his book once more. The rest of me couldn't help but feel cheated, so I glared daggers at his profile until I succumbed to sleep.

CHAPTER TWENTY-SEVEN

THE POINT OF NO RETURN

SINCE WE WERE in no hurry to head back to the castle, we decided to spend one more day in the city. I wanted to take the opportunity to learn as much as I could, so we returned to Seersthri's clinic. Riel and Seersthri both forbade me from helping, which was fine, since the menders had everything under control.

Just by observing the other healers at work, I was able to pick up a few fun facts. For example, most healers found external, physical injuries easier to mend than internal ones or illnesses. Apparently, the process was considered to be more straightforward. Some more serious cases required multiple sessions, like the people I'd helped the day before.

Also, healing usually took longer than it felt like. Sometimes, the healers would sit still for several minutes as they worked on a patient. When I asked Seersthri if that was normal, she told me that the same thing had happened when I healed the pixie queen. That came as a surprise to me, since it had only felt like a few seconds on my end. Riel explained that I was already faster than most when it came to channeling *mana*, and with practice, I'd probably be able to improve even more. The thought thrilled me.

Seersthri also explained, with some help from Riel, that mending magic couldn't always help someone who is born with a condition, because sometimes there was technically nothing to be fixed. Thinking back, I couldn't remember if I had ever tried to heal someone with a congenital disorder. I wasn't privy to my patients' medical history, but to the best of my knowledge, most of the people who came to me had some kind of terminal illness, cancer being chief among them.

In addition to the specifics of mending, being in the clinic gave me the opportunity to ask questions about aspects of fae culture. What I found out was incredibly confusing.

A majority of Miderrum's residents appeared to be the same race as Riel and his family, but the way I understood it, that didn't automatically mean they were *Ishameti*. Rather than a single race, the *Ishameti* were more a social group made up of people from various backgrounds who were united under Riel's family and lived in harmony through a shared culture, which included a common religion and language.

As if that wasn't enough, while Riel's family did have some kind of blood claim to their position, it was a bit more complex than that. This side of The Rift was separated into twelve distinct countries, each known by the name of their "leading family," or royal house. Riel's immediate family wasn't all of House Wysalar, and other members were spread throughout the country with their own smaller territories.

Thankfully, Riel was patient with me while I digested all of this.

He and I joined Seersthri and the other menders for their late morning meal, where we also took the time to say our goodbyes. Afterward, we spent the afternoon touring Main Street, and Riel insisted I get a few souvenirs. Despite my protests, he helped me pick out a pretty vest with delicate silver details for Chris and a ceremonial knife for Devon. After multiple assurances that money was no object, I also tentatively selected hair ornaments for Vivian and my stylist and a hand-bound journal for George.

I was learning that just because magic existed didn't mean that there was a magic solution for everything, and although most people could use magic, not everyone could use it to the same degree. As a result, everyone here had jobs just like anywhere else, and the economy was built on a system that relied on both money and trading skills or products.

By the time we returned to our room in the boarding house, my head spun from all the new information. As soon as I entered, I untied my cloak, let it fall to the ground, and collapsed on the bed with a long, weary sigh.

"I guess this kind of thing is obvious for most people," I said into the duvet, "but it's so crazy how different other parts of the world are. It's like, the more I see, the more I realize I've seen so little, and the more I learn, the more I realize I don't really know anything."

"Ah, my *eseri* is becoming educated," Riel commented in a teasing tone as he crossed the room. "Be careful not to give it too much thought. Your little human brain might pop like a *kainna* that's had too much nectar."

"Hey!" I made a face and sat up, supporting myself on my elbows. "We don't all have stupidly long lives and the means to travel freely. Good for you that you can cram your old man brain with all this knowledge. Assuming you also have a brain, and not, I don't know, a network of little ants crawling through your body to deliver information."

"Yes, I also have a brain." Riel's amused reply came from the direction of the bathroom, along with the sound of running water. He emerged from behind the screen with the first few buttons on his shirt undone and the sleeves folded back. "I'm preparing a bath," he stated. "If you would like to bathe as well, you're welcome to go first."

"Oh, thank you, but you can go ahead. I'll wait," I responded absently.

The glimpse of bare chest and sculpted forearms caught my attention. I attempted to avert my eyes, but they made a roundabout journey to end up right back where they started.

"Or, maybe you'd like to share."

I heard the words, but it took a moment for them to register. "Pardon?"

Riel gave me a patient smile, but something besides patience simmered behind his eyes. "The bath has plenty of space for two. Of course, only if you would be comfortable."

My brain short-circuited, producing an image of Riel and a few artfully arranged bubbles that I would never admit to seeing, not even under torture, but would be sure to file away for later. I took a deep breath before responding, taking the extra seconds to consider my options. I wasn't stupid—if we got into a bath naked together, things would go further than that. And… I wanted that. I wanted this with him.

This is it, I told myself. *The point of no return.*

"Sure," I whispered. Cleared my throat. "Sure," I repeated, my voice a little stronger. "Yeah. Save water and all that."

But when I got up and locked eyes with Riel, the length of the room felt insurmountable. Flustered, I bought another moment by leaning against the bedpost to remove my shoes. As the second shoe hit the floor, I straightened up and made my way to where Riel waited by the privacy screen.

"You can change your mind at any time," he said when I came to a stop in front of him.

"I know," I responded quietly, my hands going to the hem of my blouse. I drew it over my head and let it drop to the floor. My pants followed with a bit less grace. Standing before him in my underwear, I exhaled slowly, willing my anxiety to leave my body in the same breath. Riel made no comment, but his hands came up to unfasten the remaining buttons on his shirt.

The garment joined my clothes on the floor. The sound of the bath filling behind him pounded in my ears, an exhilarating rush of noise that blended with my quickening pulse. When his hands went to the ties of his pants, I reached out to stop him.

"Let me do it." The words tumbled out.

Riel paused and let his hands fall to his sides. "So be it."

A little awkwardly, I settled on my knees in front of him. As I started undressing him, a thought occurred to me. "Um…" I tried to think of the best way to say it. "So, I know you look pretty human, but… should I prepare for any… that is, your, um… it's not weird, is it?"

"How so?" His brows furrowed.

"Like, your… penis, you can wiggle it independently, or it has scales or something?"

"Nothing like that."

His voice came out strained. I glanced up to see that he struggled to hold back laughter, and my cheeks flushed pink. Well, so much for trying not to be self-conscious. With a determined nod, I tackled the ties of his pants with renewed enthusiasm.

"Unless the second one counts," he amended.

My hands fumbled with the string, causing it to slip from my fingers.

"Just kidding." Riel gave me a cheeky wink.

I released an exasperated huff of breath and hid a smile. With a shake of my head, I finished undoing the laces and slipped my fingers into the waistband. The fabric came down inch by inch, revealing pale, creamy flesh. This close, I could make out a light dusting of fair hair that started under his belly button and showed no signs of faltering on the way down. I also couldn't help but notice the sizable lump that formed in my line of sight.

Swallowing my nerves, I let go, allowing his pants to fall the rest of the way.

I wasn't sure if I was disappointed or relieved to see that there were, in fact, no piercings along the length or head of his sex. I was glad to see that there was nothing out of the ordinary about it, at least not that I noticed. It wasn't weirdly shaped or unmanageably large, and it was framed by trimmed honey-blond hair. It was a handsome example of male anatomy that, under my scrutinizing gaze, was rapidly reaching its full potential.

I got to my feet before I did something weird, like compliment him on his penis.

"May I?" Riel asked in a low voice, extending a hand. I felt his fingers graze against the band of my bra and nodded my permission. He reached around me to feel for the clasp. The seconds dragged on until I reached back to help. When the elastic gave, I slipped my arms out and let the garment fall. My underwear joined the growing pile of clothing at our feet.

It didn't feel as weird as I thought it would to be naked before a man. I supposed it helped that he was naked, too. It was impossible not to feel at least a little self-conscious—all the fae I'd seen were pretty much perfect, after all. *Could he see the ingrown hairs along my bikini line from his vantage point? What did he think of the freckles that covered most of my body? He'd already seen my breasts, but... were they too small? Too big? Was he a boob or an ass guy?*

Riel's expression didn't reveal much as we studied each other, but I appreciated having the chance to look my fill regardless. Eventually, I forced my gaze past him, to where water still gushed into the massive tub in the middle of the room.

"The bath is probably getting full," I whispered.

Blinking as if coming out of a daze, Riel pivoted on his heel and went to investigate. I followed, taking the opportunity to admire his backside as it moved away from me. It was shapely, toned almost to a fault, and followed by muscular thighs and calves that flexed with power as he walked.

The Goddess must really like me after all.

The bath was about three-quarters full, even with the time we'd spent getting each other naked. Riel leaned over with a little bottle in his hand to add something to the water, and the air filled with the fresh and crisp scent I always associated with him. I breathed it in with a sigh of pleasure. Straightening, Riel met my eyes before giving my body a languid, head-to-toe sweep. My toes curled into the floor as I resisted the urge to cover myself.

"You can get in now, if you like," he offered, putting the bottle of bath oil down.

I approached the tub and dipped a hand in to test the temperature. It was sufficiently warm, though not quite as hot as I usually liked it. Riel helped me in, and I settled into the contoured groove against one side, submerged up to my breasts in the water.

He kneeled by the edge of the bath and hovered over me, his hands coming around to start kneading the tension from my shoulders and neck with slow and steady pressure.

"Ohh, that's nice," I moaned, closing my eyes and letting my head fall back. I basked in the attention, especially as he ran shampoo through my hair and began massaging my scalp. His nails scraped along my hairline with aching gentleness, his fingertips melting away any dirt and oil along with the hot water. He drew away, and I dipped my head to rinse.

"Don't you want to get in, too?" I asked, angling my body toward Riel as I wiped water from my face with both hands. He responded by leaning in to skim the line of my neck with his lips. I shivered at the light contact, goosebumps breaking out across my arms.

"I'm just savoring the moment," he told me, taking one of my hands from the water and brushing his lips against the side of my wrist. He kept going, visiting each finger on my left hand before returning to my shoulder to place a lingering kiss there.

"The water's going to get cold," I pointed out, my voice coming out a bit breathless.

With a knowing chuckle, Riel released my arm and climbed

in beside me. I kept my gaze directed at the water before me rather than helping myself to another eyeful of his manhood.

"I'll do your hair too," I offered, turning to examine the bottles lined up by the tub.

"You can use the oil."

He pointed to the same bottle he'd used for the water.

I grabbed it and poured a modest amount into my hands, breathing in the scent once more. As I massaged it into his scalp, I couldn't help but appreciate the silkiness of his hair.

"Your hair is so beautiful," I marveled, unable to keep the envy from my tone as I admired the way the strands slipped through my fingers. How every single one of the long-haired fae managed to avoid frizz and split ends was a mystery to me, but I supposed it was just proof that they were chosen by the Goddess. *That or the magic bath oil.*

We both rinsed for a final time in the scented water. I got out first, going for one of the folded linens by the bath. As I wrapped it around myself, I felt a presence at my back, and the next thing I knew, I was being swept off my feet—literally.

"What—" I trailed off in a squeal as I found myself held against a very wet, very firm male body. Riel crossed the room in a few long strides and deposited me onto his side of the bed, caging me in with his arms. I froze underneath him like a deer in headlights, clutching my towel to my chest and blinking up at him with wide eyes.

Without breaking eye contact, he eased backward to stand in front of my bare legs, and his hands came down to settle on my knees. Every line of his body was tense, yet he still hesitated there, perhaps knowing that there was no going back once this line was crossed. I appreciated the courtesy of giving me a moment, but I'd already made my decision a long time ago. I forced my body to relax against the bed.

"Please," I said simply, shaking off the towel to bare myself to him. My permission was all Riel needed. As his body lowered to kneel before me, my core clenched in anticipation.

The moment his mouth made contact with my skin, sensations traveled up my spine like a bolt of lightning. Rather than going straight for the prize, he took his time, starting at my inner thigh and lining a path to my pubic mound with sensual, open-mouthed kisses.

When he finally got to my clit, he drew a lazy circle around that sensitive nub with his dexterous tongue. My hands scrambled for something to ground me, finding only rough linen and silky duvet. Riel responded to my reaction with a pleased grunt and repeated the motion, testing the waters with a little more pressure. My hips shifted in encouragement. Somehow, he knew exactly what I asked for. A stifled moan escaped me as he licked, nipped, and suckled flesh that grew increasingly sensitive under his careful ministrations.

Once he found a technique he was happy with, Riel surprised me by hefting my thighs over his shoulders and pulling me all the way to the edge of the bed. Having put me where he wanted me, he settled in and found a rhythm. I let myself fall back and relax, closing my eyes to lose myself in the sensations I was feeling—the cold air against my peaked nipples, the warmth of his hands squeezing my flesh, his wet hair tickling my inner thighs. I wanted to provide direction, but all I could manage was a series of breathless noises.

The lack of a verbal response didn't faze the prince. He feasted on me with a single-minded dedication, neither slowing nor rushing. At some point, my legs tensed around his head, and my fingers tangled themselves in his hair for better control. His hands tightened where they gripped my thighs, but he made no protest. Emboldened, I became more daring, shifting my hips upward to grind against his face. He let me, waiting patiently as I found the right spot and demonstrated the ideal level of pressure.

When the movement of my hips faltered, he didn't hesitate, taking over the proper rhythm with renewed enthusiasm. After a few more minutes of that, I could no longer draw in enough oxygen. A sound that vaguely resembled his name escaped me, along with a string of pleading words even I didn't recognize. I was scarcely lucid enough to realize that something wonderful was near. His talented tongue, better than any toy, continued its hot, slick, and insistent worship of my clit.

Then, all at once, the tension crested and snapped in a flurry of slickness and heat, and I was done for. My head went back, mouth open in a soundless cry as fireworks burst in every synapse. Riel gripped me closer to ride out my orgasm, his tongue demanding every bit of my pleasure. My legs started shaking of their own accord, but he didn't stop until my trembling ceased and I sagged against the bed. It took me several moments before I could collect my thoughts enough to manage words again.

"Fuck," I whispered.

"That comes next," Riel responded with a mischievous twinkle in his eye, rising to his feet. His tongue flicked out to taste what was left of me on his lips. Captivated by the motion, I jumped a little when I felt fingers graze against my entrance. He set his thumb against my still-tender clit with a light touch as he tested my wetness with two of his fingers. Almost immediately, they found a spot that had me shuddering in pleasure, and the muscles in my lower abdomen clenched in anticipation of round two.

"So responsive," he murmured, transfixed by what lay between my legs. Despite being completely naked and spread open before him, I couldn't bring myself to feel embarrassed. He dragged his eyes up to meet mine and the heat in his gaze was stunning.

"Goddess, you're perfect," he said, his tone reverent. *That* did cause my cheeks to warm. He cocked his head as he took in my naked form from head to toe.

When Riel made no move to continue, I grew concerned. "What is it? Everything okay?"

"Everything is much, much more than okay, *eseri*," he said, reaching out a hand to stop me as I started to get up. "Just trying to decide how I want you."

He gave me another leisurely once-over before making up his mind. He delivered his demand in a voice like a sensual purr: "Turn over, my beautiful Avery."

Heart pounding in my ears, I moved my hands underneath me to carry out the request. I turned onto my hands and knees, facing the head of the bed, and felt Riel's warmth as he leaned over me, his fingers trailing down my arm. He picked up my hand and placed it on the headboard.

"Hold on," he murmured, his low voice eliciting a shiver from me as it caressed my ear. I obediently brought my other hand up to grip the headboard alongside the first.

When he drew away, I opened my mouth to protest. But it only took a moment before his weight settled on the bed behind me, and he began trailing sensual, unhurried kisses down the length of my spine. By the time he'd made it to my tailbone, my back was arching up to meet him. I felt his fingers testing my entrance again. I didn't need to tell him I was ready—I was pretty sure I'd never been this wet in my entire life.

As I felt the tip of him tease my sex, I held my breath and squeezed my eyes shut, expecting him to invade me with one thrust. But Riel surprised me by taking his time yet again, easing just the tip inside before withdrawing and repeating the process to coat his length in my wetness. On his third or fourth repetition, he finally moved forward all the way, sinking into me with a harsh exhale. My inner walls fluttered around him, adjusting to the intrusion.

Without further delay, his hands gripped my hips almost to the point of pain, and he began to thrust into me with a punishing intensity. I gripped the headboard for dear life.

"A little... softer," I gasped, barely able to form a coherent thought in between harsh strokes. His hips slowed, which also allowed for his thrusts to become deeper, so that I could feel every inch of him and the delicious friction that came with it. I made a sound of approval somewhere between a gasp and a moan. A pleasant ache deep inside came and went each time he bottomed out, and my muscles squeezed like a vise, not wanting to let him go.

"Isha," Riel hissed. "Just like that. Ahh, *eseri,* you feel *magnificent."*

A string of fae words fell from his lips, spoken with a mix of reverence and desperation. Warmth bloomed in my chest—although I didn't know what the words meant, I could hear the affection in them. I was glad to know that this was more than just sex for both of us.

Riel bent over me then, bringing one hand up to grasp the nape of my neck and angling his hips ever-so-slightly. With the adjustment, he ground against my G-spot on every instroke. My body arched into him automatically, craving more contact, more pressure, just *more.* Skin against skin wasn't enough—I needed us to be soul to soul.

"Ohh, yes," I breathed, the words on the edge of a whine. One of my hands lifted off the headboard and started to reach back as if intending to pull him deeper inside me. I caught myself and returned it to its spot with difficulty.

"More, please. Please, more," I begged.

Without saying a word, he responded to my pleas, picking up a harsher rhythm once more. The man moved like a machine, all strength and efficiency. This time, I met his intensity as best I could. Our movements began to blend together so that all I knew was pressure, friction, heat, and pleasure. The room filled with our combined breaths, grunts, and moans, along with the indecent sounds of skin slicked with sweat and other fluids.

"So good. So good," I bit out, on the verge of babbling incoherently as I started to feel a second orgasm approaching. I let go of the headboard to roll a nipple between my fingers, desperate for the thing that would push me over the edge.

But before I could reach the pinnacle I climbed toward, Riel halted and withdrew from me. I keened over the loss, my body bowing forward.

"Why?" I practically shrieked, whirling on him. Without missing a beat, his hands came up to caress my arms and ease me down against the pillows.

"My sweet Avery," Riel crooned—only mildly breathless, damn him. "Have faith. I won't leave you wanting."

Motion drew my gaze to where he fisted his cock in his hand and my eyes widened. With his other hand, he pulled one of my legs to the side to give himself access. He entered me again with a rough thrust, greeting the deepest parts of me. Anything I might have said dissolved into a hiss and a groan as the sensation rippled through my core.

"God, fuck," I managed, frantically scrabbling for his arm, for the blankets, for anything to hold onto. I was forced to settle for raising my hands to the headboard again, and Riel took the opportunity to clutch my hip bone for better leverage. The heat from his hand was scorching.

"I'm sorry," Riel panted, not sounding sorry in the slightest, "but I wanted to see your face."

He softened the rocking of his hips to lean forward and take my chin with his other hand. Tilting my head ever-so-gently upward, he scanned my face before going in for a kiss. I threaded my fingers in his hair and let myself relax into his touch. His tongue met mine briefly before he nipped my bottom lip and began making his way down the side of my neck.

As his breath warmed the curve where my shoulder began, a full-body shudder rocked through me. "You... like doing stuff with your mouth, huh?" I mused absently, closing my eyes and angling my head back to give him better access.

"How do you feel about teeth?" came the response, muffled against my shoulder in between alternating kisses and nips. My eyes popped open in surprise.

"Do it," I said quickly, breathlessly.

Riel bit down, the motion of his hips stuttering as he did.

His teeth were sharper than I had expected, but I didn't mind the pressure and the pinch. In fact, something about the animalistic nature of the action did it for me. I gasped, clutching him closer to me with one hand and snaking the other in between our bodies to seek out my clit.

Riel soothed the spot he'd bitten with his tongue, leaving an echo of an ache behind. To my delight, he wasn't done. He went to another spot and repeated the action, making a desperate sound against my flesh, as if his instincts were telling him that he needed to be deeper inside me. I found myself strangely tempted to bite him back.

My eyelids fluttered closed, and I distracted myself by focusing on the sensations—the pleasurable pain of his bite, the heat of his body above mine, the weight of him between my legs, the length of him inside me. I rubbed my clit faster and canted my hips upward in demand.

Drawing back, Riel gave me what I was pleading for, returning his hands to my hip and leg and picking up the pace. He met my gaze and held it, and I watched with fascination as the color of his irises seemed to swirl and ripple like ink in water. He was truly a beautiful creature, even more so with his skin glowing from the barest sheen of sweat. But the thought struck me then that he was as much something else as he was a man.

"I'm going to come," I gasped as the realization of how close I was hit me with the force of a truck.

"That's my girl," Riel murmured, still holding my gaze. "Come for me, *eseri*."

Before he'd finished speaking the words, I was coming apart underneath him. I cried out in abandon as the pleasure crested, and he closed his mouth over mine, swallowing the sound. I made another sound that may have been a moan, may have been a sob, and squirmed against him in an attempt to magnify the aftershocks and wring out every last ounce of pleasure.

Riel broke off the kiss and made a similar sound. I felt him twitch inside me like a second heartbeat as he came, bathing my insides in warmth. We stayed there for a while longer, holding onto each other to catch our breaths and bask in the afterglow. Sweat plastered my hair to the back of my neck, but I couldn't summon the energy to care.

The moment was ruined when I felt the barest trickle of something down below, drawing my attention to more practical matters. Reluctantly, I sat up and began to untangle myself from Riel, nodding toward the bathroom with an apologetic smile. "Sorry, I just need to…"

"Of course." He moved aside to let me go.

I slid off the bed to do my business. Legs still weak from two fantastic, consecutive orgasms, I stumbled a bit. Riel jumped up to help me, but I waved him away. Flushing with embarrassment, I hurried to the bathroom to wash up.

When I returned, he waited for me in bed, reclining with the blankets pulled up to his waist. I ducked my head, hesitant to meet his eyes as I climbed in under the covers beside him. He lifted the blanket in invitation and I eagerly snuggled up to him.

Our bodies fit together like they were made for each other. Although I tried not to take it as some kind of sign, I hummed in pleasure and closed my eyes to savor the feeling. I was safe, warm, and surrounded by my lover. Nothing could be more perfect.

CHAPTER TWENTY-EIGHT
THE PROMISE

FAINT RAYS of dawn filtering into the room signaled that it was morning.

At first, I didn't remember where I was, but that didn't bother me. The bed was soft, and I was warm. Too warm, actually. I kicked my feet until they met air.

Much better.

Then I remembered. I shot up, the blankets falling away to reveal my naked body. Next to me lay Riel, the sight of his sleeping form making my heart melt. I softened as I took in his peaceful face, captivated by the way the sunlight through the curtains transformed his sleep-ruffled hair into strands of gold. The scent of his bath oil tickled my nose. *Would I always associate that sunny, lemon-grassy smell with sex now?*

"Like what you see?"

Riel's sleep-roughened voice brought me out of my daydream. His eyes were now open. "I know I do," he murmured, his eyes raking shamelessly over my exposed front.

Clicking my tongue in reproach, I settled back against his side and pulled the sheets up over my chest. His heartbeat thrummed under my cheek, a reminder that despite coming from two different worlds, we weren't all that different.

"Did I hurt you?" Riel frowned down at the junction of my shoulder and neck. Confused at first, I raised a hand to feel the spot he was looking at and realized that he was talking about the bites. *Is there a bruise?* I couldn't even feel them anymore.

"Oh, no," I assured him. "It was hot."

Riel responded with a stunning smile, which I returned. I snuggled up to him once more, tracing the line of his pectoral muscle with one finger. God, he was just so *firm*. I tried to think if I'd ever felt a man's chest before. *Is everyone built like that under their clothes? Certainly not.* Then again, I hadn't had much experience with the male form in real life.

After a moment, I ventured to ask, "Is... is it always like that?"

"Is what?"

"You know." For some ridiculous reason, I still hesitated to say it aloud. "Sex."

"Oh, no. I'm particularly talented."

I rolled my eyes with a soft snort. "Yeah, okay."

Riel was quiet. Then... "You... haven't had sex before? Hadn't, before last night?"

"Don't make it weird," I warned him. "No, I hadn't. But it's not a big deal."

"Perhaps not," he agreed. He fell silent for another moment before adding, "Thank you."

"Huh?" I blinked up at him. "For what, my virginity?"

"For you," he said simply, sliding an arm under my neck. I squeaked as he pulled me close. "You took a chance in crossing The Rift. You treated me with respect from the beginning. You worked hard during your training and never complained. Well, not that much."

The amendment made me frown.

"Now, you've opened your heart to me," he continued, his thumb stroking back and forth over my shoulder blade. "I'm honored by your trust. More than you know."

It was my turn to fall silent. My sinuses burned, and I

blinked back tears. *This is relief I'm feeling. Relief and joy.* I was where I belonged. Here, beyond The Rift, where not only were there no expectations put upon me, but there was someone who cared about me.

Is it okay to feel this way? Do I deserve to be this happy?

When I sniffled, Riel glanced down in alarm.

"I'm okay," I said before he could inquire. "I'm just happy. And scared," I admitted as a horrifying thought occurred to me. I burrowed into his chest to hide my face, and his arms tightened around me to provide reassurance.

"I don't want to go back," I whispered, my voice wavering with emotion. "They expect me to go back, but... I don't want to leave. I can't." While I didn't specify, I knew that he knew what I meant—it was him I couldn't bear to leave. How could I? They'd expect me to return to the White House and go back to work like nothing changed... when everything had changed. I couldn't live like that anymore, not the person I was now. And not without him.

Riel's stoic silence only made my fear intensify. My hands trembled. *What am I doing, getting caught up in these feelings?* He had a responsibility to his people too. Even more than I did, since he was one of their leaders. *What if he told me I had to leave? Could I bear it? What if I misunderstood his speech at the ball, and he only ever intended for this to be a fling?* Oh, God. *Did I just mess everything up?*

"Before you say anything," I blurted, pulling away from him. "I-I think we should just be open with each other. Communication is always best, right? Whether between friends or between l-lovers. Even if something might be hard to say, or hard to hear, it's better not to keep secrets. A-and I have to tell you something. I mean, I *want* to tell you something."

I risked a glance in Riel's direction. His expression remained impassive, but his hand fell to my arm to give it an encouraging squeeze. I reached around and held on, using his touch to ground myself as I thought back to memories that I'd buried long ago. My eyes closed.

"I had a friend once. When I was fourteen, they brought another girl to live with me at the White House. Marcia. She was another Golden Child—one of the kids born with magic. She didn't like to talk about what she went through before they rescued her, so I'm not sure what her story was like… but anyway, we were really different. Like, total opposites. She was outgoing, brave, confident, independent… everything I wasn't."

I pictured her behind my eyelids—a girl a little shorter than me, with long dark hair and bronze skin. There was a huge smile on her face, the way I always remembered her. The memory made my heart compress painfully in my chest.

"She didn't give a shit what anybody else thought," I said, my voice quivering. "Just was herself. I loved that. I was shy and a pushover. She taught me to stand up for myself and use my voice. I wanted to be like her. Even her powers were cool. She could change her features however she wanted, even things like growing fur or changing the length of her limbs. Turn herself into someone or something else with a single thought."

"Changing magic," Riel mused.

"Yeah… I guess so. I just envied that… that it was really hers, whereas mine felt like it belonged to everybody but me." Shame made my eyes fill with tears. "I shouldn't have been jealous; we were treated so well. We had basically anything we wanted—clothes, makeup, games, books, everything. We had private tutors, so we didn't have to go to school. All that, and there were just a few rules we were supposed to follow. It should have been easy.

"But… we were kids." Through the tears, I implored him to understand. "Just dumb kids. They told us we couldn't leave the White House grounds, no matter what. We had to stay behind the fence. They just didn't want anything to happen to us, I know that now. But at the time, we thought it was a stupid rule that they made up to keep us under their thumbs, you know? So, one day, we decided to sneak out."

I steeled myself with a deep breath and forged on. "We were sixteen. Marcia disguised herself as George, which got us past the guards. She had grand plans to hitch a ride to the Capital One Arena to see some pop star in concert… I forget who, but it doesn't matter. It could have been fine. The only problem was, I couldn't change my face like she could."

The words came out bitter. My hand tightened around Riel's.

"I remember following her through a crowd and losing sight of her. Before I could find her again, someone grabbed me from behind. They knew who I was. I was so startled that I didn't even fight, just let myself be pulled into some sketchy store. I don't remember their faces, I was just so confused. When I finally found my voice, I begged them to let me go. I told them I had a friend who was looking for me, but they just laughed at me. And then…

"Then they tossed me in the storage cellar, and they left me there." As I said it, my imagination kicked in with a vengeance, like it always did when I thought back to that place. It was dark, the air was musty, and the walls and ground were cold and hard. The only light I had came through the gap underneath the door at the top of the rickety, old stairs. Blinking rapidly to chase away the memories, I forced myself to continue.

"They posted that they were holding me for ransom on fucking dark web Craigslist. The Secret Service found me in four days. I was down there just four days, but it felt like a lifetime. I was afraid to even leave my room for a while after that. I thought everyone was out to get me—the servants, the sick people outside the gates, even my bodyguard at the time."

Unsurprisingly, silence followed my admission.

When Riel still didn't say anything, my gut churned in discomfort. I tried to ease the tension with an awkward laugh. "All this is to say… well, you can see why there hasn't been much opportunity to date before now. Not that that's relevant. But… since coming here, I feel like I can breathe again. I don't feel trapped or afraid every second. I don't feel like… like I have to be good, or the bogeyman will get me. It's stupid, I know, but this place… and you, it's changed everything. I can't go back and lose this. I *won't." I won't lose another person who's important to me,* I added quietly, not yet ready to say that part aloud.

I fell silent again. My hand still gripped Riel's. I let it go limp so that he could pull away if he wanted. *If this is more than what he wants from me—if he'd rather leave things here, I'll—*

"Avery."

I hadn't realized that I'd closed my eyes. When I opened them, it was to see that Riel's expression had taken on a brutal intensity, all traces of his usual humor gone.

"I won't let anything happen to you," he swore, his fingers tightening around mine. "And I don't plan on letting you go either. As long as you want to stay, you are welcome here."

My heart thundered in my chest. Hesitant to get my hopes up, I gave him a sad smile.

"I appreciate it, but… there's only so much you can do. I mean, even if everything goes well, and I stay here, and we're together… I only have, what, another seventy years to live? I know it's a weird thing to think about, but… you are going to live a lot longer than me, even though you're old enough to be my father."

"Do I feel like your father?" Riel retorted, pinning me with a look that had me clenching my hands as I recalled every single detail of the night before.

I felt my cheeks warm and averted my gaze. Feeling bold, I glanced back, looking at him from underneath my lashes. "Maybe not… but with a few tweaks, you could feel like a Daddy. With that oral fixation of yours, you're well on your way."

Riel flashed me a bemused grin before sobering.

"I should have mentioned this earlier." He sounded apologetic. "We don't always live long lives. Those who cannot use *mana* are lucky to live to a hundred years. It's the *mana* flowing through our bodies that changes us, makes us stronger and allows us to live longer. Now that you can use it freely, you will likely experience the same benefits."

"No," I breathed, thinking I must have understood him wrong. Hope soared like a songbird taking off in my chest. "So…" I didn't dare verbalize what I was thinking.

Luckily, Riel took pity on me. He sat up, reaching out to draw me closer.

"The choice is yours," he murmured against my face, nuzzling my tear-streaked cheek. "But know that if you choose to stay, I will look after you all the rest of our days."

"Riel… I…" At a loss for words, I let my forehead fall into the crook of his neck. "I don't know what to say," I admitted. Everything in me was raw and open in a way it had never been before. "Thank you. I know that's not enough, but… thank you."

Riel pressed a soft kiss to my head. "As soon as we get back, I will set up a meeting with your leaders. I'll speak to Vivian on your behalf, and we'll take it from there."

"Sounds like a plan."

Drawing back and giving him a watery smile, I wiped away what remained of my tears. Somehow, I felt ten pounds lighter compared to half an hour ago. "Well, I guess I should start packing, then. Or is there anything else we should do while we're here?"

Tilting his head, Riel pondered my question. "I can't think of anything. We can visit the market again before we leave if you'd like to make any more purchases. More souvenirs for your bodyguards, perhaps?" he suggested.

"I'm not even sure they'll be allowed to keep the stuff I already got. George might have them confiscated to test the materials or something." I thought back to the knife I'd picked out for Devon and the vest that Riel had helped me select for Chris. It had only occurred to me afterward that anything I brought back might be considered restricted, including the bracelet he'd gotten me the first day.

"Tsk." Riel slipped out of bed and collected his book from where it sat on the bedside table. "No need to worry about that until it happens, I should think."

"Yeah, you're right," I agreed. "No use stressing over it now."

Satisfied with that, I threw aside the covers and went to gather my things. As I knelt by my suitcase to pick out clothes for the day, I was startled by a light touch on my lower back. I whipped around to find Riel crouched next to me, a frown on his face.

"Geez, you surprised me," I exclaimed, putting a hand to my hammering heart. He could move like a ghost if he wanted to. *A naked ghost*, I revised, adjusting my line of sight.

"I was too rough with you," he lamented, grazing his fingers against my hip. I craned my neck to see what he was referring to. I could barely make out a few spots of shadow against my skin.

"Is it that bad? Let me see."

I got up and made for the bathroom, pausing along the way to collect the clothes I'd discarded the night before. With the bundle in my arms, I maneuvered in front of the large mirror to survey the damage. Sure enough, there were light reddish-purple marks along my sides where he had gripped me. The side of my neck also bore evidence of our passion.

"I guess we were a little rougher than we thought," I called out with a grin.

"I'm sorry," Riel said from the doorway. I could see that he was bothered by what he'd done, his brows knitted together in distress.

"Don't be." I crossed the room to him and got up on my

tiptoes to give him a kiss. "It doesn't really hurt, and I had a great time. No harm done."

My eyes went wide as a thought occurred to me. I barely refrained from facepalming. "Oh my God," I exclaimed. "I'm a frickin' healer. Hold on to these one sec."

I shoved the bundle of clothes into his arms and returned to the mirror. Since I'd never tried to heal myself before, I wasn't sure what to expect, but I imagined it wouldn't be difficult. Staring down at the bite mark on my neck didn't give me any magical clues, so I just… gave it a go, reaching for the magic in the same way I did when healing others.

Thinking it might help, I raised a hand to touch the mark and closed my eyes. While it didn't hurt, there was a whisper of soreness. If I thought of that as I tried to draw *mana,* perhaps I could rely on it to find its own way. I emptied my mind of every thought but those related to the task at hand and focused on where my magic was housed.

It took some effort, but warmth began to bloom in my chest and spread outward, tunneling through my body to find where it was needed. The sensation made me shiver. I opened my eyes just in time to see the bruises vanishing as though they were never there.

"Ha!" I made a show of dusting my hands off as I turned back around. "You be as rough as you like in the future, baby," I said with a smug smile. "Mama's got things handled."

"I think I'll still make an effort *not* to hurt you in the future," Riel responded, though he appeared relieved. He opened his mouth again and hesitated. "The… er, the references to parents in a sexual context, is that a usual thing where you're from?"

"Oh, God." I pulled a face and went to get my clothes from him. "It's just a phrase. Daddy… Well, that one's complicated, but it's not about parents. Are we going or what?"

Chuckling to himself, Riel followed me back into the bedroom.

We didn't have much with us, so it didn't take long to get everything together. I performed one final sweep, and we headed downstairs, Riel grabbing Oyanni's harness on the way out. While he returned the key to the proprietress, I waited by the door.

"Good?" I asked as he approached, bags in hand.

"Good," he answered, smiling down at me. I linked my arm in his and returned the smile.

"All right. Let's go home."

As we trotted into the courtyard, I found that I was glad to be back. It was a strange feeling to be looking to the future with optimism for once. Although I worried about sorting out my living here, those concerns weren't enough to bring down my mood. Even the weather was gorgeous; late summer in the fae world was a far cry from the unpleasant mugginess we got in D.C. this time of year. I was on top of the world.

Then something caught my eye. The gardens and sheds passed by on our left, as usual, but to the right, just in front of the field of grazing *avida,* was a tall post that had been hammered into the ground. I didn't remember that being there before, and that in and of itself was odd. The post wasn't what had snagged my attention, though. It was the person tied to the post—Neyes the seer, breathing shallowly, their strange, pale eyes open and fixed on the ground before them.

Alarmed, I tapped Riel's leg to get his attention. "Riel, what's that? Are they okay?"

"Hm?"

I felt his body stiffen behind me as he spotted what I had. "I don't know," he answered, his tone carefully controlled. "Let's find out."

He urged Oyanni to go a little faster, and we practically flew up to the castle entrance. Riel hopped down almost before we'd come to a complete stop. I went to help him with the bags, unable to tear my eyes away from Neyes until the front door flew open.

"Where have you been?" Solois demanded in English, descending the steps menacingly. Riel moved to intercept him, putting his body none-too-subtly between us. Solois drew to a halt, his eyes flaring with anger. I wasn't certain, but I could have sworn I saw him sniff the air. He shot me a look, then switched to the fae language and said something that didn't sound particularly kind. Going by context clues, it was something along the lines of "We need to talk—without that human whore of yours."

"Avery, leave the bags. Go inside, straight to your room."

Riel spoke in an even tone, without taking his eyes off the first prince. When I didn't move to obey him, he looked at me. His gaze softened at whatever he saw on my face. "I will come to you soon," he promised gently. "I just need to speak with my brother for a moment."

I took a hesitant step. I didn't want to leave him alone here —it didn't take a genius to know that something was wrong. Solois had never been pleasant, but to be this hostile…

"Please, Avery."

Riel's whispered request finally urged my feet into motion. I darted toward the steps, giving Solois a wide berth. He watched me go with narrowed eyes but didn't move.

Once I was safely inside, I fled to my room without looking back.

CHAPTER TWENTY-NINE
FAMILY MEETING

Meanwhile…

"WHAT'S GOING ON?" Riel demanded as soon as Avery was out of sight. Behind him, Oyanni pawed the ground and snorted as if to show that she had his back.

"We're having a family meeting," Solois drawled. "I realize you're barely part of the family these days, but you might like to know that certain things have come to light while you've been entertaining the human spy. *Thoroughly* entertaining, judging by the smell of her."

"We've been over this," Riel said through gritted teeth. "She's not a spy."

"Yes, yes. Trust me when I say that I *hate* having to say 'I told you so.'" Solois angled his body back toward the building. "You'd best not keep us waiting any longer. Mother and Father were displeased to learn that you'd left without warning."

"I can't imagine why, when my presence never mattered much before," Riel retorted, turning back to give Oyanni an abrupt pat before joining his brother. They headed inside together, walking briskly.

"The situation is serious," Solois revealed. "Neyes has betrayed us."

Riel's steps faltered. "Neyes—?"

"As such," Solois continued, "our family needs everyone we can get. Mother has been praying nonstop, and our army is standing by. I'm sure they'll manage to find a use for you, given the severity of the situation."

"The army?" Alarmed, Riel rushed to keep up with his brother's long, rapid strides. "Solois, please, explain. What did Neyes do? Are we going to war?"

"I'll let Father explain," Solois answered, apparently savoring Riel's panic.

They stopped in front of the master suite, and Solois raised a hand to knock. No sooner had he done so than the door swung open to reveal their mother. Although no less stunning, Elokima was visibly frazzled, with a tightness to her features that hadn't been there before. She wore a simple dress and her hair fell around her shoulders in stark contrast to how she usually appeared in public.

"Finally!" she exclaimed as her eyes landed on Riel. "Come in, quickly. We have much to discuss."

The boys obeyed, and the door shut behind them. Elokima began pacing with a fluidity that suggested she had been doing it for days. Riel surveyed the room until he spotted his father, who sat at his desk and drummed his fingers against the wood. Their eyes met, and the tension in Riel's body conveyed his many questions without words.

"Two days ago," Ralif began without delay, "we received a message from our cousin in the west. The news was... not good. He intercepted correspondence from House Leimor that was headed for us. Headed for our seer, more specifically."

"Filthy traitor," Elokima spat as she paced, her face a mask of fury. "To think that we took them in when they had nowhere to go, treated them like a beloved member of this household, and all this time they have been feeding *me*, the Right Hand of the Goddess, the enemy's lies—"

"Yes, well, that has been dealt with," Ralif cut her off. "The issue now is that there's an army on its way. I don't know what Neyes has told them, but House Leimor believes that now is the opportunity they've been waiting for. Given the timing and the contents of the letter, it appears likely that they are working with the humans. When they requested our aid with the girl, I didn't want to think that it was a trick, but to have twenty years of relative peace end now... we should be expecting a multi-pronged attack, from both sides of The Rift."

"That won't happen," Riel interjected. "Aver—the humans aren't involved in this."

"We're not asking for your advice, thank the Goddess." Solois rolled his eyes. "That girl could kill us all in our sleep and be standing over you with a knife when you woke, and you'd still be surprised when she slit your throat."

Riel ignored him. "How long do we have?"

"They will be here by tomorrow morning, if not before then." Ralif's words rang heavy with weariness. "Leimor has the benefit of advance notice on their side. They even recruited mercenaries for the occasion. Our cousin will arrive this afternoon with their men, but there's no time to call on other allies. We're at a disadvantage."

"So we send a messenger to the humans now, let them know what's going on," Riel proposed. "The Lieutenant Governor can have additional soldiers gathered in—"

"Astonriel," the king interrupted. "You've done well, and we are grateful. But the humans have never been friends. They fear that which they do not know, and they have long been envious of the Goddess's blessing. It was only a matter of time before we became enemies."

"They are wary of us," Riel agreed, "but they don't understand because we have not taught them. They knew nothing of magic; Avery knew nothing of magic." He looked to his mother imploringly. "What could she be, if not the Goddess blessing the humans as well? Her and the others like her, it's a sign that we are meant to be allies."

"Neyes has suggested the same," the queen admitted reluctantly. "But obviously, if they have been working with the enemy, we cannot trust…" She trailed off, wringing her hands in frustration. "I pray for guidance, but there is no answer. Either the Goddess has forsaken us in our foolishness, or this is Her punishment, and we must accept it with grace."

"We know that Neyes was a traitor," Solois stated. "It makes sense that they lied to protect their allies, House Leimor and the humans. The letter is proof enough that the humans are conspiring against us. It was a daring move on their part, to send a spy masquerading as a healer, but clearly, it worked. They might have gotten everything they wanted already."

"She *is* a healer," Riel argued, his voice rising, "and no danger to us."

"You took her to Neyes, and now war is upon us," Solois insisted. "Can you honestly say that you've been taking your task seriously? I've seen you two together, and she's got you wrapped around her finger. How much do you truly know about her? She may have passed along the order herself. Your denial of the situation doesn't look very good for you, brother."

A tense silence fell. Riel saw nothing good on the faces of his brother or parents.

"You can't be serious," he growled, whirling on Solois. "We have not been close in a long time, but I'm still your brother and a proud son of House Wysalar. To suggest that I…" His voice wavered. "That I would cast aside our name and my own honor…"

"I do not question your loyalty," Ralif said when Riel trailed off. "This is a difficult time for our House, and strong feelings are understandable, but Solois oversteps."

He gave the first prince a meaningful look before turning his attention back to Riel. "However, there is no denying that you are too closely involved in this matter. I think it would be best if you helped prepare for our cousin's arrival while we figure things out."

Knowing that the question of Avery's safety still hung in the balance, Riel hesitated to leave things there. "I will help out where I can," he conceded. "Avery may be valuable as well, both as another set of hands and in her capacity as a healer. I'll take her with me."

"So be it." The king waved a hand in approval. "We will keep you informed."

Riel inclined his head toward his father, then his mother. He leveled a glare on his brother before sweeping past him and making for the door.

Once Riel had gone, Ralif addressed Solois.

"We must prepare for the worst," he said. "Keep an eye on them. Regardless of whether or not she is a spy, Avery Nelson may still be a useful bargaining chip. However, she can't be allowed to return across The Rift. If she tries to escape..."

He trailed off, leaving rather valuable information unspoken.

"Of course," Solois replied, having gotten the gist of it. "Shall I prepare our soldiers?"

"They know what needs to be done, and the rest I can handle." Ralif resumed drumming his fingers against the top of his desk. "This takes precedence. If Avery is a spy, she may have information that the humans want. Hopefully, she hasn't had the chance to pass it along yet. And her abilities will prove useful in the case of an attack. It's best that she remain where she is."

"Of course." After a moment's silence, Solois inclined his head. "Then, I will take my leave. I'll inform you when our cousin arrives."

At Ralif's nod, he left the room.

Elokima collapsed into an armchair by the window and loosed a defeated sigh. "This is a miserable situation," she lamented. "Enemies on all sides, our family fracturing, the Goddess deserting us. I fail to see how this can end in anything but utter ruin."

Ralif chuckled and got to his feet. "We're not dead yet, my love," he said as he crossed the room to her. "So long as we still breathe, there is a chance for us."

Elokima reached out to him as he approached. When he bent over, she took his face in her hands and they shared a kiss. It was a beautiful moment of calm before the storm, a moment of peace before all hell broke loose.

Riel did not immediately go to Avery, but that didn't mean that she wasn't his priority. The situation was becoming dire. As such, he had to do everything he could to ensure her safety. At the same time, though, he had to tread carefully—and that meant he needed help. There weren't many people he could trust, but one came to mind. Luckily, she was easily accessible.

He found Luenki in her suite. She was not unaffected by the events of the day, but she opened the door to him without complaint. After checking the hallway for prying eyes, she waved him inside.

"Welcome back," she murmured, inviting him to take one of the armchairs by the window. As he sat, he noted the tired slump to her shoulders, unusual for the family friend and diplomat who always had a smile on her face. Indeed, she wasn't able to hide her concern, likely for Avery and the situation with the U.S. given her proximity to the issue.

"I just spoke with my parents," Riel revealed, steepling his fingers.

"I'm sure that went wonderfully," Luenki responded with a touch of sarcasm, sinking into the chair opposite him. "They told you, then, of Neyes and House Leimor?" She waited for his nod of confirmation before continuing. "I'd naïvely hoped they would have given up their foolish pursuit of our territories. Then again, honor only goes so far these days."

"Leimor has always been a threat. This outcome is not unexpected." Riel paused to consider his next words. "But... I am here to discuss a threat of a different kind."

Luenki was astute—it was a necessary trait to have in her line of work. Although the second prince's expression didn't change, she saw everything she needed to know.

"Avery," she guessed. Riel gave a curt nod in response.

"She's not the threat," he clarified. "But I believe... with the way things stand, my family is a threat to her. I am under the impression that we have a mutual interest in keeping her safe. I would not ask you to go against my family, but their attention is divided, and they are failing to consider the repercussions of starting a war with America."

Luenki worried her bottom lip.

"You are like a sister to me," Riel said quietly. "You can speak freely."

"I don't want to see her harmed," Luenki admitted. "If I am being honest, I also have my reservations about doing anything that may harm our relationship with the Americans. But you know that my loyalty is to House Wysalar."

"Of course," Riel agreed. His spirits fell a bit at that, but as important as this was, he wasn't about to force someone close to him to abandon their principles.

Slowly at first, then all at once, a mischievous smile spread across Luenki's face.

"Well, then," she remarked, "it's a good thing that you're a son of House Wysalar. What do you need from me?"

CHAPTER THIRTY

THE LULL

I TRIED to stay busy while I waited for Riel, but it was impossible to relax. First, I stared out the window for a while, as if I might be able to see him and Solois reflected in the mist outside. Then I picked up a book, but I gave up on that when I realized that I was two chapters in and didn't remember a single word I'd read.

When a knock sounded, startling me from my thoughts, I abandoned the book of crossword puzzles I was working on and flew across the room to get the door. It was Riel, and a quick head-to-toe examination told me that he was unharmed. I sagged against the door in relief.

"Is everything okay?" I breathed.

"I would love to tell you 'yes,'" Riel answered with a long-suffering sigh, shaking his head, "but I would be lying."

"Come in, come in." I stepped aside to give him room to enter. "I hope you didn't get in too much trouble for taking me to Miderrum. I didn't realize it would be such a big deal."

"Nor did I. Normally, it wouldn't have been a problem; it was unfortunate timing, but there was no way we could have known that." Riel looked around my little room as if seeing it for the first time, and a crease appeared between his brows. "In any case… Neyes has betrayed us. They are being… returned to the land, as is the custom for traitors of that degree."

"Uh…" The corners of my mouth turned down as I attempted to make sense of his words. "You don't mean…"

"They will be left outside until dead."

My hand flew to my mouth in shock.

"But that's not all," he continued, the corners of his lips turning down in a scowl. "I mentioned that we have an enemy, House Leimor. They are distantly related to our family, and they govern a province to the west, several days travel from here. We received word that they are on the way here with an army. Neyes was working with them, feeding them information and guiding our hands."

"Oh my God," I whispered. *We have to evacuate. No, we can't evacuate, what about Miderrum? And anyway, the castle has a wall. Walls are for defense, aren't they? We could barricade the doors, put the women and the children in the basement and then*—fuck, the only things I knew about defending a castle were from *Lord of the Rings*. "H-how long do we have?"

"Until the morning. I'm working on a plan. I just need you to trust me." Riel gave me a pointed look.

"Of course," I said quickly. "Whatever you need, I'm there."

"We're going to stay out of the way and provide assistance where we can. It's all we can do in the meantime, so don't stress. How do you feel about cooking?"

Don't stress… yeah, right. He had no idea… Did I hear that right?

"Cooking?" I frowned, having completely lost track of the conversation. "Whatever for?"

"We have allies coming from the west this afternoon, and more support from the city. There are going to be a lot more people around in the next few hours. The kitchen staff will be working hard to keep everyone fed, so they could use extra hands. If you're comfortable sorting deliveries and preparing food, that should be a good place for you."

A stampede of footsteps sounded from the other side of the

door. Riel tensed and angled his body toward it as if prepared to fend someone off if they burst in on us. I took a wary step back.

"They're not here already?" My voice rose with my nerves.

"No, no." One of Riel's ears twitched as the footsteps faded. He waited another moment before turning back to me. "I'm sorry. I'm just on edge. Let's go."

"Well, hang on," I protested, putting my hands up. "Are you sure there isn't anything else going on? How is your family taking all this?"

"Not well," he admitted, dropping his gaze. "That's why it's best that we stay low."

My eyes narrowed. "They don't think we're involved? America, I mean?"

Riel's hesitation told me everything I needed to know. My heart sank.

"Oh. Oh, that's bad."

Overcome with the need to sit down, I swiveled around and made for the bed, collapsing on the mattress with an audible *poof*. Once I digested that information, I spoke again. "Does... does Vivian know? And George? If you're going to war, they can help. They've got a ton of soldiers right across The Rift. I mean, I imagine they can help. There's probably a lot of paperwork involved, but I know they take their relationship with you guys seriously—"

"I appreciate it, Avery, more than you know, but you and I play small parts in all this." Riel crossed the room to join me on the bed. He reached over and took one of my hands, wrapping it in his and setting it on his knee. I met his eyes and was distraught to see little but despondency there. Slowly, I extended my free hand to rest on his.

"So, there's nothing we can do?" My voice came out a tortured whisper.

"Not right now. Just... getting things in order and waiting."

We sat there for a few minutes in silence as we mulled things over. Well, I mulled things over. Sometimes, Riel was an open book. Other times, like now, I had no idea what he was thinking. Not for the first time in my life, I wished I had the power to read minds instead of healing people; it would have been useful right then. But if there were other ways that I could be useful, then so be it. I'd do whatever was asked of me.

"Okay," I agreed eventually. "Let's help out in the kitchen. But, um… when things start going down, keep me in the loop, yeah? I'm sure I can be useful. Like, I can heal soldiers and stuff. If I'm helping your cause, then they can't think I'm a bad guy."

Riel loosed a slow sigh. "If everything goes according to plan, you'll be gone well before the fighting starts." At my look of horror, he went wide-eyed and quickly amended his words. "I meant that you'd be someplace safe. If all else fails, I'll get you back to The Rift."

"Then what happens to you?" I demanded. Riel gave me a one-shoulder shrug.

"Let me worry about that," he said lightly. Too lightly, given the gravity of the situation.

"You're going to be the death of me," I muttered under my breath as I slipped my hands out of his and got to my feet.

"I want to be many things for you, Avery." Riel's words made me jump. I didn't think he'd be able to make out what I said. "But not death. Never death."

"It's a figure of speech," I sighed, turning back to him. "You know, no one likes people who are intentionally difficult. It's not cute."

"Hm. Sounds like useful advice for a certain stubborn someone I know," Riel teased, hopping to his feet. He slid an arm around my waist as he approached and pulled me in, lowering his head as he did so. I melted into his hold and let myself enjoy the kiss, grateful for the brief reprieve. When he started to pull away, I wrapped my arms around his neck and went in for round two, making his eyes pop open in surprise.

"For good luck," I whispered with a smile as I released him.

"In that case, maybe we should do it once more?" Riel suggested.

Laughing, I pinched his arm. "How about *after* we survive the impending war?"

"As if the stakes weren't high enough," Riel quipped as we made our way to the door.

The kitchen buzzed with movement as people rushed to prepare what they could. Riel and I jumped in right away, with some direction from Juris, the head chef. Multiple deliveries arrived from Miderrum—fresh fruits and vegetables, cheeses, nuts, sacks of grains, etcetera. It was enough food to feed… well, an army. We sorted through it all, restocking the kitchen and washing the fruits and vegetables in some kind of preservative soap.

As we worked, the kitchen staff baked, put aside legumes to soak, and took a large portion of the fruits and vegetables to dry, pickle, or make into jams. At some point, one of the cooks deposited freshly baked *massiya* in our hands as they dashed past. I ate the savory pastry with great enthusiasm, burning my mouth in the process but regretting nothing.

I estimated that it had only been a couple of hours before someone came charging in with news. Riel informed me that their cousin from the west had arrived with reinforcements. My understanding was that they had a smaller territory in that other House's path, so they'd had to evacuate anyway, and figured they would be safe combining forces with ours. But I didn't pretend to know how any of this worked.

Juris got to work right away to make something for the newcomers. I wondered how things would change with them around. It would be harder for me to stay out of the way, but it shouldn't be for long. Normal wars could drag on, but magic ones? I couldn't imagine them digging trenches and lobbing lightning back and forth at each other for weeks on end.

As the day dragged on, I tried to focus on the tasks at hand and not lose myself to depressing thoughts. There was plenty to keep us busy, so it wasn't too difficult. When we went outside to gather what remained of the crops there, we saw several workers who were doing something with the walls—fortifying them, perhaps?—as well as multiple large groups running drills in the fields, some mounted on *avida* in matching leather armor.

As we sorted and washed and gathered and sorted some more, I envied Riel for the way he showed no signs of exhaustion. By that point, I was drenched in sweat and felt as though my arms were overcooked noodles. We were heading back inside with several baskets full of herbs when I thought to ask, "Wasn't there anything more... I don't know, impactful for you to do? Not that this isn't also important, but... I'm surprised you aren't working with the soldiers or something."

"I volunteered for this," Riel admitted. "I'm not much of a fighter. Honestly, I'm more suited to diplomacy and kitchen work than anything else. I can't remember the last time I participated in strategy training. It was never important for me, as the Second."

"Oh, I see. So, a younger sibling perk."

Riel was taken aback by my comment. "I'm not sure how many would see it as a perk," he said slowly. "But yes, I always had fewer responsibilities."

"Well, I'm glad they let you be my teacher." I offered him a hesitant smile.

"I am as well." Riel returned it. "We've always believed that the Goddess has a plan for Her people. I didn't think... well, a few months ago, it was difficult to see where my life was heading. I'm glad that things turned out the way they did."

"So am I. It's been fun." That was putting it lightly. "Well, everything except for literally dying to fix my magic. I could think of some other, less positive adjectives for that."

At Riel's cringe, I added, "I know, I know, that wasn't your idea."

"I don't like to remember it," he confessed. "Even with Seersthri's assurances, it was a terrifying experience. All I could think was that you weren't going to wake up, and your death was my fault for letting you attempt it."

My heart swelled with sympathy at his admission. Although I didn't regret deciding to do the *manaviri,* I did maybe feel a little guilty about the way I'd bullied Riel into it.

"I appreciated you being there. Having someone I lo—um, someone I care about there made it a little less scary. A lot less scary, really. I don't think I could have done it without you." I couldn't believe the L-word had nearly come out of my mouth. It was still too soon for that, wasn't it? My eyes scanned the floor, the walls, the windowsills—anywhere but Riel's face.

"I would not have let you do it alone," Riel responded softly.

A lump formed in my throat as it occurred to me yet again that this was temporary. Luckily, I was distracted from that line of thinking when we arrived back at the kitchens. The sense of urgency had begun to dwindle. We bundled the herbs and hung them up with others to dry, then stowed the freshly jarred goods the kitchen staff had prepared.

At that point, Riel suggested we go see if our hands were needed anywhere else. That was how we ended up carting equipment around during the evening hours. We fetched sets of spare armor from storage, dusted them off, and set them down to air out. Riel let me practice mending on some damaged pieces, and then he forced me to take a break, and I provided moral support while he put together a small mountain of arrows. They didn't use weapons in close-range combat—magic, after all—but bows were fair game. And one could never have enough arrows.

When the sun began to slip over the horizon, we had a handsome pile of supplies ready for our soldiers to make use of. I stood tall and beamed with pride as we made our way back to the kitchens for the evening meal. We passed by several groups of soldiers in the castle's stiff, white armor leaving the dining hall. When I walked into the kitchen, Riel on my heels, my optimism faded at the sight of Solois eating at the prep table where we usually took our meals. A sideways glance in Riel's direction told me that he was equally excited to see his brother.

"Astonriel, Avery," Solois greeted us both in a tone that was borderline jovial. "Come, join me for the evening meal."

"Do we have a choice?" I asked Riel in what I thought was a whisper. Solois's answering grin reminded me that I'd forgotten how keen the fae's senses were. I settled for taking a seat on the far end of the bench and kept an eye on Solois as Riel went to get us some dinner.

"Thank you for your help today," he said, sounding genuine. I blinked in surprise.

"You're welcome," I replied cautiously. "Glad I could be useful."

"Mm."

The sound of agreement he made was so like Riel that I suddenly saw the family resemblance. His features were still harsher, of course, edgier and more mature, but the shape of the eyes was the same. And maybe the point of his chin too. He wasn't at all unfortunate-looking… which stung, given that he had the personality of a stinky sock.

Riel appeared to my left, placing a plate with bean salad in front of me as he sat. "I assume preparations are going well on your end," he commented in a conversational tone, though he held himself with a vigilant sort of stiffness.

"They are," Solois agreed, scraping the sides of his bowl with his spoon. "Come what may, we will be as ready as we can be."

"That's good," I spoke up. "Let me know if there is anything else I can do to help."

He gave me what I presumed to be his version of an actual smile, a little rough around the edges but close to being friendly. "Everything is in order," he replied. "Just get some rest tonight, both of you. We will need to be refreshed for the fight."

"Do we have a strategy?" Riel asked.

"Well, it would have been handy to have a seer." Solois relaxed back in his seat. "As it stands, the plan is to meet them on the road. We will have room to maneuver but can fall back if need be. Archers will be posted westward, to have the wind on their side. Menders will remain within the walls. Mother and Father will be leading the charge, of course, and you and I will provide support. Father hopes we will have a chance to negotiate before the fighting starts, but we'll need to be ready for anything."

A little gasp escaped me. I covered it up with a mouthful of food and chewed furiously. I didn't know why it hadn't occurred to me that the family themselves would be in the thick of it. I guess I had pictured them shouting orders from the throne room. *Was it going to be dangerous? How could it not be?* I should have asked more questions.

As if knowing exactly where my mind had gone, Riel dropped a hand under the table to give my knee a reassuring squeeze.

"I'll be there," he said. I shot him a panicked look. Maybe he groped me for an unrelated reason, then—he didn't seem to understand where my thoughts were at all.

Solois pushed his empty bowl aside and got to his feet. "Good. Then I'll see you on the battlefield. Don't get distracted, little brother," he responded, the corner of his lips curving in a barely disguised smirk. With that, he headed for the exit, purposely taking the longer route around the table so that he brushed my arm on the way out. I made a face at his retreating form before turning back to the table.

"I'll be careful," Riel promised before I could say anything.

"I know you will." I set my spoon down by my half-finished meal.

I hesitated to voice my concerns, knowing that there wasn't anything I could say that would make a difference. He probably felt that he had to be there. He knew I'd worry for him, but that didn't change anything. And he would do his best to stay safe whether I told him to or not. Releasing a sorrowful sigh, I slipped off the bench. "Sorry, I'm not that hungry."

Riel quickly shoveled several large bites into his mouth and pushed the bench back as he stood. "I'll walk you to your room," he offered after a painful-looking swallow. He plucked my bowl from my hands and collected his and Solois's to add to the stack for the dishwasher.

We left the kitchen together, walking at a slow pace so as to savor the last few peaceful moments we had. As we passed the windows that looked over the fields, I could see that there were still groups of soldiers out there. *Would they get any sleep tonight?* My thoughts strayed to those who would be in the thick of it. It felt wrong to stay here, safe behind walls, while others went out to fight and possibly die. *Is there nothing more I can do?*

Unfortunately, my room wasn't far, and we were there before I knew it. I hesitated at the door. Riel couldn't stay with me tonight, not with things the way they were. But the anxious part of me was terrified that this would be the last time I ever saw him, and no matter how much I tried to push those thoughts away, they pursued me with a vengeance.

"Get some sleep," Riel murmured, reaching up to caress my arm. He stood a little closer than what would be considered proper, but I didn't have the heart to put more space between us. If someone saw us together, they would just have to deal with it. I looked up at his face, intent on burning his features into my mind, and my vision started to become blurry.

"Crap," I hissed, raising a hand to brush away the tears

before they had the chance to fall. "Sorry, I was trying not to get all emotional."

"It's fine."

The softness in Riel's voice only made it worse. I huffed a rueful laugh.

"Will I see you again in the morning?" My voice came out embarrassingly small.

Riel hesitated to answer. "We likely won't have much notice. If I have to rush out..."

"Yeah, of course," I said quickly, feeling silly. "Don't worry about it. Um... yeah."

The words I really wanted to say didn't make it out. Even if the situation sort of called for it, it was too early to be professing my love for him. And everything else had already been said. I settled for, "I guess... you get some sleep too, then. In case I don't see you, be safe."

We stayed there for a moment. I could only imagine how ridiculous the two of us might have appeared to onlookers—lovers acting like friends, standing around awkwardly because they didn't want to leave things the way they were but were too hesitant to embrace.

"All right, good night, then," I finally exclaimed, not wanting to hold him up any longer.

"Good night," Riel replied quietly.

I offered him one final smile before entering my bedroom. As the door began to swing shut, he stayed put, watching me in return. I drank in the sight freely, right up until the moment the wood grain cut off my view of him and the door latched. Then I stood there for a long while, my gaze fixed on the closed door, hands clenched at my sides. The tears at last began to fall.

Leaving him alone on the other side was one of the hardest things I'd ever had to do.

CHAPTER THIRTY-ONE
THE FALLING OUT

Later that night…

RIEL SAT on the floor beside Avery's door, his back against the wall, legs splayed out in front of him. His arms were crossed, and his head was tilted at an awkward angle, but his expression was peaceful, telling of a deep, dreamless sleep.

Solois observed this with a grimace.

Keep an eye on them, Ralif had said. Easy enough. Why the family's next head should be tasked with babysitting, only the Goddess knew. Still, he supposed he'd done well to be pleasant at dinner. At least that way, he didn't have to be sneaky about it, he could just keep them company. It was helpful to observe the human healer's responses to their plans too. When she had learned Riel would be with the rest of the family, there had been concern in her eyes. Likely because she wouldn't be able to continue manipulating him from the sidelines. Foolish man.

Solois knew the moment Riel woke, as his body tensed. He was on his feet in an instant.

"What are you doing here?" was the first thing that left his mouth.

"Keeping an eye on the spy, as Father ordered." Solois rolled his eyes. "For some reason, they don't trust you to handle it yourself. I wonder why."

Riel's gaze darted to the closed door and back.

"She's asleep."

"So? If she thinks we're asleep, she might believe this is the perfect time to slip out."

"She's not going anywhere."

"Perhaps."

The brothers stared each other down.

"You truly believe the humans are to blame for this?" Riel asked quietly.

"You believe Neyes was working alone?" Solois countered. "You think House Leimor came up with this plot by themselves all those years ago just to turn us against the humans? You think they sent one of their own to worm their way into a position of favor within our House so that they could manipulate us into a war with someone else entirely?"

"I think that's exactly what happened. It makes sense that they would want us distracted so that they could take advantage of the situation. Bringing America into this accomplishes that. They didn't have any trouble convincing our mother that this whole thing was some sort of test." Riel eyed Avery's door again, easing a few steps in the direction of the throne room. "Let's take this somewhere else," he suggested.

Solois scoffed. "Wouldn't want to wake up your pet human." Despite the spite in his words, he waved Riel along, and they headed down the hall together.

"You've changed," Riel said as they walked. "I realize we're not children anymore, but you used to be reasonable. Has a position of power gone to your head? The fact that you refuse to consider any alternatives when none of us know the whole truth—"

"You trust too easily," Solois retorted, cutting him off. "I've said it before, and I'll say it again. You should never have had faith in the humans, not when they've been envious of us since the beginning. They were bound to become more aggressive sooner or later. No doubt they want to uncover the secret behind our magic, and agreeing to teach Avery gave them hope."

"The lessons make no difference except to her. With the quantities of *mana* that still escape through The Rift to this day, they may be capable of everything we are soon enough. When that day comes, don't we want to be allies?"

"What we *want* doesn't *matter*. All that does is that a powerful nation is trying to keep us under their thumb. And if we don't take a stand, they will succeed."

"So, we make a show of good faith. We let Avery return to her people unharmed."

Solois drew to an abrupt halt on the stairs. "You're mad," he exclaimed, shaking his head incredulously. "She's our only bargaining chip. Letting her go would mean we're rolling over and practically begging them for a takeover."

"She's not a bargaining chip, she's a person," Riel argued, proceeding ahead. Once on the ground floor, he pivoted to gesture broadly to the air around them. "War is coming, Solois. She shouldn't be caught up in this. There's no reason for her to remain here."

"Father's orders were clear." Solois continued down the steps and passed his brother. "I'm not letting her leave." His tone took on a distinctive bitterness. "And you need to remember where your loyalties lie. I don't want to hurt you, but I won't let you ruin everything I've done for this family. Especially not for the sake of some traitor pussy."

"Let *me* be clear." Riel stepped in front of him. Solois drew up short, and his brows shot into his hairline, surprised that Riel would dare to challenge him. "I wasn't asking for your permission, and I don't care what Father said. I will not allow us to make this mistake. You may not be able to see it yet, but I'm doing this *for* the family."

Angry sapphire eyes clashed with determined Caribbean blue. Neither appeared likely to back down. But in fact, that didn't matter. Riel's plan was already in motion.

CHAPTER THIRTY-TWO
THE FLEEING

A HAND GRIPPED MY SHOULDER, ripping me from my dreams with a jolt of adrenaline. My eyes shot open, but only blackness greeted me. Disoriented in the dark room, all I could tell was that someone hovered by my bed. Every muscle in my body tensed. *Riel…? No, he would have said something.* I sucked in a breath, preparing to scream. *If I can get to the bathroom, maybe I can barricade myself inside—?*

"Avery?" a hushed female voice spoke up. "It is Luenki. Are you awake?"

The air gushed out of me.

"Oh my god, Luenki," I hissed. "You scared the living… I almost screamed. Jesus."

A finger met my lips.

"I'm sorry to wake you, but we must go now."

Still half asleep, it took me a moment to realize what she was saying. Once my brain caught up, I bolted upright, fear chasing away any drowsiness in an instant.

"What is it? Is Riel okay?" In my haste to get the question out, I almost forgot to whisper.

"For now," Luenki answered.

I didn't like the sound of that.

Fabric rustled from somewhere down below, where my suitcases were stowed. "Dress yourself," Luenki ordered. "We need to get you to The Rift. I have already sent word so that your people will be ready to receive you." A soft bundle was thrust into my hands. I blinked down at it, wondering how the heck I was supposed to get dressed in pitch darkness.

"Uh, can you do that thing to make light?" I asked sheepishly.

A muted, warm light illuminated our immediate area in reply. With no time to worry about modesty, I stripped out of my nightgown and pulled on the dress in my hands. It wasn't what I would have picked to flee for my life, but beggars couldn't be choosers. Rolling out of bed, I tugged the dress down over my thighs and then went to search for my sneakers.

The light winked out not even a full second after I slipped them on, and my hand was snatched up. It was all I could do to stumble along as I was pulled to my feet and led across the room to the door. Luenki let go of my hand so that she could crack open the door and survey the hallway, her figure briefly silhouetted by the lights.

Seeing nothing, she signaled me forward, and I fell into step behind her. The hallway was empty, with no sign of Riel or any soldiers. Raised voices filtered through the air from the direction of the throne room, but I couldn't make out what they were saying. She turned back to me with a somber expression and grasped both my hands this time.

"We will keep going," she said firmly, "no matter what. You will not stop."

Her ominous words barely had time to land before we were moving again. I was dragged along the maroon carpet, struggling to keep up with her long strides.

"Luenki—" I began, only to shut my mouth with an audible *snap* when Luenki shushed me.

We made our way down the stairs in silence. As we rounded the corner into the throne room, Luenki came to an abrupt halt, and I nearly crashed into her. Craning my neck to see, my eyes landed on two tall, blond men on the opposite side. They circled each other slowly, like predators sizing each other up before a territorial skirmish. I could only see the back of the one nearest me, but as we watched, the one opposite him came into view. A wall of panic hit me all at once.

I'd recognize that heart-shaped face and those kissable lips anywhere.

As if sensing my intentions, Luenki whirled about and clapped a hand over my mouth. My eyes widened in alarm as they met Riel's from across the room. His expression turned stony. He'd stopped moving, which meant that Solois's back remained to us. Their voices carried to us, harsh and argumentative. *I wish I knew what they were saying.*

Luenki caught my gaze and nodded once. I wanted to protest, but I knew that would be foolish. *He'll be fine,* I told myself firmly. *His brother wouldn't hurt him.*

We started across the room, trying to move quickly and keep our steps light at the same time. Luenki succeeded easily, gliding across the floor like a dancer; I didn't have the same luck. We made it about twenty feet before my sneakers squeaked against the marble. I looked up in horror as Solois swiveled around. His eyes narrowed on me.

Then he smiled. But it wasn't the same smile he'd given me last night, the one that bordered on friendly. No, it wasn't even close. This one was filled with dark promises, like he was glad to see me, and that was not a good thing.

Three things happened at once: Solois stepped forward. Riel lunged for his brother. Luenki caught my hand again, and she yanked me into her arms.

Someone shrieked. It might have been me.

The next thing I knew, everything was in motion. Luenki and I hurtled toward the door. Solois and Riel were on top of each other, grappling at clothing and limbs and hair too fast for my eyes to follow. One of them went flying, hitting one of the pillars with a sickening *crack* that echoed across the expanse between us. Terrified, I breathed in to scream Riel's name, to call for help, *something*—but a heartbeat later, Luenki and I were already outside.

She didn't let me go until we were in front of two waiting *avida*. My fear multiplied when I realized that the one Luenki bustled me toward was Oyanni.

"Wait, wait," I cried, struggling to speak past the confusion and panic that choked me. "What about Riel? I can't just—can't he come with us? I don't understand what's happening."

Strong arms wrapped around me and squeezed like a vise, pressing my face into a floral-smelling armpit. Luenki whispered soothing words into my hair and stroked my back while I fought to get my thoughts straight. Every instinct screamed that this wasn't right, that I couldn't leave like this, even as logic tried to convince me there was nothing I could do.

"We need to go. Solois will not be stopped for long."

Luenki's cool voice broke through the hysteria. Without any more warning, she moved her hands to my hips and lifted me up. I swung my leg over the *avida*'s back, the motion ingrained in me by now, and picked up the handhold. Luenki was mounted on her yellow *avida* in front of me before I could blink. She urged her steed into motion with a squeeze of her legs, and Oyanni followed without prompting.

As we rode for the open portcullis, tears fell in a downpour that mimicked the deluge inside me. Even swallowing great gulps of air, my lungs heaved like I was drowning. Everything felt like it was on fire and somehow numb at the same time.

My vision was blurry, but the post with the slight figure tied to the base still caught my eye on the way out. Neyes stared straight at me, no sign of sympathy or regret in their piercing gaze. In fact, a hint of a smirk teased their mouth, like they were *pleased* to see me fleeing for my life, like they were *glad* everything was falling apart.

"A pity the *manaviri* didn't kill you," they called as I passed by.

In my panic, their words didn't make any sense to me. All I could think was that they watched us go and felt nothing for the lives they had ruined.

I buried my face in Oyanni's neck and cursed their Goddess with every fiber of my being.

We rode for what felt like hours. My tears had stopped, lulled by the swaying motion and rhythmic pounding of hooves striking the earth, but the ache in my heart remained. The sky was beginning to pinken with the first signs of daybreak.

Luenki still rode in front of me, though we'd slowed from a frantic pace to a more sustainable speed some time ago. She sat tall and directed her *avida* with confidence, a natural rider. I stared at her proud back and the tears threatened again.

I knew I should just be grateful to her. I knew that, but keeping my emotions in check was another matter. At that moment, I resented her. I was angry that she forced me to leave Riel behind, and angry that she had abandoned him herself. I was upset and confused and *tired*, goddammit. The lack of sleep certainly wasn't helping things.

Now, after all that, I was supposed to go back home with my head held high and a smile on my face and… and what? *Yeah, there was an army coming, and my boyfriend and his brother started fighting each other for some reason, so I had to peace out. Hope that's okay. Anyway, that's that. It's good to be back home. When's the next healing session?*

I exhaled a forceful breath and turned my face upward. Branches formed a dark, imposing ceiling above us, only a sliver of sky visible between the twisting shadows. I was struck with a sense of claustrophobia. It was unexpected, given the open air surrounding me—I wasn't physically trapped in any way, but still, something held me in its grip.

My hands tightened on the rein strap. Every step we took was a step farther away from everything that mattered to me. Riel could be dead already, for all I knew. If Neyes convinced his family that we were both enemies, it wasn't impossible. The other House's army could be storming the castle and burning everything to the ground right now. How could I just leave? Then again, what could I do if I stayed? I'd only get in the way.

The turmoil was torture.

"Luenki," I called, my voice hoarse and weak.

Luenki angled her head to show that she had heard me but didn't slow down.

I struggled to find the right words. "I don't think I can leave things like this." It wasn't exactly what I wanted to say, but it was the best I could come up with.

"There's nothing you can do," Luenki responded, firmly but not unkindly.

"We don't know that," I protested. "I'm a healer. At the very least, I could be another set of hands, couldn't I?"

"Believe me, Avery, I understand your feelings."

With a slight shift of her body, Luenki pulled her *avida* alongside mine. She met my eyes, and I saw my pain reflected there. "I am not unaffected by this," she told me. "But choices had to be made, and Astonriel wants you safe. I intend to make that happen. Your people are expecting you, and I need to settle their concerns before we have another mess on our hands."

"Could you go tell them what happened?" I pleaded. "Maybe they can send reinforcements." Luenki opened her mouth to reply, but I cut her off, infusing my words with a little more determination. "No, I'm grateful to you and Riel, but I'm tired of having decisions made for me. I know it's dangerous, but I'm a healer. If Riel is in trouble… if he's hurt, I can help him. I can help when the army comes too."

"I understand that," Luenki began, but I forged forward, too committed to stop.

"I have to do something. I can't just run and go back to the life I had before, it's not going to work for me anymore. And I can't shake the feeling that if I leave now, I might never see you or Riel again, and I… I need him, Luenki, I know it's stupid and dumb, but I can't just let him sacrifice himself so that I can get away, not when I lo—"

The next word caught in my throat.

I tried desperately to think of something else. To reconsider and choose a word that was less emotionally charged. Nothing came to mind, and the silence became deafening. I'd backed myself into a corner. *To hell with it all.* It was the truth. Even if it was too soon, even if we were from different worlds, even if we were never supposed to be together…

"I love him!" I finished, more loudly than was necessary.

My proclamation was followed by another bout of unnerving silence. Oyanni had stopped moving at some point during my speech, and we stood still in the woods. Luenki gave me an assessing look—I'd seen the same one on George whenever I was being difficult and he was trying to think of the best way to shut me up and get me to go along with what he wanted.

In the past, he always won. But that was the past.

"I'm sorry," I gasped, breaking eye contact to turn my body away from Luenki. I yanked on the rein strap with all my strength and dug in my heels at the same time. With a charged snort, Oyanni made a beautiful about-face and took off back the way we'd come. Luenki shouted after me, but I didn't turn back —I'd made my decision.

I could only hope it was the right one.

Oyanni ran like the wind, leaving Luenki far behind us. Maybe she sensed my urgency and wanted to get back to her master as much as I did. It was also easier to see now that the sun had risen. I held on with every muscle I possessed, gritting my teeth so tightly that I thought something might crack.

Riel needs me, I thought. *I need him. I won't lose another friend. I won't lose him.*

I repeated it in my head like a mantra. We raced through undergrowth and dodged trees.

Riel needs me. I need him. I won't lose him.

It was going to be okay. He had to be okay. *Hang on until I get there.*

Would I make it? As we covered more and more ground, the sounds of the forest changed. Gone were the merry chirping of songbirds, the buzzing of working *kainna,* the rustling of *eseri* seeking their breakfasts. In their place were the braying of horns, faint whistles, and ululating war cries that echoed through the woods.

Fear gripped me with the realization that the battle had begun. *How long have we been gone? Are we too late?* The closer we got, the louder the sounds became. Dread began to cripple my thought process. I had no idea what to expect.

I'm on my way… Riel… please, be okay!

CHAPTER THIRTY-THREE
THE BATTLE

DESPITE HER FEROCIOUS SPEED, Oyanni somehow picked up the pace as we burst through the edge of the forest and into the open. In an instant, my senses were overwhelmed.

The road had become a battleground. Some fought with lightning and fire, while others had become nightmarish beasts, tearing into their enemies with teeth and claws created through changing magic. Arrows whistled through the air above our heads, and flashes of colored light chased the last remnants of night from the sky. Voices mingled together; shouted orders, howled battle cries, the wailing of the fallen and their comrades. Bodies littered the ground. My eyes squeezed shut in an attempt to ward away the horrific sight.

Luckily, Oyanni didn't hesitate. She skirted around the fighting as best she could, hooves tearing up the ground where they fell. I could only cling to her, bent close to her neck in an effort to make myself as small a target as possible. The scent of fur and sweat filled my nose.

It occurred to me at that point that this was a terrible idea. I could have headed back through The Rift with Luenki and come back with reinforcements instead of leaving her to explain the situation alone. Well, they probably wouldn't have listened to me, but I could have tried. At least then, I would have been flying in with an army, and not just a terrified me.

Someone galloped across the path in front of us, and Oyanni was forced to dodge. A jolt of pain shot through the wrist that was wrapped in the rein strap as I was thrown to one side, the breath knocked out of me. The ground loomed below, and for an instant, I thought I was about to be squashed in a rain of hooves. The world spun above me. At the last second, Oyanni managed to shift her body, getting herself back underneath me before I truly fell.

"Oh my God, oh my God," I screeched into her neck.

We careened around a few perplexed soldiers toward the entrance to the palace, but nobody tried to stop us. Once we passed underneath the portcullis, Oyanni came to an abrupt halt, sending me sprawling against her shoulder. I shimmied back into an upright position right away, fighting to catch my breath. Every part of me hurt, my hair was a mess, and I was coated with sweat, but I knew this was only the beginning. The courtyard was covered in mats for the wounded. A handful of menders were spread out among the occupied mats, tending to the most urgent injuries first. There weren't enough healers to go around.

Gritting my teeth in determination, I tilted myself to one side and half-slid, half-fell in what had to be the world's sloppiest dismount. Pain shot through both knees when my feet hit the hard ground, and I swayed on the spot. Somehow, perhaps through sheer force of will, I stayed standing. *They need me,* a little voice said in the back of my head, reminding me why I was here. *Riel needs me. I won't lose him.*

Please be okay, I begged him silently, though I knew he couldn't hear me.

Once I'd recovered from the jarring landing, I tottered across the courtyard, making my way to the injured. The one nearest me was a young woman who held her body tight with pain. An enemy's arrow protruded from the meat of her thigh.

She jumped in surprise as I dropped to my knees beside her.

"Let me help," I implored, reaching out. My hand hesitated over her wound. She looked at me with wide eyes but made no attempt to pull away. *Could I heal around the arrow? No, I probably have to take it out first. Oh, God.*

I sat frozen and trembling while my internal voice screamed at me to get it together. Sensing my internal conflict, the woman warrior reached down and gripped one end of the arrow. She breathed in, breathed out, set her jaw, and snapped the shaft into two clean pieces. The end that was lodged in her leg came out with a quick tug, accompanied by a fresh gush of too-bright blood. Bile roiled in my empty stomach. I forced down the nausea and grasped her knee. Immediately, I could sense her pain as if it were my own. The fresh wound was demanding in a way old injuries and illnesses never had been—it took my breath away.

I can't afford to get distracted. I ducked my head and focused, closing my eyes tightly against the vision of gore. Underneath my hand, the flesh twitched and spasmed in response to my magic, and muscle and skin proceeded to knit themselves back together from the inside out.

When I drew away, even her armor no longer bore a mark. She examined the area and gave me a single, firm nod before surging to her feet. I leapt back, startled, and landed hard on my hands. Pain shot through both wrists before being soothed by the residual magic that still flowed through me. My eyes followed my patient as she raced for the exit.

I did it. I can do this.

A labored moan drew my attention. I whirled around to see another bedridden fighter, this one with both arms bent at unnatural angles. My hand went to my mouth in horror. He caught my gaze and held it, and my feet moved automatically.

Several minutes and two more patients later, I realized what I was doing. *Shit, I got sidetracked.* The warriors all needed my help, but so did Riel. *Is he still inside?*

As I stumbled toward the front door, my eyes landed on someone in my path. The older man noticed me, his jaw slackening in recognition. It was Farisen, the castle's head mender. He crouched by the side of another fallen soldier. Beads of perspiration trailed down his temples, and his hands shook with effort where they applied pressure to an appalling wound. It was like the patient's armor and skin had melted away underneath one set of ribs, leaving a mess of red tissue and white bone behind. I had to look away and control my breathing.

When the nausea passed, I doggedly moved forward to join them.

"I got it," I whispered, bringing my shaking hands down around Farisen's. He hesitated before withdrawing. I got to work without delay. Everything turned gold as I channeled the largest amount of *mana* yet, forcing everything I could at the devastating trauma before me. I heard a sharp intake of breath —from the patient or from Farisen, I wasn't sure. I hoped to God it was the patient, because I wasn't sure that he was breathing at all. *Please be okay.*

Then I felt it: a life force rising to my demand to heal the shell that housed it. Relief flooded me, and I redoubled my efforts, tackling the wound in pieces from the inside out. It was a delicate process—there was more than just skin and muscle that needed rebuilding.

I wasn't sure how long it took before the gold faded from my vision, but a headache was forming behind my eyeballs. My hands shook violently as I retracted them.

"Have you seen Riel?" I asked, my voice coming out a little breathless.

Farisen just stared at me, his mouth drawn in a stubborn line. My confusion turned to anger, and then to fury. What the hell? I just helped him. *Did I not do enough? Maybe Riel told him to protect me also, and he didn't want to say?* This whole thing was infuriating.

Still shaking, I raised a threatening finger and put as much menace as I could into my words. "If you don't tell me where he is right now, for the love of all things holy, I will figure out how to unheal, and I will use your toes for practice. Then I will heal them and do it again."

The mender's eyes widened. A wary look came over his visage, telling me that the message had gotten across as intended. He finally inclined his head toward the castle.

So, Riel was still there? My brain conjured images of a bloody, vaguely man-shaped lump on the palace floor. *No.* I pushed the images away. Without wasting another moment, I jumped to my feet and bolted for the front door. It was closed, and without knowing the secret to getting it to open, all I could do was throw all my body against it. I tried twice, not sparing a thought for how it was sure to leave a bruise. Luckily, it gave way. Shoving past the half-opened door, I stumbled onto a scene not too far from what I had imagined. My heart seized in my chest.

Solois stood to one side of the room, looming over a prone form at his feet. There was no question who it was. While there was no noticeable pool of blood underneath Riel's body, and all four limbs looked intact from here, that was no comfort—he didn't seem to be moving.

"Leave him alone!" The words burst out of me in a broken cry.

Solois turned slightly. The side of his shirt was in tatters, the flesh underneath scorched and raw. If that was anything to go by, Riel had gotten at least one good hit in. A fierce surge of pride rose within me, only to be dashed by Solois's response to my arrival.

"Look, the human came to save you," Solois said in English, his tone mocking. "This is perfect. You two traitors can hang out here together while I deal with your mess." He prodded Riel's body with a foot. The motion elicited a pained groan.

He's alive! Adrenaline flooded my body, and I nearly

collapsed to my knees in relief. *I can still fix him. I just have to think fast.*

I couldn't fight Solois… but I had to get close enough to make contact with Riel. Maybe I could distract him somehow, get him to let his guard down.

"I'm surprised you're not out there," I tried. It was a miracle my voice came out steady.

"I was tasked with ensuring that the American spy does not have the chance to escape," Solois responded coolly. "I didn't anticipate that my brother would get in the way, but no matter. Once I'm finished here, I will be joining the defense of our people."

My eyes drifted to Riel. "Where does he figure into that? You're brothers. Isn't he your people?"

Solois gave a casual, one-shoulder shrug. "He defied our father's orders to let you go. Aligning himself with an enemy makes him an enemy too, regardless of blood."

"I see."

I drew out the words in an attempt to gain extra seconds. Even as I racked my brain for potential excuses, any options at all, nothing came to mind. "I won't try to escape," was my next attempt, "so let me heal him. Then you can throw us both in a dungeon or whatever."

I figured it was best to tackle one thing at a time. So long as we were both alive, we could try to plan some kind of daring escape. Maybe I could get Riel sanctuary back in America.

"Bargaining only works if you have the upper hand," Solois pointed out. He looked down at Riel and tilted his head. "From where I stand, that doesn't seem to be the case."

"I can heal that for you," I offered in desperation, nodding toward the wound on his side. "It has to hurt. I would only need a moment."

I watched his stance adjust as he considered my proposition.

"I won't let you go just for that," Solois remarked, eyeing me apprehensively.

Jesus, this guy doesn't have a decent bone in his body. But then, maybe I could use that.

I tried to appear meek and sorrowful. "I wouldn't have a chance anyway," I sighed, letting my shoulders sag. "You're too strong."

Whoever said that flattery would get you nowhere had apparently never had the pleasure of meeting someone like Solois. He grinned, white teeth flashing in the light, and spread his arms to bare his torso to me. "Have at it, then, human," he said. "But make it quick, and don't try anything. My brother was foolish enough to fall for your trick, and he's paid the price. I won't let the rest of the family suffer for his mistake."

I blinked, not quite believing my luck. *Did that actually work?* When he waved his hands impatiently, I snapped out of it and scrambled forward. I tried to keep my eyes on Solois as I approached so as not to reveal my true intentions. Tilting my head as though examining his wound, I crouched by his side, making a show of going slowly and wincing all the way.

Behind me, I felt for Riel with one hand. As a second stretched by, then two, I was terrified that Solois would hear my heart beating out of my chest and know what I was up to. When my fingers brushed against an arm, I almost cried with relief. As if picking up on my sense of urgency, *mana* flowed through me with an intensity that left me breathless. I dared a glance downward. Before my eyes, Riel's wounds were knitting shut, angry red giving way to healthy pink skin. Internally, I could feel the sharp, raw pain of his fresh wounds ebb away into nothingness. Riel breathed a sharp inhale.

The sound finally caught Solois's attention. His head snapped around, and I saw his expression darken with outrage as he pieced together what I had done.

Luckily, Riel was already moving.

He grabbed my hand and snatched me off my feet, pulling me into his chest and rolling us both out of reach of Solois before he could retaliate. The world spun around me, but cradled against Riel's body, I barely felt the motion. I clung to him and squeezed my eyes shut, breathing him in and reassuring myself that he was here, I was here; we were both alive and here together. We came to a stop some distance away, and I reluctantly let go of him.

"Are you okay?" he demanded, springing to one knee. He held me at arm's length while his eyes scoured me from head to toe, inspecting me for any signs of injury.

"Am I okay?" I repeated in disbelief, going rigid in his grip. I saw red. "Let's just recap for a moment, shall we? I come running back here to save your stupid ass with a savior complex, and not only are people dying literally everywhere, but you're getting the shit kicked out of you by your brother, and you have the nerve—"

"Yes, yes." Riel wrenched me into a brief, tight hug, and my rant died on my lips. Releasing me, he hopped to his feet. One arm remained stretched protectively in front of me as he faced down his brother, who stared us down in return.

"Thank you," he said to me, voice thick with emotion, "but you shouldn't have come."

"I wasn't just going to leave you," I grumbled, getting to my own feet and standing tall behind him. "I wanted to help. This way, we can fight together."

Solois hadn't budged from where he stood, but he gave me a dirty look, as though he couldn't believe I'd managed to pull one over on him. I was tempted to needle him further, but there were other things that took precedence right now.

"Oyanni's waiting outside," I said quietly, easing forward to grasp Riel's sleeve without taking my eyes off the enemy. "We can make a run for it. Come with me?"

Solois sneered in response. "I'm not looking to waste any more time here," he announced. "I'm sorry to say that neither of you will be leaving here alive."

Riel didn't grace him with an answer. His arm stayed raised in front of me.

"Riel—" I began, reaching out to give his arm an imploring tug.

Solois moved. Riel's sleeve was ripped from my fingers a heartbeat later as he moved forward to intercept his brother's attack. I reached for him, my mouth opening to warn him.

Except that Solois didn't go after Riel. Instead, Riel stood alone a few steps away, staring back at me with a confused look on his face. The faint presence at my back and a whisper of a breeze were all the warning I got before I was struck from behind.

Not understanding what had happened, I stumbled forward a step before catching myself. I meant to keep moving, to run to Riel and to stand at his side, but I was finding it difficult to breathe for some reason. Bewildered, I tilted my head downward. My eyes widened at the elongated fingers tipped with claws that sprouted from my ribcage.

Was that… Solois's *hand?*

The taste of copper and bile started climbing up my throat just before the pain registered. With a grotesque sound and a violent surge of uncomfortable pressure, Solois withdrew his hand. Riel scrambled to catch me, reaching me a split second before my legs finished buckling. *Thank heavens,* I thought absently. *Face-planting on the marble would have been super uncool.*

Riel's arms gripped me. He screamed something, but I had trouble understanding the words. Why couldn't I feel my legs? His fingers dug into my arms, but though I tried to shake him off, I barely managed a twitch. Then I tried to tell him that I was fine, but that he held me too tight. All that came out of my mouth was a choked gurgle and a gush of bright red blood. Riel's expression contorted in fear; I never imagined I would see that look on his face.

"What have you done?!" someone shouted.

Riel, I determined belatedly, as everything in me went blessedly numb.

"What have you done?" His voice broke.

It's okay, I tried to say. *I love you.* But my mouth refused to form the words. My limbs were growing heavier by the second, the shock and pain great and terrible and all-consuming.

"... draw it in," Riel was saying. No, commanding. "Avery, are you listening? You have to reach for your power. Stay awake! You have to heal yourself."

Something else grabbed his attention. Light flashed in the background. Riel grunted, and I went weightless for a moment. There was an echoing shriek of pain. I felt myself slipping away, but before I succumbed, I was being shaken back to awareness once more.

"Avery, focus!"

The pale blue light of Riel's magic danced over the bloody mess of my chest. It wasn't doing much—at that point, what was left of my lungs was heavy with liquid—but the pain eased slightly. I was trying to find my inner fire. I could see the flicker, a lick of candle flame, but it sputtered as if the wick was drowning. I heard a distressed sort of groan. *Was that me? God, what an unattractive sound.* Everything ran around my head in dizzying circles.

"You must, Avery, you must," Riel chanted.

He rocked me back and forth, trembling like a newborn fawn. My forehead creased in concentration as I dug hard for the thread that connected me to the river of power. It kept slipping out of my grip. I closed my eyes, reaching for the magic, and Riel's touch became more and more distant.

My last coherent thought was that if there was a God—or a Goddess, as the case may be—I could really use a miracle right about then.

CHAPTER THIRTY-FOUR

RIEL

"You must, Avery, you must."

Instructions spilled from my lips, but I didn't know if Avery could hear me at that point. There was so much blood. Her body spasmed periodically as her strength fled her, and I could feel her growing colder by the second. In moments, she would be a corpse, and my worst nightmare would be realized. Helpless, I held her close and prayed.

Valuen, grant us mercy. Goddess, give us strength.

I should have sent her home a long time ago. I should have seen this coming; this was always how it was going to end. How could I have protected her better? How did I not anticipate that Solois was bitter enough to go after her? Truly, he was no longer the brother I grew up with. Any honor he might have had was gone, hate and anger in its place. I should have known better.

My fault. My fault. My fault.

Avery's eyes were closed, which terrified me, but it was a small mercy. At least she wouldn't feel the extent of her wounds. I drew what little mending ability I possessed to her injury in an effort to staunch the flow, but her lifeblood still drained unimpeded, painting my clothes and the marble beneath us a startling shade of crimson.

"You always were so sentimental," Solois grunted from nearby as he recovered from the blow I'd dealt him and got to his feet. "It's a good thing you weren't born first—you wouldn't have been able to shoulder the responsibility of being our family's heir. She's just a human, for Valuen's sake. She manipulated you so that her allies could catch us unawares and slaughter us all. I'll admit I underestimated her, but you… what, you think you love her?"

"Be quiet," I snapped, trying to maintain my focus.

"This is how it needs to be," he continued, directing a contemptuous look down at Avery's body. "Humans were never meant to carry the Goddess's blessing. It was a divine accident, nothing more. Now, come. Our support is needed against Leimor's forces. You still have a chance to redeem yourself—don't throw it away."

Leaving Avery here to die was out of the question. But tied to duty as Solois was, he wasn't about to let me go get help. There was only one way this could end. Perhaps it was always going to end this way. My hands clenched into fists at my sides.

I assessed Solois out of the corner of my eye. The two of us weren't evenly matched—I never won when we sparred. But thanks to Avery's efforts, my wounds were gone. I also didn't miss the way he favored his left side, where I'd managed to hit him with lightning before Avery's arrival. His breathing was labored. And he didn't have someone important to protect. This was an opportunity, if I was fearless enough to claim it.

Goddess, give me strength.

I got to my feet slowly, eyes pinned on the growing puddle of blood at my feet. How long did Avery have? There was no doubt that this was a fatal wound, but Farisen had to be somewhere outside, and he was a skilled mender. If I could find him in time, maybe there was a chance. As long as I could finish this quickly, there was a chance.

With that thought in mind, I moved. Solois, apparently expecting me to come quietly, was caught by surprise. He threw his hands up to shield himself, but I barreled into him, knocking him off his feet. I called *mana,* my chest aching from the effort. That was a good sign—if I was near my limit, surely that meant that Solois was too. The air sparked with energy as I created lightning, the heat of it warming my fingers and making the hair on my arms stand on end.

My brother twisted underneath me before I could cast it, throwing off my balance and sending me skidding across the floor. Before he could get to his feet again, I was there, grasping his ankle and reaching for the marble with my other hand. As he hit the ground, I summoned another burst of *mana* for a change, turning the floor under him from solid to pliable. When he tried to get up and put space between us, his foot sank into the surface, halting his progress.

He swept an arm between us, and I leapt back as purple flames licked the collar of my shirt and seared one cheek. The attempt was weak. He was growing sloppy.

"Astonriel!"

Solois spat my name as though it were a curse. He reached down to free his trapped leg, and I surged forward for another attack, not giving him even a moment to catch his breath. We clashed so hard that the impact jarred my bones. My hand closed around Solois's neck, and I forced him back against the ground with my weight. He didn't go quietly. His fingernails gouged bloody furrows down my forearm as he struggled, but I refused to release him.

Too much was at stake. This was how it had to be.

The rage in his expression merged with fear as, resolute, I squeezed tighter.

CHAPTER THIRTY-FIVE
THE DEPARTURE

I FOUND myself in darkness with the smell of dirt and mildew in my nose. Somewhere between panic and disbelief, I reached out with trembling hands. I felt exactly what I expected: nothing but cold and ungiving stone. The cellar I had been kept in when I was kidnapped eight years ago was realer now than it had ever been in my nightmares. Was I dead, making this hell? Oh, God. I didn't think I could bear an eternity of this.

My head jerked upward as heavy footsteps sounded above me. There was shouting, and the cellar door opened with a *bang*. But instead of a member of the Counter Assault Team, there was nothing but blinding light. I threw my arms up to shield my eyes. The light dimmed enough that I could squint through my fingers without pain. There was a figure there in the doorway.

A husky female voice spoke. My brain struggled to keep up with the words; they sounded like the lilting language of the fae, but somehow I understood them as plain as day.

"Brave, softhearted human. You have used my blessing well."

A hand reached out from the light, beckoning me closer. My feet moved of their own accord. The hand remained extended, steady and patient, as I staggered up the steps. When I grasped the hand, power filled me like I was tasting oxygen for the first time. The light turned gold. I felt the presence of something living and wild underneath my skin.

"I am not supposed to do this," the voice said, almost whispering now… and sounding a bit grumpy? "If anyone asks, this was all you. Can't have them thinking that I lost my edge."

The hand tightened around mine, and the flame within me roared to life.

It took time to catch my breath. I didn't dare try to move, devoting what little energy I had to blinking the high ceiling into view. My chest tingled with pins and needles so intense that they bordered on pain. I felt cold marble against my back, along with loads of something wet and sticky that I really didn't want to think about.

Other than that, everything seemed… whole.

Eventually, I gathered the strength to turn my head. I saw blurs of color and flashes of light—Riel and Solois. By the looks of things, they weren't pulling any punches, but to my smug satisfaction, Riel seemed to have the upper hand. He trapped Solois's leg in the floor somehow and was on top of him before he could pull it out. I watched as he began to squeeze the life out of his own brother. A protest rose in my throat, only to falter.

Why should I stop him?

If it was Solois or us, there was no question. He'd been willing to kill me just a few minutes ago. I raised a shaky hand to the spot on my chest that had been a gaping hole moments before. The wound was gone; no one could have guessed that I'd nearly seen the light. Or had I? I vaguely remembered some kind of dream, a woman reaching out to me…

He *had* killed me, hadn't he? Or gotten close enough to it.

Turning my attention back to the ceiling, I tried to ignore the hot tears that trailed in rivulets down my cheeks. The throne room being empty, the sounds of the fight drifted my way. Could it still be called a fight? It was a plaintive struggle now. Riel grunted with effort, or perhaps from pain. His brother fought for breath—I could hear the heel on his free foot scuffing the floor in a panic and faint, choking wheezes emanating from that direction. Something rattled softly, like metal striking stone. The torturous sounds continued on and on.

God, why was it taking so long? It was brutal and appalling. I wished that I could cover my ears, but I also felt a strange, sick need to be present for this, as if I could support Riel throughout this terrible task by listening.

The sounds of struggle finally began to fade away. Silence fell, but not three seconds had passed before Riel let out a heart-rending cry of grief. I turned my head again to see him sitting atop Solois's still form with his head bowed, shoulders heaving with exertion. He made a twisting motion, and a sharp *crack* echoed through the room.

Eyes closed, features distorted by pain, Riel let his arms fall and turned his face up to the ceiling. His lips moved soundlessly, as though he sent up a prayer to follow his brother's soul. The moment offered a strange sort of beauty and peace. Then he stiffened, remembering why he fought Solois in the first place. He whirled about, and our eyes met.

He stared.

I stared back.

"Avery," he whispered, anguish and relief blending together in his voice like a sorrowful song. All the fight left his body in a rush, leaving him a broken but no less beautiful man. He got to his feet, hesitating only briefly before stepping over his brother's body.

I struggled to sit up and reach for him, prepared to offer whatever comfort I could. He came to me and collapsed by my side. His arms surrounded me, gripping me close, but there was little joy to be had in our reunion.

"I'm sorry," I whispered against his neck. "I'm so, so sorry."

"It's not your fault."

It kind of was. But instead of saying so out loud, I simply held him tight, and we just… were for a little while, soaking each other in.

"Ah. I got blood on you," Riel said apologetically, ending the moment. He wiped ineffectively at a stain by my right shoulder.

"Huh? I'm pretty sure *I* got blood on me."

It was then that I noticed the burn on his cheek and the ravaged flesh along his chest and arms. "When did that—" I began with a frown, before I thought better of what I was about to ask and bit back the rest of the words. "You're bleeding. Let me," I offered instead.

I tried to think of an innocent topic to fill the silence as I healed him so that Riel didn't have to be alone with his thoughts. Nothing came to mind.

We sat together for a little longer before Riel started to gather himself. He got up and helped me to my feet, making sure I had the strength to stand. I assured him I was fine, so he busied himself with straightening his messy clothing instead. When he turned back to the door, his gaze landed on the corpse nearby. His shoulders shook. It took him two tries to speak.

"What am I going to tell our parents?" he asked in a broken voice.

"The truth."

Setting a supportive hand on his arm, I told him calmly but firmly, "Solois was trying to kill us both. Hell, he almost succeeded. What you did, you did in self-defense, and there's nothing wrong with that. Your parents… well, I can't say that they'll understand right away. They'll probably need some time. You all will. But you'll get there."

I wished I could offer something better than that, but what else could I say? I was pretty sure that my abilities didn't extend to healing emotional wounds. Riel's eyes squeezed shut. When they opened again, I watched him set his feelings aside and transform from a wounded son and brother into the son of a leading family at war.

"Let's go," he said decisively. "This isn't over."

I went with him to the door. As we stepped outside, Farisen noticed us. His gaze bounced from me to Riel and back again, and it was hard to tell what he was thinking. He probably noticed that someone was missing, but if he did, he didn't comment on it. Instead, he nodded toward the courtyard, where the menders were still hard at work. Staff members were beginning to distribute food and other supplies to anyone who was present.

"The fighting is beginning to calm," he reported in English. "It should not be much longer. I have no news of your parents, only that they asked about you some time ago."

"Thank you, Farisen." Riel turned to me, and I had the sneaking suspicion that I wouldn't like what was about to come out of his mouth. "Avery… I should join them. You can stay here with the other—"

"No way," I argued immediately. "We should stick together. That way, we don't have to worry about each other. I can take care of us both with my powers, yeah?"

"Avery." The exasperation in Riel's tone was impossible to miss.

I understood where he was coming from—we'd both nearly just died, after all—but I didn't want to risk not being there if he needed me again. Didn't he feel the same?

Farisen said something in the fae language. I thought I heard Solois's name, especially since Riel's jaw clenched. He hesitated before responding. When he did, whatever he said made Farisen's eyes widen. I looked between the two of them warily. If Riel admitted to killing Solois, things could get ugly. They didn't have the full picture, and while there were some cultural differences between us, I doubted that murder was something the fae let slide.

As they continued speaking in hushed tones, a faint buzzing sound caught my attention. Normally, I wouldn't have thought twice about it, but it stirred an odd memory in me. I hadn't heard a sound like that in a long time. Not since crossing The Rift, in fact. Shielding my eyes from the sun, I scanned the sky for the source.

"What is it?" Riel asked, brows furrowing as he followed my gaze.

"That sound. It has to be some kind of…"

I hadn't even finished my sentence before a silver combat drone appeared above the woods, coming from the direction of The Rift. "Oh, shit!" I exclaimed, rushing after it. Alarmed and confused, Riel came after me. I waved my arms above my head in an attempt to catch the attention of whoever monitored the video feed. If we were lucky, they were just conducting surveillance. If we weren't, they might be about to start dropping bombs.

"We need to make sure they see us!" I was too frazzled to give a better explanation, but Riel stopped where he was and raised his hands to release a brilliant glow. I held my breath and kept my arms moving until the drone began to circle around rather than continue in the direction of the battlefield.

"Luenki!" I whirled about to face Riel and regretted it when my eyeballs were accosted by light. Groaning in pain, I turned back around, blinking repeatedly to clear my vision.

"Luenki said Vivian and the others were waiting for me," I recalled, struggling to get my thoughts together. "If she's not back yet, she probably went through The Rift. I don't know what she told them, but they might think I'm in danger." That made the most sense.

Riel let the light fade and dropped his hands. He swayed on his feet, and I saw his eyes flick toward the fighting. I wanted so badly to ask him to come with me. I was terrified of saying the wrong thing and making things even worse. I wanted him by my side while I tried to explain things I didn't understand to people way more important than me.

But what I needed was to swallow my feelings and do the brave thing, the responsible thing, like Riel did now. Otherwise, I didn't deserve him. So, instead of asking him to support me when he and his family were the ones who needed support right now, I found myself saying, "It's okay, do what you gotta do. I'll go back to The Rift and try to calm things down. Hopefully, if they can just see that I'm alive and well, they won't do anything drastic."

A winged shadow was there and gone as the drone passed by overhead.

Riel didn't respond right away, but there was a softness in his gaze that told me I had done the right thing, even though it hurt. He reached toward me, and I leaned up, expecting a parting kiss. Instead, he tousled my hair.

"Your courage is admirable, *eseri,* but someone from our family should accompany you and help Luenki smooth things over. Let me speak with Farisen before we go."

He turned away, and I stood stock still as his words sank in. Then I practically melted in relief. Although I had tried to be brave, I had been quaking in my boots at the prospect of going by myself. I thought I might be able to face anything with Riel there.

Riel approached Farisen as the mender emerged from the castle looking rather grim. Realizing that he must have seen Solois's body, I wrung my hands, expecting an accusation or worse. While I wasn't close enough to hear, the two men appeared to speak calmly, or as calmly as could be expected given the circumstances. Farisen nodded and the two clasped hands.

When Riel joined me again, it was with a stocky, antlered *avida* at his side.

"Is something wrong with Oyanni?" I asked, frowning. *Had she been wounded on our return trip, and I hadn't noticed?*

"She is well, but to The Rift and back is a long way to travel twice in one day," Riel replied. "Keersu is m—was my brother's. He will serve us just as well."

He offered his hands, and I let him help me up. The animal's back was even broader than Oyanni's, if that was possible. I tugged at my skirt to cover my legs as best I could. Riel swung himself up and settled himself behind me, and I laid a hand on his thigh for comfort.

"We've got this," I assured him, though it was as much for my own sake as for his.

"I have been dealing with your government as long as you have been alive," he reminded me, nuzzling my hair in a brief display of intimacy. "And I would rather face them than my parents on any given day, but today especially."

Unsure how to respond to that, I squeezed his thigh to show my support.

The ride to The Rift was even longer than I remembered, but I was glad that it was no longer dark. The woods were not quite so foreboding during the day. Not to mention that having Riel behind me gave me strength. In this familiar position, I could almost forget the horrors of the past few hours. Almost.

We were drawing close but had not yet left the shelter of the trees when a clear voice shouted, "halt!" Not taking any chances, my hands were in the air before we even stopped.

Armed soldiers began pouring from the brush.

"Wait, it's me!" I cried.

One of them drew up short and raised a fist, stopping the others in their tracks. "Avery Nelson?" he asked dubiously. I nodded emphatically, all my attention on the guns.

"And this is Riel, the second prince of House Wysalar." With my hands still in the air, I jerked one shoulder to indicate the man behind me.

"Please forgive the lack of notice," Riel chimed in politely.

"We came alone. The other members of my House are otherwise engaged, but we wanted to address your leaders' concerns regarding the situation here and Avery's well-being as soon as possible."

At that, the man in the lead lowered his gun, although his stance remained cautious. He nodded to another man, who disappeared into the trees, before turning his attention back to us.

"Sorry about that. We had a report from a reliable source that there was a civil war situation going on here, so we're working on securing the area. Our orders were to extract Ms. Nelson safely and provide support to the Wysalars as needed." He hesitated before addressing Riel directly. "I guess that means we're at your service. Sir."

The salute felt like an afterthought, but I didn't blame him. It wasn't too long ago that I was floundering in front of the fae myself.

Something occurred to me.

"Luenki? Was that the source?" I asked curiously.

"I'm not at liberty to share that information, ma'am," the soldier replied, not unkindly.

"Can we speak to George? Or Vivian? Are either of them available?"

The soldier gave an abrupt nod. "If you'll come this way."

He drew alongside us, casting the *avida* a wary look. A beckoning gesture had the rest of his team falling in line behind him, and we headed in the direction of The Rift.

CHAPTER THIRTY-SIX
THE NEGOTIATION

"WHAT IS YOUR NAME, SOLDIER?" Riel inquired as we walked.

"Ortega, sir. Gabriel Ortega, Sergeant First Class."

"A pleasure to make your acquaintance. Is this your first time visiting our lands?"

"No, sir." He didn't expand on his answer.

"Ah. Well, your diligence is appreciated."

Sergeant Ortega gave a sharp nod in response.

Giving up on conversation, Riel turned his attention forward. We rode in silence until the trees began to thin, signaling that we were drawing near to the river. A couple of the soldiers broke off from the others to rush ahead.

When we emerged from the woods, we were met with chaos. Soldiers filled the area, unloading equipment from a barge on the water—tents, rocket launchers, and various tools. Horses pulled materials from one side of the clearing to another. They'd even taken a tank through The Rift; it stood motionless off to one side.

"Oh my God," I whispered. "This is intense."

I couldn't tell what Riel thought, but I got the vibe that he wasn't happy to see them taking over the area. Not that I blamed him; knowing American history, seeing a bunch of soldiers getting comfortable on my land would have been pretty concerning to me too.

A group came to meet us from the direction of the tents. Most of them were in army fatigues except for a couple of people in suits. When I recognized George as being one of them, I felt many things, not all of them good. On the one hand, I was glad to see someone I knew. I'd already figured that I'd have to speak with him sooner or later. But on the other hand, I dreaded having that conversation with him. I couldn't imagine it going well.

"Hey." I greeted George with a timid smile as Riel brought us to a halt.

"Miss Avery, Prince Astonriel. So good to see that you both are alive and well." He seemed genuinely delighted to see us, which almost made me feel bad, given that I didn't feel the same way. "We have much to catch up on, don't we?"

"Yeah," I agreed, forcing a smile as I let Riel help me down. "It's been a wild few months. I've learned a lot, of course, but I've also been doing a lot of soul searching, and…" I trailed off, noticing then just how many extra pairs of eyes surrounded us. I didn't know any of these people. Anxiety began to raise its ugly head. "Well, maybe it's best that we go somewhere private to talk?"

"Actually, Miss Avery, you can wait with Sergeant Ortega and his team for now." George reached out to shake Riel's hand. "We would like to speak with the prince about the current situation before things go any further. Miss Luenki is waiting for us as well."

"Oh! Of course." My cheeks suffused with heat. As if on cue, a feminine voice called my name, and I looked up to see Luenki hastening toward us. Before I could apologize for running off, she gathered me into a hug so eager that my feet lifted off the ground.

"Luenki!" Her contagious energy made me grin from ear to ear.

"I worried for you," she sighed as she set me down. She greeted Riel with a quick, fluttering hand motion. "And you. I'm glad you were able to find each other."

"We did," I replied slowly, hesitant to imply all was well when she didn't know the rest of the story. Riel moved forward to place a hand on the small of my back.

"We should speak," he said, the quiet words directed at Luenki and George.

"Of course." Forehead creasing in puzzlement, Luenki angled her body back toward the tents. "We have set up a 'temporary base of operations' over there. I have informed Mr. Kepler of the general situation, but... it will be good for everyone to be on the same page."

Riel looked back at me. "I'll only be a moment," he promised.

"Okay, sure." I could only nod. "I'll be here if you need me, I guess."

They split off and headed for the tent, and I was left with nothing but my thoughts. *And Keersu,* I supposed, turning back to the waiting animal. The soldiers that had escorted us through the woods lingered nearby. Having observed our exchange, they eyed me with some degree of interest now. Whether it was because of who I was or my fae associates, I didn't know.

No one attempted to start a conversation as I made for the *avida.* He was tense, like he prepared to bolt. I imagined the unfamiliar sights and people were a lot for him to take in.

"Shall we go over there and find some tasty grass?" I murmured, patting the side of his neck. He lowered his head to nuzzle my thigh, and I had to lean out of the way of his antlers. Some of the soldiers stared as I coaxed him off to one side of the clearing. The horses that noticed us were also giving us apprehensive looks; even the best trainer in the world couldn't prepare an animal for what they'd find on the other side of The Rift.

We waited by a knotted tree. Keersu grazed for a while,

picking at the ground and bushes. He found the lichen growing on the tree's trunk especially tasty, which was why I was digging in one of the grooves when Riel and the others found me. I sprang upright with a guilty look. Luckily, they were all too well-versed in diplomacy to ask what I was doing.

George led with the very information I'd been dreading for weeks.

"Prince Astonriel mentioned that you've recovered your abilities," he said. "This is great news. Let's get you home for now, and we can have your things gathered as soon as there's an opportunity. Everyone will be glad to get back to work."

Excuses clambered up my throat. I had to swallow them down and put together a rational argument. The pressure was all the more intense with Riel and Luenki there. "Well, that was actually something I wanted to talk to you about," I began.

"See, I know things are a bit crazy right now, but I thought you should know as soon as possible so that you could plan accordingly. I've been giving a lot of thought to, um… the role I play currently, and I'm really grateful for everything you've done for me over the past few years, but I'd like to talk about having more of a typical employment."

I beamed, happy with the way I'd phrased my request.

George was taken aback, though he maintained a polite smile. "I see," he stated first, taking some time to think through his response. The fact that he didn't immediately shoot down the idea filled me with hope, especially as he continued to speak. "We could discuss the possibility, certainly. And, uh… what sort of terms were you thinking?"

Was this really happening?

"Well, pay, of course." I thought fast. "I think it's only fair, but I'd be open to negotiation. I can heal a lot more people in a sitting now, so maybe we could do the sessions less often? Room and board wouldn't be necessary anymore, because I'd… well, I'd find that on my own. Maybe you could cover transportation?"

I held my breath as I waited for George's response. He wasn't smiling anymore.

"How about we resume doing things as we have for now," he suggested, "and we can touch on this once things have calmed down some. There are a few more people we need to run this by, so it might take some time to circle back around. You know how government is." He gave me another smile, but this one didn't reach his eyes.

A part of me wanted to take his words at face value, but the practical side of me knew a delicate dismissal when I heard one. If that was how things were, I needed bigger guns.

"In that case," I announced, putting a hand on the *avida* next to me, "I'm not leaving."

George's expression didn't change right away. "Pardon?"

"I'm not leaving," I repeated, squaring my shoulders and raising my chin. "You can go, if you need to. I'll stay here until we get this sorted."

"There's…" George cleared his throat. "Miss Avery, with all due respect, we're looking at active combat right now. It's in everyone's best interests to get you to safety as soon as possible. We can discuss this again when things have—"

"Mr. Kepler."

Riel moved to stand at my side, so close that we nearly touched. Luenki joined us, directing the full force of her smile on George in a way that communicated she was not to be messed with.

George looked between me and Riel. I saw the moment understanding dawned, because the veins in his neck stood out starkly against his aged skin.

"This is… highly unorthodox," he muttered. Releasing a defeated sigh, he crumbled. "If you return with me now, I'll notify the appropriate parties this afternoon. We can begin negotiating the terms of your employment contract as early as next week."

I couldn't believe my ears.

"I'll have them get a boat ready," George continued. He hesitated a beat. "A few things have changed since you've been gone. I'm only mentioning this since it may be relevant now. As it happens, there was another child found with healing powers. We've been talking to her parents, but haven't yet come to an agreement. We may be able to work something out with the two of you working in shifts, if you'd be amenable to that."

My lips parted in surprise. "Another healer? You're kidding."

"I am not." George nodded to Riel and Luenki. "As I mentioned earlier, our men are at your disposal. Colonel Bradford will be your point of contact should you need anything in my absence." Turning back to me, he said, "I'll get that boat. Take your time."

With that, my mentor, overseer, and bane of my existence for the past eight years left.

Relief and worry warred within me. On the one hand—if I allowed myself to be optimistic—this could be the first page in a new and exciting chapter of my life. At the same time, I half expected that if I let George take me back through The Rift, I'd be kept at the White House by force. I understood that Riel and I had different responsibilities to tend to, but… was this our only option?

"Another mender," Luenki remarked, bringing her hands together. "Isn't that exciting?"

"Yeah." I had wondered why there were so few of us Golden Children. Maybe it was time for the magic to choose a new generation. Thinking of the girl who would find herself following in my footsteps, I cast a hopeful look at Riel. "Maybe we could…?"

"Avery." His response bore a familiar teasing tone. "I'm flattered, truly, but it may be too early to discuss children. We haven't even discussed the possibility of a coupling ceremony."

"What?" My brows came together in confusion. "Oh my

God, no. I meant that maybe we could help teach her about her magic, like you did for me."

"Perhaps when things calm down," he agreed.

Shaking my head, I turned my attention to the shoreline in the distance, where a boat was getting pulled together for me and George.

"I guess that means this is goodbye," I remarked, trying to remain light-hearted.

"Only for now," Luenki responded, bestowing an affectionate touch on my shoulder.

"For now," Riel echoed.

I had trouble looking him in the face, afraid that I would see the same fears that plagued me reflected in his eyes. We would have to fight for each other if it came down to it, but I knew that I would. And I wanted to believe he would too.

"Will you be okay?" I asked in a small voice.

Riel didn't reply immediately, perhaps knowing that the answer I wanted to hear wasn't something he could promise. "I hope so," he offered.

It would have to do.

"All right, then."

Giving the *avida* at my side a farewell pat, I swallowed the lump in my throat and worked past the misery to put a smile on my face. "I'll see you guys in a bit. Best of luck with everything. Better not throw any wild parties while I'm not here."

"You have my word." Riel mirrored my strained smile.

Surrounded by strangers as we were, I didn't dare kiss him goodbye, but I wasn't about to settle for a handshake either. I reached for him, and he enclosed me in his arms without prompting. We held each other for several seconds. It wasn't long enough, but no amount of time would have been. The moment we released each other, Luenki swept me into another hug, not as passionate but just as meaningful. I repeated my goodbyes to delay my departure.

When I couldn't stall any longer, I went to the river's edge, pausing several times along the way so that I could commit Riel's image to memory. I kept my eyes on him as long as I could see him. When I could no longer make him out, I fixed my gaze in his general direction until our boat was swallowed by the mist of The Rift, and everything dissolved into gray.

So, I returned home.

It was the same as I remembered it, yet different. After spending so long in the fae realm, the atmosphere on Earth felt strange. The comforting weight of magic was missing, leaving the air feeling oddly light and empty. I now understood the joy that Luenki felt when she returned to The Rift with me and Vivian all those months ago.

The first thing I did once George and I got to the base was seek out Felicity. While it was more difficult to draw the amount of *mana* needed on this side of The Rift, especially after healing so many grievous wounds only earlier that day, I had her ear fixed up in a jiffy. She cried many happy tears. On the outside, I joined her, but my tears were for another reason entirely.

George honored his end of the deal, and the negotiations went better than I ever dreamed. In return for preserving the once-a-month healing schedule, we settled on a salary of half a million dollars per year, to be deposited into my shiny new bank account. I used a decent portion of that to retain Devon and Chris. I would only need them when I was on this side of The Rift, and I hoped that would not be often, but I couldn't bring myself to let them go.

Although I could heal a lot more people at each session, George was not exactly happy with the new terms. However, he didn't have a leg to stand on. They couldn't control a legal adult against her will, and I had express permission from the *Ishameti* leading family to come and go through The Rift as I pleased.

Speaking of Riel. The days passed with no word from him, and the ache in my heart grew. George did tell me that his family won the battle thanks to our support, so that was a relief. I did my best to stay busy and not worry, knowing that Riel would come to me when he was able. In the meantime, I spoke to the other mender girl, Shiloh, over the phone more than once, and Chris was gracious enough to let me participate in some of his wedding planning.

I also spent a lot of time reading. I hadn't been much of a bibliophile before, but I'd developed a new appreciation for the hobby during those dull afternoons after training with Riel. The worlds in books gave me an escape when I didn't want to devote any more energy to real-world topics. There may or may not have been some fae romance and fanfiction involved.

After a week of rest, I held an impromptu healing session, partially for the sake of those who waited months for me to return, but also for a chance to test my limits. I managed to cure a whopping seventeen people before succumbing to exhaustion. The best part was that I was back to normal after sleeping the rest of the day and night away.

A week and four days after everything went down, I was reading in my bedroom when a knock pulled me from my thoughts. Chris stood by the open door with Devon behind him.

"There's someone here to see you," Chris told me. He appeared innocent enough, but there was a twinkle in his eye that told me something was up. My automatic reaction was confusion, followed by doubt. Then I realized what he meant, and I think I stopped breathing.

"You don't mean…?"

My hands dropped, letting my book topple to the floor.

He didn't bother giving me an answer, just stood there and smiled, which was answer enough. I don't remember getting to my feet, but I was suddenly running. I flew through the open door, past Chris, past Devon, and down the corridor toward the Entrance Hall. A flurry of thoughts resounded in my head, not all of them positive, but I ignored them and kept going. Nothing and no one could have held me back at that moment.

When I burst into the Hall, it was like a scene from a fairy tale. Rays of daylight streamed through the windows, lighting up the interior and making the floor gleam. The light shined on the two figures in the middle of the room. George was one of them, but it was the other man that had all of my attention. He was tall and blond, with seafoam-green eyes and long, delicately pointed ears. I couldn't move fast enough. He waited patiently for me, a warm smile on his face.

With an unrestrained squeal that expressed more emotions than I could ever put in words, I launched myself into Riel's open arms.

EPILOGUE

A YEAR PASSED, just like that. It took some time to sort things out on both sides of The Rift. With the might of the U.S. military on their side, Riel's parents were able to crush House Leimor. The aid we sent was enough to improve their opinion of humans, and they issued a grudging apology to me on behalf of Solois. He was still a sore point, of course, but I expected he would be for a long time to come. He was their beloved son, after all.

Riel was doing better. There was still a touch of shadow in his eyes, and sometimes he would stare into space when he thought I wasn't looking, but otherwise, he was back to his usual self. The two of us fell into a tentative routine. Once a month, I'd go back to the White House and heal as many people as I could. The rest of the month, I stayed with him at House Wysalar. Occasionally, we took overnight trips out to the foothills and slept under the stars.

It was like I was living a dream—one I never wanted to wake up from.

While I wasn't exactly a part of the family, I was still invited to participate in Melairos, a fall holiday with a concept similar to All Souls Day. It was a multi-day event during which everyone prayed to Valuen to ferry the souls of the dead into the Goddess's embrace. Everyone was looking forward to it as a way to make peace with the unfortunate events of the past year.

On the first day, we wore plain clothes and fasted as an offering to get the Goddess's attention. The second day, we made hundreds of little wood carvings to represent the bodies of the dead and burned them when night fell. The third and final day was dedicated to celebration, with games and a massive feast. The courtyard was filled to the brim with revelers who traveled from Miderrum to join the leading family in commemoration.

I was watching children run about and dig holes and trying to figure out what game they were playing when Riel came out of nowhere and dropped a flower crown on my head. Reaching up to feel it, I smiled up at him. He settled in the grass at my side.

"Enjoying yourself?" he asked.

"Absolutely," I replied, pulling my knees up to my chest and adjusting my skirt to fall over my feet. "It's still hard to believe I'm here, but I'm so grateful for it. I feel like I have a lot of experiences I need to catch up on, you know?"

Riel made a sound of understanding. "Have you eaten yet?"

"Only enough to feed an army. I won't be needing food again for a week."

He chuckled, and his arm came to rest around my shoulders. We sat together for a while, enjoying the sights and sounds and fresh air. The crowds started to thin as people headed home.

"Shall we go inside?" Riel asked when the sky began to take on a bronze tint.

I nodded, stretching out my arms. Out of the corner of my eye, I watched Riel get to his feet and admired the lines of his body. Specifically, the curve of his ass.

"I'm being objectified," Riel announced to the air.

Horrified, I scrambled to shush him. Luckily, there weren't many people still around, and those who were didn't seem to be paying attention. With a roguish grin, he scooped me into his arms, then peppered my face and neck with an onslaught of kisses. I failed to keep a straight face even as I protested, pushing him away without any real strength behind it.

When he finally released me, I was pink and breathless from laughter. He snatched up my hand and brought it up to his lips for one final kiss before tugging me along in the direction of home. I went without a fuss, smiling so hard that my cheeks hurt.

"I'd like to discuss something with you," Riel said then, becoming serious.

I sobered in an instant. The ambiguity of his statement unsettled me, and it took some effort to soothe my nerves before speaking. "Of course. What is it?"

"As I understand it, humans have several different types of romantic relationships and don't always stay with the same partner. Is that accurate?"

I nodded, unsure where he was going with this.

"It's the same for us. We might court several people over the course of many years if things don't work out. Then, when we find a partner that we believe is right for us, we tie our lives together in a coupling ceremony, just like you have marriage."

My lungs emptied in a rush. "With you so far," I managed.

"I'm not sure what your people consider to be the appropriate length of time for the courting period, and I understand that a lot has changed in your life recently. Do let me know if this is too forward of me. I wanted you to know that it has been such an honor for me to spend this last year with you and watch you flourish. I don't mean to suggest this too soon, but I hope you would consider joining with me in the future."

"Are you asking me to marry you, Riel?"

Surprisingly, my voice was steady.

"Something like that," Riel confirmed. "Not right now, but—"

I had to pull his head down, but I silenced him with a passionate kiss. He made no complaint, wrapping his arms around me and letting me take the lead. It went on for several seconds. When I started to feel lightheaded from lack of air, I let him go and stepped back to put some space between us. As I stared up into the face of the man I loved, I offered up a little prayer of thanks that everything worked out.

And with a sweet smile, I said, "I'll think about it."

Don't miss The Golden Children Book 2!

THANK YOU FOR READING THE TREASURED ONE!

We hope you enjoyed it as much as we enjoyed bringing it to you. We just wanted to take a moment to encourage you to review the book. Please visit The Treasured One on Amazon to leave your review.

Every review helps further the author's reach and, ultimately, helps them continue writing fantastic books for us all to enjoy.

Also in series:
The Treasured One

Want to discuss our books with other readers and even the authors? Join our Discord server today and be a part of the Aethon community.

Facebook | Instagram | Twitter | Website

Join our non-spam mailing list by visiting www.subscribepage.com/aethonreadersgroup_romantasy and never miss future releases.

Looking for more great Romantasy?

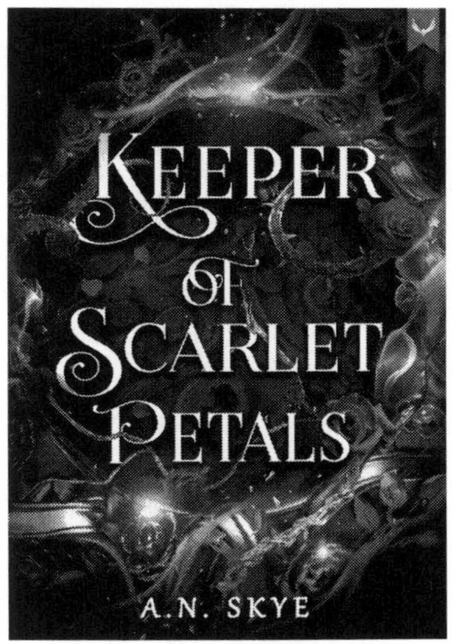

To be a Keeper is to dedicate one's life – and heart – to protecting another. *Jasmine wasn't ready for it. Less than a year into her training at Sanctuary, a college for Keepers and mages alike, and with a fresh start from a brutal life of thievery in the slums, all she wanted to do was continue mastering the sword arts and avoid her other responsibilities. Those plans are ruined when she's assigned to be the protector of a young nobleman whose family was murdered. Her new charge is cocky, smug, and drives her up a wall at every opportunity. Forced to protect a man she can't stand with her life, Jasmine needs to find time that isn't there to continue her training and keep assassins from killing both of them, all the while learning magic and discovering that there's more to life than survival. And yet, Jasmine starts to find herself inexplicably drawn to him. In the slums, Jasmine never had room to care about anything other than putting food on the table. But she's not in the slums anymore, and she can't keep her feelings tied down forever. Unfortunately, burgeoning love is the least of Jasmine's problems. As pieces of a malevolent plot start to unfold around them, she and her charge realize that there might be only one thing left that they can rely on. Each other.*

Get Keeper of Scarlet Petals Now!

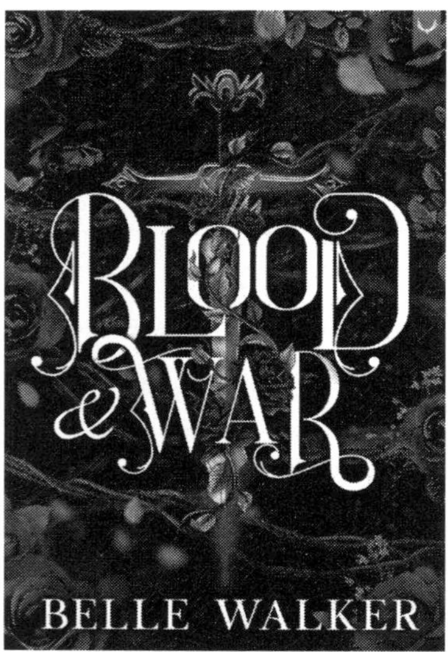

Loyalty and love can ruin you. But hope is the deadliest of all. *For ten years Demitria Collins has fought the creatures of nightmares to protect the one person she has left. With a rising string of demon attacks on the forefront, she knows it's only a matter of time until they're next. But when a routine patrol goes awry, and Demitria has a fated encounter with the legendary Horsemen known as War, everything she fought for is threatened. Including her life. Kellan, one of the Four Horsemen of the Apocalypse, has been sent to Earth by the High Council of Eden to restore the balance with his siblings. Dispatched on their newest assignment, he expected the task to be simple. Not for his charge to be human. When a split second decision leaves even more blood on his hands, Kellan has questions for the council– Ones they won't answer. The warrior should embody everything Demitria hates, but a growing darkness forces them into an unlikely allegiance to uncover a deadly truth. When an inexplicable pull complicates matters even worse, and that unyielding hostility turns into something beautiful and fiery that breaks through every belief they've ever had, both know the consequences will be deadly. But together, they might stand a chance to restore order before the ultimate destruction of a planet that she, and the High Council, hold dear.*

Get Blood & War Now!

A shattered life. A dormant power. An arms race between realms—for her. *When twenty-one-year-old Nyleeria met King Thaddeus for the first time outside her family's rickety cabin, she had no idea how irrevocably her life would change. The Spark. Magic. Spellcraft. Fae. The Great War. All elements wiped from human memory and written histories—an ignorance Nyleeria would have gladly maintained. But fate had other plans when it shattered her world with the disappearance of her siblings and the brutal murder of her parents all because of a latent power she unwittingly possessed. The primordial Spark lying dormant within her was coveted by two opposing realms who would unquestionably use its force to extinguish the other. In a war she never knew existed, where the veil between human and fae realms is becoming dangerously thin, Nyleeria finds herself in possession of the very magic that can alter the fabric of her world.* ***Don't miss this captivating adult Fantasy Romance by debut author CC Hartly. With its intricate magic systems, believable characters, and richly developed world-building, it's sure to delight romantasy and epic fantasy readers everywhere!***

Get Mythic Spark Now!

For all our Romantasy books, visit our website at www.aethonbooks.com

GLOSSARY OF FAE WORDS & PHRASES

Ishamenarin (ee-SHA-meh-NA-r / lin): A greeting translating to "The Goddess be with you." From "Isha" meaning "Goddess" and "narin" meaning "by (your) side."

Avida (AH-vee-dah): Large riding beasts that resemble colorful elk-horses.

Eseri (eh-SEH-r / lee): A small carnivorous mammal that follows predators around to clean the bones of their prey when they are finished eating.

Raast (r / lahst): A breakfast food favored by the second prince. Square chunks of chewy, mildly sweet, colorless jelly with pieces of dried fruit scattered throughout.

Mana (MAH-na): A powerful elemental force that magic users can draw from their surroundings.

Vahela (VAH-hell-ah): The state of emptying oneself of

the inner magic used to connect to the flow of *mana*, essentially death for magic users.

Keerya savessan (kee-R/LAI-yah sah-VESS-ahn): Translates to "Keerya spoke true." Used as a blasphemous expletive like "damnation," essentially discrediting the Goddess and Her authority.

Shahim (SHA-him): Colloquially "Hand of the Goddess." Magic user that can competently wield all four categories of magic: mending, breaking, changing, and making.

In virani ma onaya kessavi ki, torenna: Fae phrase meaning 'When blood is shed in the name of kindness, you have gone too far.' A reminder that you have a responsibility to yourself first and shouldn't suffer in the pursuit of selflessness.

Ishameti (ee-SHA-meh-tee): A fae group or race united under House Wysalar's rule. Translates directly to "People the Goddess is with," or more colloquially, "Goddess-blessed people."

Vali (vah-lee): A type of nut-bearing tree common in the fae world.

Kainna (KAI-ngah): Pollinating insects similar to bees.

Massiya (MA-see-yah): A semicircle-shaped pastry with savory filling, often eaten while traveling.

Vahelim (VAH-hell-im): An "empty helper," someone who offers help with questionable motives. Often used in the context of soothsayers who tell people what they want to hear rather than what their visions truly share.

Manaviri (MA-na-VI-r / lee): A technique to kickstart a mana connection through a near-death experience.

Valuen kessavi ki (VAH-loo-EN kess-AH-vi kee): "In Valuen's name / For Valuen's sake," an expression of exasperation

Lya (lee-YAH): Livestock beasts similar to cows

Epitgig (eh-PIT-gig): A rowdy goblin-like race well-known for their "music"

Aminkinya (AH-min-KIN-ee-yah): A warlike matriarchal fae race resembling pixies

Melairos (mel-AI-r / loss): A fall holiday to pray for the souls that passed on in the previous year

ACKNOWLEDGMENTS

For someone struggling with ADHD, completing any task is a challenge. Writing a 100,000-word novel? A year ago, I would have said it was impossible for me. But I guess that just goes to show that sometimes, we're stronger than we think.

This book has truly been a labor of love, but it wouldn't have been possible at all without the supporting cast: my partner, friends and family, coworkers, beta readers, critique partner, and the many writing communities of Reddit and Facebook. Take a bow—you've earned it!

I'd like to take the time to thank a few people by name. First, my beta readers: Christine, Becca, Jen, Katie, Genny, and Sierra. Your feedback not only made me a better author but also helped this book be the best it can be, and for that, I am eternally grateful. I truly appreciate every kind word and bit of brutal honesty, every brainstorming session, every pep talk. I especially appreciate that you didn't tell me to take a hike when I started blowing up your phones every time I second-guessed a plot point or wanted to get input on some ridiculously specific thing that most people probably would never notice or care about. You are all saints.

I would like to shout out the r/PubTips community, qtCritique community, and The Writing Gals Critique Group for providing support and feedback throughout the writing, planning, and querying processes. These are incredible resources for aspiring authors who are hoping to publish traditionally or simply want to finetune their skills as a writer, and I am immensely grateful for their help with my manuscript and query letter.

I'd also like to thank Aethon Books for taking a chance on my debut novel. Thanks to you, I can now proudly say that I am a published author (!!). I look forward to our partnership and sharing THE TREASURED ONE with the world.

And finally, thank you, dear reader, for picking up this book. It's equal parts thrilling and nerve-racking to know that a complete stranger is reading about a world and characters that came from my brain! If you enjoyed this book, please consider leaving me a review on Amazon, Goodreads, etc—it helps authors more than you know. Also, be sure to follow me on Instagram @authorhlevin for news of future releases. See you around!